W9-BWZ-774

Crooked
NUMBERS

ALSO BY TIM O'MARA

Sacrifice Fly

Crooked
NUMBERS

TIM O'MARA

Minotaur Books ⚹ New York

CROOKED NUMBERS. Copyright © 2013 by Tim O'Mara. All rights reserved. Printed in the United States of America. For information, address St. Martin's Press, 175 Fifth Avenue, New York, N.Y. 10010.

www.minotaurbooks.com

The Library of Congress Cataloging-in-Publication Data is available upon request.

ISBN 978-1-250-00900-5 (hardcover)
ISBN 978-1-250-00901-2 (e-book)

Minotaur books may be purchased for educational, business, or promotional use. For information on bulk purchases, please contact Macmillan Corporate and Premium Sales Department at 1-800-221-7945, extension 5442, or write specialmarkets @macmillan.com.

First Edition: October 2013

10 9 8 7 6 5 4 3 2 1

For my wife, Kate
All the proof I'll ever need

Acknowledgments

ONCE AGAIN, I AM INDEBTED to my fellow villagers for their contributions to making the writing experience so fulfilling.

I wish to thank the students, families, and talented staff members of the Computer School for their support, inspiration, and the joy they bring to my day job. I am equally grateful to the folks at P.S. 87 and the Center School for giving my daughter the education all children deserve.

A special note of thanks to Ramapo for Children. Raymond would not be around if I were not a teacher, and I would not be a teacher were it not for the summers I spent at camp. Any readers interested in children with special needs should check out their website, www.ramapoforchildren.org, and find out how they can share in the magic.

Scott Kennedy was extremely generous with sharing his knowledge of the pharmaceutical industry, as was Dave Stribling with his expertise as a pharmacist. Of course, any errors are completely my own.

Thanks to Dallas Murphy, friend and writer, for the best piece of advice I received during my introduction to the book business: "Do the writing. Don't do the math."

I am—as are writers and readers everywhere—deeply indebted to the public libraries and their fabulous librarians across the country. I especially wish to give praise to the Center for Fiction in Manhattan, Mary Barrett of the Newport (Rhode Island) Public Library, Madeline Matson of the Missouri River Regional Library in Jefferson City, the good folks of Merrick (New York) Library, and Jude Schanzer and Mary Ellen Fosso of my hometown East Meadow (New York) Public Library.

Some of the nicest and most knowledgeable folks in the business can be found working in the independent bookstores. To name a few, I am so glad the following had this new guy's back: Scott Montgomery of Mystery People in Austin, Texas; Adrean Darce Brent of Mysterious Galaxy stores in southern California; Jamie and Robin Agnew of Aunt Agatha's in Ann Arbor, Michigan; Jonah and Ellen Zimilies of [words] in Maplewood, New Jersey; Loren Aliperti of Book Revue in Huntington, New York; Otto Penzler and his staff at the Mysterious Bookshop in Manhattan; and Jenn Worthington of Word in glorious Greenpoint, Brooklyn. Support your local indie bookseller!

I've met so many fun, talented, and supportive folks through my memberships in Mystery Writers of America, Crime Writers of America, and the International Thriller Writers. Thank you all for welcoming me into the clubs.

I sold a lot of books in mid-Missouri, which would not have been possible without the help of Cece McClure of Downtown Book & Toy; Warren Krech and John Marsh of KWOS Radio; Jack and Tom Renner; the folks at Cameron's Café in Holts Summit (who needs a writer's studio?); and the incomparable, unsinkable Wyn Riley.

My agents, Erin Niumata and Maura Teitelbaum of Folio Literary, have answered all my questions with respect and clarity. Thanks to all the pros at St. Martin's/Minotaur Books, especially Hector DeJean, my publicist, who handles my many calls and requests with great patience—and editor extraordinaire Matt Martz, who simply makes my books better.

My nonbiological family is always there for me. A tip of the hat to Sharon and David Bowers, Maria Diaz and all our friends at El Azteca Mexican Restaurant, Carolyn Montgomery-Forant and Lea Forant, Teddy's, Linda Hanrahan, Jim and Josephine Levine, Ed Carroll, Dr. Nina Goldman, the Stokes Family, Kelly Ellison, Drew Orangeo Wayne Kral, Harold James, Cooper and Molly, "Aunt" Lisa Herbold, and "Uncle" Rob Roznowski.

My mid-Missouri family continues to stick by this New Yorker. Thanks to Gene and Janice Bushmann, the Bushmanns of Columbia, Missouri, and Maggie and Elise Williams. A big shout-out to my father-in-law, Les Bushmann, who's always there with pats on the back and the occasional "atta boy!" Every writer should have a mother-in-law like mine. When I married her daughter, I had no idea Cynthia Bushmann would turn out to be an amazing copy editor and proofreader. I truly stepped into a honeypot.

Thanks to my sister Ann and my brother Jack—and their families—for their support and help in spreading the word.

My sister Erin brought her considerable marketing and design skills to making her big brother look like he knew what he was doing. Her husband, Detective Will Donohue of the NYPD, was kind enough to share some of his knowledge with me. You guys produced a trio of pretty fine nephews for me, as well.

Once again, a huge debt of gratitude is owed to my brother, Sergeant Mike O'Mara of the Nassau County Police Department. It's nice to have an expert who's only a phone call away and is almost always up for a beer—or seven.

Mom, what can I say? I'll never get tired of seeing you at my readings with that look on your face. And, yes, I promise not to tell the others that I'm your favorite.

I can't believe any writer has ever had a better first-draft reader than I have in Mike Herron. I'm looking forward to seeing *Wannabe* up on the shelves real soon. No pressure.

To my wife, Kate: check the dedication. You know I don't like to repeat myself.

Eloise, you continue to amaze and amuse me—and I'm thrilled you're as proud of me as I am of you. You totally rock!

Crooked
NUMBERS

Chapter 1

IT'S NEVER EASY LOOKING INTO the face of a dead kid.

Eyes that should be tracking a fastball or twinkling with mischief, shut forever. The mouth—perfectly suited for spittin' out rhymes, lame homework excuses, or jokes about yo' mama—never to be heard from again.

Douglas William Lee was two months shy of his seventeenth birthday when he was murdered, and he used to be one of mine. He was in my class for two years—about three hundred and sixty school days—and I filled his head with math, literature, history, and science. He'd sit there and sometimes bitch and moan about the work and "Why we hafta learn this stuff anyways?" and turn around to cut on his friends, but he did the work and learned the stuff and showed up to my class every day. His mom made sure of that because she wasn't going to let Douglas William Lee make the same mistakes his father had.

I folded my hands in front of me and stood there, looking down at Dougie, lifeless in his casket, wondering what mistakes had led to this. What the hell could this boy have done to cause someone to stick a blade in him over and over again and let him bleed out on the cold, dark tennis courts under the Williamsburg Bridge? I stared at the gold crucifix Dougie's mom must have put around her dead son's neck. Right. Where the hell was Jesus when Dougie needed a little salvation?

Teachers know. We only have these kids for a short time. We throw a whole bunch of knowledge at them and hope more sticks than falls away.

They have no idea what life's going to bring, so our job is to prepare them the best we can, and then we let them go. I had last seen Dougie about a year and a half ago when he swung by my room on the last day of school to pick up his diploma. He shook my hand, thanked me for everything I'd done for him, and promised to come back and visit. He never did.

Most don't. They get caught up in high school, relationships, and family stuff. Before they know it, a year and a half has gone by and the last thing on their minds is looking back. That's the way it should be. But I'd be lying if I said I wasn't interested in seeing the results of all my time and effort every once in a while.

More than a few of the kids who graduate from my middle school never make it through high school. There are too many distractions and temptations when you come of age in and around the projects of Williamsburg, Brooklyn. You can go on up to the roof of your building and stare across the river at Manhattan—minutes away by bus or train—the skyline tempting you with the promise of adventure and excitement. You see too many examples of folks who are "gettin' by" with no education and no jobs, and too few role models who've chosen to stick with the hard work.

Dougie was going to be different.

With the help of his uncle, he'd received a scholarship to one of the top private schools on Manhattan's Upper West Side. Dougie had all the things a private school looks for when handing out free rides: a reading disability, a single mom, and brown skin. Exactly the kind of student whose smiling face you put in the glossy brochures and slick slide shows when asking wealthy New Yorkers to part with some of their hard-earned Wall Street cash. Dougie was going to be a success story people on both sides of the river would want to take credit for.

And now someone had taken all that away.

"Mr. Donne?"

I knew whose voice it was before I turned. I'd listened to it many times during the two years I'd had her son. She was dressed in black and around her neck she wore a crucifix identical to her son's. Mrs. Lee reached out and grabbed my hands, and as she squeezed them, I watched her tired eyes—Dougie's eyes—fill with tears.

"Thank you so much for coming," she said, her voice catching slightly. "You meant so much to Douglas."

"And him to me," I said. "I . . . I don't know what to say, Mrs. Lee."

She squeezed my hands a little tighter and gave them a small shake. "There's nothing *to* say, Mr. Donne. We just have to trust the good Lord has a plan and Douglas is a part of it." She closed her eyes and fought off a pained look that threatened to take over her face. "I just can't imagine what that plan would be though, Mr. Donne. I truly can't. He was not even . . . my baby boy was . . ."

Dougie's mother collapsed, and I surprised myself by catching her. Before my knees gave in to the weight and we both hit the carpet, I was able to guide her small frame to a seat a few feet away from her son's casket. We were immediately surrounded by a group of women who had been gathered somewhere nearby.

"What happened?" one of them asked, glaring at me, as if whatever had happened must have been the fault of the only white guy in the room.

Before I could answer, another woman, armed with a funeral home fan and a glass of water, said, "The poor dear's had enough is all, Wanda." The woman gave me an apologetic look as she fanned Mrs. Lee. "She has had enough."

We all watched as Mrs. Lee took a sip of water, followed by a few deep breaths, and slowly opened her eyes. A small sense of calm returned to her face and she looked slightly embarrassed by all the attention.

"I'm fine, ladies," she said. "Thank you." She blinked a few times before adding, "I would like to talk to Mr. Donne alone now, please."

Wanda gave me the glare again. "You sure about that, Gloria?"

"Yes, Wanda. I'm sure." Then to the group, "Now why don't you all get some more tea and cookies. I'll be fine."

The women mumbled among themselves for a while before each one reached out and touched a part of Mrs. Lee. After a few more reassurances and words of condolence, they walked silently to the back of the room. Wanda never took her eyes off me until she disappeared through the door.

As I waited for Mrs. Lee to compose herself, I looked at the Mass card I had picked up at the door. The Lord's Prayer was printed on one side and a smiling picture of Dougie was on the other. My throat tightened as I read his date of birth and the date he entered his "Eternal Rest." I turned to look at him again, lying in the casket. He didn't look at rest to me. He just looked dead.

"I thought I'd be stronger than that, Mr. Donne," Mrs. Lee said. "I apologize."

"You have more strength than I would have, Mrs. Lee." I sat down next to her. It was too hot in this room, and the aroma of flowers was overpowering. No wonder she almost hit the floor. *Smells like Heaven*, my uncle would say at family wakes. *But it's hotter than Hell.* "You have nothing to be sorry for."

"Thank you." She took another sip of water and let it work its magic before she spoke again. "You know how Douglas was killed?"

"Only what I read in the paper and saw on the news." I was lying. I knew much more than that because I had made a phone call to an old friend whose precinct was on the other side of the river.

"Stabbed," she said bluntly. "Eleven times. The police didn't want to tell me, but I made them. Eleven times, Mr. Donne. What's that say to you?"

I wondered if the police had told her about the twelfth wound: a two-inch shallow scratch just below his jawline, possibly made by a different weapon.

"Are you asking me as a teacher," I said, "or because I used to be a cop?"

She looked me in the eyes and said, "I'm asking *you*."

I took a deep breath of my own and chose my next words carefully. "It tells me someone was real angry with Dougie, Mrs. Lee."

"Powerful angry," she said. "You know about what the police found around Douglas's neck?"

"No, ma'am, I don't." Another lie. The cops didn't give this piece of information out to the papers, but my guy had tipped me to it.

"Purple and gold beads. Mardi Gras beads."

The colors of the Royal Family. An up-and-coming local gang known to work the public housing projects on both sides of the Williamsburg Bridge.

"And they tell me they found some marijuana. Stuffed in his socks. Five little bags." She closed her eyes again. "Know what they told me then?"

I knew exactly what they'd told her, because I probably would have told her the same thing. But I knew Dougie. What I didn't know . . . what I'd been thinking about since the call to my buddy . . . was why someone would go to the trouble of making it look like—

"Douglas's murder was the result of some drug deal gone bad." She reached into a pocket, pulled out a handkerchief, and held it with both hands. "Now, Lord knows, Douglas was no angel. He'd stay out past curfew, be up too late talking to friends on his computer, and he'd even been sassin' me a bit lately. But my boy was not in any gang. And he had nothing to do with dealing drugs."

"The police sometimes show a disappointing lack of imagination," I said. "They see what's right in front of them and don't always see the value in looking beyond that."

"You do that when you were a policeman?"

"Yes, ma'am," I said. "Then I got tired of too many unanswered questions."

"Is that why you left?"

That and a four-story drop from a fire escape. "Pretty much," I said.

"Well, they lost a good man when they lost you, Mr. Donne." Before I could correct her, she added, "And now I need your help."

I knew this was where I was supposed to say something along the lines of, "Whatever I can do," but honestly, I didn't know what I could do.

"I got *a lot* of unanswered questions, Mr. Donne. I also got a bad feeling they're going to stay that way unless someone asks them for me."

"Someone like me?" I repeated. "I'm a schoolteacher now, Mrs. Lee. The police are not going to just—"

"Douglas told me how you helped get that boy . . . Frankie . . . how you helped get him home a while back, Mr. Donne. And his sister."

"My role in that was exaggerated, Mrs. Lee." My third lie in less than two minutes. Frankie and his sister were supposed to have kept my involvement in bringing them home safely to themselves. But Milagros had blurted something out in front of a reporter, and Frankie couldn't talk his way out of it. Next thing I know, I'm being interviewed and dancing as fast as I can around a bunch of questions, which, if answered truthfully, would have landed me in a lot of trouble. "You know how kids and the papers like to make things seem like more than they are."

"Well," she said, "I believe this is going to be one of those times they make *less* out of it than there should be. The police *and* the newspapers. Just another black boy killed, dealing drugs and hanging around the wrong people."

She was right. My friend told me he'd heard Dougie's file was already making its way to the back of the detective's desk, and it had only been five days since the murder. I'm not sure what Mrs. Lee thought I could do, though, because the info I'd gotten from the one phone call was probably all I was going to get.

"Did the cops ask you what Dougie was doing out at that hour, Mrs. Lee? The news said he was killed some time after one in the morning."

"I told them what I will tell you, Mr. Donne. Douglas went to bed just after eleven. A bit later than his usual bedtime, but he's been—he was—having trouble getting to sleep for the past few weeks. I went to bed right after and didn't hear a thing until the phone woke me up. It was the police . . . telling me what happened." She paused to collect herself. "I didn't believe it could be Douglas they were talking about, so I ran into his room and he wasn't there. He was . . ."

"And they found his bike on the tennis courts?"

"Yes. They're making it sound like Douglas snuck out to sell drugs and something went wrong. That's not what happened. It can't be."

"What about Dougie's uncle?" I asked. "Can't he put some pressure on? Make a few calls as the family's lawyer?"

"Oh, I've asked him to do just that, and he will. But I thought maybe you, as someone a little less . . . colorful, well, they might be more forth-coming."

"You mean you think the police might treat a white ex-cop with more respect than the family's black lawyer?"

"Tell me I'm wrong, Mr. Donne," she said, her eyes locked on mine, daring me.

"I won't insult your intelligence, Mrs. Lee. Or your experience. But why don't you give the cops a few days? See what they come up with."

Dougie's mom reached out and placed her hand on my knee. "All I want is for Douglas's murder to mean something more than a few para-graphs and a scene-of-the-crime picture in the paper. A few days? They're going to be on to a bunch of other things in a few days." Her eyes filled up again. "That is time I do not believe we have."

We. Nicely done. Damn it.

"All right," I said, reminding myself not to overpromise. "Here's what I *will* do. I recognized the name on one of the articles about Dougie." My mind flashed on Allison Rogers's business card shoved in some drawer back at my apartment. She was the reporter who had tried to get me to say more than I wanted to a year and a half ago. "She interviewed me after we got—after Frankie Rivas came home. Maybe she'll be interested in doing a human-interest piece. A teacher's point of view on the story."

With that said, Dougie's mom gave me a smile. There was no joy in it, but I did detect a little relief.

"See," she said. "You *are* a good man, Mr. Donne. I knew that when you were Douglas's teacher, and I know it now." She put the palms of her hands together. "And the good Lord knows it, too. Thank you."

"You can thank me when I've actually done something, Mrs. Lee." *And the good Lord can keep on minding His own business.* "I have to make the call first."

"Well, thank you for that, sir."

"You're welcome," I said, uncomfortable with a grown woman calling me "sir." She reached out and grabbed my hands again.

"Gloria," a booming voice announced. "There you are."

Mrs. Lee and I turned to see a large man in a dark blue suit making his way toward us. "My brother-in-law," Mrs. Lee whispered, with a touch of annoyance. "Douglas's uncle."

When he reached us, he put his hand on Mrs. Lee's shoulder. The gesture did not look affectionate. "The ladies told me you had fainted," he said. With his eyes on me, he added, "I think it may be time for you to go downstairs and rest."

Ignoring that, she said, "This is Mr. Donne, Douglas. Douglas's teacher from the middle school."

Uncle Douglas considered that for a few seconds before offering his hand. "Yes, of course. Hello, Mr. Donne. Douglas Lee." I waited for him to add, "Attorney at Law," but he didn't.

"I am very sorry for your loss," I said. "And, please, it's Raymond," I said to both of them, pretty sure the request would go ignored. "Dougie enjoyed that he and I had that in common, by the way. Both of us being named after our uncles."

"Yes," Uncle Douglas said, not interested. "Gloria, you need to rest now."

"I was just finishing up with Mr. Donne, Douglas. And you can tell the ladies I did not faint. I'll be down in a minute."

It was clear Uncle Douglas wanted to disagree with his sister-in-law. Get her away from the schoolteacher, maybe? But he decided not to push it.

"Very well, Gloria," he said. "Remember, there *are* other people who wish to pay their respects before visitation is over for the evening."

"Yes, Douglas. Thank you."

"Nice meeting you, Mr. Donne," he said. "It was kind of you to come."

"Absolutely," I said. "Is Dougie's father here? I'd like to offer my condolences."

Douglas Lee took my hand again and held it in a tight shake. It wasn't painful, but it did make me feel as if I were being controlled. "My brother," he said, "has chosen to mourn the loss of his son in private, I'm afraid."

When he released my hand, I said, "Please let him know I asked for him."

"I'll be sure to do that."

As he walked out of the room, I saw Mrs. Lee relax just a bit. "This has been hard on all of us," she explained. "I apologize if Douglas was rude."

"No need," I said. "I can't imagine what your family is going through."

"Thank you. Again."

I reached out and touched Mrs. Lee on the elbow. "I'll be in touch."

"Yes," she said. "I know you will."

After she turned to go downstairs, I went over to Dougie's casket again. The tightness in my throat turned into a lump as I ran my fingers over the smooth brown wood. Unburdened by any desire to pray and not wanting to tear up in a roomful of strangers, I gave Dougie one last look, tapped the casket twice, and walked away.

The crisp November air felt good as I stepped out onto the street. It was a week after Thanksgiving, and after an unseasonably warm fall, it was finally starting to feel like the holiday season. *A bad time to lose a loved one,* my mother would say. As if there's ever a good time.

I was zipping my jacket when I noticed a couple of men in suits—fellow mourners, I figured—taking a cigarette break on the corner. We exchanged nods and forced smiles and then went back to minding our own business.

"Yo, Mr. D!"

I spun around to see two kids—one black, the other Hispanic—walking toward me. I recognized them as graduates from two years ago—not my kids, but friends of Dougie. I couldn't come up with their names.

"Hey, guys," I said, taking them up on their offer to bump fists.

"Hey," the black one said. "You still teaching the speddies?"

I ignored his insult referring to the special education class I used to have. The one his recently murdered friend had been in. "No," I said. "Mr. Thomas asked me to be the dean for this year."

"Whoa," said the Hispanic kid. "Mr. W quit? He finally get too old to run up and down the stairs chasing kids and breaking up fights?"

"Something like that." They probably didn't want to hear about Mr. W's wife and her breast cancer coming back hard, and how he wanted to spend their last six months together at home. I gestured with my head toward the funeral home. "Did you guys still keep in touch with Dougie?"

Their looks turned serious. "Yeah, kinda," the black one said. "Tha's fucked up, y'know? We seen him every once in a while at McCarren Park or around the way, but we didn't hang all that much no more."

"He was all into his private school friends." The Hispanic kid wiped something off his upper lip. "Not 'cause he was stuck up or conceited about it, he was just real busy keepin' up with all that shit."

"Yeah," I said. "He ever say anything to you guys about the Royal Family?"

"Dougie?" the Hispanic kid said, and then they both laughed. "Dougie didn't roll with no gangs, Mr. D. Why you think that?"

"I heard a rumor," I said, deciding to take a chance and divulge a little inside info. "The cops may have found some beads on Dougie. Royal Family colors."

"Shit," they both said at the same time.

"Yeah."

The black one spoke next. "Tha's fucked up, Mr. D. You know who'd know, though, is Junior. Remember him?"

We'd had a lot of Juniors in my years at the school. "Which one?" I asked.

He gave that some thought. Last names were not as easily recalled as nicknames or tags. "Truck's half-brother."

I immediately knew which Junior he was talking about.

"Yeah, right," the Hispanic kid agreed. "Their cousin. He's like some bigwig in the Family. They call him Tio, I think."

"What's Tio's last name?"

"Shit. I dunno. You should ask Junior. He lives right around the school."

"Okay," I said. "Maybe I'll do that. You guys go on in. Dougie's mom's probably downstairs. Make sure you say hi. She'll appreciate it."

"Yeah, Mr. D," they said.

"Be good."

They both gave a quick laugh and went inside the funeral home. As the door closed, I couldn't help but think that, statistically, one of those two was not going to make it out of high school. But today they both stood a better chance than Dougie.

"Yo, dude. You got a light?"

I turned to face two kids walking my way. Two white kids. They both had on ski jackets with lift tickets hanging from the zippers. Some people were enjoying this recent cold weather. The taller of the two kids had long blond hair and an unlit cigarette between his lips.

"A light?" he repeated, miming striking a match. Speaking to me like I was slow.

"No," I said. "I don't smoke. And you don't look old enough to, either."

"Yeah," he said, grinning, and then putting the cigarette in his jacket pocket. "I get that a lot. I'm actually much older than I look."

He gave his buddy, who was a good foot shorter than he and sported a militarylike crew cut, a playful slap on the upper arm. They both smiled.

I motioned with my head toward the funeral home. "You here for the wake?"

"Yeah," the smoker said. "Douglas was a buddy of ours from school."

"Upper West?"

"That's the one." He looked past me at the funeral home. "Fucking incredible, man, what happened to Douglas."

"Yes," I said and stuck out my hand. "I'm Raymond Donne. I used to be Dougie's teacher, back in middle school."

The smoker took my hand and said, "The cop, right?"

"Ex."

"Yeah, Douglas told us about you. Said you were pretty cool."

"I still am."

"So how does that work?" the kid asked. "Going from one civil service job to another. You have to take a test or something?"

I was not in the mood to explain to this Upper West Side kid that neither job was "civil service." For all he cared, I probably could have been a doorman.

"No," I said. "I actually had to go to college."

"Oh, sorry," he said. "I'm Jack. Jack Quinn." He looked at his buddy. "This is Paulie Sherman."

I shook Paulie's hand. He gave me a weak smile and an even weaker handshake. He was a bit jumpy and obviously uncomfortable in this neighborhood.

"We were real good buds with Douglas," Jack Quinn explained as he gave the intersection a complete three-sixty. "Jesus. Is this where Douglas lived?"

"Close enough," I said. "About ten blocks away from here."

They both looked around. Jack said, "Cool," as if he were getting a backstage tour of a movie set. "We took the subway here."

"That was very brave of you."

It took a few seconds for my sarcasm to sink in. When it did, Jack laughed. Paulie did not.

"Yeah," he said. "We met the height requirement and all." Again he gave his friend a slap on the jacket. "Paulie just made it."

The three of us stood there for a while, hands in our pockets, trying to think of something else to say. I looked at my watch. "I gotta head out, guys. It's nice to see some kids from Dougie's school dropping by. Do me a favor and make sure you see his mom when you get inside."

"Yeah," Jack said. "We've done the wake thing before. We know how it goes."

"Good. Then you shouldn't have any problems with the whole respect thing." I looked up at the red traffic light just as a truck rumbled by. "Be safe going home."

Jack winked at me. "Yeah. You, too, Mr. Donne."

When the light turned green, I crossed. Behind me, I heard one of the kids say something and then the sound of one of them laughing. Probably Jack.

Nice to be young, wealthy, and alive, I thought.

Chapter 2

"MR. DONNE ASKED YOU A QUESTION, Angel."

Angel Rosario held his father's glare with increasingly watery eyes. When the first couple of tears hit the floor, Angel's dad said, "Oh, now you gonna cry? Big man brings a box cutter to school." He turned to me. "*My box cutter.*" He looked back to his son. "And now you gonna cry? Shit."

The three of us were sitting in my office with me between the two of them, making a kind of stressed-out equilateral triangle. Experience had taught me not to sit an angry father next to the source of his anger. I reached over to my desk and grabbed a tissue off my desk for Angel. I kept a box there for meetings like this.

"Mr. Rosario," I said, "I don't really care much for the *where* in this situation. We need to concern ourselves with the *why.*"

"Yeah," Mr. Rosario said. "I'd like to know that, too, Angel. What the hell were you thinking? I don't tell you enough stories 'bout what I see at my job?"

Mr. Rosario was a school safety officer at one of the more undesirable high schools in Brooklyn. The sort of school where they can never find the money for sports equipment or art supplies, but always seem to have more than enough for the latest in metal detectors and security cameras.

"Angel," I said, leaning toward the kid, "tell your dad what you told me."

Angel sniffled and then wiped his nose. His eyes were back on the floor. He took a deep breath. He was having trouble speaking, but finally mumbled something that ended with the words, "bus stop."

Now his dad leaned forward. "What's that? Speak up."

Angel looked up and stared at his father. "Those kids at the bus stop," he hissed. "The ones I told you 'bout two weeks ago."

"What about them? You told me they stopped botherin' you."

"They started up again," Angel said. Then, in a much lower voice, "And they took my iPod."

"They took your— Jesus, boy. When were you gonna tell me?"

"I wasn't," Angel said. "I was gonna get it back."

"With that?" his dad yelled, pointing at the box cutter on my desk. "You were gonna get your iPod back with a box cutter? Goddamn, Angel. If your mother's lookin' down right now, she's shaking her head at the both of us. I taught you better. Why you think I tell you those stories about work?"

"To scare me. Make sure I don't become one of those kids."

"And here you are," Mr. Rosario said. "About to get suspended—*or worse*—for bringing a box cutter to school. Damn."

He was right about the "or worse" part. If the school wanted, we could push it and have Angel transferred to another school in the district. This was the Year of Zero Tolerance for weapons of any sort, and that was the system's imaginative way of dealing with this type of problem: move the kid to another building. That'll teach him.

"Your dad's right, Angel," I said. "I'm supposed to suspend you. Bringing a weapon to school—for any reason—is a serious offense."

"I know," Angel said to the floor.

It took Mr. Rosario a few seconds to pick up on what I had said. When he did, he leaned forward. "What do you mean, 'supposed to'?"

"Well," I said. "The only three people who know for sure that Angel brought a box cutter to school are sitting in this room. I know Angel, and I don't believe any of our students were in any danger from him."

"So what are you saying?"

I stood up and went around to the other side of my desk. I took the box cutter and stuck it in my bottom drawer. "I'm saying you and Angel have enough to worry about without having to deal with a suspension." I shut the drawer with my foot and held my hands out like a magician who had just made something disappear.

"You're not supposed to do that," Angel's dad—the school safety officer—said.

"Do what?"

Father and son looked at me, then at each other, and then back at me. After a few more seconds of awkward of silence, I said, "Angel. You have math this period, right?"

"Yes," he said.

"Then why don't you head off to class?"

Angel stood up and slipped his backpack over his shoulder. "So," he said, "that's it? I can just . . . go?"

"I think you and your dad are going to discuss this at home tonight, but, yeah. For right now, get to class."

He turned to leave, and his dad grabbed his elbow. "You got something you wanna say to Mr. Donne, Angel?"

"Yeah," Angel said, offering his hand and looking me straight in the eyes like I'm sure his dad taught him to. "Thanks, Mr. D."

"Get to math, Angel."

After Angel left, Mr. Rosario glanced over at my desk and gave me a concerned look. "You're takin' a chance with that, Mr. Donne."

"Why?" I said. "You planning on telling my boss?"

He shook his head. "I appreciate it. I don't know what I'd do with him if he got suspended. Daycare for the week? And a transfer? He likes this school."

"He'll be fine here, Mr. Rosario. I'm concerned about those knuckleheads at the bus stop."

"Yeah," he said. "I gotta figure something out about that."

"Call the cops," I suggested. "Or tell your supervisor. Maybe he can contact the school nearest the bus stop, and they can put someone over there in the afternoons. I'm sure your son's not the only one being hassled."

"Right. I'll talk to my sergeant when I get back to school." He removed his jacket from the back of the chair. "Don't got enough things to worry about."

"Have a good one, Mr. Rosario."

"Yeah. You, too," he said. "And thanks again."

After he left, I reached into my shirt pocket and pulled out Allison Rogers's business card. She was the reporter I had promised Dougie's mother I'd call. I had tried earlier and left a message. I took out my cell phone and tried again.

She picked up after two rings. "Allison Rogers."

"Allison," I said. "Raymond Donne. I called earlier."

"I was just getting ready to call you back. How long have you been reading minds, Mr. Donne?"

"It's Raymond or Ray," I said. "What are you talking about?"

"I just got out of an editorial meeting with my bosses," she explained. "They made it quite clear that if I don't get something new on this Douglas Lee piece, I'm on to writing about the living conditions of the animal acts at the circus over by Lincoln Center. Then, I get your message." She paused. "I remembered you worked over in The Burg, but, Christ. Douglas was one of yours, huh?"

"Yeah. Graduated a few years ago. With Frankie Rivas," I added, hoping she'd pick up on my angle.

"Right," she said. "I have to say, Mr.—*Raymond*—you just might be saving my ass here. The idea of a teacher's take on the case, and what with your history. . . . Let's just say it beats the hell out of smelling horse shit and carnies for the next few days."

"Glad I could help."

"How's four o'clock look for you?"

"*Today,* four o'clock?"

"Raymond," she said as if talking to an eight-year-old, "this story's dead—sorry, bad choice of words—by tomorrow if I don't get something tight to my editor by eight tonight. So, yes. *Today,* four o'clock. At the crime scene."

"Does it have to be there?"

"I'll need some art. A photo of the hero schoolteacher at the site of a student's brutal murder? No offense, but that shit's gonna fly." Before I could say anything, she said, "I know. I sound heartless and cold. Talk to my ex. But your take on the victim, *plus* a picture of you looking all sad and pensive, places Douglas's murder squarely on page four. Let's see the cops ignore that, Raymond."

Now who's the mind reader? "Four o'clock is great, Allison."

"I'll see you there. Be on time. I don't wanna lose that light."

Less than five minutes later, I was in the main office going through old yearbooks, trying to get a last name to go with "Junior." The process re-minded me a little too much of when I used to go through mug-shot

books as a cop. After ten minutes, I found the photo and name I was looking for. Junior Alvarez graduated three years ago. Under his picture, where
it said "Future Aspirations," it read "Businessman." That's what it always
said when the kid didn't fill out the questionnaire the yearbook advisor
sent out.

I went over to the file cabinet where we kept the old contact cards
filed by year. School policy used to require us to hang on to them for three
years. I hoped that was still the case. It was, and Junior Alvarez did indeed
live close to the school. Two blocks away. At least that's where he lived
three years ago. I copied down the address, along with the number listed
for his home and his mother's cell. Then I put the card back.

On the way back to my office, I took out my cell phone. This wasn't
exactly school business, and I didn't want anyone in the main office over-
hearing my conversation. I dialed the home number, and after five rings I
was outside my room, listening to a computerized voice tell me I had dialed the right number and to leave a message at the beep.

"Hello," I said. "This is Raymond Donne from the middle school.
I'm looking for Junior Alvarez. If this is the right number, please have him
give me a call back at—"

"Mr. Donne?"

"Yes. Is this Junior?" It shouldn't be. Junior should be in school.

"Yeah," he said. "What's up? Emily okay?"

"Emily?" I asked as I unlocked my office and stepped inside.

"My cousin," he said. "She goes to the school now, and her moms put
my moms down as an emergency number. What's up? She okay?"

"No. I mean, yeah. She's fine." As far as I knew she was fine. "I'm
calling about something else."

"Emily's okay, though?"

"Yeah, Junior. Everything's fine. I called to talk to you."

He waited a few seconds. "Me? What do you wanna talk to me
about?"

"Your cousin," I said, then realized I probably sounded like a crazy
person. "Your *other* cousin. Tio."

Silence again. Then, "I don't talk much about Tio, Mr. D."

"I understand, Junior," I said. "And I know you and I didn't have a
lot to do with each other when you were here, but . . ." I decided to go

with the truth. "One of my kids was killed the other day under the bridge. Dougie Lee?"

"Yeah," Junior said. "I heard about that. What's that got to do with Tio?"

"That's what I want to find out. The cops found some beads and a few bags of pot on Dougie, and they're making some noise it might be gang-related."

"They mention Tio?"

"They mentioned the Royal Family."

"Shit." He paused again. "You know where I live?"

"You still at the same address?"

"Yeah," he said. "Whyn't you come over?"

"I don't know, Junior, I'm kinda swamped here, and I don't want to impose."

"No worries, man. My moms went crazy with the food. We can eat some lunch. It's cool. Half hour, okay?"

I looked at my watch, and it was almost one. "I guess I can do lunch."

"I just remembered something, Mr. D."

"What's that, Junior?"

"Back in eighth grade. The time I punched the kid in the playground."

I remembered. Alex Something. He'd been bothering Junior's girl-friend and Junior wanted him to stop. I was on afterschool yard duty and saw the whole thing. One good old-fashioned punch in the nose. "What about it?"

"How come you didn't get me suspended?"

"Because Alex deserved it. And you made your point." No cheap shots, no weapons, no threats. "I also remember you helping him off the ground, Junior."

"Yeah," he said, reminiscing. Good times. "See you in thirty, Mr. D. Peace."

After he hung up, I spent some time in the office putting some papers away and closing out my computer for the day. Then I walked around the halls, checking the bathrooms and staircases for any unauthorized extra-curricular activities. All quiet. I headed down to the boss' office to let him know I'd be leaving early. I found Ron Thomas, the principal, as I always did: in front of his computer.

"Everything's okay, I hope," he said.

"Yeah. Got a few things to do before heading out to the Island for the weekend."

"Good, good." He stood up from behind his desk and stretched. "What was Angel Rosario's father doing here?"

I was surprised he knew who Angel Rosario was.

"Angel's been having some trouble with some kids at the bus stop. *By home*," I emphasized, knowing Ron hated when trouble got too close to his school. "Just wanted to make sure none of the kids were ours."

"And . . ."

"They're not."

"Good." He sat down again to stare at his computer screen. "Have a good one, Raymond."

"You, too, Ron."

I left his office, then headed over to Junior's for lunch to get some information on a gang leader who may or may not have been involved in Dougie's murder.

Chapter 3

I DIDN'T REALIZE HOW HUNGRY I was until the front door to Junior's building buzzed open and I stepped inside. The aromas of meat and garlic and spices filled the hallways. It was like walking into the middle of a cooking competition, and if Junior's mother had indeed gone "crazy with the food again," I was in for enough of that to last me until tomorrow morning.

By the time I got to the second floor, Junior was already standing in the doorway to his apartment. He was a few inches taller than I remembered, and his upper lip was sporting a bit of brown hair I'm sure he called a mustache. His right arm was in a sling.

"Yo, Mr. D," he said, offering me his left hand. "What's the haps?"

I looked at his wounded arm. "I should be asking you."

"Ah, this?" He stepped aside to let me in. The smell of food grew stronger, and so did my hunger. "You remember that chick from school? Gladys?"

I thought back a few years ago. We may have had a lot of Juniors, but I could recall only one Gladys. "Big girl?" I said. "Dyed her hair blond? Socially awkward?"

"Yo," Junior said. "You bein' kind. She was fat and crazy, and she's even fatter and nuttier now. She's like a Snickers bar on steroids."

The kid knew how to drop a simile. "What about her?"

"We was all hanging out a couple a weeks ago, at McCarren. Playing handball, bustin' each other's balls, shit like that." He closed the door behind me. "Anyways, one of the guys makes a crack about Gladys's weight and shit, and I guess I laughed the hardest, and she pulls this fuck-ing blade outta nowheres and cuts me right under the armpit."

"Ouch," I said.

"Yeah. Doctor says she got a big chunka the muscle and some of the tendon, and I'm gonna be in this sling for a few more weeks."

"That why you're not in school?"

He gave me a look like a little kid caught in a lie. "Nah, Mr. D," he said. "I ain't been going to school this year. I got a job at the car shop I been working at. I mean a real job, not just sweeping and shit. My boss, he's training me on the computers and how to do them state inspections. I'm making real money, Mr. D." He touched his free hand to his chest two times. "Help my moms out around here, y'know?"

As if on cue, and before I could give him the requisite shit about go-ing back to school, his mother stepped into the room. She was wiping her hands with a towel and gave me a big smile.

"Senor Donne," she said. "Come in. Time to eat."

Junior took me by the arm. "It's always time to eat around here." He patted his stomach. "That's how she takes care a my arm. She cooks like a crazy woman."

"I can think of worse ways to heal, Junior," I said.

"I hear that."

He took me over to the small table inside the kitchen. I put my jacket over the back of a chair, and the two of us sat down in front of two empty plates. A pitcher of iced tea was in the middle of the table, and Junior poured us both a glass as his mom went over to the stove. Every burner on the stove was occupied. I could make out chicken, beans, rice, and some-thing that looked like yellow potatoes. Within thirty seconds, portions of each filled my plate.

"Eat," Mrs. Alvarez said.

"Thank you, Senora," I said. "Are you going to join us?"

"No. You two eat. I eat later."

Junior put a piece of chicken in his mouth. "I swear. She don't ever eat until supper. Just drinks her Café Bustelo and cooks or talks on the phone all day."

His mother hit him with the towel. "You do not worry about me, Junior."

With that, she left us two men alone at the table. With a lot of food. We ate in silence for a few minutes. Chicken, chorizo, rice, beans, yucca, potatoes. If I ever got my arm cut by some crazy girl with dyed hair, this was where I wanted to do my rehab.

"So," Junior said, after taking a sip of the tea, "the cops think the Royal Family's got something to do with the kid why?"

I pushed my plate a few inches away to take a break. "They found beads around his neck. Purple and gold."

Junior nodded. "Prob'ly a wannabe."

"Not Dougie," I said. "He wasn't the sharpest kid, but I don't think he'd do something stupid like pretending to be in a gang."

"Then what?"

"That's what I've been thinking about. One of two things. Someone wanted to distract the police. Get them looking in the wrong direction."

Junior smirked. "That's not too hard."

"Or," I said, "someone wants to put undue attention on the Royal Family."

"Why someone wanna do that?"

"I don't know," I said. "I'd like you to ask Tio about it."

"Tio likes to keep things with the Family on the down low."

"Maybe he'll agree to talk to me. Can you get me a sit-down?"

Junior thought about that. Then a smile crossed his face.

"What?" I asked.

"I just remembered something." He took another bite of sausage before telling me what that was. "Kids used to say you was a cop before coming to the school."

"That's because I was."

"Damn," Junior said. "You still sound like one."

"I get that a lot." I stood up to get my blood flowing. All the food was making me a little tired. "Tell Tio I've still got some connections on the force. If he can convince me The Family had nothing to do with Dougie's murder, maybe I can convince them and help him avoid having to talk to the cops."

"You can do that?"

"Absolutely," I said, surprised by how confident I sounded. I looked at my watch. I was going to have to get moving if I was going to get to the

Manhattan side of the bridge by four o'clock. "Can you help me out, Junior?"

He stood. "I can try. You got a number I can reach you at?"

I gave him my cell number. "Call me anytime," I said.

"A'ight, Mr. D. No promises, though. I'll talk to Tio, but it's up to him what he does with the info."

"That's all I'm asking for. Thanks, Junior." I grabbed my jacket. "And thank your mom for lunch."

"Let me go get her," he said. "She'll be pissed she doesn't get to say good-bye."

I put my jacket on and waited by the front door. Just below the peep-hole and to the left of three locks, there was a crucifix. You can never have too much security.

"Senor Donne," Mrs. Alvarez said as she came toward me. "Please, you take some food home for dinner."

I patted my gut. "I think I already had my dinner, Senora. Thank you."

We exchanged a quick hug. I stuck out my hand for Junior.

"I'll call you, Mr. D. Either way."

"Thanks."

As he opened up the door, he put his hand on my shoulder. "Be careful."

I looked at his arm in the sling and said, "You, too." Then, just to remind us both of the here and now, I added, "And go back to school. Get that diploma."

"Right," he said, and shut the door. I looked at my watch again. I had thirty minutes to get to my meeting with Allison Rogers.

Chapter 4

I GOT THERE IN FORTY-FIVE. The walk from the subway to East River Park was longer than I remembered. And I'd picked up a cup of coffee at the last deli before the river.

The air coming off the water somehow smelled better on this side of the bridge. Colder, but fresher. A reminder that maybe winter wasn't going to be too bad when it officially arrived in a few weeks. When I got to the tennis courts, I saw a woman standing near the fence, her hands deep inside her coat pockets. I hadn't seen her in a year and a half, but it had to be Allison Rogers. Her blond hair was cut shorter than I remembered, and a pair of striking blue eyes were doing a bad job of hiding behind her librarian eyeglasses. I must have been more stressed out than I thought when we met a year and a half ago to have missed those eyes.

"Sorry I'm late," I said.

"No worries." She looked at the cup in my hand. "You didn't bring two of those by any chance?"

"Sorry." I held it out to her. "Sugar with half and half. I don't mind sharing."

"Thanks." She took a sip and placed the warm cup against her cheek. "I just got here myself." She looked around. "Wish I'd thought to bring a hat. Bosses kept me waiting to see if they could get me a photographer."

"And?"

She handed back my coffee, reached into her pocket, and pulled out a small, but professional-looking, camera. "Double duty. Same pay." She looked up at the sky. "Let's get a shot of you before we lose this light."

I looked up. The sun was just about gone, and the little light that remained was sneaking through the buildings and turning the Williamsburg Bridge orange. I followed Allison through the gate and onto the tennis courts as a subway train rumbled by overhead on its way to Brooklyn.

There were three sets of four courts, each set separated by a fence with a little walkway cut out. We took the first walkway. I picked up a slight limp in her walk just before Allison stopped on Court 6 and walked toward the net. There was a piece of black electrical tape on the ground. She pointed to it. "That's where they found the—where they found Douglas. Maintenance guy called it in right after he opened the courts at seven A.M."

I knew the courts were supposed to be closed at one A.M., because the sign on the gate said so. That, plus the ME's report, is how they figured Dougie was killed sometime after one. What the hell brought him out here at that time of the morning?

"If you don't mind," Allison said, "stand on the tape and turn toward me. I want a shot with the DOMINO sign in the background." She had planned this out before I got there. "It'll help make the connection between Manhattan and Williamsburg."

I looked over at the old Domino Sugar factory on the other side of the river. "'Dougie's Two Worlds,'" I said out loud, imagining the headline.

"Sorry, Ray. It's cynical, I know, but it works." She moved about ten feet away from me and looked through the lens. She adjusted the focus and started taking pictures. "Good, good," she said. "Just like that."

"Just like what?" I asked, then realized I must have looked sad and pensive. Just what she wanted, without even trying.

I looked at the surface of the tennis court. The normal scuff marks you'd expect—three- to four-inch swooshes—made by the stop-and-go of sneakers. There were other marks, too. A foot or so in length. Tiny skid marks.

"That's it." She shut off the camera and put it back in her pocket. From the other pocket, she pulled out a small notebook and a pen. "So, you went to the wake."

"How'd you know that?"

"I swung by the funeral home this morning, hoping to get some quotes for the article. I went inside and read the guestbook and saw your name. I missed the family by half an hour. Just as well. Saved me from having to ask a bunch of stupid questions I already knew the answers to."

"Like you're about to ask me?" I said.

She smiled and her eyes brightened even more. Maybe answering some inane questions wouldn't be so bad after all.

"Yeah," she said. "I suppose so."

"Shoot."

"Tell me about Dougie. What kind of student was he?"

"Not . . . outstanding," I said, keeping in mind my words would probably be showing up in the next day's newspaper. "He struggled with reading and math. Most of my kids did, but they brought other things to the table."

"Special ed, right?"

"Yeah, but it's not what most people think. Dougie had a quick mind. He could be funny as hell." I smiled at the thought. "He'd dis another kid so . . . effectively, the kid felt honored to have been his target. Dougie always seemed to know where the line was. He never pushed it." I realized what I had said and looked down at the black piece of tape. "At least not when I had him."

"You think he could have pushed someone too far this time?"

"Don't put words in my mouth, Allison. I'm just saying, Dougie knew how *not* to piss people off. I'll take those kind of smarts over working the Pythagorean theorem any day in the real world. What happened here . . . *this* . . . is off the charts."

"Any idea what he was doing out here at that time of night?"

"Not a clue. His mom told me he went to bed just after eleven and, the next thing she knows, she gets a call from the cops."

"Shit," Allison said. "Hell of a wake-up call."

"Yeah," I agreed. "I told her I was going to ask you to look into this a bit more."

"She *wants* this story pushed? She trusts the news to get this right?"

"More than she trusts the police. She wants the truth, Allison. Something—some*one*—got him out here that morning. We want to know who it was."

" 'We'?"

She caught me. "Yeah," I said. "She's got me talking like that."

"Who doesn't trust the police?" a voice said.

Allison and I turned to see a man in sunglasses and a dark blue overcoat walking toward us. The coat was open and underneath was a blue suit with a white shirt and a red tie. He looked as if he'd just walked out of the NYPD Detectives' Winter Catalog. When he got close enough, he offered his hand to Allison.

"Ms. Rogers," he said. "A pleasure. Again."

"Detective Murcer, thank you for coming. I know you're very busy."

"Never too busy to pass on an opportunity to see you, Allison." He turned to me and removed his shades. "Raymond."

Holy shit. "Dennis," I said, and turned to Allison. "Why didn't you tell me he was going to be here?"

"You two know each other?"

"Graduated from the academy together," Murcer explained.

"Why didn't you tell me that over the phone, Detective?"

"Thought I'd surprise old Ray here," he said. "And I wanted to see the look on your pretty face, Allison."

"This is your case, Dennis?" I asked.

"Yep," he said. "Can't catch a winner every time." He paused. "Sorry, Ray. Allison told me you knew the vic."

"Dougie," I said. "He was one of my kids for two years." I turned to Allison and gave her a what-the-fuck look.

"When you said you would meet me," she explained, "I called Detective Murcer, and he agreed to come on down and hear your side of the story. I obviously had no idea you two—"

"My side . . ." I struggled for the right words. "I don't *have* a 'side of the story,' Allison." I looked at Murcer. "The Douglas Lee I knew would not leave his house late at night without a good reason. Whatever brought him out here must have been real important. And it was not drugs. That's *my side* of the story. What did his teachers tell you when you spoke to them?"

Murcer cleared his throat. "Douglas was an above-average student with no disciplinary issues."

"How long did that phone call take?" I asked, and immediately wished I hadn't. "What did his classmates say?"

The look on Murcer's face went from slight embarrassment—he realized Allison was paying close attention—to something close to indignation. Not the righteous kind. The pissed-off kind. I'd seen that look many times years ago.

"Is this why I'm here, Allison?" he asked, his eyes on mine. "So I can get lectured by Chief Donne's nephew?"

"Oooh." Allison faked a shiver. "I love it when boys get all . . . testy." She took another sip of my coffee and handed back the cup. "I asked you down here, Detective, because I know a good story when I see one. This one," she looked down at the black tape, "has a lot of unanswered questions and requires a tad more . . . imagination."

Those words were a lot more polite than the ones I was thinking, but they were close enough to push the conversation in the direction I wanted it to go.

"What unanswered questions?" Murcer asked.

"How'd he—and his bike—get into the courts if they were locked?" I said.

Murcer gave that some thought. "Maybe the attendant forgot to lock up."

"Is it the same guy who's on duty now?"

Murcer shrugged. Allison said, "Let's go find out."

We found the guy inside the little attendant house outside the gate. He was sitting in a chair next to a portable heater, reading a newspaper. Some light jazz was coming from a small transistor radio on the table. The gold stitching on his green Parks Department shirt said his name was TER-RENCE, and Terrence didn't look too thrilled at having visitors, especially one with a badge dangling outside his jacket.

"Help ya, officers?" he asked.

Allison and I waited as Dennis reached into his jacket and pulled out a small notebook. He flipped through a few pages. "You were the attendant on duty last week?"

Terrence gave us a bored look. "Which day?"

"The night the kid was killed, Terrence."

Terrence considered that and nodded. "Yes, I was. I left here just after one. *In the morning.* Officer."

"Detective," Murcer corrected. "And you told the responding officers the next day you had locked up the night before, correct?"

"At one A.M. That is correct. Yes."

"And you're sure of that because . . ."

"Because I don't got too many complicated duties around here," Terrence said. "I sweep up the leaves and the garbage, move along the loiterers, every once in a while I get the thrill of removing a dead animal. Mostly pigeons and squirrels. Last thing I do is lock up. One A.M. Every morning. Like clockwork."

"And you found the body?" Murcer asked.

"Yes, sir."

"So you locked up at one," I interjected, "and you opened up at seven. Doesn't leave you much time for sleep."

Terrence grinned. "OT, my friend. I don't sleep when I'm *tired,* 'cause I'm gonna sleep when I'm *re*tired. You cops know all 'bout overtime, don'tcha?"

"He's the cop," I said, pointing my thumb at Murcer. "I'm just a schoolteacher."

"Bet you two get invited to lots of parties." He glanced over at Allison. "How about you, Miss? Police or teacher? You too cute to be either."

Allison held up her notepad. "Press."

"Ooh. You gonna put me in the papers?"

Allison turned to Murcer. "You didn't interview Terrence last week, Detective?"

"By the time I arrived," Murcer said, "my partner'd concluded the interview. I did a canvass of the park."

"And . . . ?" I asked.

"Not too many people around, and those that were didn't see anything." Murcer looked at the attendant and handed him a card. "You think of anything else . . ."

Terrence took the card and flipped it onto the table. "Right."

We all turned to leave when a thought hit me. I turned back to Terrence as Murcer and Allison stepped out of the building. "Those black marks out there," I said.

"Sneakers," he said. "Tennis shoes, my mother called 'em."

"I figured that. What about the longer ones?"

Terrence shook his head. "Damn kids with their skateboards. That's the main reason I gotta lock this place up. Think the city worries about people sneaking in and playing a late-night tennis match? Maybe stealing some nets? Shit. It's those brats doing three-sixties and whatnot. All we need's some kid to crack his head open 'cause I left the gate unlocked, and the city's got themselves a big old lawsuit and I'm back shoveling shit at the dog runs."

"So they climb over the fence after you're gone?"

"Pretty much."

"Any way a kid could sneak a bike through the locked gate?"

"Houdini's kid, maybe," he said. "I lock that thing tighter than a nun's legs."

Nice. With no more questions, I said, "Thanks for your help, Terrence."

"No problem, Officer," he said. "I mean, Detective."

"I'm the teacher."

"Whatever."

When I got outside, it took me a few seconds to find Allison and Murcer. They were standing with their backs to me, arms folded, watching a tugboat make its way up the East River. I heard Murcer say something about coffee and Allison mention she had to head back to the paper and write this piece up. They heard me coming and turned.

Murcer smirked. "Learn anything new from Terrence?"

"Said kids sometimes use the courts for skateboarding, usually after hours. That's what those longer scuff marks are from. Kids just hop the fence."

Allison thought about that. "But the gate was open when they found Douglas."

"Somebody must have unlocked it to let Dougie in with his bike." I looked at Murcer. "You ever find the murder weapon?"

"Nope."

"The ME give you any indication what it was?"

Murcer took out his notebook again and flipped through it. When he got to the page he was looking for, he said, "Eleven small entry wounds. 'Punctures' was the word he used. Shallow penetrations. Ten to the torso, front and back, one to the upper thigh. That one was not so shallow. One superficial two-inch wound to the upper neck. Not much internal damage. Vic just bled out. Jacket soaked up most of the blood."

"The victim's name was Dougie, Dennis," I reminded him. "The wound on his neck. Was it made by the same weapon as the other wounds?"

Murcer checked his notes. "ME didn't think so." Dennis tilted his head and squinted at me. "How'd you know to ask?"

"Two different types of wounds," I said. "The gate was unlocked, I'm thinking maybe the murder weapon was a lock pick. Also, the killer most likely knew where Dougie lived and knew Dougie could get here fast by bike."

Allison took out her notebook. She started writing so quickly her hand was almost a blur. Murcer reached out and touched her arm.

"You can't put that in the paper, Ms. Rogers."

"The hell I can't. This is the kind of stuff that'll keep this story—sorry, the investigation—moving in the right direction." Allison read the look on Murcer's face and said, "We may have different jobs, Detective, but I'll tell you one thing we do have in common: bosses who will not be able to ignore this information."

"That's not information," he said, pointing at Allison's notebook. "It's *Mr.* Donne's imagination. You print that and—"

"And what?" Allison asked. "You've got more important stuff on your desk than a dead black teenager?"

She might as well have kicked Dennis between the legs. He turned away from us and let out a large grunt. This was not why I came across the river.

"Okay," I said. "Everyone take a breath. It's not a competition. At least it doesn't have to be." I turned to Allison. "How's this?" I said. "After returning to the scene of the crime and taking a fresh look at the details, Detective Murcer agreed to pursue another course of investigation into the death of Douglas Lee."

Murcer spun back around. "I don't need your help, Raymond."

"And I don't want to make you look bad, Dennis," I said. "But I know what happened here and so does Douglas's mother. You got handed a loser, and you want to see it go away. *Yesterday.* That's not going to happen. You can either take our help, or we can just wait and see how your bosses react after reading the story Allison's dying to write." I lowered my voice. "We both know how they love a good cops-screwed-up piece next to a picture of the victim's grieving mother."

Allison tried to object, but I kept going.

"And, Allison, that kind of story is too easy for you. This new information—whatever you want to call it—came to light as a result of Detective Murcer agreeing to look further into the facts. What could have become another routine unsolved is now an ongoing investigation. *That's* a better story than what you came here with."

Allison knew I was putting a shine on the situation, but after a while she realized what I was saying sounded pretty good.

"Okay," she said. "I can see it playing. And it *is* the truth."

Murcer still didn't look happy. I remembered that look well.

"Leave out the part about the murder weapon possibly being a lock pick," he said. "It is an ongoing investigation, and we don't want to give the killer a reason to get rid of any evidence." He looked at Allison's face. "Please."

Allison nodded. "And you keep me on the top of your call list when you become aware of any new developments."

"I can do that," Murcer said and looked at his watch. "The school's closed for the weekend. I'll head over there Monday and talk to some of the kids and teachers."

"What about the rumor of a gang angle?" Allison asked. "The Royal Family?"

"How'd you— We're looking into that," Murcer said. "Off the record?" Allison gave him a reluctant nod. "They keep pretty much on the down low, and their structure's a bit hard to get a read on." I kept my mouth shut as he went on. "From what we are hearing"—he looked at me—"it doesn't seem like Douglas fits the profile of a gang member. But we've got our feelers out just in case."

The three of us stood there silently for a few moments. When it became obvious none of us had anything to add, Allison flipped her notebook shut. "Thanks for your time, gentlemen. I've got to head uptown and write this baby up. I'm gonna try and catch a cab." She pointed north to the entrance ramp of the FDR Highway.

Murcer buttoned up his coat. "I'm going to see if I can catch the ME before he heads out for the weekend and run this lock pick idea past him."

Dennis was getting on board. At least in front of Allison.

"Thank you both," I said. "Dougie's mom will find some comfort knowing the press *and* the police are taking this seriously. It'll mean a lot to her."

I shook their hands. Murcer held on to my hand a bit longer than customary. "You got a few minutes to stay and chat, Ray?"

"Yeah, Dennis." I turned to Allison. "This'll be in tomorrow's paper?"

"It damn well better be."

"Okay."

With nothing else to say, Allison walked north. Murcer and I watched as she did. I noticed the limp again. When she was out of earshot, Dennis turned to me.

"What the fuck, Ray? You think I can't handle this myself?"

"Dennis," I said, "I had no idea you caught this case. Shit, I had no idea you'd been assigned to the Lower East Side. When did that happen?"

"Your Uncle Ray didn't tell you?"

"We don't see each other all that much, and when we do he doesn't talk much about his Boys, Dennis."

He grinned and shook his head. "You're still smarting over that, huh?"

"Over what?"

"Me getting that gig. That I got to spend six months as 'Chief Donne's Boy.'"

"Why the hell would I resent him picking you?"

"Oh, I don't know, Ray. Maybe because you wanted it."

"Yeah, that would've looked good: Chief Donne picking his nephew to be on the fast track to promotion."

"I earned my fucking promotion, Ray."

"I'm not saying you didn't, Dennis. I wouldn't have put in a good word for you if I hadn't thought you were a good cop."

"I didn't need your *good word*."

"Dennis," I said calmly. My hands were getting cold so I stuck them in my pockets. "We had a graduating class of a couple of hundred cadets. Everybody he considered needed a good word."

"And yours was the best, right?"

"I'm his nephew. Yeah, it carried a lot of weight. You deserved it."

Dennis looked out at the water, the lights from the bridge twinkling in the approaching darkness.

"How fast you get your shield?" I asked.

"Year-and-a-half after I left your uncle. He wanted to place me in Midtown North after I left him."

"The Cuff Link Crew?"

He laughed. "Yeah. Told him I wanted the Ghetto Squad. Make my bones the old-fashioned way. Working case after case, getting my hands dirty. Made second grade two years ago."

"That's why I put in the good word, D. I didn't take you as someone who'd take the easy route."

He looked back at the river. "You don't have any regrets?"

"About . . . ?"

"What if he *had* helped you out, and you were the one with the special assignment six months after the academy? All nepotism aside. You don't think about that? About how your future as a cop would've changed?"

I let out a deep breath. "You talking about my accident?" My legs tingled when I flashed back to the fire escape.

"Yeah, Ray. I am. I can see why you couldn't take the gig with your uncle. Let's say you let him throw something else your way. You're not on the streets of Williamsburg, and you don't take that plunge. And that kid don't get himself killed."

"Dennis," I said, "there's not a day that goes by I don't think about my accident. My body won't let me. And there's also not a day I don't think of Raheem Ellis and how he'd probably still be alive if I hadn't chased him into that building. But I've moved on, man. I got a new life. I'm working on being good with that."

He turned to look me in the eyes. "That why you came out here today, Ray? Because you've moved on?"

"I came out here today to help keep Dougie's story in the paper, Dennis. No offense, but you and I both know the shelf life of this kind of case. As long as the press is on it, so are your bosses."

He smiled, but it wasn't the happy kind. "So I won't be seeing you butting your nose around, right?"

"Don't see any reason why you would," I said. "I got what I wanted."

"Because I know what happened with that other kid of yours a while back. The kid from the Clemente Houses."

You don't know everything.

"Frankie. Yeah. I don't know what you think you—"

"I still talk with Chief Donne, Ray. He may not talk about his Boys, but he *does* speak quite highly of his nephew."

"A different time, Dennis. Different situation."

"I hope so." He stuck out his hand. "Maybe I'll swing by The LineUp some night. You still doing time working the stick?"

"Every Tuesday night," I said, shaking his hand. "That'd be cool."

"Yeah," he said. He turned to go and then stopped. "Maybe you could ask Rachel to come around."

I was wondering how long it'd take for her to come up.

"You know how I said you're a good cop, Dennis?"

"Yeah?"

"You were a fucking lousy boyfriend."

"Jesus. We're not gonna have this conversation again, are we, Ray?"

"I'm not," I said.

"Maybe I've changed, Ray. Learned to keep the shit at the precinct before heading home."

"I'll see you at The LineUp, Dennis. Tuesday nights."

I could tell he was thinking of something else to say. When he couldn't come up with anything, he raised his hands. "Whatever." He turned again to leave, and this time he didn't stop.

I looked over at the East River and took in a bit of clean, cold air. The lights from the bridge were dancing across the water. I found myself wanting to smile at the beauty of the whole image until a thought hit me: That bridge and those lights might have been the last things Douglas Lee ever laid his eyes on.

Chapter 5

"YOU SURE YOU DON'T WANT a burger?" Mikey asked me. "I can have the kitchen throw one on the grill, be ready in ten minutes."

"Just the pint of Brooklyn," I repeated. "I had a late lunch."

"Okey dokey." Mikey slipped a coaster under my pilsner then headed down to the other end of the bar. That's when Edgar Martinez O'Brien lifted his glass to me.

"Four, one, two," he said. Edgar's daily toast to the years, months, and days he had until retiring from the New York City Transit Authority. He was on his regular stool—the one with the best view of the TV—drinking his regular pint of Bass with tomato juice. Tonight, like every other recent evening, he had his laptop with him.

I clinked my glass against his. "I don't know what they're going to do without you, Edgar." My usual response.

"Hire me to consult." His usual response. "And how was your day, Raymond?"

One thing about Edgar: when he asked how your day was, he meant it and wanted all the details. Another thing is, Edgar was a cop junkie, which was why he hung out at The LineUp as much as he did. This is a cop bar, owned by Mrs. Mac, a cop's widow, and quite often staffed by ex-cops. My shift was Tuesday nights. Edgar never got enough of listening to the stories the cops—past and present—tell each other. There was a time when I used to find Edgar more of a pain in the ass than anything else, but a year and a half ago he'd come through for me big-time and now we were—for lack of a better word—buddies. So when he asked me about my day, there was no holding back.

When I had finished with the details, Edgar leaned back, folded his arms, and smiled. He took off his glasses and wiped them with a napkin.

"The detective," Edgar said. "He let you check out the crime scene?"

"Wasn't up to him," I said. "Dougie was killed almost a week ago. The courts are open for public use."

He slid his glasses back on. "Pretty slick how you figured out the murder weapon mighta been a lock pick. They checking for similar MOs?" Edgar loved that cop talk.

"Yeah," I said. "I'm sure they are."

"Cool." He leaned closer to me. "So what do you do next, Ray?"

"Well," I said, lowering my voice, "I'm going to finish my beer, go home to bed, wake up tomorrow, and see if the story made the paper." If it did, I'd have to call two mothers: Dougie's and mine. Dougie's mom would thank me, while mine would go out and buy all the copies at the corner deli by her house.

"Come on, Ray. You know what I mean. About the Royal Family connection."

"Probably nothing, Edgar. I reached out to Junior, and he made it clear Tio does not talk about Family business with people outside the Family." I took a sip of my beer. "I promised Dougie's mom I'd call Allison and see if she could keep the story alive. I did that. Whatever Murcer comes up with in regards to the gang stuff, I hope he checks it out. My guess, it doesn't come to much."

Edgar let out a disappointed sigh and then opened his laptop. He played with the keys for about fifteen seconds and turned the screen so I could see it.

"This," he explained, "is all the news that's fit to print about the Royal Family. Every piece containing their name and the word 'gang' written in the past six months. I could go back further if you want. A year, maybe?"

I slid the computer closer to me, looked at the screen, and scrolled down. Not a lot of press on these guys. Four pieces over the past half year. Junior was right: Tio did keep his business on the down low. I clicked on one of the stories, and it was all of six short paragraphs. Even the headline was sketchy: LOCAL GANG SUSPECTED IN DRUGSTORE BREAK-IN. Not much info in the four paragraphs, and what there was sounded more like what people thought than what they actually knew. The rest of the stories were pretty much the same. Light on details, no names, no actual evidence of anything. Gang gossip.

Edgar was reading along with me. "Not much, huh?"

"Like they barely exist," I agreed.

"You still know anybody in the gang unit?"

"Edgar," I said. "There's no one I know who's going to be more helpful to me than the guys Murcer can reach out to. Like I told Dougie's mom, let's see what they come up with. Murcer's got a pushy reporter more than interested in this story. I know him. He'll exercise due diligence." I took a quick sip. "At least for the next few days."

"I guess you're right," Edgar said, not even trying to hide the disappointment in his voice. He was probably hoping this was going to be the beginning of another adventure. He looked at my almost-empty pint glass. "You ready for another?"

I drained what was left. "Yeah. Why not?" I knew this was his way of keeping the conversation going, but if it got me another beer, where was the harm?

Edgar waved down Mikey, who brought another round over.

"You two doing okay?" he asked. Mikey was still amazed at my friendship with Edgar. Most of the other regulars did their best to stay clear of his constant questioning and his inability to let go of a train of thought.

"Doing well," I said. "Thanks."

I slid my empty glass away to make room for the new one. My cell phone started to vibrate in my pocket. I pulled it out and didn't recognize the number on the screen. Usually I'd let it go to voice mail, but curiosity got the better of me and I answered it.

"Hello?"

"Mr. D?" a voice said.

"Yes?"

"Yo, Mr. D. It's me. Junior."

"Hey, Junior," I said, and once again had Edgar's full attention. "What's up?"

"I called Tio and explained the sitch. You know, with the cops and the beads around the dead kid's neck?"

"Yeah."

"Said he knew 'bout that already. But then I told him you was looking into it, and at first he got all pissed, but then I told him who you was, and he remembered you from the papers when you helped that other kid, y'know?"

"Okay . . ."

"Anyways," Junior said, "he says he'll meet with you."

I sat up straighter. "Really?"

"Yeah. He said better you than the cops. You can do that, right?"

"Absolutely, Junior," I said, starting to believe my own spin. "When?"

"Tomorrow, man. He said nine o'clock. You know the pizza place next to the dollar store a block away from the hospital?"

"Yeah."

"A'ight, then. Be there at nine."

"Junior," I said, "thanks a lot for this. I owe you one."

"Nah, Mr. D. This is me payin' you back for not jacking me up when I decked that kid in the playground."

"Okay, Junior. Thanks again."

"Later, Mr. D."

I hung up and looked at Edgar's curious face. If his tongue had been out, he would have looked like a puppy waiting for a treat. I raised my glass and touched it against his.

"Looks like I'm meeting with a gang leader tomorrow," I said.

Edgar gave me his biggest shit-eating grin. "Pretty cool."

"Yeah," I said, feeling a buzz I hadn't felt in a long time. "I guess it is."

Chapter 6

THE LIGHT-SKINNED HISPANIC kid who showed up at the locked door of the pizza shop was just over four feet and looked like he was still in elementary school. He was wearing a black and gold New Orleans Saints football jersey with the number seven on it, matching do-rag, baggy blue jeans, and a nice, new pair of purple sneakers. The watch on his left wrist was big enough to serve spaghetti on. He looked me up and down, paused after putting his hand on the lock, and said, "Who you?"

"Raymond Donne," I said through the glass door. "I'm here to see Tio."

The kid shook his head. "Ain't no Tio here, mister. You sure you at the right pizza place?"

Yeah. I was sure. Calmly, I said, "Junior told me to meet Tio here."

The kid smiled and nodded. "Whatcha say your name was?"

Fucking with the white guy. Enjoy it while you can, little man. "Raymond Donne," I repeated. "Tio's expecting me."

"Hold on a minute," he said. "I be right back."

He turned around, did a nice, slow walk to the back of the restaurant, and disappeared through a set of swinging doors. I looked over my shoulder across the street and noticed a teenager at the corner on a cell phone. Same Saints jersey—his with the number eleven—same do-rag as the kid. I held on for about a minute and was about to knock again when the kid came through the swinging doors, followed by a larger, older Hispanic male wearing a similar outfit, without the do-rag. His jersey had the number one. *Subtle*. Number One put away his phone and took a seat at a booth, while the kid came back to the door. This time he unlocked it and held it open for me.

"C'mon in, mister," he said. "Tio say he *expecting* you."

"Thanks, kid," I said as I stepped inside.

"Name's Boo," the kid said. To make his point, he showed me the gold chain around his neck that did indeed say BOO. I also noticed some purple and gold beads peeking out from under the neckline of his jersey. Boo relocked the door. "Follow me."

He brought me to the booth where the older guy was sitting. I stood there as Boo went through the swinging doors again; doors I could now see led to the kitchen. The guy at the booth took a big sip from the steaming cup he had in his hands and motioned for me to sit down. I did. Today's paper was opened to the page with Allison's story about Dougie. My picture was staring back at me.

"Can I get you something, Mr. Donne?" the guy asked.

"If that coffee tastes as good as it smells, I'll take some."

"Boo!" The kid stuck his head through the service window of the kitchen. "Coffee for the teacher." He turned to me. "How you take it?"

"Cream and two sugars," I said.

"Thank you, Boo." Boo's head disappeared. "You hungry?"

"I'm good, thanks. You're Tio?"

"Yes." He tapped my picture in the paper. "And you . . . have you read this?"

"Not yet, no. I woke up and came right here."

Tio closed up the paper and slid it to me. "For later then."

"Thanks." I put the paper on the seat next to me. "I appreciate the meeting."

"My cousin says you cool, I'm cool." Tio took another sip of his coffee. "That was your boy killed over by the river, huh?"

"Former student of mine, yeah. Junior explain to you why—"

"I heard about the beads around your boy's neck," he said. "Junior told me you could keep me and the cops from having a conversation. That's why you and me are having *this* conversation."

"That's about right."

"What's that mean?"

Before I could answer, Boo came back with my coffee and placed it in front of me on a napkin. While I waited for him to leave, I took a sip. Perfect.

"It means," I said, "the detective investigating Dougie's murder is an old friend of mine. If I like what I hear from you, I think he'll listen to me."

"What's that mean? If you like what you hear? You think I invited you here so I could spin you some fairy tale?"

"I know how these guys think. I used to be one of them. They smell smoke, they don't always want to know where the fire is." I waited a few seconds for that to sink in. Then I came out with the purpose of my visit. "Was Dougie Lee a member of the Royal Family?"

Tio took a moment to rub the palms of his hands over the tabletop. Then he drained the rest of his coffee, took a napkin out of the dispenser, and wiped his lips. After taking a deep breath, he said, "You sure you're not hungry? Boo makes a good omelet."

"He doesn't look big enough to reach the stove."

"Boo!" Again, Boo's head appeared at the window. "Bring the teacher the same as me. And more coffee, please."

I had the feeling I'd just passed some kind of a test. Instead of getting kicked out on my ass, I just got invited to brunch.

"So," Tio said. "Used to be a cop, now you're a teacher. Ain't you just a bit curious about why we're meeting in a pizza shop?"

I looked around the restaurant. "You want to know what I think?"

"That's why I asked."

"My guess," I said, "The Family's got a deal with the owner. You get the space when he's not open for business, and he gets what amounts to the best security system in Brooklyn. I watch a lot of old gangster movies, though, so I could be wrong."

Tio smiled and rubbed his chin. "That's good, Teacher Man. Junior was right about you. No bullshit."

"So, no bullshit. Are you going to answer my question?"

"I don't talk about Family members. Junior told you that, right?"

"I'm not asking about Family members. I'm asking about Dougie."

"That's good, too," he said, now running his index finger and thumb over his mustache. "You pretty sure this kid of yours was not a part of my crew. Why's that?"

"Dougie wasn't the type of kid to join a gang."

Tio leaned back and folded his arms. "What type of kid joins a gang, Mr. Donne?"

"Again," I said, "the truth?"

"Please."

Before I could answer, Boo came through the swinging doors with two plates filled with omelets, toast, and home fries. He placed them on the table and went back for the coffees. After he left the second time, Tio said, "Go on."

I took a bite of my eggs before speaking. Red and green peppers, mushrooms, and cheese. Again, perfect.

"Take Boo," I said. "Single mom, my guess in her upper twenties. Probably has a little brother or sister—different dad—so he doesn't get a hell of a lot of attention at home. Mom still likes to go out and have some fun, though, so Boo's babysitting the little one more than he should and, as bright as he is, he misses a lot of school." I took a sip of coffee. "How am I doing so far?"

"Like you been working The Burg too long." We both took a few bites of our food. "Boo's my cousin. His moms is my mom's cousin. Had Boo when she was sixteen and dropped outta high school. Had his sister two years later. Same guy, but now he's gone. Not exactly a family man."

"And that's where you come in?"

"Somebody's gotta teach the boy about life." Tio sipped his coffee. "Teach him a skill. Keep his ass in school as long as it takes."

"You should talk to Junior."

"Boy's earning, Teacher Man," Tio said. "Junior doesn't need what Boo needs. His moms set him on the right path young. College doesn't come into that picture, so Junior and a high school diploma don't necessarily need to be on a first-name basis." I must have had a look on my face, because Tio added, "I say something charming?"

I shook my head. "Just trying to figure you out, Tio." I took the last bite of my toast as I chose my next words carefully. "You're obviously a smart, articulate guy. You switch back and forth between English and Street, but you've been schooled."

"I got my GED. So what?"

"And yet here you are . . ." I stopped, searching for the right word.

"A gang leader?" he filled in for me, with the serious tone of a bad newscaster.

"Yeah," I said. "You *don't* fit the type."

Tio smiled again, took one more bite of his omelet, and pushed his plate away. It was a good half-minute before he spoke.

"I grew up 'round here. Coupla blocks away. My dad did the restaurant thing in Manhattan and my mom was part-time home health care. I was ten when they split. *Legally separated.* Just like the white folks do it in the burbs. No big deal. Lived with Mom during the week and Dad on the weekends, but 'cause he worked as a cook, I didn't see him too much. Weekend was my time to be a street kid, hang out late, run around with the wannabe bangers, know what I mean?"

I nodded. "Until your mom figured it out."

"Got that right. No more Saturdays bouncing 'round The Burg, no more Monday mornings always being late and dragging my tired ass to school. Got me back on track, she did. But not before I saw the need." He pointed toward the front door of the pizza place. "Kids out there that shouldn't be, y'know? Running nowhere fast, my moms would say. Soon's I could, I dropped out, got my GED, and started making some real moves of my own to earn some green."

"Restaurant gigs?" I guessed out loud.

"Dishwasher, busboy, line cook. You name it. Always worked the daytime shift. Made sure I kept my nights free, though, so I could fill the need I saw." He sat back. "Ever read Dickens?"

I leaned forward. "Excuse me?"

"Charlie Dickens, Teacher Man. *Great Expectations? Oliver Twist?*"

"Yeah," I said. "I've read him."

"Last book I checked out before droppin' out. Thought it'd be cool to be like Fagin, y'know? Buncha kids following me around, doing my shit, learning from me."

"Stealing and dealing?"

Tio spread his hands out. "I ain't saying. But I tell my kids to get their asses home by ten and stay in school and respect the folks you got putting food on your table."

"What does your mom think of all this . . . Dickens stuff?"

"I don't know," he said, his eyes locked on mine. "She died four years ago. Got stuck by a needle shouldn'ta been where it was."

"I'm sorry."

"Is what it is."

I finished up the last of my coffee and piled fork, knife, and napkin on top of the plate. As if on cue, Boo came out and cleared the table. He didn't ask if I wanted more coffee, and I took that as a cue it might be time to leave.

"So," I said. "Dougie Lee?"

Tio stroked his mustache again. "Name don't ring a bell."

"Any idea why someone would want to point the cops in your direction?"

"A couple," he said. "But that's Family business."

"And you don't discuss Family business outside the Family."

"Man's nothing without some rules."

"I understand," I said, feeling like a bit player in *The Godfather*. I grabbed the newspaper and slid out of the booth. Tio didn't move to get up, so I stuck out my hand. "Again, I appreciate the meet, Tio. I know you didn't have to agree to this."

"We all do things we don't hafta every once in a while," he said, looking at the newspaper in my hand while shaking my other one. "Got a feeling you know that."

"Life's like that sometimes," I said. "I'll see ya around, maybe."

"Maybe. By the way, the owner of this place?"

"Yeah?"

"You looking at him."

I smiled and nodded. "Cool."

"Yeah," Tio the gang leader said. "It is."

I was a few blocks from the subway station, wondering what to do with the rest of my Saturday, when I realized I was being followed. I normally wouldn't have noticed, but after seeing black-and-gold jerseys this morning, it was hard to miss the two behind me, one on my side of the street and one on the other. Maybe Tio wanted to make sure I wasn't going straight to the cops with what little info I'd gotten from our meeting. I was about to turn around and say something, when I noticed another black-and-gold heading my way. The one coming at me was wearing a matching baseball cap and speaking on a cell phone. When we were about half a block from each other, I saw she was female. Asian-looking. She ended her call, stopped walking, and waited for me to get closer.

I stopped a few feet in front of her and said, "Tell Tio I'm just going home. And thanks again for breakfast."

She sucked her teeth. "Don't give a shit about breakfast," she said. "You need to come for a walk wit' us."

I felt the other two moving in behind me and I turned around. Two more girls, both Hispanic. They spread out so I was in the middle of a triangle.

"I'm going home," I repeated, and tried to move past the one with the cell phone. She stepped in front of me, and the other two closed in from behind.

"You wanna get stomped, Mister Man?" the one in front asked. I could see now she was Hispanic, not Asian. "Right here on the avenue? By a buncha girls?"

"Not if I can help it," I said, trying to figure a way out of this. Before I could come up with something, a van pulled up alongside us. The windows were tinted, so I couldn't see inside.

"Then you either let us walk you to the subway, or"—she gestured with her thumb toward the van—"you go for a ride."

I considered my options and knew from experience nothing good would come from me getting in the van. I thought about running, but with my fucking knees, and three young girls and a van chasing me, I didn't think I'd get too far.

"I guess it wouldn't hurt to have you all walk me to the train," I said.

"Yeah," the girl said. "And it might hurt if ya didn't." She linked her arm through mine as if we were a couple. "Let's go."

And we did: the two of us arm-in-arm, the other girls staying a couple of steps back. The van followed along slowly, a block away.

"So," she said, "what'd you and Tio conversate about?"

"Why don't you ask him?" I said, and she dug her nails into my wrist. "Jesus!" I pulled my arm away.

"You want me to ask you again?"

"Not if you're going to ask like that," I said, looking at the red crescents forming on my wrist. "I asked him if he knew an old student of mine."

"Kid who got hisself killed on the tennis courts?"

"Yeah."

She smiled. Without the toughness, she might have been pretty. "We seen you over there yesterday. But you ain't no cop. Why you all up in this business?"

"I promised someone I'd look into it for her."

She seemed to consider that for a bit and then nodded. "What Tio tell you?"

"He didn't know Dougie."

She grabbed my arm again and tightened her grip. "Anything else?"

"It was my only question."

"Long meeting for one answer."

"I got invited to stay for breakfast."

She nodded again, understanding. "Then we shouldn't be seeing you over on the other side of the bridge no more, right? Or having no more brunches with Tio?"

"I don't know why you would." Those were almost the exact words I'd said to Dennis Murcer the day before.

She loosened her grip a little, ran her fingertips over the area she'd just dug her nails into. "That wasn't so bad now, was it, Mister Man?" Her voice was lower now, trying for seductive.

"Could've been worse, I guess."

"Yeah," she agreed. "Coulda been a lot worse." We were a half a block away from the subway. She woke up her cell phone, punched a number, and said something in Spanish. She spoke too fast for me to understand it. After she ended her call, the van pulled over in front of us, and the side door slid open. "You sure you don't want a ride? Getcha home real quick."

"No," I said. "I'm good."

"Whatever," she said, and slid into the van, taking a seat in the front as the other two climbed in the side. The van took off, speeding through a yellow light. I pulled out my cell and found Junior's number.

"What's up?" he said. "How'd it go with Tio?"

"Good," I said. "Thanks again for hooking me up. Any idea why I was just accosted by a group of girls wearing Family jerseys?"

A brief pause. "Ah shit, Mr. D. What'd they look like?"

"Three girls," I said. "Hispanic. Another one in a van. The one who did all the talking looked kind of Asian. Almost pretty, but a bit quick with the nails." I waited for a response. After ten seconds, I said, "Junior? You still there?"

"These jerseys," he said. "Same as Tio's?"

"Black and gold, yeah."

"Even numbers?"

"I don't remember, Junior. What the hell does—?"

"Tio's boys," he said. "They all sport odd numbers."

He was right. I wasn't paying much attention at the time, but now I recalled the girls all had even numbers on their shirts.

"Sounds like it was probably China," he said.

"Who?" I asked.

"China," he repeated. "Chee Nah."

"Okay. Who's China?"

A longer pause. This time I waited. "Ahh, Mr. D," he finally said. "I told you, I don't like talking 'bout Family business."

"Come on, Junior. The girl threatened to toss me in the back of a van and practically drew blood from my wrist. The least you can tell me is who the hell she is."

Again, I waited. Junior was probably wishing I'd never called him.

"She's Tio's cousin," Junior said. "She's from the other side."

The other side? "What? She's a vampire?"

That got a laugh. "Other side of the bridge, Mr. D. She kinda runs things over there. I don't know how much she and Tio talk these days."

"Not too much, I'd guess. She pretty much told me she'd been watching me the last two days but didn't know why I was talking with Tio."

"And you told her?"

"Yeah, I told her. It was either that or risk the nails again."

"Sorry, man. I'm gonna give Tio a call and let him know."

"Whatever," I said. "Thanks again, Junior. Tio said he didn't know Dougie. His mom'll be glad to hear that."

"All good, then," Junior said. "See ya 'round, Mr. D. Stay cool."

"I'll do my best. You, too, Junior."

I was about to go down to the subway but decided to walk the rest of the way home. I needed the air.

• ꞏ •   •

I got back home about twenty minutes later. A large man wearing a trench coat, standing with his back to me, was waiting in front of my apartment. He held a rolled-up newspaper and tapped his leg with it. His other hand was up by his face, and then a plume of smoke rose above his head. *Oh, boy. What the hell was he doing here?*

"Uncle Ray?" I said.

He turned to face me and grinned. He spread his arms out and said, "My nephew. The famous Raymond Donne."

I stepped into his arms, and we gave each other a hug. He patted me on the back a few times, and I knew I'd be feeling that spot for the next hour.

"Why are you here?" I asked after we broke the embrace.

He held up the newspaper. "Had to swing by and congratulate you on your appearance in one of our fine city's respected papers of record. What's this? Something you do every eighteen months or so?" He stuck his cigar in his mouth, opened the paper, found the page he was looking for, and folded it over. "There you are, Raymond. Your mother must be so proud."

"I haven't spoken to her yet," I said.

"Well . . ." He folded the paper back the way it had been and handed it to me. "I see you've got your own, but take mine, too. For your scrapbook."

"Thanks." I took the paper and put it under my arm with the copy Tio had given me. "You came all the way to Greenpoint just to give me a newspaper?" I asked, both of us knowing the answer to that question.

"Actually," he said, then took a long drag from his cigar and let out a smooth stream of smoke. "Having lunch at Peter Luger's this afternoon. Bunch of us from the academy—those of us still alive and not in Florida—still keep in touch, try to get together once a year before the holidays. Reminisce, shoot the shit, you know."

I smiled. "That's cool."

He pointed to the newspapers. "Seems like you've been taking a little stroll down memory lane yourself, Nephew."

"Yeah. I ran into Dennis Murcer yesterday. The reporter covering my kid's—"

"I read the paper, Raymond." He looked at the tip of his cigar and blew off the one-inch layer of ash. Eyes back on me, he said, "Had the weird feeling of déjà vu after reading that story. Made me very uncomfortable."

"And why's that?"

He grinned. "A year and a half ago, Raymond. Didn't we have this very conversation a year and a half ago?"

I considered that for a while. "Absolutely, Uncle Ray. This has nothing to do with that, though. This was just me—"

"Sticking your nose into police business."

"Keeping Douglas Lee's story in the papers for another day or two."

"Raymond," he said, still grinning. "Don't bullshit the man who taught you how to bullshit. It's insulting."

"Uncle Ray, all I wanted to do was get the reporter to do another piece on Dougie. I had no idea Dennis was the detective in charge. Even if I had, it wouldn't have mattered. I'm glad he caught the case. He's a good cop."

"Damn straight he is," said the man who had the most invested in that idea. "So your involvement in this case is over?"

"My involvement in this case is over," I said, knowing my uncle liked to have his exact words repeated back to him to make sure I got it.

He dropped his cigar to the ground, stepped on it, then kicked it into the gutter. "Good," he said. "Because I have no desire to go through what we went through the last time."

"I have no intention of that happening either, Uncle Ray."

He let out a big laugh. "The road to Hell, Raymond. I believe you had *no intention* the last time, as well." He held up his hand, anticipating my next words. "I know. This time is different."

"It is," I said.

He looked me in the eyes for a few seconds. "Okay," he said. "We going to see you and Rachel for Christmas dinner?"

No one changes a topic faster than Uncle Ray. "That's the plan," I said.

"Good." He stepped over and pulled me into another hug. "Your mom's gonna be there. And Reeny's brother, Max."

Reeny was my uncle's second wife, and her single brother was always invited to family functions—I think with the intention of him and my mom getting together. Not only was this never going to happen, I had the strong feeling Max was gay. An issue never discussed at Raymond and Reeny Donne's very Catholic kitchen table.

"I'm there," I said.

"Outstanding," my uncle said. He motioned with his head up the block at a black town car illegally double parked, and said, "There's my ride. Don't wanna keep the boys—or my steak—waiting. Stay in touch, Nephew."

"I will, Uncle Ray. Thanks for the extra copy."

When I got upstairs, I threw the papers on the couch, and went to the kitchen. I needed something hot to drink and started up the coffee machine. It probably wouldn't be as good as Boo's, but it'd have to do. My kitchen is almost all windows, and they provide me with an outstanding view of the Manhattan skyline. A mess of gray and white clouds was coming in over the buildings from Jersey, and I remembered the guy on the radio this morning saying we were probably in for some flurries.

I took two steps back from the counter and got into a runner's stretch position. My knees were starting to feel the walk home in the cold. A hot shower would help, but I knew I needed to get my ass—and my knees—over to Muscles's and do some real rehab. It had been over a year since I'd last had to use my umbrella as a cane. If I didn't keep ahead of it, I knew I was going to be right back where I had started.

When the coffee was done, I took a cup into the living room to check out the paper. I was about to open it, when I noticed the message light blinking on the phone. The number next to the light blinked, "9." Uncle Ray wasn't the only one to read about me this morning. I took a sip of coffee and pressed the PLAY button.

Ten minutes later, I had listened to messages from my mother, my sister Rachel, Edgar, a few others from The LineUp, Uncle Ray, and Elaine Stiles, the school counselor. Edgar thought the article and picture made me look "cool." My mom was proud and had already bought out all the papers in her neighborhood. Only Elaine and Rachel asked me how I was feeling. *Good question.*

I opened the paper and turned to the article. It was a half page—Saturdays are slow news days in the big city—and the picture of me looking down at where Dougie's body had been found took up a chunk of that. Allison had done a good job recapping the story, connecting me to Dougie, and commenting on how the cops were conducting a thorough investiga-tion. All in all, exactly what I had hoped for. I grabbed my cell phone off the coffee table, scrolled down to Allison's number, and dialed.

"Hello, hero," she said.

"Don't start. I just called to say thank you."

"I was about to do the same, Ray. Really. My bosses loved the piece, and they promised to let me get at least one more in. How about Dougie's mom? She happy with the way we handled it?"

"She's my next call," I said.

Pause. "You called me first?"

"To say thanks."

"Okay." She cleared her throat. "Hey. What are you doing tonight?"

In a day full of surprises, here was another one. "I'm not sure," I said. "I guess I don't really have any plans." *Great, Ray. You don't sound too much like a loser.*

"Well, now you do," Allison said. "You know the new club on Metro-politan Avenue? Used to be a kosher deli or Laundromat or something?"

"I can't say that I do."

"I gotta be there tonight. The paper's doing a new series: Saturdays at Eight. They want to spotlight the new hot spots around the five boroughs. Get the young readers turning the pages. Bullshit, if you ask me. All the hipsters get their info electronically or by word of mouth, but when your editors went to journalism school with Cronkite and Murrow, what do you expect?"

"So," I said, "you're a crime reporter during the day and a trendspot-ter at night?"

"The cheap fucks won't spring for another reporter, so those of us still lucky enough to be hanging on to our jobs get to take turns club-hopping. And you, my friend, get to tag along. Come on, whattaya say?"

"They serve beer?"

"And apple martinis."

I laughed and grabbed a piece of paper off the table. "What's the address?"

She gave it to me. "Eight o'clock, Ray. And dress . . . hip."

She'd never seen my closet. "I'll see what I can do."

"Later."

After she hung up—and I got the smile off my face—I called the Lee home. A woman's voice I did not recognize picked up. "Lee residence."

"This is Raymond Donne," I said. "Is Mrs. Lee home?"

"The teacher from the newspaper?" A slight Southern accent.

"Yes." I was already getting tired of this. "Is Mrs. Lee there?"

"Oh, no," the woman said. "They're all still at the cemetery. You didn't go to the church, young man?"

"No, ma'am. I didn't."

"That's okay," she reassured me. "Gloria told me you didn't strike her as a church-going person. But you seem nice just the same."

"Thank you," I said. "When's a good time . . ." There was no way to finish that without sounding stupid. "When would I be able to speak with Mrs. Lee?"

"She wants everyone to know she'll be expecting them at the apartment tomorrow afternoon. Anytime after one. I'm back here taking calls and cleaning, getting the home ready for tomorrow."

"That's very nice of you."

"It's what family does," she explained. "I went to the church, but I don't much care for cemeteries."

Like the rest of us enjoyed them. "Okay, then. Thank you, Miss . . ."

"Dutton. Missus Sarah Dutton. Gloria's cousin from Virginia."

"Thank you, Mrs. Dutton. I'll see you tomorrow."

"You better, young man. I know Gloria's expecting *you* especially. And I'm sure there's a whole buncha others who would like to meet you."

"I guess that settles it then."

"It most certainly does. Oh," she said. "Don't eat a big breakfast."

"I'll keep that in mind."

I hung up the phone, threw my sneakers, a pair of shorts, and a shirt into my gym bag, and grabbed one more cup of coffee before heading out to Muscles's. I was trying to locate my keys when I remembered one more call I wanted to make. It took me a minute to find his card.

"Murcer," he said.

"Dennis, it's Raymond."

"What can I do for you, Ray?"

So much for small talk. "I just wanted to check in, see how the article was received on your end."

He laughed. "My end received it just fine. Any piece that says how hard we're working to solve a case gets received just fine. It didn't hurt to have your name—your uncle's name—attached to it."

"Yeah," I said. "It gets me into restaurants all the time."

He waited a few beats before saying, "What's that?"

"Nothing. Hey, about the gang angle?"

"I told you yesterday," he said, "the Family's got a loose structure. It's hard to get a handle on it, and the word on the street ain't been much help."

Okay, I thought. *Let's see how he receives this.* "I may have some information related to the Family."

I thought I heard him swallow. He may have been eating. "What's that, now?"

"A former student of mine," I said. "He turned me on to a guy who has an inside track on the Family."

"Interesting, Ray. And what did you do with this *inside track*?"

"I had breakfast with a guy this morning."

"And . . . ?"

"The guy I spoke with said he—the Royal Family—had no connection with Douglas Lee."

"And I should believe that why?"

"Because the guy didn't have to meet with me, and had no reason to lie."

"Everybody's got a reason to lie, Ray. Your uncle taught us that. This guy you spoke with, he a member of the Family?"

"I promised not to tell."

Another laugh. "Jesus. You've had quite an astounding two days keeping your nose out of this business. You get to check out a crime scene with a reporter *and* the investigating detective, your name and picture get in the papers, and now you're cultivating confidential informants. Tell me again what you do for a living these days."

I ignored that. Largely because I knew where he was going, and he was right.

"I did find out something I *can* tell you, Dennis. If you're interested."

He swallowed again. "Enlighten me."

"One reason it might be hard to get a read on the Royal Family is they seem to have different leadership on each side of the bridge."

"You're going to have to explain that. I'm just a cop."

"One of the people I spoke with," I explained, "told me there's Family on both sides, and they don't exactly see eye-to-eye on Family business."

"This just hearsay, or you got something to back it up?"

I gave him the sketchy details of my meeting with Tio—without mentioning his name or the location—and about my encounter with the ladies. I had to pronounce China's name twice.

"Rhymes with Tina."

"Doesn't ring a bell," he said.

"Can you check her out with the gang unit?"

"What the fuck, Ray? Why don't you just come across the river and do my goddamn job for me?"

"You're right, Dennis. I'm sorry. Sometimes my mouth gets ahead of the brain. I was just thinking out loud."

As I waited for him to answer, I took another sip of coffee and walked over to the sink. The clouds were really coming in now.

"Okay. I'll run her name by my guys. You done playing cop now?"

"I'm not playing cop," I said. Then, to prove my point, I added, "Can I ask about Dougie's phone records?"

"You're too much," he said, but a few seconds later he added, "The call he got that night was made from a disposable phone. Not traceable."

"Shit." Just to cover my bases, I thought of something else to tell him. "I'm going to the Lees' tomorrow. The family's holding a . . . I don't know, a reception."

"Enjoy," he said.

Before I could come back with an answer, he'd hung up.

With too much Dougie in my head and nothing to keep my mind occupied at the apartment, I tossed my phone into my gym bag and was about to head off to Muscles's when it rang. I would have let it go to voice mail, but the caller ID told me it was Rachel.

"Little sister," I said. "I got your message and was going to call you later."

"I'm sure," Rachel said. "How'd you get mixed up with Denny again, Ray?"

"Wow," I said. "That didn't take long. Fate, I guess."

I explained the situation to her, and she seemed to believe me. After a few moments of silence, she said, "How'd he look?"

"Excuse me?"

"Denny. How'd he look?"

"The same, I guess. Little bit of gray in the goatee, and he's wearing a better quality of suits these days. Why is that your first question?"

"It was my second, actually. Just curious. We were pretty close for a while."

"And then you weren't," I reminded her. "Things didn't end so well, Rachel. Remember? You asked me to step in and break it to him."

"That's not exactly how I remember it, Ray. I seem to recall you asking me if I wanted you to talk to Denny."

"And you said yes, so what's the difference?"

"The difference," she said, "is that it was my responsibility to end it. I shouldn't need my big brother to come in and do it for me."

"But you did."

"No. I *needed* to do it myself. I just couldn't."

"Again, Rachel. What's the difference?"

"I was a big girl, Raymond. You made me feel like I was back in high school, unable to protect myself."

"The point is, Rachel, the relationship needed to end, and it did. Case closed."

"Real sensitive. Maybe it never felt closed to me. Did you ever think of that?"

"Oh, come on. You've dated lots of guys since Dennis."

"And look how well those turned out."

I took a deep breath. "So, what are you telling me? You shouldn't have ended things with him?"

"No," she said. "I don't know. Maybe it just feels like I didn't end it with him. It feels like you did."

"I don't get that, Rache. I'm sorry, but I just don't."

She paused. "That's because you have a penis."

Not knowing how to answer that one, I just said, "Sorry."

"You should be." She laughed. "You all should be."

"We are." I looked at the clock. "Listen, I got to head off to the gym, get back home, and be showered and out of here before eight."

"Hot date?"

"Sort of. I'm not sure how hot it's going to be."

"Want me to call up the girl and ask for you?"

"Drop it, Rachel."

"I love you, Raymond."

"Yeah," I said. "Me, too."

Chapter 7

I HAD BEEN WALKING BACKWARD on the treadmill for ten minutes before Muscles finished up with one of his clients. He came over with a clipboard in hand and a disapproving look on his face. He wore his usual outfit: a black T-shirt and black track pants with his name and his logo on both—MUSCLES over a bright orange bicep. He watched me for a half minute, wrote something, and spoke.

"Saw you in the paper this morning."

"Really? I didn't get to the sports section yet."

He laughed, but not like he meant it. "That's almost funny. What's not funny is I haven't seen you in here since Monday. You too busy playing cop again?"

He sounded just like Murcer and my uncle. "I'm not playing anything, Muscles." I gave him the rundown of why the article was in the paper and how that was the end of it for me.

"Good," he said. "Because my biggest fear with you is, you get distracted from the rehab and find excuses not to come here. I don't have to remind you what'll happen to your knees and the surrounding area if you don't come here three times a week."

You don't have to remind me, I thought, *but you just did*. I kept walking.

"How's it feeling, by the way?" he asked.

"Like I haven't been here for five days."

He smiled his I-told-you-so smile. "You taking any of the supplements I recommended? Omega–3s? Hyaluronic acid?"

"No," I said, like a kid being asked where his homework was.

"Good. Wouldn't want to speed the process along any faster than this."

I gave him a hard look and missed a step, almost slipping off the tread-mill. "I just think I'm a little young to be taking pills for the rest of my life."

"*You* may be young," he said. "But your knees are in their sixties. I'm not sure exercise alone is going to do the job. Especially if you only come when you feel like it."

"I'll get better at coming."

"Right." He looked at his clipboard again. "You got any interest in making a thousand dollars?"

"Who do I have to kill?"

This time his laugh was real. "A company I know, they make supple-ments. I have some for sale behind the desk. They got a new product they been working on, and they've been approved to start some limited clinical trials here in the States."

"What's the product?"

"Supposed to help rebuild damaged cartilage. You'd be a perfect sub-ject with the damage you did to your knees. They want to see how it works in conjunction with a rigorous physical therapy regimen, though."

"Oooh," I said. "I love it when you talk like that."

He ignored me. "You'd have to undergo some tests, another MRI. If you're chosen to participate, you go into one of two groups. One gets the supplement, the other doesn't. It's all legit and, except for the MRI, very little hassle on your part."

I considered that. "You sure it's safe?"

"Hell, yeah. They have to go through a bunch of hoops to get to this point. They run it through computer models, study past models of similar supplements, and then test it out on animals. Mostly rats. The FDA goes over the results and determines whether it's safe to proceed to the next level."

"And this is the next level?"

"Yep. Most drugs and supplements don't even get this far. It's a good company, Ray. I wouldn't do business with them if they weren't, and I definitely wouldn't ask anyone I care about—even you—to get involved in a trial if I didn't trust them."

"Let me give it some thought, Muscles."

"Sure. Just let me know as soon as you can. They wanna start the trials after the first of the year, and you'll need to go through some blood tests beforehand."

"What's that about?"

"They have to be real careful you're not taking anything that might interact badly with their product. They have to know what you've got in your system, even if you're just taking ibuprofen or some other over-the-counter meds."

I raised my hands. "I'm clean."

"Stay that way," Muscles said, making a few notes on his clipboard. "Okay. Now finish up this easy stuff and hit the machines. You got a few days to make up for."

"Sir, yes, sir," I replied. He didn't find that funny, either.

It was after two when I got back to the apartment. I took a long, hot shower, made some iced coffee out of what was left in the machine, and sat in front of the TV, surfing the channels until I found a show about animals surviving winter in the Himalayas. The next thing I knew, an old couple was telling the story of how their border collie saved their lives during brush fires in Los Angeles. I looked at the clock. It was almost seven. An hour before I had to meet Allison at the hot new club.

I went to my closet and found the hippest clothes I owned: a long-sleeved black shirt, my newest jeans, and a pair of sneakers with a blue stripe across the side.

Oh, yeah.

Chapter 8

ALLISON'S CAB DROPPED HER OFF just as I approached the back of the line outside the club. There were a few dozen—much younger—people in front of me. I hate lines, which is one of many reasons I don't do the club thing. Or Disneyland. I waved to Allison. I noticed she wasn't wearing her glasses tonight. Contacts? She stepped over to me, surprised me with a kiss on my cheek, and leaned into my ear.

"You clean up well," she stage-whispered.

"You, too."

"We don't have to stand on line, Ray," she said. "I *am* the media."

"Don't you want the full club experience?"

"Normally, sure. But in thirty-degree weather, I find my press credentials keep me very warm." She took me by the hand. "Let's go."

We walked to the front of the line, and Allison flashed her press pass at the guy working the door. He checked his clipboard, checked us, apparently liked what he saw, and let us in. Just like how my uncle used to get us into Yankee Stadium.

Inside the club, we were assaulted by blaring house music, flashing lights, overheated air, and the distinct smell of desperation. The line at the bar was three-deep and looked to be made up of busloads of kids from Long Island, New Jersey, and an MTV reality show. Allison grabbed my hand again.

"I bet you absolutely hate this," she said, getting close to my ear again.

"No," I said. "This is totally my kind of scene." I looked around. "Except I'd probably be teaching half these kids if I worked in the suburbs."

She laughed. I liked that. "Thirty minutes," she said. She saw the look on my face and added, "C'mon. That's one beer."

I looked at the crowd by the bar. "That's standing in line for one beer."

"Don't be so negative, Ray. It's not your best quality." She let go of my hand. "Get us a couple of beers while I walk around and soak up the vibe. I'll be right back."

She left, and I realized she was right. Being negative wasn't going to make this any more pleasant. Besides, I was out on a Saturday night with an attractive woman. It could be a lot worse.

After only a few minutes, I got the bartender's attention. It must have been the mature, relaxed aura I was giving off. I pointed to the guy next to me who—I was pleasantly surprised to see—was drinking a Blue Point Toasted Lager. I raised two fingers. He gave me the universal bartender's double-finger-pistol shot. A minute later, I had my two beers and was out eighteen bucks. The price of maturity, including tip.

"Somebody in trouble?"

I turned to face a young, attractive brunette standing less than a foot from me. Her brown hair had streaks of pink running down both sides. Her T-shirt—and her bare midriff—advertised a gym, which was located on the other side of Brooklyn. I did my best to keep my eyes on hers when I shouted, "What's that?"

She leaned in closer. "Is somebody in trouble?"

I looked around the bar and checked out the customers. Young men and women in various stages of dress, leaning all over and into each other, some of them making me wonder how carefully the guy at the door was checking IDs.

"My guess would be yes," I said. "Why are you asking me?"

She smiled. "You're a cop, right?"

I shook my head. "No. I'm not."

She looked at the beers in my hands. "I didn't think you guys were allowed to drink on duty. Way cool."

"I'm not a cop," I repeated.

"Okay," she said, then looked me up and down and nodded her approval. She leaned in again. "Undercover suits you, man. Keep it real." Before turning to leave, she flashed me the peace sign.

Allison returned before I was forced into another conversation. She grabbed one of the beers and read the label. "This is the good stuff?"

I touched my bottle against hers. "Almost worth the experience of coming here."

"Now that's a positive outlook." We both took sips. After looking around a bit, Allison said, "You know what I don't like about this place?"

Ignoring the straight line, I said, "What's that?"

"The lack of diversity. It's all white kids. Maybe a few Asians and a token black or two, but out of over a hundred kids here, it's ninety-five percent white."

"Yeah," I said. "It's like prom night at a talented and gifted school."

She laughed again and then held up her beer bottle. "Drink up, Teach. The night is young, and your half hour is over."

I took a long pull and drained half the bottle. I got a little closer to Allison so she could hear me. "You have enough for your piece?"

She leaned in. I thought she was going to whisper something again, but instead she kissed me on the cheek. "You," she said, "are going to take me to your bar. What's it called? The All Points Bulletin?"

"The LineUp," I said, finishing up the beer. "You sure? It's not exactly a hot spot, and we might actually be able to hear each other talk."

"I'll take my chances."

The average age of the customers at The LineUp was about ten years older than those at the club we'd just left. The beer was half the price and colder, and the lights were not going to cause any seizures. A Springsteen tune was on the jukebox, loud enough to hear, but not like he was in the bar with us. Allison and I had grabbed a couple of stools at the corner of the bar, giving us a view of the whole place. There seemed to be half a dozen copies of today's paper scattered around the bar.

Mikey came over with our pints of Brooklyn Pilsner. He looked at Allison, then at me, and gave me his raised-eyebrows look.

"Better-looking company you're keeping these days, Raymond." He offered his hand to Allison. "Usually he sits with Edgar," he explained. "I'm Mikey."

"Allison Rogers."

"Nice to meet you, Allison." He slid the closest paper over to her. "You see Ray's picture in today's paper?"

"No." Allison gave me a playful slap on the arm. "Raymond. You didn't tell me you were in the paper. What for?"

"I killed a nosy bartender," I said. "Mikey, Allison wrote the piece in the paper."

"And took the picture," she added.

"Excellent," Mikey said, even more impressed with Allison now. Someone made some noise at the other end of the bar. "I'll be right back," Mikey said.

When he was out of earshot, Allison said, "He seems cool."

I took a sip of my beer. "You get a chance to look into the Royal Family yet?"

"Ah, back to business. Yeah, I did a quick search and found a few articles over the past year." I knew that, but kept my mouth shut. "I'm gonna ask some of the other reporters. See if they have anything in their notes, stuff that didn't make it into the paper. Maybe," she said, "I can check with some of my own people on the street. Cops aren't the only ones with confidential informants, you know."

"Can I tell you something?" I asked. "Off the record?"

"Better do it now, before the beer goes to my head."

"I met with this guy this morning." I almost mentioned his name, but decided not to. "He runs the Royal Family on this side of the bridge."

"How'd you arrange that?"

"That's not important. What I want you to look into—please—is the Family's activity on the other side. Particularly this girl named China. She seems to be in charge over there. The guy told me he didn't know Dougie. I believe him. China didn't say anything." I showed her the marks on my wrist. "She just asked."

"My God, Raymond." She took me by the wrist and ran her fingers over the bruises. Just like China had done. Only this time, I liked it. "Did you call the cops?"

"No," I said. "But I did speak with Dennis Murcer after calling you. He was somewhat pissed I was still involved."

"I'm sure he was."

"But he listened and said he'd look into what I just told you."

"Good," she said. "What's your deal with him, anyway?"

I cleared my throat. "We went through the academy together."

She waited for me to go on. When I didn't, she said, "And . . ."

I gave her the edited version, from my recommending him to Uncle Ray all the way up to his dating my sister for half a year.

"He wasn't what you had in mind for Rachel?" she asked.

"A lot of cops make lousy boyfriends," I said.

"You're very protective of her. That's sweet."

"It's not that. Dennis was one of those cops who couldn't leave the job at the precinct. It wasn't good for either one of them."

She gave me a quizzical look. "Was that your decision or your sister's?"

"Both," I said. "When Rachel had difficulty breaking things off, I gave her a hand. I took Dennis out for some beers and had a long talk with him."

Allison smiled and shook her head. "You broke up with your sister's boyfriend?"

"He wasn't listening to her and I—we—needed it to stop before he crossed the line."

"You don't think he would've hurt her, do you?"

"No, I don't think so. It wasn't like that." I took a sip of beer.

"So, he did what you wanted him to?"

"He did what needed to be done."

"Why do you think so many cops make shitty boyfriends?" she asked.

"Let's just say a bad day on the streets is a hell of a lot different than a bad day in the greeting-card business. Kinda limits the empathy thing."

"Did you ever have any—?"

I put my hand on her arm and said, "Let's just leave it at that, okay, Allison?"

She put her other hand on mine. "Okay."

"How about you?" I asked. "How'd you get the limp?"

"Wow," she said, cringing a bit. "That's both rude *and* observant."

"I used to be a cop."

"Right. I used to be a track star. Back in high school."

"You didn't run in college?"

"Didn't get a chance to." She took a long sip of beer and studied the label for a few seconds. "Had an accident halfway through my senior year."

"Sorry," I said. "I shouldn't have—"

"It's okay," she said. "I'm cool with it now." She ran a finger up and down the bottle. "Got hit by a Jeep while running before school. The only reason I walk so well now is I was in great shape at the time."

"You're still in pretty good shape," I said.

"Yeah," she said. But not like she believed me.

"They get the driver?"

"Well . . ." She picked up her bottle and started tapping the bottom against the bar. "That's where the story gets better."

"What do you mean?"

She closed her eyes. "Before I passed out, I looked up and saw the driver had stopped and staggered out of the Jeep. I could tell he was drunk. He got about five feet away from me before running back into the car and taking off."

"Were you able to identify him?"

"Better than that," she said. "I saw the last three numbers of his license plate and the color of the Jeep."

I waited for her to go on. When she didn't, I said, "So they got the guy?"

She laughed. "Oh, yeah. They got the guy."

"Good."

"Yeah, *real* good. Except for the fact he was a cop."

"Shit." My turn to cringe. "How'd it play out?"

"He denied everything. Said he was still at work at the time of the accident and had witnesses to back him up. A bunch of *cop* witnesses against the word of a high school girl who'd just been run down. I think you know the rest of the story, Ray."

I shook my head. "I'm sorry. That sucks."

"Yep." She put her hands on her lap and rubbed her legs. "Lost my track scholarship. Couldn't sue 'cause I didn't have a case, and I'm still paying off my student loan ten years after graduating. But don't think that soured me on cops or anything."

We both got silent for a while. She brought her beer up to her lips and held it there. Before taking a sip, she said, "So what are you thinking? *Did* Dougie have something to do with the Royal Family?"

"Or they had something to do with him," I said. "At least, on the other side of the bridge." That sounded confusing. "I'd love to know why Dougie was there at that hour. If he was meeting someone, it would make sense if that person was somehow connected to the Family." I thought about the beads around Dougie's neck. "Wouldn't it?"

She nodded and put her glass down. "The cops didn't find a phone at the scene. So . . . whoever killed him . . . either took it, or Dougie left it at home."

"I'm going to Dougie's tomorrow," I told her, explaining the situation. "I can ask Mrs. Lee if she knows about his phone. Murcer told me the last call Dougie got was from a disposable."

"Damn, Ray," she said. "It's like investigating a crime."

"Not much different, I'd imagine, than chasing down a good story."

"Kind of. Except this one has a dead kid."

"Yeah," I said, finishing up my beer. "There is that."

Allison drained the rest of her pilsner and raised two fingers. "Hey, Mikey," she said. Mikey looked over his shoulder. "Two more." She turned to me. "You want a date for tomorrow? Y'know, the thing at the Lees'?"

"I wouldn't call it a date thing, Allison."

"And I wouldn't call that an answer, Raymond."

Before I could respond, Mikey came over with the beers. "You guys hungry?"

I looked at Allison. "Are we staying for a bit?"

She raised her glass. "I've got nowhere to go."

"Yeah, Mikey," I said. "Maybe some calamari and two pretzels. Thanks."

"You got it."

"So," Allison said after Mikey left us. "What about tomorrow?"

I thought about that. "How about I call you in the morning?"

"Or," she said, eyes on mine, "you can just nudge me."

Had there been beer in my mouth, I would've spit it out. For the first time in a long time, I couldn't think of a thing to say.

"Oh, my God," Allison said. "You've never been propositioned before?"

"That's your third beer, Allison. I don't want to take—"

"Oh, cut the shit." She looked at my glass. "That's your third beer, too. Maybe I want to take advantage of you. I hate that guy shit." She spun her glass around a few times. "Truth be told," she said, "I wanted to hit on you after the Rivas story broke."

"What stopped you?"

"You had 'damaged goods' written all over you."

"Wow," I said. "That's honest. How do I look now?"

"Not so damaged," she said. "Kinda cute, actually."

I looked up at the TV, which was tuned to the Weather Channel. I pretended to watch the local radar before responding.

"Okay," I said. "You can go to Mrs. Lee's with me tomorrow. But not as a reporter. Or a date. As a friend."

"Okay, friend," she said. "What about my other . . . suggestion?"

"Let me think on that a bit."

She put her hand on my knee. It felt good there.

"One thing I learned from my accident? Live for the moment, because you never know what's gonna happen tomorrow."

"I'm not arguing with that," I said. "I learned the same thing from my accident. It just took me a few years."

"So what's the problem, tough guy?"

I took a sip of beer as I stalled to find the right words.

"I guess I still see myself as damaged," I finally said. "It's been a long process for me."

She leaned forward and looked around to see if anyone was listening. She lowered her voice and asked, "So, what? You haven't gotten laid since your accident?"

I laughed. "*Now* who's being rude?"

"I'm a reporter. It's a habit."

"I've had a few one-night stands, if you must know. Nothing serious."

Allison put her hands back on her legs and rubbed them again.

"Well, I guess if we're being honest—or tipsy—truth is, that's about all *I've* had since the accident. Dated a guy in college for a few months, but he was gay."

"How long did it take you to figure that out?"

"Oh, I knew from the start. I just thought having a boyfriend was cool, and it provided great cover. For both of us."

"At least you both got something out of it."

"Yeah. At least."

Mikey came by with our food and quickly spun around to handle the small crowd forming at the other end of the bar. I recognized a few of them as semi-regulars, cops who'd swing by for a quick one on the way home. Which immediately made me think of Allison's accident.

"So," I said. "I guess we're both still a bit damaged."

"Yeah," she said. "But I'm willing to do something about it."

"So am I. Just not tonight."

"Why don't you think of me as a one-night stand?"

"I could do that, but I'm already starting to like you."

She leaned back. "What if it's a one-time offer?"

I dipped a piece of calamari in the red sauce. "I'm willing to take that chance."

"You sound pretty confident there, Ray."

"Like I said, it's been a long process."

Chapter 9

I AWOKE THE NEXT MORNING to the sound of the church bells from across the street. The curtains were pulled, and my eyes were too blurry to see my clock, but if I had counted the number of rings correctly it was nine o'clock. Time to roll out of bed, put on a pot of coffee, and take a long, hot shower. I thought back to Allison's offer last night and was pretty sure I'd made the right decision.

After my shower, I put on some decent clothes and poured myself a cup of coffee. I took it over to the windows, watched the city skyline for a bit, and thought about my plans for the day.

Douglas William Lee was in the ground now. His final resting place. And somewhere out there, beyond my kitchen windows, was the person responsible. How do you live with yourself after doing something like that? We see and read about these guys who murder and rape and swindle folks out of their life savings. We see them caught and led off in handcuffs. We watch their trials, then we watch them go off to prison. But how do they live with themselves?

I heard the church bells again. Ten o'clock. When I was younger, I was taught that those who crossed God's line would spend eternity in Hell. That was just to scare the shit out of me. So that I'd stay in line and be the good kid, the good Catholic. Now that I no longer had any faith, it was times like this when I missed the concept of Hell. It would be some sort of cruel comfort to believe the person who had killed Dougie would be spending eternity somewhere south of where I was sitting.

Or maybe, if I still believed what I learned in Sunday school, I would have to show forgiveness. That had been one of the first cracks in my foundation of faith. How could people go to Hell if we were supposed to forgive them? Didn't God forgive, or was forgiveness just for those of us here on Earth? I remembered asking that question after church one Sunday, and my dad's answer was a hand to the back of my head. The Lord, my mother would invariably say, worked in mysterious ways.

I had given Allison Mrs. Lee's address, and I got there five minutes before she did—just before one o'clock. According to the buzzers on the front of the five-story building, the Lees had the entire first floor, while each of the other floors had three apartments each. I wondered how Mrs. Lee had swung that. There was no reason to use the buzzer since the front door was open for anyone to walk right in. We did.

After a brief walk through a small, undecorated hallway and past a door that presumably led to the basement, we were in the Lee apartment.

"We're friends," I reminded Allison. "You're here for support."

"I'll keep that in mind."

The room we were in—the living room?—was filled with well-dressed people wearing what would have to be called their "Sunday best." Every flat surface held either a plate of food or a plastic cup. A few people turned to acknowledge our presence, and more than a few eyes lingered on the only white people in the room.

I raised my hand. "Hi. Raymond Donne."

A woman came up to me. She looked familiar, but I couldn't quite place from where. Until she spoke.

"You're the man from the wake the other night." *Hello, Wanda.* "The one who upset Gloria so."

"Nice to see you again, Wanda." She seemed shocked I knew her name. "This is Allison Rogers."

Allison offered her hand. "Nice to meet you."

Wanda looked at Allison's hand like it was a questionable piece of fish. To her credit, though, she took it, politeness winning out.

"The man from the papers." Another woman was coming our way, saving us from further conversation with Wanda. "Mr. Donne," she said, taking both my hands. "Sarah Dutton. From the phone yesterday."

"Of course. Thank you for having us, Ms. Dutton."

Ms. Dutton turned to Allison. "Mrs. Donne?"

Allison laughed. Hard. "No," she said. "I'm just a friend."

"Oh, darlin'," Ms. Dutton said, taking Allison in. "You are not *just* anything. You are gorgeous." Then to me she added, "Don't you think so, Mr. Donne?"

"Absolutely," I said, not missing a beat.

"Yes," Ms. Dutton said. "Yes, she is. Have you two eaten?"

"We just got here," I said.

"Well, let me show you where the food is." She took me by the hand. I took Allison the same way, and we followed Ms. Dutton into the next room, which was also filled with people. This was the dining room, and there were two tables filled with all sorts of homemade and store-bought foods, and one table loaded with bottles of soda, water, and more than a few bottles of wine. "You two go on ahead and help your-selves."

"I'm not hungry right now," I said, looking at Allison, who nodded her agreement. "We'd really like to say hello to Mrs. Lee."

"Not hungry?" Ms. Dutton gave me a look as if she'd never heard that sentiment before. "Maybe later then. I believe I saw Gloria in the back. This way."

We followed her again, deeper into the apartment. *This was a lot of rooms for two people*, I thought. I couldn't help but wonder if Mrs. Lee would be staying here now that her only son was gone. We were in the kitchen now, and through the window over the sink I could see into the small back-yard. There were a couple of men out there smoking, maybe the same two from the other night outside the funeral home.

"There she is," Ms. Dutton whispered, pointing into the adjacent room. Sure enough, there was Mrs. Lee in quiet conversation with an-other woman. "You two go on ahead and pay your respects. I'm gonna make sure the kids've eaten. They're probably all down in the basement playing those video games. Those kids forget to eat, and they got a long drive ahead of them. Recipe for disaster."

"Thank you, Ms. Dutton," Allison said.

"Oh, thank *you* for coming, darlin'." She touched me on the arm. "And don't you let this one get too far away, now."

Allison looped her arm around mine, and I was reminded of the previous day's stroll with China. "I'll do my best," I said. As Ms. Dutton walked away, I turned to Allison. "You ready to pay your respects?"

She looked around. "I'm as ready as I'll ever be."

"Just remember, no questions."

"I'm not a reporter twenty-four seven, Ray."

We walked over to Mrs. Lee, and she stood up when she saw us coming. She put her hand on the shoulder of the woman she was talking with for support. She even managed a small smile for my benefit.

"Mr. Donne," she said. "I knew you would come." She looked at the other woman. "Didn't I say he'd come, Marilyn?"

The other woman smiled. "You did, Gloria. You most surely did."

I reached out to take Mrs. Lee's hand, and she turned the gesture into a hug. I could feel her take two deep breaths as she held me. "Thank you, Mr. Donne. Thank you for everything."

I gave her back a pat. "You're welcome," I said. "And, again, I am so sorry for your loss. This . . . should never have happened."

"No," she agreed. "It should not have." She stepped back from the hug and looked at Allison. Another look of approval. "And who is this?"

Allison took Mrs. Lee by the hand. "Allison Rogers," she said. "And I am so sorry we have to meet like this."

"Thank you, Allison." Mrs. Lee's face turned pensive and then a thought hit her. "Allison Rogers? The reporter from the paper who wrote the story about my Douglas?"

Allison hesitated. "Yes, ma'am," she said.

"You are most welcome in our home, young lady." Mrs. Lee grabbed Allison's hands as her eyes filled up. "You kept my boy's story alive. I will be forever grateful to you. Forever grateful."

"That's very kind of you, Mrs. Lee." Allison looked at me. "It was really Raymond's—Mr. Donne's—doing, though. He would not let it go, in fact."

"I know that, Ms. Rogers. I know that." She turned to me. "Have you eaten, Mr. Donne?" Before I could answer, tears fell from her face, and Marilyn was there with a fresh tissue. Mrs. Lee wiped her eyes. "That's a silly question, I know, but we do find some comfort in food, don't we? In feeding others?" She handed the tissue back to her friend, who tossed it into a wastebasket that already held quite a few others. "Maybe it's because it's something we can control. We cook it, we serve it, and then we clean up after it's been enjoyed." She took a breath. "The illusion of control, at least."

"Makes sense to me," I said. "Seems to be universal."

"Yes, it does. Yes, it does. It brings us together." She put her hands up to her lips as if she were about to pray. Instead she said, "Would you do me a favor, Mr. Donne? A big favor, I'm afraid. Feel free to say no, if you want."

Right. Just like the other night at the wake. "Tell me what you need, Mrs. Lee."

"I need"—she took another breath—"to go into Douglas's room." She let out the breath. "I need to go into Douglas's room. I have not . . . gone in since . . ." She trailed off.

I watched again as her eyes filled up with tears. This woman's strength did not come easily. It was impressive to watch.

"Are you sure you want to do that now?" I asked.

"I am not going to be one of those women who can't . . . can't bear to be reminded of their loved ones. The sooner I go in there, the better. The longer I wait, the stronger its control over me and then . . . I become one of those women." She took me by the hand. "I will go in with you." She turned to Allison. "Would you mind if I borrow him for a few minutes?"

"Not at all, Mrs. Lee," Allison said. To both of us, she added, "Take your time."

"Are you ready, Mr. Donne?"

"If you're absolutely sure."

"Don't try and talk me out of it. If you do—." Whatever words were to come out next got stuck somewhere in her throat. I let her pull me in what I assumed was the direction of Dougie's room. I looked back at Allison, who mouthed, "Good luck."

The room was down yet another hallway. *How big was this place?* As if hearing my thoughts, she said, "My brother-in-law owns the building, Mr. Donne. He has generously given us the entire floor, the basement, and the use of the backyard. He himself lives up in Rockland County and has an office up there as well as down here. He rents out the other floors and does quite well by them."

"That's nice," I said.

"Yes. It is."

We stopped when we got in front of Dougie's room. The door was unadorned with the normal teenager door stuff: no KEEP OUT—THIS MEANS YOU! signs, no stickers of athletes or musicians. Just a door. Mrs. Lee put her hand on the knob and turned. Before pushing it open, she bowed her head.

"You're okay with this?" I asked one more time.

"I am."

She pushed open the door. The room was dark and had the slightly unpleasant smell a small space acquires when it has been closed up for a week. From the doorway, it was hard to make out anything for half a minute. That's how long we stood there before Mrs. Lee said, "The shades are pulled. The light from the neighbors' always bothers—" She stopped when she caught herself using the present tense. The loved ones of recent victims do that all the time. "There's too much light at night if you don't pull the shades. Makes it hard to sleep."

"Would you like me to go in and open the shades?" I asked.

"Please. And open the window a crack, as well. Please."

I walked to the window, careful not to step on anything on the floor. A sneaker almost tripped me, but I moved it aside with my foot. I raised the shade and pulled up the window two inches. Mrs. Lee was still in the doorway.

"Take your time," I said. "There's no rush."

"Thank you."

The floor looked like a normal teenager's floor: two mismatched sneakers lying on a rug; a pair of underwear near the bed next to a pair of balled-up socks and a few sports magazines; the bed itself unmade, the blanket shoved to the foot end, and a sheet hanging over the side.

His desk was remarkably well kept. He had a laptop, a holder for his pens and pencils, and something that looked like an "in" box, which held some papers. A printer rested on a side table, the desk too small to hold it. This was the space of a kid who took his work seriously. I couldn't help but feel a bit proud and a deep ache for the kid I'd had in my class two years ago.

I looked over at Mrs. Lee. She had taken her first steps into the room. She looked around as if taking it all in for the first time. She closed her eyes, and I got the feeling she was sensing her son's presence. Imagining him back in the room, studying or listening to music, or sitting on the floor, leaning against the bed to read. When she opened her eyes again, she looked at me. "I apologize for the mess." *Still Dougie's mother.*

"You should see mine," I answered.

I walked over to the wall by Dougie's bed. He had a cork bulletin board, which held a few photos of some basketball players, a couple of Post-its reminding himself about upcoming school assignments, and a few photos of Dougie with some other kids about his age.

"Those are some of his new classmates," Mrs. Lee explained. "I met a few of them the other night at the wake. Nice kids. Some of them have too much, though. If you know what I mean."

"I think I do," I said, remembering some of the spoiled kids I had gone to high school with on Long Island. Kids who didn't have to get the weekend or afterschool job, who applied to any college they wanted to, not having to think about tuition. I taught in the inner city for a reason. I did not want to teach the kids I'd grown up with.

Mrs. Lee went over to the desk and opened the drawers, looking for something. Then she stepped over to her son's bed and moved the blanket and covers around.

"What are you looking for?" I asked.

"His phone," she said. "The police never found it. At least it wasn't in his . . ." Struggling with the words. Words never uttered in happy times. ". . . his personal effects." She looked at the floor. "I thought maybe it'd be in here." She moved over to his closet and started going through the pockets of the jackets and pants that were hanging in there. She mumbled something.

"Excuse me?" I said.

"I'm going to have to donate all this." She choked back the tears. "His clothes. They're doing nobody any good just hanging here."

"I'm sure the church will know what to do with them, Mrs. Lee. I don't think it's something you have to worry about now."

"The sooner the better," she said. "No phone. He never went any-where without his phone. It was always either in his pocket or clipped to his waist."

"I'll ask Detective Murcer about that if you'd like," I offered.

"Yes, please." She took two steps toward me. "I watch those police shows on TV. They don't need to have the phone to find out who called Dougie that night. They can check his cell phone records, right?"

TV made everybody a crime investigator these days.

"They did that already," I said. I explained how the last call Dougie received was made from an untraceable disposable cell. "By the way," I said. "I spoke with someone yesterday who has a strong connection to the Royal Family."

"That's the gang?" she said. "The one with the beads they found?"

"Yes. The person I spoke to said, as far as he knew, Dougie was in no way involved with the gang. And he's in a position to know."

"Well, of course he wasn't, Mr. Donne." It sounded like she was saying that as much for her own benefit as mine. "Thank you."

"You're welcome." I glanced at Dougie's desk, and another thought hit me. "Did the police ask for his computer?"

"No," she said. "Should they have?"

I went over to it and checked to see if it was off. It was. "He was on this a lot, you said?"

"Even after his bedtime, every once in a while I'd find him . . . surfing the web."

"You should call Detective Murcer and offer him Dougie's computer."

"Can *you* do that?"

"I can," I said, thinking about how thrilled Dennis would be to hear from me again so soon, "but it would be more effective if it came from you."

"I'll do it tomorrow," she said.

"Good." I opened the center drawer of the desk and found the usual: paper clips, a mini stapler, some erasers, and loose change. There was also a bunch of business cards gathered in a rubber band alongside a separate, single card. I picked up the one that wasn't part of the pack. It was for something called Finch's Landing, with a picture of a bird in front of a computer screen, over which was printed an email address. I handed the card to Mrs. Lee. "Any idea what this is?"

She took the card from me. "The name 'Finch' sounds familiar. It's probably something he got from one of his friends at school. Somebody was always starting up a new club."

"May I have that?"

She handed it back to me. "I don't see why not."

I slipped the card into my shirt pocket and turned back to the desk. I opened the center drawer a little more and found a small walkie-talkie. It looked like a good one, well made and probably expensive, the kind Edgar would use. It reminded me of the kind I took off a few corner boys back when I worked the streets. They'd use them when acting as lookouts, letting the other boys know five-oh was around. Not a good sign that Dougie had one. I turned it on and got static. All the channels gave me the same.

"Dougie ever mention why he had this?" I asked.

Mrs. Lee gave it a quick look and said, "No."

"Can I take it?" I said, well aware of the fact that I was crossing the line between curiosity and interfering with an investigation. "I'd like to show it to a friend."

She nodded. Then she put her hand to her face and rubbed her eyes.

"This is a bit too much, Mr. Donne," she said. "Would you mind?"

"Not at all." I closed the drawer and clipped the walkie-talkie to my belt. "Let's go outside and get something to drink." I took her by her elbow.

"Yes," she said. "Some tea would be nice."

Before leaving the room, Mrs. Lee went over to her son's bed, picked up his pillow, and fluffed it up. She brought it up to her face and breathed it in. From where I was standing, I couldn't see the look on her face. I didn't have to. She stayed that way for almost a minute. Finally, I put my hand on her shoulder. "Let's get that tea."

She placed the pillow down gently and ran her hand over it. "Yes," she said.

We left Dougie's room, closed the door soundlessly, and made our way back to the main area. It was even more crowded than before. I found Allison sitting on the edge of a couch, listening to one of the guests explain how rain and snow and traffic had made for such a terrible trip up from Virginia. Allison stood and excused herself from the conversation when she noticed Mrs. Lee and me.

"How are you?" Allison asked Mrs. Lee.

Dougie's mother considered the question. "I don't know." She turned to me. "Thank you, Mr. Donne. I needed to go in there."

"Sure." I looked at Allison. "Maybe we should go."

"Oh," Mrs. Lee said. "But you haven't eaten anything yet."

"I'm not hungry," I said. "And you have so many visitors you need to be with."

She looked around the room and shook her head. "None more important." She took one of my hands and one of Allison's. "You both have done so much. Thank you."

"You're welcome," we both said.

"And stay as long as you wish. My own mother used to say, 'If you ain't hungry now, stay until you are.'"

"That sounds very nice, Mrs. Lee," I said.

"Yes. Mother was very Southern." She hugged us both.

On the front steps, Allison and I closed up our jackets and breathed in the fresh air. I hadn't realized how hot and stuffy it had been inside the crowded apartment until we stepped outside.

"What's with the walkie-talkie?" Allison asked, noticing my belt.

"It was Dougie's," I said. "Mrs. Lee gave it to me. I'm going to show it to a friend." She put her hand in mine as we walked down the stairs. "Thanks for coming with me today. It made it easier."

"You'd have done all right by yourself, Mr. Donne. But you're welcome." She took in the neighborhood. "Your school's around here, right?"

I pointed west. "A few blocks that way. Most of our kids live within walking distance. Keeps our school's attendance rate up, at least."

"But not very diversified."

I laughed. "Kind of the opposite of the club last night." We walked about a block before I said, "I need another favor, Allison."

"Ask. The worst I could do is say no."

"I need you to call Murcer tomorrow and ask if he found anything interesting on Dougie's laptop."

"I didn't know he looked into the computer."

"He didn't."

She smiled. "So this is your way of getting him to investigate a little harder." She slapped me on the shoulder. "And using me to do the dirty work."

"If I call him/. . ."

"It looks like you're butting in or, worse, telling him how to do his job."

"You're good at this," I said. "You should look into a career in journalism."

"The pay sucks," she said. "And job security? Please."

"So, you'll call Murcer?"

"I'll call Murcer." She looked at her watch. "How far are we from the subway?"

"A few blocks," I said. "You have to head right home?"

"I have to write up last night." We both considered that and she laughed. "The club, Raymond. Not the part where I got shot down by you."

"Oh, good," I said. We continued walking to the train. "So, I'll call you tomorrow?"

"To see if I called Murcer?"

"And to see how you're doing. Maybe make plans to get together again?"

"Try me in the afternoon," she said. "I'll call Murcer in the morning. As for getting together again, I never know what my schedule for the week's going to be. The life of a reporter and all that. We did have our chance last night, though."

"Okay, I get your point." We stopped at the entrance to the subway, and I realized I had no idea where Allison lived. I saved that for another time. "You okay on your own from here?"

"Yes," she said. "I think I can make it home."

We put our arms around each other and hugged. The hug turned into a kiss. We stopped when a guy behind us cleared his throat. After he passed, Allison looked at me. "That was nice." She gave me one more kiss on the cheek and headed down to the train.

"Tomorrow," I repeated, watching as she disappeared underground.

There was an unfamiliar feeling in my gut. It took me a while to recognize it. It was that feeling you get at the beginning of something you think might turn out really good. A new job, a trip someplace you've never been. I didn't recognize it at first, because it was mixed with that other feeling in my stomach.

The one caused by loss.

•   •   •

"This is sweet," Edgar said, examining the walkie-talkie I had taken from Dougie's desk. We were sitting at The LineUp a few hours after I'd said good-bye to Allison, sharing a couple of after-dinner beers. "My uncle's got one. Goes for a hundred and a half easily. Why'd your boy have this?"

"I don't know," I said, surprised at the price. "But one's no good without a second one, right? There must be a match out there?"

"Oh, yeah. You just gotta find it."

"And how would I go about that, Edgar?"

Edgar leaned back and closed his eyes, relishing the idea of me asking for his assistance. I looked up at the TV, which was tuned to the Weather Channel, longing again for some baseball. Edgar kept his eyes closed as he said, "Could run a search, see which stores sell this particular model in the metropolitan area, and track down the purchaser that way. Of course, that wouldn't help if your boy wasn't the purchaser or if it was a cash transaction."

"Or . . . ?"

"Or you could hang out around your boy's known—"

"His name was Dougie, Edgar."

"—Dougie's known hangouts, tune to all the channels, and see who picks up."

"Sounds time-consuming," I said, thinking of all the places Dougie might have hung around.

"It can be. Or maybe you get lucky." He moved his eyebrows up and down. "You know . . . lucky."

"Something on your mind, Edgar?"

He leaned into me and lowered his voice. "Mikey told me you had a date last night. Here."

"Yes, Edgar. I did. That's what grown-ups do sometimes."

"How'd it go?"

"Fine," I said. "Thanks for asking." I couldn't help myself from adding, "You seeing anyone special?"

That shut him up, but it also made him pout. I might have pushed a sore spot this time.

"Thanks for your help, Edgar. Maybe I will check out Dougie's hangouts."

"Should probably start with his school first," he said, recovering quickly. He slid his laptop over. "Where'd you say he went?"

"Upper West Academy. Manhattan."

Edgar ran his fingers over his keyboard. "Here it is," he said. "Hmmm."

"What?"

"It's right off Central Park West. In the seventies."

"So?"

"That's a real popular spot for bird-watching. The Ramble, inside the park."

"I really don't think Dougie was into bird-watching, Edgar."

"I think there's even a birding walkie channel in the park. I can check with my uncle. He's up there all the time. That's why he's got one of these."

"Bird channel?"

"Yeah," he said. "Uncle Bob spots a red-headed woodpecker, and the rest of the crew come running before the bird flies off."

I looked at Edgar. "Your whole family nerds?"

"We have varied interests, Raymond. No need to judge." He shifted his body. "You find yourself up that way, take the walkie-talkie with you. Hit the park, go through the channels. Maybe you'll luck out, and someone'll pick up who knew Dougie."

"What're the odds of that happening?"

He shrugged. "Better than if you don't."

"Good point. Thanks, Edgar. I wouldn't have come up with this line of . . . this idea without your help."

"Your friendly neighborhood nerd." He tipped an imaginary hat to me.

Chapter 10

MONDAY MORNING. THERE WAS a thin layer of snow on the steps leading up to the school. I stepped carefully and headed to the main office. It was surprisingly quiet this morning. No parents waiting to see me. No teachers milling about, killing time. I took some papers out of my mailbox, gave a quick wave to Mary, who was on the phone, and stepped back into the hallway. I was almost to the staircase when someone called out my name. Ron Thomas, Principal. He was speed walking toward me, holding a rolled-up newspaper.

"You see the paper this morning, Mr. Donne?" he asked, practically choking the one he had in his hand.

"Not yet, Ron." It occurred to me I always called him by his first name, and he always referred to me as Mr. Donne. I could live with that.

He unrolled the paper and held it so I could see the front page. The headline read, NOT SO SAFETY, OFFICER! Underneath was a blurry picture of a man standing over someone lying on the ground. The man standing seemed to have his fist in the face of the other person.

"Okay," I said. "So . . . ?"

"So read closely, Mr. Donne." He ran his finger along the text below the picture and handed me the paper.

" 'School Safety Officer Angel Rosario'—*shit*—'standing over victim of alleged assault.' What the hell happened, Ron?"

"Seems your kid's dad tried to get Angel's iPod back from this guy," he said, pointing at the blur on the ground, "and ended up assaulting him. As luck would have it, one of the guy's friends recorded the whole thing from his cell phone." Ron opened the paper to the story on page three. "And . . . the article mentions the school that his son attends. *Our* school. Is that what Rosario was here about the other day? What the hell did you say to him?"

"I didn't tell him to assault anyone, if that's what you mean. I told him to get the cops involved, maybe his boss." I looked at the article. "When did this happen?"

"Friday afternoon," Ron said. "It took the kid with the video a while to realize he had something worth some money. It hit some Internet sites yesterday, and the papers picked up on it today."

Shit. "Did you call the home?"

"And say what?" Ron said. " 'Way to go, Slugger'?"

"Check out how Angel's doing," I said, and realized Ron didn't know which Angel I was talking about. "The son, Ron. *Our student.*"

Ron thought about that. "No, I didn't. Maybe you could do that, huh? You guys seemed to be all chummy the other day."

"Yeah," I said. "I'll take care of it."

"Thanks," he said. He looked at the paper in my hand and scowled. "You can keep that."

I went up to my office to call the Rosario home. I found the dad's cell number on my clipboard.

"Yeah?"

"Mr. Rosario," I said. "Raymond Donne, from the school."

"Oh, hey," he said. "I guess you heard."

"Just. My boss showed me the paper."

"Guess we got something in common now, huh?" He paused. "I saw you in the paper on Saturday. Sorry about that kid."

"Yeah," I said. "How're you and Angel doing?"

He thought about that before answering. "Not too good, y'know? Had to disconnect the landline, all the papers and TV calling. What the fuck? Nothing else happening in the world, they gotta make this front-page news? Woulda been a nothing story except for that knucklehead taking the video."

"I hear you," I said. "Sometimes the story doesn't matter, just as long as they got it on video. What about Angel?"

"What about him?"

"Is he coming to school today?"

More silence. "I don't know, Mr. Donne. I don't want him catching shit for what his old man did."

"What exactly *did* you do?," I asked. "What happened?"

I could hear him as he let out a deep breath. This was not the first time he had retold the story. "I clocked out early on Friday," he began. "To go meet up with Angel at the bus stop. I thought maybe I could talk to these guys who are hassling him, y'know? Man-to-man. Tell 'em I've been there, grew up on these streets, and did my share of hustling. But this is my boy, and I'm in a uniform, so how about cutting him some slack?"

"I'm guessing that didn't work?"

"Guys were there. Angel wasn't five steps off the bus before they started in on him. I'd been standing there for a few minutes before the bus came, watching the bunch of 'em hanging around, but kept quiet. Didn't know if they were the same guys or what." Another deep breath. "They were. Soon as they started in on Angel, I stepped in and told them who I was."

"And?"

"They didn't give a shit. Looked at my uniform and called me a rent-a-cop. Nothing I ain't heard before. I work in a high school, y'know? I figured I'd get Angel outta there and take your advice. Talk to my sergeant, maybe call the cops."

"Why didn't you?"

"Didn't get the chance," he said. "The chief knucklehead—the guy Angel told me later took his iPod—stepped in front of me. Grabbed Angel by his book bag and . . ."

I waited for him to finish. When he didn't, I said, "And what?"

"This motherfucker," he began, "this piece of shit . . . grabbed Angel, looked me dead in the eyes, and said, 'Why don't you go home and get your momma, boy?'" He was fighting back tears now. "Before I could react, Angel kicked the guy. Right below the knee." I sensed a little bit of pride in that last part. "Fucker took Angel by the shoulder and threw him down. Next thing I know, I got him by the neck, and I drop him. That's when the cops showed up. Every fucking time my boy's getting hassled, nothing. But the one time I mix it up with some punk-ass, and there they are."

"Did you explain the situation?"

"I tried, but . . . Shit, it didn't exactly look good. And the guy who assaulted Angel . . . ?"

"Yeah?"

"Three weeks away from his eighteenth birthday. Twenty-one days later, and we ain't having this conversation, Mr. Donne. But because I 'assaulted a juvenile'—who's got about three inches on me—I get taken in and charged, while my boy has to wait around the precinct."

"Shit," I said.

"Yeah," Rosario agreed. "Shit. I'm just lucky they let me go with a DAT."

Desk Appearance Ticket. I guessed the judge didn't consider Mr. Rosario a genuine threat. He did catch a break there. Get some judge in a bad mood, or one who doesn't like school safety officers, and you're spending the weekend behind bars.

"What happens now?" I asked.

"I'm on suspension," he said. "Without pay. That's the first thing what happens now. I gotta meet with my union rep and one of their lawyers tomorrow. I don't wanna go with the union's lawyer, but how the hell am I gonna pay for one on my own?"

"That's what we pay dues for," I said, going for a little brotherhood-of-union-guys thing. "All right. Keep Angel home today, but walk him in tomorrow. He misses too much school, and you're just making a bad situation a little bit worse."

"Yeah," he said. "I guess you're right. And thanks for calling. For checking up on Angel. I appreciate it."

"Not a problem. Good luck tomorrow."

"I'm gonna need all the luck I can get, Mr. Donne."

Uneventful days are few and far between in my new line of work as the school's dean. This Monday was one of them. Maybe it was the snow falling or the temperatures dropping, but the school was subdued all day. No kids running the halls, no small parties in the bathrooms, and not one teacher sent an unruly student to my office. I was able to catch up on the paperwork from last week's incidents and accidents, make a couple of phone calls to homes of kids we hadn't seen for three consecutive days, and drop by Elaine Stiles's office to see if our school counselor had any kids she needed me to touch base with. She didn't, so we had coffee as I filled her in on Angel's situation.

"Suspended without pay?" she asked.

"That's what he told me. I think normally they would've just reassigned him, away from any kids, but with the video all over the place now, they had no choice."

"Damn." She took a sip of coffee. "Maybe we should take up a collection. Help them get through the next few weeks."

"I'm not sure how Mr. Rosario would respond to charity. He seems like the proud, self-reliant type."

Elaine nodded. "We'll have Lizzie handle it," she said. "No one says no to her."

I smiled as I thought of Elizabeth Medina, our parent coordinator. She was everything a job like that in a neighborhood like this needed: a college-educated Latina with two public school kids of her own and who took shit from no one. I reached into my pocket and pulled out two twenties.

"You can start off with that," I said, handing Elaine the forty bucks.

"Thanks." She opened the drawer to her desk and put the money inside an envelope she labeled ANGEL'S FUND. "How was it at Dougie's house yesterday?"

"Not bad." I told her all about it, including details about Allison and the walkie-talkie I'd found in Dougie's desk and brought with me to school today.

"You took a date?" Elaine asked. "To a memorial service?"

"It wasn't a date, Elaine. She asked to come, and I said yes."

Elaine gave me a look as if she didn't quite believe me. "Whatever," she said, sounding more like one of our kids than I'm sure she wanted to. "What are you going to do with the walkie-talkie?"

I told her Edgar's idea. "In fact," I added, looking at my watch, "if I leave now, I can get up there by three thirty."

"Be careful," Elaine said.

"Of what? I'm just taking a little trip uptown."

"Your little trips sometimes lead you to places you don't want to go, Raymond."

Even though I'd never told Elaine the full story of how I had helped Frankie get home a year and a half ago—how deeply involved I'd let myself get and the laws I'd broken to get there—I think she knew I was holding something back.

"I'll be fine, Elaine. Thanks. And thanks for the coffee. I'll see you tomorrow."

"Have an uneventful afternoon, Ray."

Chapter 11

IF YOU LOOK AT THE NEW YORK City subway map, you'll see that if you want to get from Williamsburg, Brooklyn, to the Upper West Side of Manhattan, all you have to do is jump on the L train, transfer at Eighth Avenue to the C, and you'll be there in only forty-five minutes. Maybe less. Five miles. *Geo*graphically.

*Demo*graphically, the Upper West Side might as well be on the other side of the world. It is an area where real estate is valued by the square foot, not by how many people you can squeeze into a two-bedroom apartment. Doctors and lawyers are your neighbors, not professionals you go to on really bad days. In this part of the city, the first sign of spring is not robins, but women on cell phones suddenly walking alongside their own babies' strollers, as women whose skin is a few shades darker push their children for them.

As I made my way around pockets of tourists and a school group outside the Museum of Natural History, I remembered the field trips we used to take to the museum when I was in school. How we had traveled by yellow bus all the way from Long Island to see dinosaurs, gemstones, and mannequins depicting early America. I didn't appreciate it back then. Even when I was working in the classroom and took my own students, I was too busy keeping an eye on them to fully enjoy the museum.

I headed south toward Dougie's school, Central Park on my left. Looking over at the snow-covered trees in the park, I could almost understand why people spend so much of their hard-earned money to live here. Almost.

I took Dougie's walkie-talkie out of my bag and turned it on. I tuned to the first channel and got static. As I got closer to the school, I flipped through the channels every half block or so, getting nothing but white noise. When I got to the corner of the block where Upper West Academy was, the static changed to silence. I pressed the button to talk. "Hello?" No response. "Hello?" Nothing. I was about to try again, when a kid on a skateboard rode by about a foot in front of me.

"Gotta watch yourself, mister," he said, as he raced over the curb and into the traffic of Central Park West. He looked back from the street and showed me his middle finger. He then skillfully skated between two parked cars, jumped the opposite curb, and disappeared into the park. Young, invincible, and stupid. We all were at that age.

I was about to turn the corner toward the school, when a voice came over the walkie-talkie. "I said ten-five."

Cop talk. Whoever it was wanted me to repeat my message. I hoped I hadn't gotten the police frequency. I maintained radio silence, hoping the speaker would say something else. I thought he sounded too young to be a cop.

"Ten-five," the voice said again. Definitely a kid. *Good.* "What's your twenty?"

I pressed the TALK button and stated my location.

"Ten-four," he said. "Cross over to the park side, and I'll meet you there. Over."

I waited for the light to change and did as instructed. The sidewalk on the park side was busy with people, many taking pictures. A few folks were holding out peanuts, trying to get a squirrel to come in for a close-up. I figured them for Europeans. They didn't have squirrels over there and, unlike New Yorkers, found them to be quite photogenic. I looked up and down the sidewalk and saw no one carrying a walkie-talkie. I took off my book bag and was about to lean against the stone, waist-high wall that separated the park from the sidewalk, when a voice behind me said, "Who're you?"

I turned to see a kid—fifteen, maybe?—on the other side of the wall. He was wearing a white baseball cap over his long, brown hair. Around his neck hung a pair of binoculars, and he was holding a walkie-talkie in his right hand. Edgar's bird-watcher. He adjusted his eyeglasses and gave me a good look-over.

"How did you get Robin's walkie-talkie?" he asked.

"Who?" I asked.

"The walkie-talkie." He pointed at it. "How did you get that? I gave that to Robin. You are not supposed to have that."

"I don't know any Robin," I said. "I got this"—I held up the radio—"from Douglas Lee's mother. Do you know Dougie?"

The kid took off his hat, looked up, and scratched his head, emphasizing how hard he was thinking about my question. "I do not know Dougie," he said. "I know Robin, and that is his walkie-talkie. How did you get it?"

I stepped closer to the wall, and the kid took two steps back, almost slipping on the snowy dirt. He grabbed onto a tree, frightened. I held up my hand, signaling I'd stop moving toward him. I was starting to sense something else about this kid.

"It's okay," I said and watched as the kid squinted at me from behind his glasses. "I'm a friend of Dougie's—Douglas Lee? I used to be his teacher." I took a breath. "He goes to . . . he went to school right down the block. Upper West Academy." I pointed behind me. "He was killed last week."

The kid squinted harder and put his whole body behind the tree. "I go to Upper West Academy, and I do not know Dougie. I know Robin, and you have his radio." He shook the tree. "Why do you have Robin's radio?" he asked loudly. "Where is Robin?"

I took the walkie-talkie and clipped it on my belt under my jacket. Some of the passersby stopped and looked at me. I smiled that everything was okay, and they smiled back. I doubted they spoke English, which was good. I turned back to the kid.

"What's your name?" I asked. "Mine's Raymond. Raymond Donne."

"You do not need to know my name, Raymond Donne," he said, his voice getting higher. "Why do you want to know my name?"

"When you're having a conversation, it's polite to know the name of the person you're talking with."

"We are *not* having a conversation, Raymond Donne. I asked you a question, and you have not answered. Why do you have Robin's radio?"

This could go on all day.

I waited a few seconds before speaking again. "You go to Upper West?"

"Yes," he said. "But I should not have told you that."

"And you don't know Douglas Lee? Dougie?"

"I told you I do not."

"Well," I said, "the walkie-talkie I have belonged—" A thought came to me. "What does Robin look like?"

The kid thought about that and moved from behind the tree. "Why do you want to know what Robin looks like? You should know. You have his walkie-talkie."

"I think, maybe, the kid you're calling Robin is the one I'm calling Dougie." I waited as he considered that. "Tell me what Robin looks like."

He squeezed his eyes completely shut. "He is African–American. Black. He is taller than I am by five inches. He was just starting to grow a mustache, and he is my best friend at the school, and that is his radio." He opened his eyes again. "What does Dougie look like, Raymond Donne?"

I nodded. "Pretty much like Robin, I'm afraid."

"Why does that make you af—?" He stopped himself. "Oh. You said . . ." He looked up into the trees and held his breath. When he let it out, he said, "The school told us one of the students had been killed last weekend. That was the name they used, but I did not know Douglas Lee. I know Robin." He closed his eyes again.

"I'm sorry," I said. "But I think Robin was Dougie."

"And he is dead?"

"Yeah."

He stepped out from behind the tree and turned off his walkie-talkie. Then he removed his baseball cap and placed it over his heart. "I am not sure why people do this," he said looking at me.

"Me, neither," I answered. "Are you okay?"

"No," he said. "I am not okay. You just told me my best friend at school is dead. I thought he was out sick. Why would I be okay?"

"You wouldn't be," I admitted. "It's just another thing people say in a situation like this, I guess."

He took a step toward me and the wall that separated us. "Have you had a lot of situations like this, Raymond Donne?"

I nodded again. "Too many, I'm afraid."

He clipped his radio to his belt, came all the way to the wall, and put his hands on the stones. "You seem to be afraid a lot. Do you know that?"

I had to choose my words very carefully around this kid. "I'm not, really," I explained. "I guess it's just something I say too much." I took a step closer to the kid. "What is your name, by the way?"

"Elliot," he said, trusting me a bit more. "Elliot Henry Finch."

I stuck out my hand. "Raymond Donne. Raymond."

He looked at my hand. "I do not shake hands with people," he said matter-of-factly. "And you have already told me your name."

I dropped my hand. "I guess I did." Something occurred to me. "Are you involved with Finch's Landing? I saw a card in Dougie's desk."

For the first time since we met five minutes ago, Elliot Henry Finch smiled. "That is me," he said proudly. "It is a website I started. I took the name from my last name and also *To Kill a Mockingbird*. Have you read it?"

"A couple of times," I said.

"Me, too," he said. "Thirteen times, to be exact."

This kid was nothing if not exact. Then why . . .

"Why did you call Dougie 'Robin'?"

He shook his head and lifted the binoculars that were hanging around his neck. "I am into birds, Raymond." He didn't add "duh," but he might as well have.

"I can see that," I said. "But why 'Robin'?"

He climbed on top of the stone wall and threw his legs over the side. As he sat there, I got a much better view of his eyes behind the glasses. They were moving from side to side, up and down, like he didn't want to miss anything. They settled down before he spoke again.

"Robins," he explained, "are a generalist species. *Turdus migratorius*." He chuckled to himself on the last part.

"I understood the word 'robins.'"

"They can survive in almost any habitat. *Turdus* is Latin for thrush." He barely controlled himself this time. "But the name makes me laugh." Then he got serious again, somber almost. "I called him Robin, and he called me Finch. Because of my last name and other obvious reasons. I do not usually like the names parents give to their kids, so I give them new ones. Names that fit. Especially my friends."

I thought of the way Dougie had handled himself in Williamsburg and how his mother told me he was fitting in here at the Upper West Side private school. Elliot was spot-on. Dougie *was* a generalist.

"What's the website?" I asked.

"Finch's Landing," he said with obvious pride, "is a website exclusively devoted to the social needs of exceptional children in the private school setting." He'd given this pitch before. "We have thirty-one members as of this morning."

Exceptional: one of the many politically correct euphemisms for kids with special needs. Dougie had a reading disability. It wasn't crippling, but it did slow him down when acquiring and processing new information. It was apparently enough to get him into his new school. I must have been looking a bit too long at Elliot without speaking, because he gave me a look and said, "I am an Aspy."

"Excuse me?"

"An Aspy," he repeated. "I have been diagnosed with Asperger's syndrome. Are you familiar with the diagnosis? You should be. You are a teacher, right?"

"Right. And yes, I am familiar with Asperger's." I thought of Edgar. "I have a friend who has many of the characteristics."

"Is he highly intelligent?" Elliot asked.

"Very much so."

"Does he have few friends and trouble reading social cues?"

"Absolutely."

"Is he now a successful adult in a field a lot of 'normal people' might not be drawn to due to its lack of human interaction and its technical requirements?"

I laughed. "Have you met my friend Edgar?"

He gave me a serious look. "Not that I remember."

Kids with Asperger's don't always get the joke. "Did Dougie have a lot of friends at the school?"

"Yes, he did. As I said, he was a generalist. He fit in with every group at school."

That's going to make Murcer's job harder, I thought. *There'd be fewer kids to interview if Dougie hadn't been so damned popular.*

"Did you hear," Elliot said, "about our student who was killed a few days ago while skateboarding?"

"No. I didn't."

"On Riverside Drive," he said, pointing west. "He was going down a hilly street and skated directly into a city bus."

"Shit," I said. "He went to your school?"

"Yes. I did not know him well, but he was a friend of Rob—of Douglas. He was obviously quite upset about Douglas." He paused for a bit. "I miss Douglas. We used to talk a lot about bird-watching."

"What else did you and Dougie talk about?" I asked.

"You sound like a police detective, Mr. Donne."

"I get that a lot."

"Why do you want to know what else Douglas and I talked about?"

I took a chance and moved a few steps closer to Elliot. If he was still afraid of me, he was hiding it well.

"The police are saying Dougie's death was gang-related and—"

"Then the police are stupid," he blurted out. "He did not belong to a gang."

"I promised his mother I'd ask some questions and see what I could find out."

He leaned forward and squinted at me. "You sound like a detective again."

"I used to be a cop, Elliot. Many years ago. That's the reason Dougie's mom asked me for help."

"And now you are a teacher." He continued his squinting. "You . . . are a raven, Mr. Donne. Do you know much about ravens?"

"They're like big crows, right?"

"Hardly, but most people do make that same connection. Ravens are of the family *Cordivae* and among the smartest of birds."

"I'll take that as a compliment."

"Ravens are also symbols of mystery and death. As a teacher, you have most likely read Poe's poem."

"Once a year," I replied. "At Halloween."

He gave me a disappointed look. "Ravens also take pleasure in bothering other birds for no other reason than their own amusement. Does that sound like you?"

"Depends on who you ask."

"I am asking you, Mr. Donne."

"I do not believe I do that, no."

Elliot smiled. "Of course you would say that. Would you like an example of how intelligent ravens can be?"

"I'd love one."

He cleared his throat as if he were about to present a report to his science class. "Ravens are scavengers mostly. They will hunt when necessary, but they prefer to find their food ready to eat. Ravens have been known to come across a large, dead animal—let us say a deer. Unable to get at the good parts, they will proceed to make enough noise to attract other carnivores—those with sharp teeth and the ability to get at the flesh of the deer—and let those animals rip off the outer layer, exposing the meat of the animal. They then wait patiently until the carnivore is satisfied and leaves, so they can enjoy whatever remains."

I nodded, impressed. "They let the wolves do the dirty work."

"That is one way of putting it," he said. "Another, more *precise* way, would be to say that ravens are intelligent enough to understand and accept their limitations. By locating the food source and sharing with other animals, they benefit the whole community."

I gave it some thought. "I like your way better, Elliot."

"Call me Finch," he said. "And I will call you Ray." He held up his hand as if to stop me from talking. "Before you tell me not to get presumptuous, Ray is short for Raven, as well as the name your parents gave you."

This kid was good. "Tell me about Finch's Landing."

As he considered his response, he again cleared his throat.

"You are," he began, "aware of the popularity of social networking sites among the students you teach."

Not sure if that was a question, I just nodded.

"The most popular of these sites are quite attractive to those in my demographic group," he explained. "Initially. We are seduced by the ability to make 'friends' easily and often without much effort. You can understand how those such as myself, Asperger's kids, would . . ."—he paused for effect—". . . flock to such sites."

I nodded and smiled this time, enjoying his choice of words.

"After a while," he went on, "the same social issues arise nonetheless, and those of us who are not your 'typical,' 'normal' kids feel left out. We may not pick up on social cues very well in face-to-face situations, but online we pick them up better than our non–Asperger's counterparts."

"So," I said, "you still find yourselves on the outside, looking in."

He gave me an approving look. I was learning.

"Yes. So, I did the only logical thing and created a site for those of us who do not fit in. A site where we do not have to concern ourselves with saying the right thing or with the subtleties and nuances that are so confusing to us in the so-called real world." He flourished his arms like a magician. "Finch's Landing."

"I'm impressed, Finch."

"Yes. As I said, we have thirty-one members as of today." He stopped, realizing what he'd just said. "I guess that . . . we have thirty now. I was counting Douglas." He swallowed hard and rubbed his eyes. "That is just from three schools on the Upper West Side. All private, all special needs. I plan to expand in the new year."

"Did Dougie hang out with any of the other members?" I asked.

"In real life?"

"Yes, in real life."

"I observed him 'hanging out' with a few of my members. Boys who go to this school. The student who was killed was one of them. I was not personal friends with them, but they met membership criteria."

"You didn't care much for them?" I asked.

"They were part of the popular group," he said.

I detected what sounded like disappointment in his voice. "Did that bother you?"

He gave that some thought before speaking. "Do you know much about finches, Ray?" he asked, pretending to brush more snow off his shoulders.

"About as much as I know about ravens."

"The more colorful the male finch," he explained, "the more mates he attracts."

"Okay," I said. "That makes sense."

"The less colorful males eventually become aware of this difference and make a conscious choice to hang out with their more colorful, more attractive counterparts in the hope they will have more opportunities to mate."

"Kind of like social networking."

"Very good," Finch said. "I started my site in an effort to be more popular."

"You don't strike me as someone who cares much about popularity."

"I do not, in theory. But I was interested in seeing if it would work in practice."

"Did it?"

"No, Ray. It did not. The only true friend I had on Finch's Landing was Robin. *Douglas.* That was enough for me." He pulled up his jacket sleeve and looked at his watch. "I have to go now."

"Was Dougie close to any teachers here?" I asked.

"My train is coming." A touch of urgency in his voice. "I have to go now."

He started off in the direction of the subway. I followed him.

"Finch," I said, picking up my pace, "was Dougie close to any teachers?"

He looked at his watch again. "Four forty-seven. Yes, he and I both got along well with Mr. Rivera, the computer teacher. He was also our advisor." He started walking faster. "He might still be at the school. He is in charge of the afterschool computer class. I have to go now."

"Thanks, Finch," I called as he flew away toward his train.

A group of four boys was coming out the front door of Upper West Academy when I got there a few minutes later. They seemed to be talking about something serious, until they all broke out into laughter. The school seemed to be made up of four brownstones connected to one another. The steps leading to the main entrance had recently been swept clean of the light snow. Behind the boys was a man of about thirty, talking on his cell phone as he looped his computer bag over his shoulder. We caught each other's eye at the same time.

"Mr. Rivera?" I asked.

He held up his hand in a give-me-a-second gesture and said good-bye to the person on the other end. He slipped his cell inside his jacket. "You a reporter?" he asked. "Or another cop?"

"*Another* cop?" I asked.

"I spoke with a Detective Murcer a couple of hours ago," he explained. *Good for Dennis,* I thought. "I really don't have much more to say."

"Actually," I said, "I'm Raymond Donne, Douglas Lee's old teacher. From Williamsburg."

He gave me a long look and then smiled. "Oh, yeah," he said, offering his hand. "I saw you in the paper over the weekend. Looks like the article got the cops off their asses a bit, huh?"

"Actually," I said, "Murcer's a pretty good cop. He'd have made his way up here eventually. The article just sped up the process."

"Good for you," he said. "Douglas used to talk about you. Said you helped a friend of his a couple of years ago. A runaway kid or something?"

"Yeah," I said. "How well did you know Dougie?"

"Damn shame about Douglas." He took his phone out again to check the time. "You mind if we walk and talk? I gotta tutor a kid downtown in forty-five minutes."

"Not a problem," I said, and we headed west.

"Why are you here, Mr. Donne?"

"I was returning a walkie-talkie that belongs to one of your students. Dougie's mom asked me to get it back to the kid," I lied then realized it was still attached to my belt. "Wow. We had a whole conversation, and I forgot to give it to him." I handed him the walkie. "Would you mind?"

"That would be Mr. Finch, I assume. Our bird-watcher." He slipped the radio into his bag.

"It would be."

"Interesting young man, Elliot." Rivera gave me another look as we crossed Columbus Avenue. "So why are you *still* here, Mr. Donne?"

"Raymond. I also promised Mrs. Lee I'd ask around a bit. See if I could find out anything the cops should know about. That was before I knew Detective Murcer had come up this way." I wanted to keep this guy talking. "Were you able to tell him anything useful?"

He paused before answering. "I don't know. He asked how Douglas was doing in school, how'd he'd been acting before he was killed, who his friends were. Stuff like that. Kinda questions the TV cops ask, y'know?"

"The same questions I would have asked."

"Well, I'll tell you what I told him. Douglas was doing great in school. Top of his class, as a matter of fact."

"How many kids are in a class?"

"Fifteen. We've got four grades, two classes per grade, and fifteen kids in each class. He was becoming a standout. You prepared him well."

"Thanks." I thought back to the group of boys I'd seen coming out of the building. "One hundred and twenty kids," I said. "How many non-whites?"

Rivera grinned. "You picked up on that, huh? Not many," he said. And then with a joyless smile added, "It's time for ABC."

"I don't follow you."

"ABC," he repeated. "Another Black Child. We're a private school, Raymond. Come fund-raising time, we can't be too white, you know what I mean?"

"It's a different world from what I know," I said. "I understand Dougie hung out with the popular kids. Any best friends?"

"Elliot tell you that? 'The popular kids?'" I nodded. "Yeah. Dougie was tight with . . ." He lowered his voice to just above a whisper. "The *not-so-special* kids, as we call them in the faculty lounge."

"Because . . ."

"This is the Upper West Side, Raymond. Parents do what they can to give their kids any advantage over their friends' kids. Let's just say their idea of a 'learning disability' is not the same as yours and mine."

"Don't kids have to be evaluated to get into the school?"

"Pay six thousand bucks for a private eval up here, the evaluator will pretty much tell you what you want to hear."

I ran that concept through my head. "So the parents get their kids tested and then placed in a school for kids with special needs . . ."

". . . And Junior does better than his cohorts at the other private schools. When it's time for the college application game, who do you think gets more attention? The rich, white kid with decent grades at a non–special ed school or the rich, white kid who has struggled to overcome his learning disability to succeed at Upper West Academy?"

"Shit," I said.

"Of the bull variety."

We were silent for a while, as a group of young girls giggled their way past us. We got to Broadway, just across from the subway station. As we waited for the light to change, I said, "So. Dougie's best friends?"

"Probably . . ."—he paused to think—"Jack Quinn and . . . damn, I guess Paulie."

"Why 'damn'?"

"Paulie Sherman was the boy who got hit by the bus."

Shit. I'd met Paulie and Jack outside Dougie's funeral home.

Rivera zipped his jacket against the cold breeze coming from the Hudson River a few blocks away. "It's been a rough couple of weeks around here," he said.

"Yeah, Elliot told me about that. Sorry." I gave him a minute. During that time, the light changed, but he made no move to cross the street. "Jack and Paulie," I said, "you'd consider them . . . nondisabled?"

"Unless you count overprivileged and overanalyzed as disabilities," he said. "And in their cases, you probably should. I was their advisor. Douglas's as well. Jack and Paulie were both on ADHD medication, when all they really needed was their folks to step up and realize the word *parent* is a verb, too. Paulie . . ." His words caught in his throat. "I'm not blaming the victim, but what the fuck was a sixteen-year-old doing out after eleven o'clock on a school night . . . skateboarding?"

I nodded. "I hear ya."

"The three of them," he continued, "the last few weeks, I swear, it looked like they hadn't been sleeping at all."

Mrs. Lee had said something along those lines. "They say what that was about?"

"Gave me a load of crap. Staying up late to study, reading. I wasn't buying it. There's tired," he said, "and then there's *wired and tired,* you know what I mean?"

"You think they were on something besides their meds?" The thought of Dougie taking drugs was not something I could get my mind around. His mother didn't say anything about him taking prescription medications, either.

"I wouldn't put it past them. Jack and Paulie, anyway. As for Douglas, sometimes he'd go along with those two when he should have known better. Nothing big, just things like cutting last period or showing up late for first class with breakfast from Mickey D's. One time I caught them on the roof—we got a green space up there—smoking. Jack and Paulie acted like it was no big thing, but Douglas was upset for the rest of the day. Couldn't stop coughing, either." He laughed at the thought as we crossed to the Seventy-second Street subway station. "I wouldn't put him in the same category as the other two, but you know how kids can change in the right—or wrong—environment."

"Yeah," I said. "But who'd think a private school on the Upper West Side would be the wrong environment for a kid from Williamsburg?"

"Hey, man," Rivera said, "I grew up in Bedford–Stuyvesant." He gave his chest a playful double thump. *"Bed–Stuy. Do or Die.* I've seen kids pull shit up here my boys back in Brooklyn wouldn't think of doing. They eat their own in this zip code."

I let out an uncomfortable laugh. "What happened with the Paulie kid?"

He shook his head. "The hell if I know. Some of those streets over by Riverside Drive, the kids take their boards, ride down the slopes. But not at night, man. Not around those blind corners. And not alone." He reached into his pocket and pulled out his MetroCard for the train. "They go with their buddies, so they got someone looking out for them."

"Paulie was by himself?"

"Far as I know. No one's come out to say otherwise."

"What did Detective Murcer have to say about that?"

"What do you mean?" Rivera asked.

"Did he think it was strange Paulie was by himself? Or did he say anything about the coincidence of two kids who went to the same school getting killed within a week and a half of each other?"

"He didn't say anything about anything. You know how cops are: 'I'll ask the questions here.' Whatever he was thinking, he kept it to himself." He reached out to shake my hand. "I know what I'm thinking, though."

"What are you thinking?" I asked.

"Upper West Academy's been around for, what, fifty-something years? I asked some of the old-timers. Only two kids had ever died while students there. One in the sixties—a drug overdose—and one ten years ago in a skiing accident. To have two more killed in less than two weeks . . . I don't know."

"Too much of a coincidence," I said, as much for myself as Rivera.

"You're the one who used to be a cop. How do you feel about coincidences?"

I thought about that and nodded. "Thanks for taking the time, Mr. Rivera," I said. "Dougie's mom will appreciate it."

"Give her my condolences again, Raymond. She's a good woman."

"I'll do that. Thanks."

I watched as he made his way toward the busy subway entrance. He stopped and turned around. "Hey," he said.

"Yeah?"

"You speak with Douglas's girlfriend?"

I took a few steps toward him, maneuvering around people coming up from the underground. "I didn't know he had one."

"Oh, yeah. Jack's twin sister. Alexis. I think they were getting hot and heavy there toward . . . you know."

"Does she go to Upper West?"

"Oh, no," he said, the sarcasm practically dripping from his lips. "She's an academic superstar. One of Dayton's best and brightest," he said, referring to the exclusive all-girls' private school on the east side of the park. He took a few steps closer and lowered his voice. "With all the difficulties these kids have to face, one of the worst is an overachieving sibling. And a twin? Shit. Jack's got a hard road ahead of him."

Yeah, I thought. *Good thing he's probably got a trust fund to ease his way.* A family with two kids in private school was not hurting for bucks.

"I gotta go," Rivera said. "Tell Murcer to talk to the girlfriend." With those last words, he disappeared inside the station with a few hundred other riders.

Obviously, I was in no position to tell Detective Murcer anything. But I did know someone who could drop a strong hint that might get him motivated. I pulled out my cell phone and dialed Allison's number.

"Hello, Mr. Donne," she said, picking up after the second ring.

"Whoa," I said. "You got me on caller ID already? I'm flattered."

"Don't be too flattered. You're a source. I'm a reporter, Ray. What's up?"

Ouch. Right down to business. "A kid was killed the other night up on Riverside Drive. Rode his skateboard into a city bus. You know the story?"

She was quiet for a bit, but I heard clicking in the background. She was pulling the story up on her computer, I guessed.

"Yeah," she said. "We ran it. Kid was killed Thursday night. Got a half page with art the next day, a few paragraphs on Saturday about the cops not charging the bus driver. We plan on running a small piece on today's funeral services. That's it. Why?"

"The kid was a friend and classmate of Dougie's," I said. Thursday night. That's when I met Paulie outside the funeral home. "The driver say how it happened?"

Ten seconds went by. "It's not in the piece, but I can ask Tony. He wrote the piece, and we're both back at the office." Another pause. "I don't see him right now, but I know he's here. Let me find him and call you back."

That was a good idea, but I had a better one. "I'm on the Upper West Side," I said. "You want to meet up for dinner?"

"Dinner with a source, huh?" she teased. "But which one of us is the source?"

"We'll figure that out over dinner."

"Okay," she said. "I'll be another half hour here. Why don't we meet downtown by my place? But don't get any ideas, Ray. You know Bar 82?"

I closed my eyes and tried to visualize it. "Second and St. Mark's?"

"Very good, Brooklyn Boy. Be there at seven."

I looked at my watch. "I may have to start without you."

"Then I may have to catch up. Don't get too far ahead. See you at seven."

I put my phone away, pulled out my MetroCard, and headed in the same direction Rivera had a short time ago. I was looking forward to a little alcohol and more than a little Allison.

Chapter 12

I WAS SITTING AT THE CORNER of the bar, looking out at the snow falling on Second Avenue, when the door opened and Allison Rogers walked in. Without saying a word, she came over, kissed me on the cheek, and glanced down at my half-finished beer.

"All you need is a smoking jacket and a dog at your feet."

"I asked for a fire," I said, "but they have a stupid rule about requiring a fireplace or something."

"Damn government." She slid into the empty stool next to mine and, as she was undoing her coat, the bartender came over. "Hello, Meghan," Allison said. "The usual. And back up my friend here, if you will."

Meghan tapped the bar twice. "You got it, Ally."

"Ally?" I said, ready to give Allison a little shit.

"Yes," she said. "Ally. And, yes, I *do* come here often. Any more questions?"

I shook my head. "Not at the moment."

"Smart choice, tough guy." Her drink came—Meghan placed an upside-down shot glass in front of me—and Allison touched her glass to mine. "Here's to the first real snow of the season."

"You like this weather?"

"I love when it snows in New York. Kinda quiets everything down, especially when we get one of those blizzards." She looked out the window. "Nothing shuts this city down like a good snowstorm."

"You're in a good mood."

"I am in a hungry mood. How about you?"

"I could eat," I said, and then looked at the shot glass. "But I think I've got another drink coming."

"We'll order in."

"Your place?"

"You wish," she said. "Here." She waved to Meghan, who came right over. "Can you call us in an order of ribs and onion rings?"

"You got it," Meghan said. Then to me, "You ready for another pilsner, friend?"

I drained what was left of my first and slid the glass over. "I guess I am."

After Meghan walked away, Allison picked up our conversation of over an hour ago. "So the bus driver said the kid who rode his board out into Riverside Drive? Paulie Sherman? . . ."

"Yeah?"

"Said it almost seemed like the kid was waiting for the bus."

"I don't get it. You mean, like waiting to get on the bus?"

"No," Allison said. "Actually waiting for the bus to come by so he could . . . you know . . . skateboard out in front of it. He was on the corner, a block from the stop."

"Shit," I said, just as my second beer was placed in front of me.

"Nice mouth, friend," Meghan said. "You can pick 'em, Ally."

"Not now, Meg," Allison said. "Thanks."

Meghan raised her hands in mock defeat and stepped away to take care of some customers at the other end of the bar.

"So the driver thinks it was—what?—intentional?" I asked.

"That's what he told us, Ray. 'Suicide by bus.' How fucked is that?"

"Pretty." I took a sip of beer. Allison turned to the window. She had a look on her face that made me think she was remembering her own accident. "What'd the family have to say?" I asked.

"Nothing to us." She turned back to me. "We—and the family's lawyer—decided to keep that part out of the piece. Out of respect."

"Really?" I added, not hiding my cynicism.

"Yeah, Ray. Really. Jesus. We're not completely heartless. A lot of us have families of our own."

I reached over and touched her arm. "Sorry." When she didn't pull away, I said, "Your guy talk to any of the friends? Kids from school?"

"Nope. Just the driver. Tony's not known for his dogged pursuit of the truth."

"But," I said, "you are. So you've got to be more than curious about two friends from the same private school getting killed so close to each other."

"Hell, yeah," she said. "That's why I marched into my editor's office today and told him what I wanted to do, and he told me to run with it."

"Just like Lois Lane and Perry White?"

"Great Caesar's ghost," she said. "First thing I want to do is get Detective Murcer—" A buzzing noise came from her pocket. She removed her phone, gave it a look and said, "Shit." Then, in a much nicer voice: "Hello, Peter." Pause. She looked at me and rolled her eyes. "Yes, I can be if I have to." Pause. "Fifteen minutes. You got it." She hung up. "Hope you're really hungry."

"You have to go?"

"One of our local college basketball players is involved in a bit of a paternity scandal, and I gotta get over to the Garden and get some reaction quotes. Sorry."

"So that was Perry White on the phone."

She slid off her stool and put on her jacket. "Yeah." She kissed me on the cheek. "And this is the price for marching into his office earlier. Rain check, okay?"

"I can go with you. Keep you company?"

"It's my job, Ray. I'll be there for a few hours. It's harder than you think to get three or four usable quotes. And outside the Garden? Could take a while."

"Let's talk tomorrow?" I asked. "About Detective Murcer?"

"Yeah," she said, leaning in to give me a quick, friendly kiss. "This is what I meant the other night about living for the moment, Ray."

"I get the point, Allison. Again."

Meghan came back over. "You guys done already?"

"Work," Allison said. "Take good care of my friend here, okay?"

"You got it."

We both watched as Allison zipped her jacket and made her way out of the warm bar onto the snowy street. When I turned around, Meghan was down at the other end of the bar, serving two customers who seemed to be arguing. One was a tall black guy with white hair, and the other was white and about a foot shorter with spiky hair. Kind of like watching Billy Dee Williams argue with Sting's little brother. Meghan headed back to my end of the bar.

"What was that about?" I asked.

"Ah, they run a reading series here every other Monday night. They're like brothers who love each other except when they don't. Thank God they got the third guy working with them."

"We all need someone to keep the peace," I said.

Meghan smiled at that and kept on smiling.

"What?" I asked.

"Allison likes you. Maybe she'll keep you around longer than the others."

I grinned back. "I'm not going to ask how many *others*."

"And I wouldn't tell you. Just enjoy the ride."

"That was my plan all along."

"Smart man," she said and went back to tending bar.

A really smart man would've known how to get the lead detective on a murder case interested in talking to the bus driver who ran over his murder victim's friend.

"We'll see about that," I said to no one in particular.

Chapter 13

TOMORROW CAME QUICKER than I wanted it to. There's a reason I don't usually hang out late on school nights, and this morning my head reminded me why. I had two cups of coffee and three ibuprofens before heading off. By the time I got to my office, I was feeling better. After making sure the halls were clear after homeroom, I checked to see if Angel Rosario had made it to school. Outside his first-period class, I looked through the glass part of the door and saw Angel sitting in the first row. I knocked, stuck my head in, and asked the teacher if I could talk to Angel for a minute.

"Your dad bring you to school today?" I asked, once outside the classroom.

"Yeah," Angel said, somewhat embarrassed.

"It's okay," I said. "This'll blow over soon enough, and things will get back to normal. Any kids give you a hard time?"

"Not really. I got some looks in homeroom, but nobody said nothing."

"Good. Dad picking you up after school?"

"Yeah."

"If anybody gives you any grief, try to ignore it. If it gets bad, come to my office." I watched as a pout crossed his face. "What is it, Angel?"

"I don't wanna be treated like a baby, that's all. Dad taking me to school and picking me up. You telling me to come to your office if I get any shit." He looked down at his feet. "I feel like a little kid."

I put my hand on his shoulder. "I understand, Angel. I do. You and your dad are in a bad situation right now, and we don't want it to get any worse. Let's just get through this week, okay?"

He looked up, his eyes wet. "Yeah," he said. "Okay."

"All right," I said. "Get back to class, and I'll see you in the lunchroom."

"Okay, Mr. D." He wiped his eyes. "Thanks."

He went back inside the classroom, and I returned to my office, where I spent the next hour and a half making phone calls and finishing up some paperwork. The last call I made was to Dennis Murcer. I got his voice mail and left a message asking him if he'd get back to me at his earliest convenience. I wanted to discuss the kid killed by the bus but didn't want to leave that message on his machine. Just as well. It would probably be better if Allison asked him about it. I used that as an excuse to call her.

"Allison Rogers."

"You get your quotes last night?" I asked.

"After three hours of trying. What's up?"

Again, no small talk. "I just wanted to see if you had a chance to talk to Murcer yet about Paulie Sherman."

"Who?"

"Paulie Sherman," I repeated. "The skateboarder killed by the bus."

After a brief pause, she said, "Not yet, but I just made myself a note on it. I've been kinda busy with the basketball story. Turns out now the kid may have had a similar problem in high school. I have to track down some people who knew him back in the day and maybe head out to the Island. Why can't these athletes keep it in their pants?"

"Probably because no one ever told them they had to."

"Good point," she said. "It seems the better you are at sports, the less you hear the word 'no.'" Silence for a few seconds. "Let me get back to it, Ray. I'll call Murcer later and let you know what he says."

"Any chance of finishing our date from last night?"

"Have to get back to you on that one, too."

"So," I said, "we'll talk later?"

"I'll do my best. Let me get back to this piece, okay?"

She hung up without saying good-bye. *Okay.* I went out to check the hallways, staircases, and bathrooms: all the places kids would be if they were not where they were supposed to be. All clear, so I went down to the cafeteria and waited for the first lunch period to begin. *Exciting times.*

The rest of the day passed without incident. After making sure most of the kids had left the building and were heading home, I went back inside to check my mailbox. I found a pink "While You Were Out" slip. *When was I out?* It seemed Elliot Finch had called me—how did he get this number?— and the message was that it was "important" I get back to him "ASAP." I stepped over to the office phone and dialed the number on the slip. Elliot picked up after two rings.

"Ray?" he said.

"Yeah, Elliot. I'm returning your call. What's so—"

"Remember I told you that Douglas was friendly with Jack Quinn?"

"Yeah, I remember. I met him outside the funeral home."

"Well," he said, pausing for effect, "Jack is in the hospital."

"What? What happened?"

"I do not have all the details, Ray. His sister posted a message on the Finch's Landing site. Jack is a member, and he must have shared his password with her. *Against* the terms and conditions of the site."

"What did the message say, Elliot?"

"Just that Jack is in the hospital, and we should pray for him. It would seem the Quinns are a religious family. I do not pray, Raymond."

"Me, neither," I said. "Was Jack in school today?"

"I did not see him, and we have some of the same classes. So I would have to say he was not in school today."

"Okay," I said. "Do you know the sister?"

"No. She is not a student here. I believe she goes to Dayton."

Right. That's what Mr. Rivera had told me yesterday. "Did she say what hospital her brother's in?"

"New York–Presbyterian," Finch said. "On the other side of Central Park. Why do you want to know that?"

"I'm going to call the detective in charge of Dougie's case. He needs to know another person associated with Dougie is . . . I don't know . . . in trouble?"

Elliot was silent for a few seconds. "You are right, Ray. It does seem statistically improbable that three friends from the same school have all had . . . trouble in a short period of time. The odds of that are . . ."

"Pretty long, Elliot. Thanks for calling."

"Will you let me know if you find out anything?"

"Sure. I'll call you later."

I hung up and immediately called Murcer. Again I got his voice mail and asked him to call me as soon as he could. This time I mentioned Paulie Sherman *and* Jack Quinn. I wasn't sure when Allison would get the chance to call him, and I wanted him on this as soon as possible. He could yell at me for playing cop as much as he wanted. I just hoped he believed, as I did, that these three friends and their problems were worth looking into. Sometimes it's all about seeing the connections. If he needed help, I was more than willing to make that happen.

My day was over, so I went to my office. I started filing an online suspension report, all the while thinking about Jack Quinn and what might have put him in the hospital. I could wait for Murcer to find out and share the information with me, but I didn't think he'd do that. I could call Allison back, but she'd already told me how swamped she was. My third option was to head back across the river and visit the hospital myself. Which was the one I chose.

Less than an hour later, I was standing outside New York–Presbyterian, trying to figure out a way to get up to Jack Quinn's room and find out what was going on. It wasn't like I could just walk into his room and look at his chart. The nurses and doctors certainly were not going to give me any information, and security at the front desk seemed pretty tight. I realized I hadn't thought this trip out completely and was about to cut my losses and go home, when I saw a teenage girl with a blond ponytail exit the building. She was dressed only in a long-sleeve T-shirt that read DAYTON VOLLEYBALL, jeans, and white sneakers. She didn't seem to realize or care how cold it was. She stepped over to the bushes and pulled a pack of cigarettes out of her front pocket. After she lit up and took a few deep drags, she pulled a cell phone out of another pocket. It didn't take long before she started talking, loud enough for me to hear.

"Hey, it's me," she said as she pulled her ponytail around her neck for a scarf. "No, they won't know anything more until he stabilizes." She listened for a while. "That's what they think, but they had to do a blood test to be sure." Pause. "I don't know. He didn't tell me if he was." Another pause. "Okay, I'll call you later. Bye."

She hung up the phone and slipped it back into her pocket. After she took another pull from her cigarette, she noticed me looking at her. I decided to take a chance.

"Excuse me," I said as I walked over to her. She was taller than I'd expected. "Are you Jack Quinn's sister?"

She gave me a long look through bloodshot eyes. "Who the hell are you?"

I stopped a few feet away from where she stood. "My name's Raymond Donne. I was a . . . friend of Douglas Lee."

"Dougie?" she said. She took another drag, dropped the cigarette to the ground, and stepped on it. "What do you mean, you were a friend of Dougie's?" She slurred the last part of the sentence.

"His old teacher, actually," I admitted. "You knew Dougie, right?"

"He was good friends with my brother."

"How is Jack, by the way?"

She gave me another look that made me think she was deciding whether to keep this conversation going. Her eyes told me she hadn't slept much. After a few seconds, she said, "He's . . . stable. How did you know he was here? Why are you here?"

Good questions.

"Elliot Finch called me," I said, as if that were enough to explain my presence. "You posted a message on his website?"

"Oh, yeah," she said, her tone a bit more unsure now. Confused. I wondered if she was on something, or just tired. "I forgot about that."

"Do you need to sit down?" I asked.

She rubbed her eyes. "Why are you here?"

"Honestly?" I said.

"No," she said, her red eyes doing their best to stay focused. "Lie to me."

"I don't know. I know Jack was good friends with Dougie, and when I heard he was in the hospital . . ."

"Hey," she said. "You're that guy from the paper the other day." She smiled as she made the connection. "Used to be a cop, helped save that kid a couple of years ago. Dougie told us about you."

"How well did you know Dougie?"

"He," she said slowly, almost like she was drunk, "was my brother's best friend. So that's how well I knew him."

"I heard you were his girlfriend," I said. "Alexis, right?"

"I was not his *girlfriend,* Mr. Raymond. He was my brother's best friend and we were friendly . . . but not romantic friendly. Who told you we were boyfriend–girlfriend?"

"Maybe I misheard. Sorry."

"Yeah, you should be. Maybe you misheard." She was having a little difficulty standing up now. "You misheard."

I stepped closer. "Do you need to sit, Alexis? You seem a little . . . out of it."

"You'd be out of it, too, if it was your brother upstairs with tubes coming out of his arms. I got no sleep last night, so I took a little something to help me through. I'm not sure it's working."

"What did you take, Alexis?"

"God," she said. "You ask a lot of questions, don't you?"

I took another chance and touched her elbow. When she didn't shrug me off, I said, "Why don't we grab a seat on the bench over there?" I thought about taking her inside, but thought she needed the air. "I think whatever you took is starting to kick in."

"It's about time," she said, allowing me to lead her over.

When we got to the bench, she grabbed the iron armrest, turned around, and slowly sat down.

"Yeah," she said. "Now I feel better."

"Is there anyone here who can take you home?" I asked, standing above her. "Your mother or your father maybe?"

"Don't know where my mom is," she said, not even trying to keep her eyes open now. "Daddy's upstairs with Jack. Told him I was going out for some air. I don't think he's gonna wanna leave Jack and take me home."

"Does he know you took . . . some medication?"

"No. It's one of my mom's pills, and I just took it. I do it all the time, when I need something to get me through." She smiled real big now, proud of herself. "They never count their pills, Mr. Raymond."

How nice for you. "Is there someone I can call who can come and get you?"

"I can't leave," she said. "My brother's up there in intensive . . . I need to be here."

"You need to get some sleep, Alexis. And not outside on a bench."

"Well, whattaya gonna do, huh?"

This girl was full of good questions. I wished I had some answers. And then one came to me. "Can I borrow your cell, Alexis? I need to make a call."

She reached into her front pocket and pulled out her phone. When she handed it to me, she didn't let go. "Who ya gonna call?"

"It'll be a surprise."

She opened her eyes and thought about it. "Okay."

I took the phone and tapped at the screen until I brought up the names and numbers of her most recent calls. The name "Daddy" showed up. I scrolled down and pressed the DIAL button. He picked up after three rings.

"Yes, Alexis," he said. "What is it now?"

"Mr. Quinn," I said. "My name's Raymond Donne and—"

"What the hell are you doing with my daughter's phone? Where's Alexis?"

"We're right outside the main entrance to the hospital. Your daughter's about to pass out on a bench."

"What the hell do you mean, she's 'about to pass out'?"

"She told me she took one of your wife's pills. It's obviously starting to work, and I think you should come down and get her, sir."

"Jesus Christ," he said. "Put her on the damn phone, will you?"

I looked down at the man's daughter. Her chin was on her chest.

"She's in no condition to speak right now, Mr. Quinn. I really think you need to get down here right away and get her some help."

Silence from the other end, and then, "Okay. I'll be right down."

"Thank you," I said. "And bring her coat." He'd already hung up. I reached over and gently shook Alexis's arm. "Your dad's coming to get you."

"Uh-oh," she mumbled. "I'm in major trouble now."

I took my jacket off and draped it over her shoulders. I stuck my hands in my pants pockets and hoped her dad would get here soon. Two minutes later, the front doors to the hospital opened, and a man in a dark blue suit came out. Judging by the redness of his face and the girls' coat he was clutching, this was Alexis's dad.

"What the hell do you think you're doing, Alexis?" he said as he came over to the bench. "Do you have any idea how embarrassing this is?" When his daughter didn't answer, he looked at me. "You're the man who called?"

"Yes," I said, handing him his daughter's phone. "Raymond Donne."

He took the phone and put it into his pocket. "John Quinn. That your jacket?"

"Yes. I thought she needed it more than I did at the moment."

He shook his head and rubbed his eyes, much like his daughter had done a few minutes ago. "Thank you, Mr. Donne. I'm sorry you got involved in this."

"Not a problem," I said. "Any idea what she took?"

He looked down at his daughter. "If what you said is correct, more than likely one of my wife's antianxiety pills. They can have a sedating effect."

"Alexis mentioned that. How's your son?"

He gave me a quizzical look. "How do you know about my son?"

"Alexis told me," I lied. "She said he's in ICU."

"Alexis," he said, "talks too much." He offered me his hand, and I took it. "Thank you, Mr. Donne. I'm only glad my daughter ran into someone . . . responsible."

This was clearly not the first time he'd received this kind of phone call. "You're welcome," I said. "You'll take her home?"

"I have someone coming to do that, yes. My son needs me here. She"—he looked down at Alexis again—"just needs to sleep this off." He handed me my jacket and put her coat over her shoulders.

She's going to need more than sleep, I thought. I put my jacket on.

"Good luck, Mr. Quinn."

He gave me a weak smile. "Thanks." He then sat down and put his arm around his daughter. "I didn't ask, sorry. Are you visiting someone in the hospital?"

"No," I said. "I just happened to be passing by."

"And aren't you glad you did."

I smiled at the forced humor. "Good-bye, Mr. Quinn."

"Good-bye, Mr. Donne."

Alexis stirred. "He's a teacher, Daddy," she said. "He's Dougie's old teacher."

Mr. Quinn gave me an odd look. "What's that, sweetie?"

"He's. A. Teacher." She sounded drunk again. "He knew Dougie."

With his arm still around his daughter, but his eyes firmly on mine, he said, "Is this true, Mr. Donne?"

Unable to come up with a quick lie, I just said, "Yes."

"I don't understand," he said. "You said you were just passing by, and now it turns out you knew one of my son's best friends?" He paused for a few seconds as he processed this new information. "What the hell are you doing here?"

"He came by," Alexis mumbled, her eyes still closed, "to see what happened to Jack. Elliot called him. Isn't that right, Mr. Raymond?"

"Who the hell is Elliot?" Quinn demanded.

When Alexis didn't say anything, I figured it was my turn to talk.

"A mutual friend," I said. "A classmate of Jack's. And Dougie's."

"And that brings you here *why?*"

With no way forward but the truth, I thought about a way to explain that wouldn't make me sound crazy. It took a little while. "When I got the call from Elliot," I began, "it struck me as too much of a coincidence that your son was in the hospital after what happened to Dougie and to Paulie Sherman."

"What the hell does Paul Sherman have to do with my son's . . . condition?"

"I don't know. I was hoping to talk to Jack. I didn't realize he was in ICU."

"Oh," Quinn said. "Your buddy Elliot didn't know about that?"

"He only knew what your daughter posted online, Mr. Quinn. He knew I was . . . looking into Dougie's murder and thought I'd be interested in whatever happened to your son."

Quinn slowly removed his arm from around his daughter, who seemed to be sleeping again. He stood up with a confused, angry look on his face. "You're a schoolteacher," he said. "What the hell are you doing 'looking into' Douglas Lee's death? And how dare you involve my family?"

"I didn't mean to involve—"

"No," he snapped. "You just show up at the hospital. What were you trying to accomplish, if not involve my family?"

"I was hoping to find out what happened to your son and maybe ask him some questions about Dougie."

"Jesus Christ. Do you hear yourself?" He took a step closer to me. "You're a fucking schoolteacher." His face turned red again. "And my son is in no condition to answer any questions. From anyone." His eyes filled with tears as he backed away and slowly sat down next to his daughter.

"I understand," I said. "And I apologize for intruding. You should know, though, the detective assigned to Dougie's murder will be contacting you."

He looked up at me. "And how did he find out about Jack?"

"I called him."

"Of course you did," he said. He pointed his finger at me. "Something's wrong with you, Mr. Donne."

I thought about offering him a quick comeback, but decided against it. "Good-bye, Mr. Quinn. And again, good luck with . . . your kids."

"If I see you around my kids again, Mr. Donne, you'll be hearing from the police and my attorney."

Of course I would.

As I made my way to the street, a black Lincoln Town Car pulled up in front of the hospital. Same car as my uncle's. The back passenger door opened, and out came a large black man. *Damn.* Looked like I'd be hearing from Quinn's attorney sooner than we both had thought. The man who emerged from the car was Dougie's uncle. He gave me an odd look once he realized who I was. He considered stopping for a second, but chose to go over to where his client was trying to wake his drugged-up daughter. They spoke in hushed tones and, when they were done, looked over at me. Douglas Lee called out my name, and we met halfway.

"Mr. Lee," I said. "How are you?"

He stuck out his hand. When I took it, he squeezed harder than he had to.

"What are you doing here, Mr. Donne?" he asked, maintaining his grip. "We have a family in distress, and you choose to add to their problems?"

"That was not my intention, Mr. Lee."

"Your intention doesn't quite matter at this moment. What should matter to you is my client has every right to charge you with harassment."

Didn't take long to get into that Lawyer Speak.

"You think he'll bring his daughter to court to testify against me?"

Douglas Lee didn't smile. "That's very clever, Mr. Donne."

"Thanks," I said. "Can I have my hand back now?"

He looked down at our hands and relaxed his grip. I pulled my hand back to where it belonged. I'd be feeling that for a while.

"You're fortunate, Mr. Donne, that my client has much more pressing matters to attend to at the moment."

"Are you the call he made to get his daughter home?" I asked.

"That is none of your concern. None of this is your concern. You would do well to remember that. You are not a policeman anymore."

"Maybe *you* better ask him then—before the cops get here—about the connection between your nephew, Paulie Sherman, and Quinn's boy, Jack."

He shook his head at me and grinned, like I just didn't get it. "Who says there's a connection, Mr. Donne?"

"Oh, come on," I said, noticing he didn't ask me who Paulie Sherman was. "I know you're a lawyer and sometimes you have to think like that, but really? Your nephew's been murdered. One best friend lost a fight with a bus, and the other's in intensive care. You don't see a connection here?"

"As a lawyer," he said, "I see only the facts, and the facts are that those are three separate and unrelated tragedies. Unless you have evidence that proves otherwise?" He paused for a beat. "Do you have such evidence, Mr. Donne?"

"No, Mr. Lee," I admitted. "I don't. But once the police start looking into this, I believe that will change."

"Then my client and I will deal with that when the time comes. That's why people have lawyers."

"And taking home semiconscious daughters is just a part of your personal service?"

That got him. He tried not to let it show, but his eyes gave him away. He wasn't just a lawyer. He was an employee. A highly paid babysitter at the moment.

"Good-bye, Mr. Donne," he said. "Stay away from the Quinns."

"Don't worry about me," I said, looking past him and over at the father and daughter on the bench. "You might want to get the driver to help you with Alexis. It doesn't look like she's gonna be able to make it on her own."

I turned to the street and started walking. I pulled out my cell phone and dialed Murcer's number. Again, I got his voice mail, and I hung up without leaving a message. Didn't want him thinking I was stalking him. While I had the phone out, I tried Allison one more time but got the same results. I slipped the phone back into my jacket pocket.

With no one else to talk to, it seemed like a good time to head back to Brooklyn and try to find some people who would be glad to see me.

Chapter 14

BY THE TIME I GOT TO THE LineUp, the early evening rush was in full swing. Mikey was behind the bar, mixing something that required a shaker—more than likely for the pair of young cop groupies talking to the two off-duties down at the far end. Mikey had asked to take my shift for the night, because he needed the extra cash with the holidays coming up. I had no problem taking the night off.

The usual retired cops were in their regular seats. The TV above the bar was showing an old—I mean, *classic*—Yankees game. Every seat at the bar was taken except one: the one next to Edgar, who was busy with his laptop again. I patted him on the back as I slid into the empty seat.

"How's it going?" I asked.

"Raymond!" he said, surprised to see me. "Mikey told me you wouldn't be showing up tonight. Any more news about the dead kid?"

And that's why the stool next to Edgar is usually open. I got Mikey's attention by raising my index finger, and I knew within the next sixty seconds a Brooklyn Pilsner would land in front of me.

"No, Edgar," I said. "No more news about Dougie. But you were right."

"I was?" he said. "About what?"

"The walkie-talkie he had. Turns out Dougie *was* into bird-watching."

"You went up to Central Park?" he asked, pleased I'd taken his advice.

"Yep. I did just what you told me to, and I found his partner."

"All right," Edgar said, offering me his fist to bump. I bumped it. "Kinda like a couple of detectives, huh?"

"Kinda."

Mikey came with my beer. "Thanks again for the extra shift, man. You eating tonight?" he asked. "Or just the beers?"

"Chicken sandwich," I answered. "No fries or rings, though."

"What's up with that? You're thin enough as it is."

"Just not that hungry tonight. Okay?"

"You got it, Ray."

After Mikey left to put in my order, Edgar picked up right where we had left off.

"So," he said. "Tell me about this bird-watcher."

I took a long sip of pilsner. "He went to school with Dougie. Takes his bird-watching very seriously."

"They all do, Ray. You should hear my uncle talk about it." He made a big deal out of rolling his eyes. "You ever listen to someone go on and on about something, and you have to sit there, faking interest?"

"Yeah," I said, enjoying the irony. "Every once in a while. Anyway, the kid's really into birds and computers. Started his own social website for kids with special needs who go to private schools."

Edgar grinned. "I like this kid. What's the site?"

I told him, and within seconds we were looking at Finch's Landing on Edgar's laptop. I asked him to click on the "Recent Postings" link. He did, and there was Alexis's message about her brother. There were two postings after hers, both expressing best wishes to Jack and his family.

"This website's pretty good," Edgar said. "But your friend really should put in a better security system. I mean"—he waved his hand over his laptop—"anybody can just get right on and cruise the site."

"I'll make that recommendation next time I see him."

I went on to tell Edgar about my trip to the hospital and my experience with Alexis, Mr. Quinn, and Dougie's uncle.

"That's one hell of a coincidence, huh?" Edgar observed. "Your kid's uncle is the lawyer for the ICU kid's dad."

"Maybe not so much of a coincidence," I said. "This guy Quinn might have been Dougie's connection to Upper West Academy. Can you get onto their site?"

Edgar gave me a look like I was disrespecting him for even asking. Half a minute later, we were looking at the school's home page. There were links for everything from "Campus Life" to "Make a Donation." I pointed to the one that said "Board of Directors" and asked Edgar to click on it. He did and, sure enough, halfway down the list of names was *John R. Quinn Sr.*

"Right again, Ray." Edgar squinted at the computer screen. "What's a Board of Director do, anyway?"

"I'm not sure," I said. "If the private schools work the way the Catholic ones do, I'd say they're involved in fundraising and recruitment."

"And scholarships?"

I nodded. "Yeah, probably scholarships, too."

"So," Edgar thought out loud, "Uncle Douglas is Quinn senior's lawyer, and your boy Dougie just happens to get a free ride to an exclusive private school. What's this guy Quinn do when he's not a Board of Director?"

"I don't know," I said, then pointed to the empty search field in the upper-right corner of the screen. "Why don't you tell me?"

As Edgar was typing John Quinn's name into the box, Mikey came over with my chicken sandwich. He looked down at the plate and shook his head. "Just doesn't look right with no fries or rings."

"If it makes you feel any better," I said, "you can bring Edgar and me another couple of beers."

"Yes," Mikey said. "That would make me feel better."

As he left to get our beers, I took a bite of my sandwich and looked over at the computer screen. Edgar was frowning and shaking his head.

"Too many *John Quinns*," he said to no one in particular. "I'm gonna put in the middle initial and the *Sr.* and see what pops up." He did, and his frown quickly turned to a grin. "There we go. *John R. Quinn Sr.* Looks like he's a big wheel for some pharmaceutical company in Jersey."

"Which one?" I asked.

"Ward Fullerton."

"Never heard of it," I said.

"Me, neither. Probably because they don't advertise during baseball games."

"Which means they don't treat erectile dysfunction."

Edgar laughed. "Wanna check out their site and see what they do make?"

"Absolutely," I said and took another bite of my chicken. Mikey came over with our beers and a small can of tomato juice for Edgar. He gave me an up-and-down wiggle of the eyebrows.

"You two enjoying yourselves?" he asked.

"Oh, yeah," Edgar said, his fingers practically dancing across the keyboard. "Give me my computer and a few beers, and I can stay here all night."

Mikey grimaced. "No need to make threats, Edgar."

"Give us a minute, will ya, Mikey?" I said. "Edgar and I are right in the middle of something."

"Yeah," Edgar said, his eyes glued to the screen. "Right in the middle."

Mikey rolled his eyes, but took the hint and went to the other end of the bar. I glanced over at Edgar's screen and watched as an impressive web page came to life. The faces of children—all different colors—scrolled beneath the heart-shaped corporate logo of Ward Fullerton Pharmaceuticals, the company name written in green capital letters. Under the pictures of the kids floated various words and phrases, including *Childhood Cancer, Rare and Neglected Diseases, Attentional Issues, Juvenile Vaccines.*

"These guys are involved with a lot of heavy stuff," Edgar said.

I nodded. "Is it all kid-related?"

"I don't see any pictures of grown-ups. Maybe that's why we've never heard of them. Who advertises kiddie drugs on TV?"

I looked at links at the top of the page and pointed. "Click on the one that says *Board of Directors.*"

As he did, he said, "You think . . ."

"I don't know, Edgar. That's what we're going to find out."

Within seconds, the screen was filled with pictures of Ward Fullerton's Board of Directors. It didn't take long to recognize John R. Quinn Sr.'s face in the middle of the pack. Without having to be told, Edgar clicked on Quinn's name so that his bio came up. We both read silently for a bit before Edgar said, "This guy's pretty impressive. Head of research and development."

"I guess he does pretty well for himself," I said. "Got his own driver—and a lawyer—who come when he calls." I read more of his bio. "Master's in International Relations and Biology."

"Smart guy."

"Not smart enough to keep his wife's drugs away from his daughter. But, yeah, I guess he'd have to be pretty sharp."

I took another bite of my sandwich and followed it with a sip of beer. Edgar continued to navigate around the website but didn't seem to find anything that held his interest for more than a few seconds.

"You wanna hear about their corporate citizenship or how their stock's been performing over the last financial quarter?"

"Not really," I answered. "Just wanted to see who the guy was."

"Okay." Edgar closed out of the site, and the screen returned to Upper West Academy's page. "We done here, too?"

"Yeah. Thanks." My cell phone rang. I took it out of my pocket and looked at the number I had dialed three times that day. I got off my stool and walked away from the bar for a little privacy. "Dennis," I said. "Thanks for getting back to me."

"Something on your mind, Raymond? I got three missed calls from you this afternoon. Who is Jack Quinn, and why should I care?"

"He's—*was* a friend of Dougie's," I said. "He's in the ICU over at New York–Presbyterian. He was also a friend of Paulie Sherman."

Silence from the other end and then, "The kid killed on the skateboard?"

"Yeah. Doesn't that strike you as too much of a coincidence?"

As I waited for an answer, I looked over at Edgar, who was giving me a "What's up?" look. I held up my index finger to let him know I'd be done soon.

"It does," Murcer finally said. "How'd you hear about the Quinn kid?"

"I got a call from a friend of Dougie's," I said. Then I told him about my visit to Dougie's school and how I met Elliot.

"You've been busy again, Raymond. Anything else you think I should be made aware of while I have you on the phone?"

I paused for a bit and figured he'd probably find out anyway.

"I went to the hospital today," I said. "To see Jack Quinn."

"Please tell me you are shitting me."

"I felt like I had to do something. I did try to call you first, though."

"Fuck, Raymond." Dennis went silent again, struggling for the right words. Before he could find them, I went on.

"I met the sister and the father," I said, then gave him the rest of the details up to and including my conversation with Dougie's uncle.

"He's right, y'know," Dennis said. "This Quinn guy can charge you with harassment. Shit, *I* can charge you with interfering with an investigation. What the hell were you thinking? No, no. Forget I asked that. I know exactly what you were thinking. You're not police anymore, Ray."

"Maybe not," I said. "But if I were, I'd have known enough to check Dougie's laptop and talk to his friends and teachers at the school."

"How'd you know about the laptop?"

"I was at the Lees' the other day. The reception after the funeral."

"So you had the mom call me to—"

"It was her idea," I lied. "I agreed with her."

He mumbled something I didn't quite get. I think I made out the word "asshole."

"So," I said. "You'll go to the hospital and speak with Quinn?"

"Are you hearing me, Raymond?"

"Yes, Dennis," I said. "I'm hearing you. When I got to the hospital I realized I shouldn't have been there. I was about to leave when the sister came out."

"And then you just couldn't help yourself, right?"

"I figured, what the hell? I'd come all that way. What harm was there in talking to the kid's sister? Shit, they're lucky I was there. The condition she was in, she was another tragedy waiting to happen."

Dennis laughed. "Careful there, Ray. With all the spinning you're doing, you're gonna get dizzy. And, yes," he said, the lightness in his voice disappearing, "I will take a ride up to the hospital and speak with the family. What you did was stupid, but I do think you're right about this being too much of a coincidence."

"You're welcome," I said.

"I never said thank you. I just said you were right. See the difference?"

I didn't care about the difference. I was just happy he was going to look into Jack Quinn.

"Thanks, Dennis."

"You're welcome," he said. "Enjoy the rest of your night." I thought he was going to hang up, when he said, "Just out of curiosity."

"Yeah?"

"You still doing those Thursday night dinners with Rachel?"

"You've got a good memory, Dennis."

"Helps with the job."

"Yeah, we're still getting together. Why?"

"Just asking," he said. *Liar.* "Hey, Ray?"

"Yes, Dennis?"

"You mind if I give her a call?"

"Why would I mind?"

He laughed. "I believe you referred to me as, quote, 'A shitty boy-friend.'"

I thought back to my last conversation with Rachel. The one where she'd told me I'd overstepped my bounds and that she could handle things herself.

"You go ahead, Dennis. You're both grown-ups."

"Thanks, Ray," he said.

"You're welcome."

"And stay the hell away from my case." Now he hung up.

I put my phone into my front pocket and went back over to Edgar. Before he could ask, I said, "Murcer's going to the hospital."

"So he appreciated your help?"

"*Appreciate* is not the word I would use, no. Let's just say he reluctantly agreed with me and made sure to remind me of my obligation to stay out of his way."

"He's just afraid you'll show him up."

"No, Edgar, he's right." I sat down and grabbed my beer. "I was out of line this afternoon. I'm lucky that—"

My cell rang again. *Mr. Popularity all of a sudden.* I saw it was Allison and stepped away from the bar again.

"Hey," I said.

"Hey back." She seemed to be in a good mood. "You at The LineUp?"

"Yeah," I said. "Taking the night off."

"And spending it at the place where you should be working. I know I've only known you for less than a week, but you are a creature of habit."

"I am?"

"Don't worry about it. It's not a bad thing." She paused, waiting for me to respond. When I didn't, she said, "And how was your day?"

"Not bad," I said. I told her about the trip to the hospital and my phone call with Murcer. "So all in all, a productive day."

"Maybe I should head over to the hospital myself tomorrow."

"I wouldn't expect much cooperation from the family, Allison."

"No, probably not, but maybe I can find a chatty nurse or doctor. It's amazing what people will tell you when they think they're going to be quoted in the paper."

"On or off the record?"

"Both. Mostly off, but I can get around that by quoting a 'hospital spokesperson' or a 'source close to the family.' Either way, my editor's going to dig this new angle. Two dead kids and another on the edge."

"You guys really get off on other people's tragedies, don't you?" I said.

"Don't start with that, Ray," Allison said. "You were the one who called me and asked for the piece on Douglas. Mom wanted something in the papers, and you were more than willing to oblige her." She waited for me to respond. When I didn't, she continued. "This is a good story. Shit, it's turning into an actual mystery. You know how often that actually happens in a reporter's career? Excuse me for getting excited, but this is what I do for a living. Do you really want to debate this, Ray?"

She was right. She did me a solid when I asked for one. It wasn't her fault the case got complicated. I was the one who called *her* about Jack Quinn. "No. I don't." I rubbed my eyes. "I want to find out what happened to Dougie."

"The same thing I want," she said. "And the info you just gave me is going to help me to do that. If we have to put up with a few flashy headlines to get there, that's the price of the ride, tough guy."

"Yeah," I said. "I get it."

"I hope you do. I wouldn't want this story to get in the way of . . ."

I smiled. "No. Neither would I. Speaking of which . . ."

"Let me call you tomorrow, Ray. Between the basketball player paternity story and now Jack Quinn, I'm not going to have a lot of time for socializing, I'm afraid."

"Right." *And here I am with nothing* but *time.* I looked over at Edgar. "Let's talk soon," I said to Allison.

"You bet, Ray. Thanks for understanding. See ya."

"Yeah. See ya."

After we both hung up, I stared out the front window for a while, watching the headlights of the cars and trucks heading toward the entrance ramp of the BQE. My phone started to vibrate in my hand. I again recognized the number and looked over at the bar. "What do you want, Edgar?" I said into the phone.

"Hey, Ray," he said, laughing. "Just thought it'd be funny if I called you."

"And how'd that work out?" I hung up and walked over to him. "I was trying to get my thoughts together."

"Sorry. You just looked like you needed a laugh."

I got back on my stool. "It's okay, Edgar. It's been a long day."

"I hear ya, brother." He raised his glass. "Here's to the working man."

I picked up my glass and tapped his. "Here's to him," I said. "That was Allison," I explained. "She's going to follow up on her end with Jack Quinn."

"Excellent," Edgar said. "Between her and your detective friend, you've had a pretty good day, huh?"

"Yeah," I said. "I guess I have."

"You guess? You got the newspaper and the cops backing your play, Raymond. You are the man."

I shook my head. "Don't make too much out of it."

"I won't," he said. "But, Jeez, don't *you* make too little out of it." He raised his hand to get Mikey's attention. "At the very least, it deserves another round."

"It's a school night, Edgar." I thought back to the morning's hangover. "I don't know."

"Yes, you do, Ray." Edgar looked at me and gave me what I guessed he thought was his all-knowing smile. "Yes, you do."

I looked back at him and had to admit it. He was right. This did deserve another round. "All right," I said. "One more."

"Cool." He got Mikey's attention and motioned with two fingers that we needed another round. "Besides," Edgar said, pointing up to the TV, "they're playing the Yankees–Red Sox game from 2003. Clemens against Pedro?"

I looked up at the set. "Pretty good game."

"Yeah." Edgar's smile got bigger. "Remember? Roger put one up high and tight to Ramirez, and Manny almost went nuts."

"Nothing like a little chin music to back a guy off the plate," I said.

"Yeah. Pitch wasn't even that close, but it did its job. Got things going, all right. It was a different game after that."

Edgar is right, I thought, as Mikey put our drinks in front of us. Amazing how one moment—one fraction of a second—could change the whole ballgame.

Chapter 15

WEDNESDAY WAS ONE OF THOSE school days that went by so fast it was three o'clock before I remembered I hadn't eaten lunch. I'd had a lot of days like that these first few months as dean, and I must have lost at least ten pounds. Who needed the gym when I had to patrol all over the building looking for kids cutting class, go up and down three flights of stairs, depending on where the latest crisis was; or walk at least two miles around the cafeteria during my lunch duty? Depending on whom I talked to, I was either in the best shape since I'd left the force, or I was too thin. Either way, there was a big part of me that was glad for the busy days, because I wasn't much for sitting around, waiting for stuff to happen.

After making sure the kids had moved away from the building and the playground was not being used as a wrestling ring, I went back inside to make a call to Dougie's mom. I wanted to see how she was doing and also felt obligated to give her a heads-up about the story that might show up in the papers about Dougie's two friends from school. She picked up after two rings and seemed genuinely happy to hear my voice. She told me she had just gotten back from church.

"It's good to have support at times like this," I said.

"Yes," she agreed, not sounding too convinced. "It is."

I proceeded to tell her the stories of Paulie Sherman's death and Jack Quinn's hospitalization. I also told her about running into her brother-in-law outside the hospital. She let out a heavy sigh and said she remembered the boys from the wake, and knew her brother-in-law was John Quinn's lawyer.

"Did Dougie have a girlfriend, Mrs. Lee?" I asked.

"If he did," she said, "he didn't tell me about it. You know how teen-age boys are with their mothers. It was all I could do sometimes to get him to tell me what he wanted for dinner." She paused. "Last couple of weeks, he spent most of his time in his room on the computer. I barely saw him except when he came out to the kitchen or bathroom."

"Did he ever mention an Elliot Finch?"

"Oh, yes," she said. I could practically hear the smile on her face. "He was very fond of that young man. He told me he joined just to be nice to Elliot, but I think he came to enjoy his time exchanging messages with the other members. He 'chatted' with them more than he talked to me, I'm afraid." I could hear her catch her breath. "Maybe if he knew . . . if he had any idea how little . . .." She started crying. I stayed quiet. Half a minute later, she said, "I'm sorry."

"That's okay, Mrs. Lee. I think you're handling this very well. Better than most people, I would say."

"Thank you for saying that, Mr. Donne. I'm sure you heard lots of crying when you were a policeman."

"And even more now that I'm a teacher."

She laughed. "I don't know why that's funny, but it is."

We both got quiet for a while—me thinking of what else there was to say, and Mrs. Lee thinking whatever the mothers of recently murdered children think. I couldn't even imagine. The silence was uncomfortable, but I didn't want to be the one to end the conversation.

As if reading my mind, she said, "You know, I've been thinking about something you and the detective both asked me."

"What's that?"

"You both asked if Douglas's behavior was any different before . . . what happened."

"Yeah," I said. "I'm sorry if the question bothered you. Sometimes I slip back into cop mode without even thinking about it."

"No, it's quite all right. It got me to thinking." She paused again to collect her thoughts. "I mentioned Douglas was having trouble sleeping the past few weeks."

"Yes, I remember you said that."

"There was something else, though."

I waited for her to say what it was. When it took too long, I said, "Something else, Mrs. Lee?"

"He'd been talking more to his father the past month or so. He'd call him on his cell phone and talk for quite some time."

"How often did he talk to his father?"

"A few times a week, from what I could tell." Anticipating my next question, she said, "Before that, they'd go months without talking. Douglas never seemed to have much need to talk to William, and William was not the type to reach out much."

"What did they talk about?"

"Oh, I don't have any idea. Most of the time, Douglas would take the phone into his room or out on the back steps. I didn't want to be nosy, so I never asked."

"Where does his father live?" I asked. "Dougie rarely talked about him."

"I'm not sure of that, either, I'm afraid. I think I know where he spends most of his time, though."

"Where's that?"

"Do you know the old bar on Graham Avenue?" she asked. "Right on the corner. The one with no sign? I think it might have been called Ruth's a long time ago."

I closed my eyes to try and picture the place she was talking about. It didn't take long. Back in the day, I'd been called there a few times to clean up a mess and ended up giving more than one patron a ride home. A few I'd taken straight to the hospital.

"Yeah," I said. "I think you're right. It might have been called Ruth's. I don't even know if it has a name anymore. I'm surprised it's still there."

"Oh, it's still there, Mr. Donne. I don't keep tabs on William, you understand, but I hear from folks he still goes there. They've seen him outside smoking or leaning up against the wall, talking with another drunk."

"Did Dougie ever see his father drunk?"

"Not that I know of, and not if I could help it. I saw the writing on the wall and told him to get out before Douglas got old enough to know what his daddy was up to when he should've been home being a father."

"So," I said, "if I wanted to talk with him . . ."

"Don't know why you would, but I'm sure you'll find him there."

"Any time of day in particular?"

"Knowing William?" she said. "Sometime between opening and closing."

I looked at my watch. Almost three thirty.

"Well, Mrs. Lee," I said. "I don't want to take up any more of your time."

"Don't you worry about that, Mr. Donne. It was nice of you to call. And thank you again for keeping the papers interested in Douglas. How is that lovely young reporter, by the way?"

Mothers. "She's fine, Mrs. Lee. I'll tell her you asked for her."

"You do that," she said. "And be sure to tell her I said thank you."

"I will. Take care."

"Good-bye, Mr. Donne."

After we hung up, I slipped my phone into my pocket and grabbed my coat. I had plans to meet my sister at seven, but I decided it was time to finally meet Dougie's father.

Chapter 16

AS I ENTERED THE BAR THAT may or may not have been called Ruth's, I understood why it might very well have had no name. It was dark—depressingly dark—with the only sources of natural light being the small front window that held the broken neon Budweiser sign and the small window on the side that faced onto the alley. There were three hanging lamps above the bar that gave a yellowish hue to the half dozen or so customers. As my eyes adjusted, I stepped over to the bar, where I was immediately greeted by a man of about sixty who was wiping out the inside of a pint glass with a classic white bar rag.

"What can I get for ya?" he asked.

I looked over at the three taps. "What do you have on draft?"

He told me. I was not impressed. "Anything interesting in a bottle?" I tried.

"If ya find Bud and Bud Light interesting, yeah. Me? I find 'em all fascinating."

"I'll take a Bud Light. Thanks." I pulled a twenty from my pocket and sat down on a wooden barstool that had seen better days. The TV behind the bar was tuned to a sports channel. The sound was off, and the colors were not what they were supposed to be. At the moment they were showing a soccer game being played on blue grass. The bartender came over, placed my beer on a napkin, and slid it over in front of me.

"Thanks," I said.

"Two fifty," he answered, picking up the twenty and leaving to make change. I watched as he punched the keys on an old cash register. When the drawer slid open, the thing actually made the *ching* sound. He grabbed some bills and some coins out of the register, closed the drawer, and came back.

"Seventeen fifty change," he said.

"Happy hour?"

"Look around, friend." He made a sweeping motion with his hand. "Every hour around here's happy."

I gave him another smile and a nod. After taking a sip of my beer, I asked, "You know William Lee?"

He placed his hands on the edge of the bar in front of me and squinted. "Who?"

"William Lee," I repeated. "I heard he comes here a lot."

"Ah, see," he said. "Here I thought you were just a beer snob. Now I'm guessing you're some sort of cop."

"Why? Do a lot of cops come around here looking for William Lee?"

"Not that I know of," he said. "Don't get too many people around here asking for no one. Why you want to know about Spaceman?"

" 'Spaceman'?"

The bartender smiled again. "Oh, yeah. You're probably too young to know 'bout that, huh?" He paused, leaned back, and crossed his arms. "Red Sox used to have a pitcher. Tall guy, great fastball, better curve. Bill Lee. People called him Spaceman because he was really out there. On the field and off."

"I've heard of him," I said. "But why did you call—"

"Our *Bill* Lee is a bit like that himself," he explained. "He's got some weird ideas, and sometimes the craziest shit comes outta his mouth. Just made sense for folks to start calling him Spaceman. Compliment really, if ya think about it. But nobody calls him William."

I took another sip of beer. "So you do know him?"

"You ain't a cop?"

"Not anymore," I said. "Just asking if you know William—Bill Lee."

"Know him?" The bartender's grin got real big now. "Shit, he's the one sitting at the other end of the bar, pretending he's watching the soccer game."

I took notice of the other customers: two pairs and a single. The pair closest to me was busy reading the same newspaper. The other two seemed to find their glasses of beer to be the most fascinating things they'd seen in a long time. And then there was Bill Lee. *Spaceman.* A blue baseball cap firmly fixed on his head, and his eyes glued to the soccer game on the TV.

"You think it's okay if I talk to him?" I asked the bartender.

"I don't know," he said. "He's not been real chatty these days. Lost his kid recently. Shot or something. The other side of the bridge."

"Stabbed," I said. "That's what I want to talk to him about."

"Ah, shit. You're not a reporter, are ya?" He made a big gesture of pointing at the front door. "'Cause if that's the case, you can just—"

"I'm not a reporter," I said. "And I'm not a cop. I'm just someone who wants to talk to Bill Lee about his son." I took another sip. "I knew Dougie. I was his teacher."

"Teacher?" The bartender gave that some thought. "Well, it's still a free country. You can talk to just about anybody you want. Don't mean they hafta talk back, though."

"I hear that," I said, picking up my beer and sliding a ten-dollar bill at the bartender. "Get Mr. Lee another of whatever he's drinking. Thanks." I got off my stool and headed over to Dougie's father.

It's hard to tell the age of someone who drinks a lot. Mr. Lee could have been anywhere between thirty and sixty. He was a bit lighter-skinned than Dougie, but I could see the resemblance in the shape of his nose and in the way his eyebrows were set on his forehead. He might have been handsome a while ago. The booze took care of that. The wrinkles on his face made me think of a poorly drawn road map. I immediately felt guilty about buying him another drink.

I put my hand on the back of the barstool next to him. "This seat taken?"

He just shrugged, not taking his eyes off the soccer game.

I pulled out the stool and sat down. I placed my beer and the rest of my change on the bar. Mr. Lee had his left hand wrapped around a cocktail glass that held a bunch of melting ice cubes and a brown liquid. I could tell by the aroma it was bourbon.

I motioned with my head at the TV. "Who's playing?"

He shrugged again just as the bartender came over with a fresh bourbon and ice.

"This is on your new friend, Spaceman. He gave me enough to pour the good stuff, including tip." He winked at me. "Not that crap you always ask for."

After the bartender walked away, Mr. Lee drained what was left of his old drink, pushed the glass away, and brought in the one I had bought for him. He raised the glass and mumbled something that might have been "thank you."

"No problem," I said. "My name's Raymond Donne, and I was hoping I could talk to you for a bit, Mr. Lee."

Another shrug. "About what?"

I took another sip of beer and said, "Your son. Dougie."

He placed his drink down and gently touched his glass with all ten fingers. After a few seconds, he pulled his fingers away and rubbed them together as if making the international signal for money. He turned, allowing me to see his full face for the first time. His eyes were teary and red; the left one was looking slightly off to the side.

"Never trusted this game," he said, taking a quick glance at the TV and then looking back at me. "Don't understand how people all over the world can get so damned excited about a game that could possibly end up zero to zero."

I took some time to digest that and said, "I never thought about it that way."

"Most people don't," he said. He reached over and picked up his drink. He put the glass to his lips. "Whatchoo wanna talk about my son for?" Then he completed the act of taking a sip.

"I was his teacher, Mr. Lee."

"Ain't nobody calls me that anymore. You can call me Spaceman like everyone else around here, or you can call me Bill."

"Okay," I said. "Bill. I was Dougie's teacher back when he was in middle school. I don't believe we've ever met before."

"Probably not. Let his mother take care of that kind of stuff."

What kind of stuff? Parenting?

"Yeah," I said. "I got to know Mrs. Lee pretty well."

"Good woman," he said. "Real good woman. Sometimes I'm amazed she put up with me for so long. Gotta love them good Christian women, know what I mean?"

"I guess," I said, half smiling. "My mother's one of them."

He raised his glass. "Here's to good Christian women." He took a sip of his bourbon and slid one of the ice cubes into his mouth. He rolled it around for a bit and then crunched. His face turned serious. "Why you wanna talk about my son, Mr. Donne? Obviously you heard what happened."

"I did, and I first want to offer my condolences. He was a great kid."

"Yeah. Got his mother to thank for that, I guess. But . . ." His attention was drawn back to the soccer game, which now seemed to be taking place on purple grass.

"Dougie's mom said he'd been calling you lately," I said, trying to refocus the conversation. It wasn't working. I raised my voice a touch. "Before he died? You and Dougie had talked on the phone a few times?"

"Yeah, yeah," Mr. Lee said, still watching the game. "We'd talk on the phone a coupla times a week. He got himself one of them cell phones."

"Did he call you or did you call him?"

"Sometimes I'd call him from here." He motioned with his head at the pay phone near the rear door of the bar. "I'd tell him I was here, and he'd call me right back so as I didn't hafta keep putting quarters in the phone. Good kid, my Douglas. I even let him meet me here once. Just before he . . . you know . . . before what happened to him."

"They let a seventeen-year-old into a bar?"

"Just for a few minutes," he explained, his watery bloodshot eyes now on me. "Just wanted to show him off a bit. Let everybody see there was more to me than just whiskey and ice, know what I mean?" He picked up said drink and swirled the ice around a few times. "Let them see a bit of what I used to be." He touched the glass to his lips and moved it back and forth a few times. His glance went off over my shoulders, to someplace far beyond his barstool.

After a suitable amount of time, I spoke. "What did you two talk about?"

"You ask a lot of questions, you know that?" He took a sip. "We talked about what fathers and sons talk about. School, sports . . . and shit. What do you think we talked about? Nuclear energy?" He smiled at his own joke, and then the smile went away. "Talked about life, Mr. Donne. Life."

"Did he ever mention any friends? Jack Quinn? Paulie Sherman? Elliot Finch?"

He squinted as he thought about the question. Then he opened his right eye. "Elliot?" he said. "He's the bird-watching kid?"

"Yes."

"Yeah, he mentioned him once or twice. Always thought it was kinda funny a bird-watcher had the last name of Finch. Knew a veterinarian years ago named Katz. Or was it Fisch? Kinda stuff makes me laugh. Don't recognize the other names, though. Why you asking about his friends?"

"I met them this week."

"You been getting around, haven't ya?"

"I guess. I'm sorry I missed you at Dougie's wake."

He turned back around to face the TV set. "Yeah," he said. "I chose to do my mourning in private. Don't go in for all those flowers and prayers and shit. Always felt if I had something to say to God, I could say it any damn place I pleased, and it did not please me to do it in some sweet-smelling funeral home."

"So you didn't go to the church, either?"

"No, I did not. I said all I got to say to God." He slowly looked up at the bar's ceiling and sucked his teeth. "He heard me."

I took a sip of my beer and let that last thought hang in the air for a bit.

"If you don't mind me asking," I said, "what *did* you say to God?"

"Why you wanna know that?"

"I'm not religious. I just wonder what people say to God when something like this happens." I thought back to Dougie's mom at the wake. "What is there to say?"

He picked up his glass and swirled the ice around a few times. "Well," he said, raising his glass to me, "you bought me one, so I guess that entitles you to ask one personal question."

He sipped from his glass and stayed silent for half a minute. I waited.

"Said what every parent who loses a child says, I guess. 'Why'd you take my boy? Why not me?' I mean, the kid wasn't even seventeen yet. What the hell did he do to deserve what happened to him, huh?" He paused. "Ain't nobody can give me an answer to that one, Mr. Donne. Not even the good Lord himself. Now, me? I done plenty coulda cashed my ticket early. But here I still sit, drinking my whiskey and ice, watching stupid shit on the TV, and cashing my disability check twice a month.

Nobody expects shit from me. Now, Dougie . . ." His next words got caught in his throat. He had a little more whiskey to loosen them up. "Dougie was different. You seen the fancy school he was going to?"

"I did."

"He was doing all right. Hanging with the right kids, learning the right stuff. Reminded me of myself when I was that age. Before . . ." He pointed at his left eye. "Y'know what I mean?"

I shook my head. "No, Mr. Lee. *Bill*. I don't."

"Dougie never told you?"

"Told me what?"

He smiled, lifted his glass to his lips, and downed what was left of his bourbon and water. He raised his hand to get the bartender's attention. The bartender waved and fixed Spaceman another drink.

"Don't worry," Mr. Lee said. "I won't make ya pay for any more. I can buy my own drinks, and I don't want you feeling like you're contributing to the delinquency of an alcoholic. I'm guessing you noticed the eye, huh?" He pointed to it again. "The way it goes off a bit? You seem like a pretty observant guy."

"Yeah," I said. "I noticed."

"Well," he began, taking a deep breath, "the man who sits before you was not always the man who sits before you. Believe it or not, there used to be a time when I was pretty sharp. Used to be a time when I had the world where I wanted it."

The bartender came over with the new drink and winced. "Spaceman," he said. "You ain't telling the story about how you got that eye again, are ya?"

"And what if I am?"

The bartender waved his hand as if shooing away a fly. "Just keep your voice down." He turned to me. "The rest of us have heard the story a dozen times, mister. I'll be down at the other end if ya need me."

"Thanks," I said. And then to Mr. Lee, "Go on."

"Maybe I didn't have it all," he said, "but I was pretty damned close. College scholarship, pretty girls, enough cash money to do something about them pretty girls. I was living the life."

"What was the scholarship for?"

"Baseball. Got clocked one time at ninety-five miles per. Not many kids doing that back in the day. Got me a free ride to school. I never was as smart as my big brother. You meet Douglas?"

"Twice."

"Yeah, he got the scholarship for what he had up here." He tapped his temple. "I got mine 'cause of my right arm. Anyways, I was halfway through my four years, started noticing some scouts coming around, checking me out with their clipboards and radar guns. None of them came up and spoke with me, just sat in the stands working their numbers. That's when I figured one thing out for sure."

After the required pause, I said, "What was that?"

He grinned. "Gotta get me one girl and stick with her. I figured I'd be getting paid real soon with all them scouts floating around. Didn't think it'd be wise to have too many irons in the fire, if you know what I mean. Not that I was ready to settle down, but I had to keep my focus on what was important. Too many young beauties around can distract a guy. So"—he raised his glass—"I picked the prettiest and the smartest one and said adios to all the others."

"Dougie's mom?"

"You got that right. Glorious Gloria. That's what I called her back then. And she was. Best damn decision I ever made, that one."

His eyes went off again, back over my shoulder and somewhere far away. I finished my beer and let him stay there for a minute before I spoke.

"What's all that got to do with your eye?"

His eyes came slowly back to me. At least, the right one did.

"I'm getting to that," he said. "So we're together. I mean, I'm upstate in school and she's down here in Brooklyn, but we're together. See each other every coupla weekends. She comes up to me. I come down here. Liked it better when she came up, because then I could show her off around campus. Anyways, we do that for a coupla months and one time she comes up, says she's got something real important to tell me. Shit. I was barely twenty. What's real important to a kid just outta his teens, right?"

I nodded.

"Tells me she's pregnant. Boom!" He clapped his hands together. "Just like that. Well, long story short, I don't react right away the way she wants me to react, and she takes off. Walked herself all the way to the train station before I finally caught up with her. She's all crying and shit, saying

I don't love her. I said bullshit. I love you. Just didn't expect the news you dropped on me, baby. We sit there for a while—ain't no train coming 'til the next day anyway—and we work it out. Go back to my dorm and fall asleep together. Just like everything was normal."

"But it wasn't," I said. "Normal."

"Shit, no, it wasn't. I'm twenty years old with a future in the bigs staring me in the face, and I'm gonna be a daddy? Damn. That's a lot to stick in my head, y'know?"

"I can imagine," I said.

"Hmmm," he said, taking a sip of his drink. "Don't know if you can, Mr. Donne. Anyways, that's what's in my head, and I got all distracted. Got together with Gloria in the first place to avoid distractions, and she ends up giving me a big one. Hard to keep my head in the game, y'know?" He closed his eyes and ran his tongue over his lips. "So a few days after I get the news, I'm pitching against a school in Jersey. Had everything going that day: curveball, changeup, fastball. My arm was alive. Think there mighta been a scout or two in the bleachers, checking me out. They saw me at my best."

He stopped and smiled, eyes still shut. After thirty seconds went by, I spoke.

"The eye?"

The smile faded. "I'm getting to that." He opened his eyes. "Fifth inning, we're up, two–zip. I'm shutting them down, ain't walking no one. I am in control. Gave up only one hit and the guy who got it steps up to the plate. Digs in, makes a big show of taking his practice swings. Gets himself settled in a bit too close to home plate, know what I'm saying? He's in my territory. First pitch, I throw him an outside curve off the plate, but he gets enough wood on it to foul it off. Shouldn't of come close to that pitch, but he's all over the plate. *My plate.* So next pitch, I put a fastball high and inside, back him off."

"Chin music," I said, remembering the Yankees–Red Sox rerun Edgar and I watched the other night.

"Yeah," Mr. Lee said, the smile returning. "So he settles in again, this time an inch or two back from where he started, so I decide to throw him the slow curve again. I'm looking at the outside corner, but the damn thing didn't break. Just hung there like a goddamn batting-practice pitch.

Guy's eyes get as big as cue balls, and he jumps all over it." He shuddered, as if touched by a cold breeze. "Came right at me faster'n anything I ever got hit back to me." He paused for a few seconds and lowered his chin almost to his chest. "Next thing I know, I'm waking up in the emergency room at some Jersey hospital surrounded by white people in white coats. Couldn't understand most of what they were saying, but the general idea seemed to be I was lucky to be alive.

"Long story short—*ha*—that was the last pitch I ever threw. The headaches and blurriness pretty much put an end to my college career, too. Came back home to Brooklyn with nothing. No school, no baseball, no job. Just another unemployed black man who's gonna have a kid."

"Wasn't your fault, though," I said.

He laughed. "Life don't give a shit if it's your fault or not, Mr. Donne. You old enough to know that."

I thought about my accident and how it had changed my life. How it turned me from a cop to a teacher. How Allison went from runner to reporter. "Yeah," I said. "I am."

"So," Mr. Lee continued, "we do the right thing and get married, move in with her folks until we can get a place of our own. Gloria's the one with the real job. I'm over at the ninety-nine-cents store stocking the shelves. We did it, though. Just before Dougie was born, we got ourselves a two-bedroom over by the J train, and we bring our baby back to *our* house."

"How long were you married?"

"Dougie was three when she told me she couldn't take it no more. I couldn't hold a job, 'cause the headaches never stopped and the eyes couldn't stay focused for too long. I figured someone as bright as myself didn't need a doctor to tell him what was wrong, so I started medicating myself. A little pot at first, then some harder stuff. Never did that shit in front of Dougie, though. Never. After a few years of that, I switched to this." He tapped his glass. "I guess somewheres along the line, I just forgot about everything else. She didn't want me around no more, and I couldn't blame her."

He spun around and returned to the soccer game. With his eyes glued to the TV, he said, "Pretty boring story, huh?"

"I've heard worse. So you and Dougie had been talking lately?"

"Yep." He nodded. "Last coupla conversations got weird, though."

"Weird how?"

"I don't know. He was going on about how he was gonna help me get better. I tried to tell him this was the best it was gonna get for me, but he kept saying he was learning about some shit . . . I don't know . . . something to do with the brain. Like I said, I ain't the bright one in the family."

"What else did he say?"

"Ah, I don't know. That he had 'connections' through his school. People who knew stuff. Who helped people like me get better."

"And you have no idea what he was talking about?"

"Nope. Said he couldn't tell me too much; I'd find out soon enough." He turned to face me. His eyes were tearing up again. "That kid," he said. "I think he really believed he could help me. I tell ya, Mr. Donne, that school and those people he was hanging with, they put some ideas in his head. That ain't always a good thing." He shook his head. He turned back to the TV set and got that lost look again.

"You may be right." I put my empty pint glass on the bar and looked at my watch. I had a couple of hours before I had to meet my sister, but it looked like this conversation was over. I put my hand out to Bill Lee. "Thanks for talking to me, Bill. I know you didn't have to, and I appreciate it."

He took my hand. "And I 'preciate everything you did for Dougie. I might not've been around much, but I know you helped put him on the right track. Not like the one I found myself on, know what I mean?"

"I'm not sure I agree with you," I said. "I'm also old enough to have learned most people choose their own paths. Like you said: life doesn't care about fair and unfair or who's at fault. Most of us end up where we put ourselves."

He placed both hands on his knees. "So, you're saying *I'm* the reason I'm here? At this bar, living from paycheck to paycheck?"

"I just think we have more control than most of us think we do. Like when you were pitching."

"Yeah, well," he said, taking a long look around the bar and giving me a pathetic smile. "I ain't pitching no more, am I?"

"No. You're not." I gently touched his shoulder. "Take care of yourself."

"I am and I will, Mr. Donne. You make sure and do the same."

With that, I turned, threw a good-bye salute to the bartender, and made my way to the front door of the bar that may or may not have once been called Ruth's.

Chapter 17

"BIG BROTHER," Rachel said as she slid into the empty stool next to mine and placed a sisterly kiss on my cheek.

"Little sister." I gave her a kiss on her forehead.

"Thanks for your flexibility, Ray."

"Not a problem."

Rachel had some sort of office holiday thing, so we had moved our date up a day. As per our agreement, I had chosen the place tonight, so it was my check to pick up. The place I picked could not have been more different from the bar where I'd met with Mr. Lee. Beers here were three or four times the price, and all the TVs were high-def.

"I'd much rather hang out with you than the bunch I work with and those other assholes," Rachel said.

"I believe those other 'assholes' are called 'clients,' and they pay your salary."

"I know. And once a year I have to be rudely reminded of that fact." The bartender came over, and Rachel ordered herself a dirty martini and another beer for me. "What's that you're drinking?"

I looked at the bartender and said, "Brooklyn Pilsner."

As the bartender walked away, Rachel patted me on the back. "Way to expand your horizons, Ray."

"Hey," I said. "If I find a better beer, I'll drink it." I raised the almost-empty pint glass in front of me. "Until then . . ." I drained what was left.

"So . . ." She slapped her hands on her thighs and rubbed them. "Are we eating here, too, or just drinks?"

"We can eat here." I reached over and pulled a bar menu out of its holder and handed it to her. "The wings are really good. The fried calamari is excellent. And they make an amazing sliced sirloin sandwich."

"One-stop shopping," she said. "I like it. Besides, I'll probably be pigging out tomorrow night. Good idea to take it easy tonight."

"Glad I could help you out."

The bartender came back with our drinks. I put in our food order, and Rachel and I touched glasses.

"Here's to the assholes," she said. "Long may they continue to employ my services and write me big fat checks."

"Here's to them," I agreed.

We sipped, and something registered on Rachel's face.

"Hey," she said. "Mom got a lot of calls about you being in the paper. The poor kid. And his family."

"I've been keeping in contact with Dennis, and he's got a lot more questions than answers at this point."

"He told me," she said. "He called me last night."

That didn't take long, I thought. "What'd you two talk about?"

"You, mostly. A little me, a little him. How it ended between us, and how much we've both changed." She looked for a reaction. I gave her none. "Change is good, Raymond."

"Most of the time."

"Anyway," she said before taking a sip of her drink, "we're getting together one of these nights. Dinner."

There were half a dozen responses to that. The one I chose was, "Really?"

"Yes, really. Just dinner."

"It's never 'just dinner,' Rachel."

"Well, that's what it is, Ray. Two *adults* having dinner. Just like we're doing right now."

She was right. I knew it, but still, the thought of her back with Dennis. . . .

"What?" she asked.

"Nothing," I said. "I hope you have a good time."

"Thank you. Now we can enjoy *our* dinner. When did you talk to Denny last?"

"Yesterday," I said, leaving out the part where he asked me if it was okay for him to call her. "I had some info about the case I thought he should have."

"Of course you did. Far be it from you to let the police do their job without a little help from Raymond Donne. Didn't you learn your lesson the last time?"

"The last time?" I spun my pint glass around a few times before picking it up and taking a long sip. I loved my sister, but she was starting to sound like Uncle Ray. I didn't want to talk about last time. Hell, I didn't want to talk much about *this* time. "He was my kid, Rache," I said. "His mom asked me to give the cops a little push, so I set up the interview with Allison. It worked. She got Dennis to put in a little more effort, and we've made some progress."

"*We?*"

"We. They. What does it matter? Some new developments came to light, which may help Dennis."

"New developments?" She did nothing to hide her sarcasm. "Ray. The last time you behaved like this, I had to leave town and you had to get Uncle Ray to help pull your ass out of the fire. Remember?"

"This time is different, Rache."

"Different how?"

I told her about what had happened with Paulie Sherman and Jack Quinn and how it seemed to me—and Allison—that they were more than just a coincidence. I told her how I just wanted to point Murcer in the right direction and then back off. I'm not sure she was buying it. But, being my sister, she chose to focus on something else.

"Allison, huh?" she said. "Is there something going on I should know about?" I took too long to answer. "Oh, there is, isn't there? You in with the lady reporter from the newspaper, Ray?"

I waited for her to stop laughing before answering. When Rachel finally settled down to just a smirk, I said, "You'd like her. She's a bit of a smart-ass, too."

"Are you seeing each other?"

"We had . . . a date, I guess. But I haven't seen her since Monday.

She's been busy with the story on Dougie and this basketball player thing."

She slapped my knee. "Well, okay. She's got a life of her own."

"So?"

"So don't try to push things, Ray. She's a woman and a reporter. She smells the tiniest bit of desperation coming off you, and that'll be all she wrote." The smirk got a touch bigger. "Pun intended."

"I am not desperate, Rachel."

Rachel took a quick sip of her martini. "I know I'm your *little* sister, Ray, but I know about these things. Women with jobs—especially jobs they like—don't want to feel pressured."

"I'm not pressuring her."

"I'm not saying you are, but let's be honest. It's been a while for you."

"Thanks for the reminder. Anyway," I said, trying to shift the conversation back, "she's been real good at keeping this story in the paper, so Dennis has gotta be on his toes. He can't just push it aside."

"And you're more than willing to help put some pressure on him."

"Yeah, you know what? I am. And it's got nothing to do with Dennis. Hell, I used to be part of the system. It's sad, but it's true: If it's in the press, the top guys pay attention and the guys on the street hear it. Everybody works a little bit harder. Pressure from the brass runs downhill. Like shit when it rains."

"You sure it has nothing to do with my ex being the detective in charge?"

"Positive."

"Well, then," Rachel said. "It sounds like you've done your part. Now you can just back off and let everybody do their job, right?"

"That's all I want. Believe me."

I could tell she didn't believe me.

"What?" I said.

"You like it, Ray. Admit it. At least to yourself. You like the excitement, the thrill." She wiggled her fingers. "The mystery of it all."

"A kid of mine was murdered, Rachel. That's what this is about. Not me."

She gave that some thought and took another sip. "I know, Ray, and I'm sorry about the boy. Really. But come on. There's a part of you—"

The bartender interrupted her thought by putting our food in front of us. I didn't realize how hungry I was until I smelled the barbecue sauce on the wings and the fried calamari.

"Yes, Rachel," I said. "There is a part of me that wants to know the truth." I touched my cold pint glass with two fingers and a thumb. "I guess if I'm being real honest here, I *need* to know the truth. Maybe it's a flaw in my character, I don't know. I got involved because I wasn't the only one who needed to know."

"The boy's mother?"

"Yeah. Dougie's mom. She's seen stuff like this her whole life. It probably never got this close, but she's seen it. She knows how these things go. Why do the missing white girls get all the media attention? No black or Hispanic girls ever disappear? You watch the news, read the papers. Tell me I'm wrong."

She reached over and put her hand on my knee. "You're not wrong, Ray. I guess I just wanted to hear you say it. It was obvious back when Frankie went missing. But it all happened so fast, I don't think you had time to process it all."

"Now you sound like your shrink."

"Don't start with that," she said. "I know you haven't told me the whole story about Frankie, and I don't expect you ever will. But I'm sure you pushed the envelope as far as you could. Learn from that. And be careful. Remember, some of us actually love you."

I smiled. "Thanks. I love you, too."

"I know." She picked up a fork and speared a piece of calamari. "Now, let's eat, and you can tell me more about whatever her name is."

"Allison," I said. "Allison Rogers."

"Right. Now start talking."

Chapter 18

"I THOUGHT WE WAS GOING TO talk to the principal."

"Mr. Thomas waited as long as he could," I said. "He had to go to a meeting at the district office. He asked me to speak with you and your son, since I'll be Jerome's dean." I looked over at fifteen-year-old Jerome Dexter, in his sunglasses and black sweatshirt, standing next to his mother. One of them—maybe both—reeked of cigarettes. I gestured toward the conference table. "Have a seat. Please."

"Don't know why I hadda come by anyways." She pulled out a chair, eased her large frame into it, and let out a deep sigh. "Transfer's a transfer, far as I'm concerned."

Jerome took the seat next to his mother, while I went over to the window and raised it as far as it would go. The room we were in had an overactive radiator. It was uncomfortably warm, and the smell of smoke was getting to me.

"Jerome," I said. "Why don't you take off your sunglasses and hat?"

He grinned at me, slouched, and shoved his hands into his pockets. "Don't feel like it."

I took the seat at the head of the table, rested my hands on the folder containing the file of Jerome Dexter, and leaned forward. "How about doing it just the same?"

"Why?"

I waited for a response from his mother. I probably could have gone on waiting for another day or two. She just sat there looking through me, then made a big deal out of glancing at her watch as if *I* were the one who had been an hour late.

"Because," I said, "you're inside a school, it's ninety degrees in here, and . . . a grown-up has asked you to."

Jerome sucked his teeth, reached up with both hands, and slipped his sunglasses off. His eyes were bloodshot. He was either on something or had forgotten to go to sleep the previous night.

I opened the file and flipped through the pages. I already knew what I'd find, because I had spoken with my boss after he got off the phone with the district office that morning. Jerome Dexter wasn't exactly sent to us because he was an academic superstar. They never are. How he'd ever made it as far as the eighth grade was amazing. He'd been suspended from another middle school for fighting. Ordinarily, that wouldn't be enough for a transfer, but Jerome had held up his end of the schoolyard scuffle with a box cutter. After missing a week and a half of school and admitting to what he had done, the district office exercised its option and shipped him to us. As if that was going to make any difference in his life.

"Cut this other guy a little, huh?"

Jerome Dexter stroked the little wisp of hair above his lip and smiled. "Punk tried to play me in fronta a whole buncha people. He won't do that no more."

"This punk have a blade, too, or was that just you?"

"Hey. You bring it on, you best be prepared to battle."

I flipped through a few more pages and then closed the file.

"You like middle school, Jerome?"

He squinted at me. "What's that supposed to mean?"

"Bright guy like yourself. You must like the eighth grade. You should be in high school by now. But here you are, ready to repeat the eighth grade. Again."

"Jerome's fifteen," his mother chimed in. "Gotta go to high school next year."

"You're thinking of the old rules, Mrs. Dexter. There are no more social promotions."

Jerome straightened up, and I heard a small *click* as his ankle brushed against his chair leg. It was then that I saw the gold and purple beads around his neck. *Terrific.* "The fuck's a social promotion?" Jerome asked.

I ignored the profanity. "That's where they used to just move you on up to the next grade because of your age. Didn't want kids shaving in middle school." I placed my hands back on the folder. "Those days are over. I'm surprised you didn't know about that. It was in all the papers."

The two of them considered that for a while before the mother spoke.

"What's he gotta do to get into high school then?"

"Pass the state exams this spring," I said. "Demonstrate he can read, write, and do math on something approaching the eighth-grade level."

Jerome let out a burst of air. "Fuck that," he said, dismissing me with a wave of his hand.

I looked over at his mother. "Are you going to speak to him about his language?"

"Boy's got a minda his own, Mr. . . ."

"Donne."

"Mr. Donne. He don't pay me no mind."

"And yet you expect us to teach him enough to get him into high school?"

"That's your job, right?"

I looked at mother and son, and took a deep breath. "I'm going to explain how this will work. Jerome will have exemplary attendance from now until the end of the school year."

Mrs. Dexter looked at her boy and nodded. "Okay."

"He may or may not participate in graduation ceremonies, depending on his behavior."

She leaned forward. "But he will graduate?"

"If he passes the exams. If not, he's looking at summer school. At a minimum."

"I ain't going to fuckin' summer school," Jerome said.

Again, I waited for Mom to say something. When she didn't, I said, "If your son does not control his language, I'm going to end this meeting and you can reschedule for some other time."

Mrs. Dexter reached over and gently smacked her son's arm.

"You hush up, Jerome."

"You don't have much of a choice, Jerome. It's either pass the exams, summer school, or you're back in the eighth grade come September."

Jerome Dexter sat there next to his mother and shook his head from side to side. "Fu—uh-uh. No way."

"Jerome," I said, "this is not a battle you can win with a box cutter." I tapped the side of my head with my index finger. "Got to use your brain for this one. Try to play the system, and you're going to lose."

He reached out, pushed himself away from the table, and got to his feet. He stood next to his mother, but his eyes were on me. He unzipped his sweatshirt, revealing the Saints jersey he had on underneath. The number on it was ten. *Wrong number for Brooklyn.*

"You can't make me do nothing."

There comes a time in many a disagreement when one of the parties involved gets a little too close to the edge. Jerome Dexter took very little time getting there. I stayed in my seat.

"You sound like you're ready to do battle again, Jerome."

"If I have to."

I looked up at the kid. All of fifteen years old, and the only way he could see out of this situation was violence. His mother just sat there, blank-faced and helpless. The thought of Jerome Dexter in this school made my stomach hurt.

There was a look in Jerome's eyes that I had seen more times than I could count. The look of someone whose fear is ready to take him places he doesn't understand. Another time, I might have found myself feeling sorry for the kid. Right now, I didn't want an angry, wannabe gangbanger in my school. It was time to play hardball.

"What's that in your sock, Jerome?"

He took a step around his mother. A step closer to me. I remained seated.

"Ain't got nothin' in my sock, man."

I eased my chair a few inches away from the table.

"Guy like you. Just waiting for someone to 'bring it on.' You got something in your sock right now. The left one. I heard it when your leg hit the chair."

"You're crazy." He put his hand on his mother's shoulder. "Let's get outta this punk-ass school, Ma."

Mrs. Dexter reached up and put her hand on her son's. She closed her eyes.

"Go ahead and show your mom how you came prepared for school, Jerome." I pushed my chair back a little more. "Roll up your pant leg. Show her what you got."

He locked his eyes on mine. "You pushin' it, man."

I stood slowly and looked around the office. "Bit different than the schoolyard, huh? Not quite that many people around who are scared of you."

"Don't need nobody scared a me. And I ain't scared a you."

"Then go ahead and show your mom."

He took a step toward me. "Listen, mister—"

"Do what the man says, Jerome," Mrs. Dexter said, her eyes still closed.

Jerome looked down at his mother. "Ma. You gonna listen to this—"

"Do it, boy." Her eyes were wide open now.

Jerome looked down at his mom again and then back to me. After about thirty seconds, he lifted his leg and put his foot up onto the table. He rolled up his pant leg, removed a yellow box cutter from his sock, and slammed it down on the table.

"There," he said. "Happy?"

"Thrilled." I grabbed the box cutter and put it in my pocket. I stepped over to the door, pulled it open, and kicked the wooden doorstop into place. "Mrs. Dexter," I said. "Find your son another school."

"Excuse me?" she asked.

"Jerome will not be attending school here. Go back to the district office. Tell them anything you want. The school wasn't to your liking, it's too far from home, whatever. I don't care what you tell them."

"You can't do that. The district told us—"

"That's because the district didn't know Jerome would be showing up on his first day at his new school with a weapon in his sock and gang beads around his neck."

As she stared at me, Jerome stood at the table, silently going over his options.

"You lucky we in school, man."

I stared back. "I think we're probably both lucky, Jerome. Does Tio know you're sporting Royal Family colors?"

"Who the fuck's Tio?"

"That's what I thought. You wear the colors, you best know the players."

He had no answer for that. He waited a few seconds, thinking maybe I'd challenge him. When I didn't, he mumbled the word "pussy" under his breath and stormed past me out of the room. Jerome's mother slowly got up from her seat. I walked her out into the hallway.

"You're going to have to do something about your boy, Mrs. Dexter. He's going to have more problems than getting out of the eighth grade."

She gave me one last blank look, shook her head, and followed the path her son had taken out of the building.

Chapter 19

AS THE LAST OF THE KIDS STARTED to make their way home, I decided it was time for me to do the same. But first, I had a phone call to make. I checked the Yellow Pages in the office and got the number for Tio's pizza place. Someone picked up after two rings.

"Pizza."

"Yeah, hey. This is Raymond Donne. Is Tio around?"

"Who this?"

"Raymond Donne," I repeated.

"Who Tio?"

I thought I recognized the voice. "Boo?"

"Who's askin'?"

This was turning into an Abbot and Costello routine.

"Boo, this is Raymond Donne. I met with Tio Saturday morning."

Silence from the other end and then, "The white guy from the paper?"

"That's the one, Boo. Can I talk with Tio?"

"He ain't here."

"When do you expect him?"

"Not my job to expect him," he said. "You gonna be at that phone a while?"

"Yeah."

Boo said, "Okay," then hung up.

I put the phone back down, and less than half a minute later it rang.

"Mr. Donne," I said.

"Teacher Man," Tio said. "What's the haps?"

"Thanks for getting back to me so quickly. I want to tell you something, but I need you to promise me you won't take what I say and react with violence."

"Now you sound like a cop, Teacher Man."

"Do I have your word, Tio? No violence?"

He was silent as he thought about it. Probably thinking, who the hell was I to tell him how to react to something?

"Yeah, okay," Tio said. "Talk to me."

I told Tio about Jerome Dexter, the box cutter, and his beads and jersey. Again he was silent as he thought about what I'd just said. I heard him let out a long sigh.

"You know where this Jerome lives?" he asked.

"I do."

"You wanna tell me?"

"I have your word, right? No violence?"

"I don't promise things twice."

"Okay." I opened the file and read off Jerome Dexter's address. "It's near the subway."

"I know where it is," Tio said. "Good lookin' out, Teacher Man. Me and one of my boys'll go have a face-to-face with young Jerome. Can't have no wannabes going around rockin' our colors and makin' us look bad. Cause us all sorts of trouble."

"That's why I called, Tio. I appreciated our conversation the other day," I explained. "Just talk to the kid, all right?"

"Oh, we talk to him, all right. Scare the boy straight, know what I'm sayin'?"

"I think I do."

"Okay. Good lookin' out. See ya 'round."

After we hung up, I had my doubts about having made the call. I eased them by telling myself Jerome Dexter was an act of violence waiting to happen. Someone had to stop him, and it wasn't going to be a teacher, and certainly not his mother. If Tio kept his word, and I believed he would, maybe Jerome *would* be scared straight. At least enough to cut the shit with the jersey and beads.

I looked at the clock. I had some paperwork up in my office that I thought about knocking off, but I was too damned tired and could think of little else except lying on my couch, watching TV while I ate some dinner, and then dozing off. So I left for the day.

I had barely made it to the corner, when a black town car flashed its red grill lights, whooped its siren, and pulled over to where I stood. I first thought maybe Dougie's uncle was dropping by to read me the riot act again. That thought quickly disappeared as the rear passenger window rolled down, revealing Uncle Ray. He looked too large for the back of the car.

"Nephew," he said, removing the ever-present cigar from his mouth and blowing the smoke out the window. "Surprised?"

"Yeah, Uncle Ray. A little." I placed my hand on the top of the car to lean into the window. "Twice in one week? You got business at the nine-oh?"

"Nah. Just wanted to cross the river and pay another little visit to my favorite nephew." He paused for effect. "*The schoolteacher.*"

The way he said those words, I knew someone had reached out to him. The only question was whether it was Dennis Murcer or Dougie's uncle. I chose to play dumb for the moment and just say, "Cool. You got time for a beer?"

He looked at his watch. "Some of us are still on the clock, Raymond. Not every employee of the great City of New York gets to go home at three thirty. But I guess with all your after-school activities these past few days, you might not be going home just yet. What's it going to be this afternoon? Back to the private school? Maybe a home visit to a family in crisis? Huh? Whatcha got in mind, Nephew?"

I took a deep breath, let it out, and watched as it disappeared into the chilled air. Uncle Ray did not invite me to have a seat inside the car, and I knew damn well he wasn't going to come out in the cold just to chew on my ass. No, he could do that just fine from the back of his warm and cozy town car.

"Who called you, Uncle Ray?"

"Who didn't call? First, I hear from Dennis Murcer. Said—real respectfully—he appreciated your help the other day, but would I please suggest to my nephew that he allow the investigation to proceed without his assistance from this point."

I nodded. "Yeah, I got the message. I was only trying to—"

"Then," he interrupted me, "I get a call from a lawyer. Douglas Lee, Esquire. He said—again, with all due respect to me—my nephew would do well to stay away from a certain family." He paused to flick some cigar ashes out the window. "Quinn, I believe the name was."

"Yeah," I said. "I can explain that."

"I knew you could, Raymond. You've always been so good at explaining things." He turned away from me and spoke to his driver. "Didn't I tell you, Smitty, my nephew would be able to explain the situation?"

"Yes, sir," Smitty said, without turning around. "I believe you did."

For the first time, I noticed the driver. From the way he barely fit behind the steering wheel, Smitty appeared to be quite large himself.

"It's okay, Raymond," my uncle said. "I don't need to hear your explanation. I just need to hear you're through messing around. Both of those phone calls were a courtesy to me. If we didn't have the same name, you might very well be in a lot of trouble at this point."

"I understand that, Uncle Ray. I just—"

"Good," he said. "Then I don't need to remind you of what happened last time you went down this road." He turned back to Smitty. "My nephew here is one of the few teachers in the New York City public schools who ever needed police protection."

"What else did Dennis tell you?"

Uncle Ray took another drag from his cigar and blew the smoke out the window. He rubbed his eyes before speaking.

"That you were very helpful. Up to a point. Said you also handled the press thing well, too. Shame about that situation."

"Yeah," I said. "It is."

"Good kid gone bad. How many times we seen that?"

"Dougie was not a good kid gone bad, Uncle Ray. He was a good kid who got involved in something that . . ." I realized I didn't know how to finish the sentence.

"Come on, Raymond. Good kids don't end up under the Williamsburg Bridge after midnight. A good kid wouldn't put himself in that position. You know that. You work with these kids."

"Which is why I know Dougie . . . why we think he was meeting somebody there. His mother said he was already in bed for the night.

He must have gotten a phone call and then snuck out without her knowing."

"You're making my argument for me," Uncle Ray said. "What did Murcer say when he checked the kid's phone records?"

"The last call Dougie received was from a disposable, so they have no number to go with it. Dougie's phone can't be found. The working theory is the killer took it."

Uncle Ray smirked. "Oh, is that the working theory? Listen to him, Smitty. Sounds like he's still wearing the uniform." Back to me. "Let Dennis do his job, Raymond. He's a good investigator."

"I never said he wasn't."

"Now," Uncle Ray said, "about the Quinn family."

"Yeah, I know. I realized my mistake when I got to the hospital and before I could get out of there, I got into a conversation with the sister."

"Just couldn't help it, huh? Couldn't just walk away?"

"I guess I could have, but we got to talking and I noticed she was high on something and needed help, so I used her phone to call her father."

"Who's also the father of the kid in the hospital?"

"Yeah. And a client of Douglas Lee, Dougie's uncle."

"So let me guess," he said, holding his cigar so the smoke streamed out the car window. "All this is too much of a coincidence to you."

"Yes," I said, accenting the point by gently slapping the top of the car. "And we've also got Paulie Sherman, the kid killed by the bus. That's three kids—three friends—all from the same school. Two are dead and the other's . . . who knows?"

Uncle Ray stuck the cigar in his mouth and shut his eyes. I knew this was his way of processing what I'd just said, so I stayed quiet.

"And Murcer knows all this?" he said after a half minute of silence.

"He does now that I've told him."

"Careful with the sarcasm, Ray." He opened his eyes. "Murcer's right. You've done good, but that's as far as your involvement in this case goes. Understand me?"

"Yes, Uncle Ray. I understand."

"Good." He graced me with a smile, and then it was gone. "What's this other story about? The school safety officer. Paper said the kid goes to your school?"

"He's one of ours, yeah. I spoke with the dad. Told him to get his supervisor or the cops involved, but he thought he could handle it himself. He was wrong."

"Big-time," Uncle Ray said. He closed his eyes again. When he re-opened them, he said, "You know where the bus stop is?"

"The one where Angel was having trouble?"

"That's the one I'm thinking of."

"Yeah," I said. "Why?"

"I'm just thinking—since I'm out this way—we might want to take a ride over there. See if we get lucky. Talk a little sense into the kid pressing charges. Maybe convince him to give Officer What's-his-name a break."

"Rosario," I said, slightly wary of my uncle's definition of "a little sense." "You okay with doing that?"

"Hey," Uncle Ray said, as if he were offended by the question. "School Safety's a division of the NYPD, and we gotta look after our own, right?"

"Absolutely."

"Then get in." He opened the back passenger door and slid over to make room for me. "Let's go for a ride."

About five minutes later, we pulled in front of the bus stop where Angel and his dad had their problems. It was empty, which shouldn't have come as a big surprise. School had been out for almost an hour, and there were no businesses open in the area. This was one of those Williamsburg blocks that used to be busy with small factories and a couple of tiny restaurants serving breakfast and lunch to the workers. That seemed like a long time ago. Right now, it looked like an urban ghost town.

"Not much going on," Uncle Ray said, getting a firm grip on the obvious.

"Nope." I looked over at the whitewashed wall behind the bus stop, where some local artist had spray-painted a penis with something dripping out of its tip. Below the drawing were the words IT'LL COME WHEN IT COMES. *Brilliant.* "I guess we should have had this idea half an hour ago."

"Give it time, Nephew." He slapped my left leg twice. Hard. "You seem to have forgotten one of the first lessons of law enforcement."

"And what is that, Uncle Ray?" I could hear the pain in my voice.

Uncle Ray now slapped the back of his driver's seat. "Tell him, Smitty."

Smitty cleared his throat, but again did not turn around. "Half of this job is waiting around for shit to happen."

"And the other half?" Uncle Ray prompted.

"The other half is cleaning up the shit," Smitty concluded. "Sir."

"And so we wait." Uncle Ray lowered his window and let some of the cigar smoke out. "Tell me about this kid of yours, Raymond."

"Which one?"

"The one who was getting harassed. Why didn't he just get off at the next stop?"

"He told me he tried that for a while, and after a few weeks he thought the problem was over."

"Why'd he think that?"

"He'd stay on the bus and not get off here. For a couple of days he didn't see the guys who were bothering him. He figured they moved on to some other location. The day he got his iPod jacked, there was no one at the stop when he got off."

"And . . ."

"Soon as he got off, they turned the corner and he ran right into them."

"Wrong place," Uncle Ray said. "Wrong time." He turned to the window and again let out a long stream of cigar smoke. "Common theme here, wouldn't you say, Raymond?"

It took me a few seconds. "You're talking about Dougie now?"

"Yes, I am."

"Uncle Ray," I started, but then I realized he was right. No matter what sent Dougie to those tennis courts after midnight, he was in the wrong place at the wrong time. And obviously with the wrong person. "I think we'd do well to focus on the 'who' and not the 'why' at this point."

"There you go again," Uncle Ray said, tapping about an inch of his cigar ash out the window. "Using the word 'we.' There is no *we* here. There is Dennis Murcer, and there is the New York Police Department of which *you* are no longer a member."

There are times I think my uncle just waits for moments like this to remind me of my current job. I know it's partly because he wants to keep me from getting myself in trouble, but the other part is because he's still smarting over my decision to leave the force after my accident. If he'd had his way, I'd be sitting behind a desk, telling other cops how to do their jobs. It's not all that rare for cops who've been injured on the job to be given promotions and higher paychecks. It wasn't how I pictured my career path, so I left. A lot of people—my uncle included—didn't get that.

"Sir," Officer Smitty said from the front seat.

Uncle Ray and I both answered, "Yes?"

Smitty clarified. "*Chief* Donne."

My uncle looked up front. "I see them, Smitty."

I turned to look out the windshield as well and saw what they were talking about. A group of three boys—young men almost—had turned the corner and were heading in our direction. They got about twenty feet from where we were parked and stopped. After putting their heads together and surely discussing the presence of a town car at the bus stop, they looked over at us and waved.

"Sir?" Smitty said again.

"Show 'em the lights, kid."

Smitty leaned over slightly and flipped on the grill lights. The group of three seemed surprised—but when Smitty shut the lights off five seconds later, they started laughing. *It's great to be young,* I thought.

"How do you want to handle this?" my uncle asked.

"Really?" I said. "You're asking my advice?"

"Hey. Just because you're not a cop anymore doesn't mean I don't respect your skills and judgment. You're more experienced at dealing with this . . . age group than I am." He let that sit for a bit. "How do you want to handle this?"

I stayed silent. First, I had to get over being complimented by my uncle. Second, I needed to make sure what came out of my mouth next made a whole lot of sense. I looked out the front window again and assessed the situation. There were three of them, all in their upper teens at least. Odds were, one of them had the scrape with Angel's father. I couldn't tell which one from the back of the car, but my money would be on the big guy in the middle. They'd seen the flashing lights, so there was no doubt in their minds we were law enforcement. Or two of us were.

"How about," I began, "I go out and talk to them? Just me. They know I got backup, so I don't think they'll try anything physical."

"What are you planning to say to them?" Uncle Ray asked, as if I were a new recruit and he was quizzing me.

"I'll explain who I am, why I'm here, and see if we can come to some sort of mutual agreement where both sides feel they got something they wanted."

My uncle grinned. "You learn that on the force or from some staff development the Department of Education made you take?"

"A little of both," I said. "There are two sides to every conflict, but one thing is always the same: both sides want something. The trick is to figure out what that is."

"And you're representing Officer Rosario?"

I took a deep breath. "I know. It's best to have both parties present, but given this small window of opportunity, it's the best I can come up with."

"I could just have Smitty go out there, show them his badge and gun, and politely ask that all charges be dropped."

"There's always that," I said. "Let me try it my way first."

"Okay, Nephew. You're the expert." He sounded like he meant that.

"All right," I said, zipping my jacket and putting my hand on the door handle. "I'll be back in a few minutes."

"We'll be waiting right here," my uncle said.

"Which is what gives me such unwavering confidence." I pushed open the door and stepped out of the car. It seemed colder than before. Maybe it was the slight breeze blowing between the buildings. I leaned back inside and said, "Thanks." I shut the door and walked slowly over to the group of three young men.

As I approached, the three of them spread out. I had my hands out of my pockets, palms facing out front: the international sign for "I come in peace." I stopped when I got five feet away. At this short distance, I recognized the biggest of the three from the front page of the paper. It took a few seconds of staring and silence before I could summon up his name.

I looked him square in the eyes and said, "Hector, right? Hector Ferrer?"

"That's right, officer," he said, removing the earbuds to his iPod—probably Angel's iPod—and draping them around his neck. He looked at both his boys and smiled. He was missing one of his top front teeth, but, to his credit, it did nothing to diminish the shit-eating quality of his grin. "What can we do for you?"

"Actually," I said, "I'm not a cop." I pointed over my shoulder with my thumb. "They're the cops."

All three looked over at the town car and then back to me.

Still smiling, Hector said, "What that make you, then?"

"I'm a teacher."

Five seconds of silence. Then the three broke out into laughter.

As I waited for the boys to settle down, I watched a plastic grocery bag make its way down the street, blown by the breeze.

"That what this is about?" Hector said. "We ain't been going to school, and they send a attendance officer with the cops? That's some real bullshit, man."

"I'm not an attendance officer. I'm a teacher." I paused. "A dean, to be exact. Angel Rosario's dean."

The three of them looked at one another and did a group shrug. The short guy on Hector's left said, "We supposed to know who is that?"

"He's the kid whose iPod you took," I explained. "And when his father came over to get it back, an altercation ensued."

"Shit, man," Hector said. "For a teacher, you talk like a cop." They all laughed over that, then Hector spoke again. "So what about Angel Rosario and his pops? Came 'round here accusing me of stealing some shit. Old man gets all up in my face and knocks me to the ground." He shook his head and placed his right hand on his chest in mock seriousness. Like a bad actor doing *West Side Story*. "Me . . . a poor little minor."

After hearing that, the boys returned to laughing. This was one hell of a fun group. I stuck my tongue to the roof of my mouth as I waited for the laughing to stop. It took almost a minute.

"I came here," I said, "to see if we could come to some sort of agreement."

Hector made a big deal about considering my comment. He even rubbed the little bit of hair he had on his chin and looked to the sky as if deeply pondering the question.

"What kind of 'agreement' you talkin' about?" he said.

"We can start," I said, "by you telling me what you want."

"What I want?"

"Yes."

"What I want?" he repeated, and then playfully slapped both his boys on their upper arms. "What I want is to sue that fake cop for all he's got. And I'ma sue the New York City Board of Education and the NYPD, because they in charge of security."

"School safety," I corrected. "Security works at Kmart."

"Whatever," Hector said. "I'ma sue *all* their asses, and then we see who pulls up in front of a bus stop in a town car." He smiled again. "Funny, ain't it?"

"What do you mean?"

"Here I is, a high school dropout, and I'ma have more money than all my teachers combined. That's why they told me to stay in school, right? So's I could find a good-paying job?" He slapped his boys again. "Well, looks like I found me one. Right here on this broken-down, busted-ass, bootleg street."

That got the three amigos going again. I turned around to face my uncle's car and gave an exaggerated shrug. A few seconds later, the left side passenger door opened, and Uncle Ray stepped out. His long, dark blue coat flapped in the breeze, and I watched as he slowly buttoned it closed. He began walking toward me. The laughter started to die down as the three young men noticed him approaching. Uncle Ray is a big man, and the way he carries himself says just one thing: police. He stopped when he got to me.

"Raymond," he said. He then looked at the small group in front of us. "Boys."

For a moment, a flicker of fear crossed all three faces. That look was quickly replaced with nervous smiles. Hector, again, was the first to speak.

"Now you," he said, pointing at my uncle, "are definitely po-po."

Uncle Ray smiled back. "Most definitely." He looked around, and the grins disappeared. "You boys come to an understanding?"

"Not the one I was hoping for," I said.

Uncle Ray shook his head. "That's disappointing, Nephew. Very."

"*Nephew?*" Hector said and then looked at me. "You brought your uncle to watch your back, Teacher?"

"Actually," my uncle said, "it was my idea to come around. See if we could come to some sort of arrangement." He put his hand on my shoulder. "It was my nephew's idea to do so diplomatically."

"This is good," Hector said. He looked at his two buddies. "First we got a teacher talks like a cop and now we got a cop talks like a teacher." He looked back over at the car we'd pulled up in. "What's your driver talk like? A doctor?"

"If you'd like," Uncle Ray said, "I can bring him out here and you can listen to him yourself." He leaned his large frame into Hector's space. "Real close."

Hector locked eyes with my uncle. He tried not to look intimidated, but it wasn't working out so well. He turned away and looked at his friends. "You guys have your phones with you?" he asked.

The two of them nodded. Both reached into their pockets and pulled out their cells.

"Another time and place," Uncle Ray said, looking around, "different lighting, lots of confusion, that kinda move would get you a whole lot of dead."

The three of them looked at my uncle in silence. Hector's buddies were starting to look like they knew they were getting in over their collective heads. Hector did his best to remain cool and seemed to be thinking of what he could say to impress his boys.

"That's pretty tough talk, Cop," Hector said. "You mind saying that again so's my boys can get it on video?" He looked at the two of them, and both held up their phones. "I believe you just violated my rights. Maybe my lawyer could add you two in on the lawsuit. The more, the better, right?"

My uncle shook his head and looked down at the cracked asphalt. When he looked up again, he said, "How is it, Raymond, that every high school dropout in this city seems to know all about his rights?"

"I think they teach it early to some kids," I said. I looked at the three knuckleheads. "Some teachers just know who's going to need that kind of knowledge."

"That's good," Hector said. "Make all the jokes y'all want. I get my day in court, we see who's laughing then." He held out his hands for his boys to slap. They did.

"You might be right about that, son," Uncle Ray said. "It's one thing to have money, though, and quite another to live long enough to enjoy it."

"Shit, man," Hector said. "You guys getting this? He just threat-ened me."

Now it was my uncle's turn to laugh. "Son," he said. "That wasn't a threat. It was an observation by someone who's seen a hundred punks like you not make it to their twenties because they thought they were smarter than everyone else."

"The hell you know about me, old man? You don't know me!"

My uncle leaned in closer to Hector. I knew that lean-in from my childhood. It's the one when Uncle Ray is about to tell you something real important.

"Boy," he began, lowering his voice now. "I was working these streets before your daddy even knew how to jerk off. Keep pushing your luck. It *will* run out some day. Sooner than you think. Right now, what're you? Oh, right. In a few weeks you'll be eighteen. Old enough to enlist and old enough to vote. I doubt either one of those things'll happen." Uncle Ray took a long drag off his cigar and blew the smoke directly into Hector's face. "You keep being the king of your little corner here. Enjoy it while it lasts. Good luck." Uncle Ray put his hand on my shoulder again. "Let's go, Raymond."

We both turned and headed back to the car. I looked up and watched as a small group of pigeons took off from the roof of the building to our right.

"I don't need no luck," Hector yelled after us. "I already got my luck. I got me a lawyer, and I'ma have more money than all y'all."

"Keep thinking there, Hector," Uncle Ray said softly enough so only I could hear. I smiled at the reference to *Butch Cassidy and the Sundance Kid,* one of my favorite movies. "That's what you do best."

Chapter 20

BACK IN THE WARMTH of the car, my uncle unbuttoned his coat and extinguished what was left of his cigar in one of the built-in car door ashtrays. We both watched as Hector and his boys decided it was too cold to hang at the bus stop, especially when there was no one around to harass. They put their hands in their jacket pockets, turned, and headed back in the direction they'd come from, disappearing around the corner.

"Well," Uncle Ray said, "we did what we could. That boy'll get *his* someday. They all do."

"In the meantime," I said, "he's fucking with a family's life."

"There is that. Sometimes, Raymond, you can only do what you can do. This could very well be one of those times."

"Still sucks, though."

"Big-time." He looked at his watch. "It's getting to be that time, Nephew. You want us to drop you at home, or is this one of your LineUp nights?"

"Home, I think." I pulled out my cell phone. "Let me just check my messages."

As I checked, Uncle Ray tapped the back of Smitty's seat. "Greenpoint Avenue," he said. "Just like the last time."

"Yes, sir," Smitty said, and proceeded to do a U-turn.

The recorded-lady voice on my phone informed me I had one message.

"Hello, Mr. Donne. Gloria Lee. If it's not too much trouble, can you give

me a call when you get this?" There was a three-second pause. *"I'm not even sure why I called. I guess I just wanted to see if . . . there were any new. . . . I don't know."* Another pause. *"I guess it's not all that important. I'm sorry I bothered you. Good-bye."*

I deleted the message and rubbed the time display with my thumb. It was just after five. "Dougie's mom," I said out loud.

"What'd she want?" Uncle Ray asked.

"I don't know." I thought I did. "Maybe just someone to talk to."

I found Mrs. Lee's number and pressed the CALL button. She picked up after three rings.

"Hello?"

"Mrs. Lee. Raymond Donne. I got your message."

"I'm sorry about that, Mr. Donne. I'm not sure why I even called."

I waited a few seconds for her to go on. It started to feel awkward, so I figured maybe she was waiting for me to speak. It took me a while to come up with something.

"Listen," I finally said. "I'm kind of in your neighborhood. If it's not too inconvenient for you, would you mind if I dropped by for a bit?"

I waited for a reply. "No," Mrs. Lee said. "I wouldn't mind at all."

"Good. I'll see you in a few minutes then."

"Thank you, Mr. Donne. Thank you."

"Not a problem."

I ended the call and asked Officer Smitty to drop me off at Mrs. Lee's house. After giving him the address, I turned to my uncle. "I think she just needs someone to talk to."

"And that someone has to be you?" he asked.

"It doesn't have to . . . She called me, Uncle Ray."

"Of course she did, Raymond." He leaned closer to me. "Remember, you are not to be involved in this investigation."

"That's not why I'm going over there," I said somewhat convincingly.

"Of course not." He faced front again and stared out the windshield. "How's your sister?"

"Fine. We had dinner last night."

"Excellent. It's nice you two keep in touch like that."

"She's got dinner plans with Dennis Murcer."

"Is that so?"

"Yep. Two adults having dinner."

"You don't approve, Raymond?"

"It is what it is," I said, remembering Tio's words from the other day.

"That's very wise of you."

"Sir?" Smitty said from up front.

Again, my uncle and I both answered, "Yes?"

"*Mr.* Donne, sir. We're here."

I looked out my window. "That was quick," I said. "Thanks, Smitty."

"Have a good one, sir."

"Thanks, Uncle Ray." I held out my hand. "I appreciate your trying to help."

"I wish we had a better outcome," he said.

"Me, too."

"See you soon, Raymond."

"Absolutely." I opened my door and stepped out, then leaned back in. "Say hi to Reeny for me."

"Most definitely. Mind yourself."

"Always." I shut the door and headed across the street to Mrs. Lee's house. I took the steps two at a time, slowly, and gave my knees a little stretch. I needed to get back over to Muscles's place tomorrow. I rang the buzzer and waited.

A half minute later, she greeted me at the front door with a weak smile and quickly ushered me in out of the cold. I followed her into the living room, and she offered me a seat on the couch. She sat down in the chair to my right. I took my coat off and placed it next to me on the couch. Between us was a small coffee table with a pot of something and two mugs.

"I took the liberty," she said, "of making some hot chocolate. Would you care for some, Mr. Donne?"

"Yes, I would. Thank you."

She poured the hot chocolate into the two mugs and slid mine over to me. I picked it up and, before taking a sip, enjoyed the heat as it warmed my cold hands. Mrs. Lee smiled approvingly as I took my first sip.

"This is very good," I said.

She nodded. "I make it myself. The stuff from the packages is no good. You noticed I haven't offered you any marshmallows."

"I did notice. Yes."

"That's because my hot chocolate has nothing to hide, Mr. Donne." She took a sip then placed her mug back on the coffee table. "Thank you for coming over. I didn't feel like being alone and—may the good Lord forgive me—I'm getting just a little bit weary of the women from the church. It's always the same conversation with them." She gave me an apologetic smile. "And how was your day?"

Just two regular folks sitting around talking.

I took another sip and placed my mug next to hers. I went on to tell her about my visit with her ex-husband the day before. She listened closely and quietly, saving any questions she had until I was done.

Her first question surprised me. "How did William look?" There was genuine concern in her question.

"How'd he look?" I said. She sounded like Rachel asking after Dennis Murcer. What was it with women and their exes? "Fine, I guess. I found him at the bar you told me about, and he'd been there for a while."

"So he was drunk."

"He was . . . maintaining a desired state."

Mrs. Lee smiled. "You are a kind man, Mr. Donne." She took another sip. "Did William have anything interesting to say?"

I told her about the meeting and the phone conversations her ex-husband had with their son and that Dougie had said some curious things about getting his father help.

"What did Douglas mean by that?" she asked.

"Mr. Lee said he had no idea. Just that Dougie sounded like he really believed he could help his father and that he had connections through the school. Did Dougie ever mention anything along those lines to you?"

"No. I can't remember the last time we even talked about his father." She took another sip. "Do you think these conversations actually took place, or did William imagine them?"

"He believes they happened. I'm not a psychologist but, yeah, I think Dougie and his father had those conversations. It seems as if Dougie was being deliberately careful about how much he told his father—like he didn't trust his father with too much information."

Mrs. Lee smiled. "If Douglas was just beginning to let his father back into his life, I'm . . . glad to hear he was doing so with caution."

"Dougie was a pretty sharp kid, Mrs. Lee."

"I know that. It's just boys and their dads. You never know, especially at this age. Did you talk to your father much when you were Douglas's age?"

I picked up my hot chocolate and again held it with both palms.

"My father died when I was thirteen," I said. "We didn't speak much before that. I doubt anything much would have changed in my teen years."

Mrs. Lee shook her head. "I am so sorry, Mr. Donne. It must have been hard on you. Going through your teenage years without a father."

"I tried not to think much about it," I said. "It became the new normal for me. My mom used to say we had to deal with the hand the Lord gave us." I took a sip of hot chocolate. "That's when I started to question my faith."

She reached over and touched my knee. "Your mother did a fine job of raising you nonetheless. Faith or no faith, you act more Christian than many Christians I know."

"I appreciate that. Thanks."

We both got silent for a while. After about a minute, Mrs. Lee said, "Are you hungry, Mr. Donne? I've still got so much food left over from . . . the other day. It would be no trouble at all to fix you a plate."

"Thank you," I said. "But I'm not hungry." The truth was, I *was* hungry. I just wasn't comfortable with Mrs. Lee serving me.

"I could send you home with something."

"Maybe. Right now this hot chocolate is doing me fine."

She smiled. "Good."

We both looked up as we heard the front door open. I looked over at Mrs. Lee.

"That's Douglas," she said, her voice barely above a whisper. "He said he might be dropping by this evening, but I didn't think—"

We heard the front door shut and then, "Gloria?" That was definitely Douglas Lee's voice, and I could just imagine how happy he was going to be to see me in his sister-in-law's living room, drinking hot chocolate.

"In here, Douglas," Mrs. Lee said.

We both stood as the sound of his footsteps got closer. "I'm sorry I didn't call first," he said from the hallway, "but a meeting got canceled at the last minute and—"

He stopped as he entered the living room and tried to process my presence. He didn't strike me as a man who was easily surprised, but he looked surprised now. Then the look turned to annoyed. He took a deep breath before speaking.

"What is Mr. Donne doing here?" he asked.

"I invited him, Douglas," Mrs. Lee said. "He's my guest. *That's* why he's here."

"Hello again, Mr. Lee," I said.

The attorney just shook his head. "Seems like every time I turn around these days, there you are, Mr. Donne."

"I think that's a bit of an exaggeration, Mr. Lee. I believe this is only the third time we've met this past week."

"Somehow it seems like more."

"I have that effect on some people."

"Is there something wrong with Mr. Donne being in my home, Douglas?" Mrs. Lee asked.

"I believe, Gloria," he said, looking right at me, "there may be something wrong with Mr. Donne."

"And just what does that mean?"

Mr. Lee took a few steps into the living room. He looked down at our mugs of hot chocolate and shook his head.

"Did Mr. Donne tell you about his trip to the hospital the other day?"

"As a matter of fact, he did."

"So, I imagine he also shared his conspiracy theory with you."

I had something to say about that but decided to keep my mouth shut. For now.

"I don't know, Douglas," Mrs. Lee said. "Three boys—three *friends*—from the same school. And all this tragedy? I think I understand Mr. Donne's interest. I believe you would do well to listen—"

"Mr. Donne's interest?" His voice was getting louder now. "Mr. Donne is a schoolteacher, Gloria. His interest should have been met when he attended Douglas's wake." He looked at me and lowered his voice. "Which was greatly appreciated. But this continued involvement of yours is uncalled for, and you're lucky my client did not wish to press charges."

"And again," I said, "your client's lucky I was outside the hospital when his daughter was tripping on whatever was in her system."

"That was fortuitous, yes. But I cannot tolerate your coming over here and filling Gloria's mind with these conspiratorial thoughts of yours."

"Filling my mind?" Now it was Mrs. Lee's turn to raise her voice. "You talk as if I'm a child, Douglas. I asked Mr. Donne for his help, because he was the only one I knew I could turn to."

"You could have turned to me, Gloria," Mr. Lee said.

"I did." Her voice was a bit shaky now. "But you either didn't hear me or didn't like what you were hearing. Mr. Donne got Douglas's story in the newspaper, and that got the police moving in the . . . well, it got them moving. I called him this evening because, out of all the people I've asked for help, he's the only one who *has* helped." She took a breath. "You're right. He is a schoolteacher, and maybe he *shouldn't* have involved himself the way he did." She looked at me. "Doing well more than I asked of him. But I'll tell you right now, my hand to God, I'm glad he did. Nobody else seemed to be stepping up!"

Douglas Lee looked exasperated. "There's a line, Gloria, between 'stepping up' and interfering with an active police investigation. Mr. Donne is well aware of that line." He looked at me. "It doesn't seem to concern him, though."

My turn to speak. "It does concern me, Mr. Lee. I've spoken with the detective on the case, and we've agreed my involvement is over. I'm here tonight as a friend."

"Gloria has enough friends."

"Don't you speak for me, Douglas," Mrs. Lee said. "You're my brother-in-law, not my attorney. Or my father."

Mr. Lee had no immediate comeback for that one. So the three of us just stood there in silence. After a few moments of awkwardness, Mr. Lee spoke.

"Is there any food left over?" he asked. "I was supposed to have a dinner meeting with some clients, but . . ."

"There's food in the fridge," Mrs. Lee said. "I'll be more than happy to make up a plate for you, soon as I'm done speaking with Mr. Donne."

Douglas Lee looked down at the tray. "Any more hot chocolate?"

That brought a small smile to Mrs. Lee's face. "I'll get you a mug, Douglas."

As Mrs. Lee left the room, Douglas Lee removed his coat and draped it over the back of one of the living room chairs. He sat down in the same chair and let out a long, deep breath and closed his eyes. I had the feeling he was trying to wish me away.

"Long day?" I asked.

With his eyes still closed, he said, "They're all long days. I'm sure you know all about those, Mr. Donne."

"I hear that," I said. "In fact, I probably should be heading home."

"Don't leave on my account." A small grin crossed his face.

"Wouldn't dream of it, Mr. Lee."

The man looked as if he could fall asleep where he sat. Mrs. Lee came back into the room with a mug. She went over to the tray and poured some hot chocolate.

"Douglas," she said.

Mr. Lee opened his eyes, saw the mug, and said, "Thank you, Gloria."

She took the mug over to her brother-in-law then turned to me. "Would you care for some more, Mr. Donne?"

I finished off what was in my mug. "No, thank you, Mrs. Lee." I looked at my watch, even though I was pretty sure of the time. "I should probably head home."

"You sure you don't want me to fix you a plate? It's no trouble."

"I'm good. Thanks." I grabbed my coat off the couch and slipped it on. "I'm glad you called," I said. "Please feel free to do so anytime."

She looked over at Mr. Lee sipping his cocoa. "I will," she said. "Thank you."

"Mr. Donne," Mr. Lee said as he rose out of his seat. "I'll walk you to your car."

"I got dropped off. I don't have a car."

He put his coat on. "Then I'll walk you out."

"I'll be okay," I said. "I appreciate the offer."

"I do not believe I *made* an offer."

Lawyers. "I guess you didn't." I stepped over to Mrs. Lee and took her hand. "Thank you again."

"Thank you, Mr. Donne." She glanced over at her brother-in-law as she let go of my hand. "I'm sure we'll be in touch."

"Absolutely."

"I'll be right back, Gloria," Mr. Lee said.

"I'll get your plate ready, Douglas."

Mr. Lee and I watched as she cleared the tray and headed toward the kitchen. When she was gone, Lee motioned toward the door with his right hand. "Mr. Donne."

Outside on the steps, I buttoned up my coat. Mr. Lee kept his open. Whatever he had to say, I guessed, would not take too long. I decided to speak before he did.

"How're the Quinn kids?"

He gave me a frustrated look, but chose not to ignore my question.

"Alexis is fine," he said. "She just needed to get home and sleep it off."

"And Jack?"

"When I left the hospital this afternoon, he was still in ICU." He rubbed his eyes. "The doctors are uncertain as to how long he'll remain there."

"What happened?" I tried.

Mr. Lee shook his head and gave me a tired grin. "That's family business, Mr. Donne. It is no concern of yours. Didn't we just discuss this?"

"I'm sure Mr. Quinn appreciated your help."

"Mr. Quinn is an important client of my firm. I'm sure you wouldn't understand, but there's often more to a client-attorney relationship than just legal matters."

"And the more needy the client, the more accessible the lawyer."

"I never said John Quinn was needy."

"I kind of picked that up on my own, Mr. Lee."

Mr. Lee buttoned up his coat halfway. Maybe this conversation was going to take longer than he'd thought. I looked up at the clear night sky and could actually make out a few stars. Somewhere close by, a truck driver was playing his horn.

"Mr. Donne, I'm not going to stand here in the cold and discuss my relationship with the Quinn family."

"Was John Quinn the reason Dougie attended Upper West?" I asked.

"John . . . smoothed the way for Douglas, yes. But Douglas's grades and his interview were the reasons for his acceptance."

"I'm sure he charmed the very expensive socks off of them."

"Yes. And before you ask, the fact that Douglas was African-American did help in the process. Upper West could fill every seat they have with a white student if they wished and still have a waiting list stretching into Central Park. The board decided years ago they wanted their student body to better reflect the city in which their students were to be educated." He brushed something off his coat sleeve. "Douglas's skin color helped in that regard."

"Must have been a tough transition for him, though."

"It was," Mr. Lee agreed. "To come from this . . ."—he motioned with his head toward the street—"and to enter a private school on the Upper West Side of Manhattan would be stressful for any young man. Douglas was handling it with poise."

"And that's what you wanted for him?"

"That's what *we* wanted for him, yes. Gloria, more than most mothers, understands the importance of a good education and the proper school environment. When the offer came, she accepted enthusiastically."

"And Douglas?"

"What do you mean?"

"Did *he* accept enthusiastically?"

"He accepted," Mr. Lee said. "The enthusiasm came later."

"Must have been hard at first."

"More than you can know."

"What does that mean?"

The attorney smiled. "With all due respect, Mr. Donne, you have no idea what it's like growing up black in this city."

"I never claimed to."

"And to *raise* a young black man," he said. "Just as hard. Douglas was a bright young man, but there was so much he didn't know."

"Like what?"

"Are we really having this conversation, Mr. Donne?"

"Seems like it to me. Like what?"

"Like how it's twice as important," he began, a touch of anger in his voice, "for a young black man to say 'please' and 'thank you' and 'sir' or 'ma'am' than it is for a white kid in the same situation. Or when an Upper West Side white kid wears a hoodie, he looks like a track star. But when a black kid wears one, he fits the profile."

"That's got to be tough," I said.

"I had to explain to Douglas that to some people, he'd always be the black kid who got in on a scholarship and there's nothing he could do to change that image."

I let that sit for a few seconds and took a chance.

"Must be the same for black lawyers."

"You got that right," he blurted out. "You don't think I have to work fifty percent harder than the white lawyers at my firm? You don't think that was on my mind the other day when John Quinn called *me* to help clean up his most recent mess? If I hadn't done it, he would have found someone else to, and maybe I'd stop getting called at all." He let out a deep breath. It looked like my uncle's cigar smoke in the cold air. "I didn't learn that until college. And law school? I made sure to sit in front of my white classmates and raise my hand twice as often." He paused to catch his breath. "I wanted Douglas to have that experience earlier than I did so he'd be more prepared than I was. I lost too much time learning that particular lesson." His eyes went off over my shoulder to somewhere far away, and for the first time I saw the resemblance to his brother. "Too much damn time."

I tried to think of something to say, but came up empty. There was nothing for me to say. I'd grown up white, in middle-class Long Island, and even with all my years in Williamsburg as a cop and a teacher, there was no way I'd ever truly understand what Douglas and his uncle had to go through. After about a minute of silence, I realized the only thing I could say.

"I have to go, Mr. Lee."

His eyes came back to me.

"Yes," he said. "I think you should."

I offered him my hand, and he took it. There was no tight grip this time.

"Listen to Gloria," I said. "She needs you to do that."

"I'm well aware of what my sister-in-law needs, Mr. Donne." He let go of my hand. "But thanks for the advice."

"Be well, Mr. Lee."

Before I got to the bottom of the steps, I heard the door shut and lock behind me. I looked at my watch. It was still early, and I was still hungry. Big surprise, I decided to head over to The LineUp before going home.

Chapter 21

"I'VE BEEN DOING A LITTLE research," Edgar explained as he pulled a bunch of papers out of his laptop bag.

"I can see that," I said. "I don't remember assigning any homework, though."

Edgar faked a laugh. "Good one, Ray." He pushed his empty plate to the right, moved his pint glass to the left, and put the papers down in the vacant space. "I don't know. I just got curious about that guy Quinn and your boy's uncle."

"Douglas Lee."

"Yeah, and their relationship. So I did a rather extensive search."

I looked at the half-inch pile of paper he had in front of him. "How many hours did you spend on this 'research,' Edgar?"

"Doesn't matter," he said. Then he quietly added, "Five and a half."

"And what new information did you acquire?"

"Well," he began, "some of this stuff we actually knew. Douglas Lee's firm has been representing Ward Fullerton Pharmaceuticals for about six years. It must keep Mr. Lee quite busy, because I was unable to find any other recent—within those six years—cases he was involved with. So I assume he is the firm's main attorney when it comes to WFP."

"Okay," I said. "Go on."

"I didn't realize it until . . . this," he said, pointing at his stack of papers, "but it seems as if pharmaceutical companies are constantly involved with one sort of legal matter or another. Not that they've done anything wrong. It's just with copyrights, licensing, drug trials. I mean, according to what I read in the business sections and trade papers, representing a drug company is a lawyer's wet dream. The work never stops."

I remembered the exhausted look I'd seen an hour ago on Douglas Lee's face.

"I guess that makes sense," I said. "It's one of the biggest businesses in the country, and one mistake could put you under. What was that drug a couple of years ago? Caused heart attacks when it was supposed to be lowering blood pressure?"

"Yeah," Edgar said. "I don't remember the name, but I remember the story."

"I imagine suing these companies is pretty lucrative, too."

"Big-time. There's less info on that, though, because most of the time the drug companies settle out of court and that stuff's all hush-hush. The only time they want to see their name in the papers is when they're introducing a new product or in a full-page ad for their latest cholesterol-fighting drug."

"Did you find anything on lawsuits against Ward Fullerton?"

"Not much. They seem to know what they're doing." He flipped through his papers. "Their specialty seems to be psychopharmacology."

"Drugs that deal with psychological problems?"

"That's an oversimplification."

"Sorry," I said. "I didn't have five and a half hours of spare time to do my research, Edgar."

"Not to worry, Raymond." He patted my arm. "That's what you got me for. Psychopharmacology deals with how drugs affect our moods, the way we think, even how we behave. It's fascinating stuff, really. The big bucks come from antidepressants and ADHD meds."

"And that's what WFP does?"

"For the most part, but in a limited way. They have a few drugs currently on the market and a few more under development. They're not one of the big boys—which explains why they have outside counsel—and they seem to be comfortable with that."

"Okay," I said, getting a bit bored with the conversation. "Looks like that was five and a half hours well spent."

Edgar picked up the pages. "There's more, Ray. Lots."

"I'm sure there is, Edgar. It's just been a long day, and I don't think there's any more room in my brain for new information. But it's good stuff. Thanks."

Ignoring me, Edgar went on. "I couldn't find much about that kid, Paulie Sherman. I figured a story like that would have gotten more coverage, but I only found two days' worth."

"Probably because he comes from a well-to-do Upper West Side family who values its privacy. If it *was* suicide-by-bus, you think they want it spread all over the tabloids in this city?"

Edgar nodded. "You're right. It's a different world up there, huh?"

"Families with lawyers generally get what they want."

"I wouldn't know. Oh, by the way, I contacted that little friend of yours."

"Who am I? Mr. Rogers? I don't have 'little friends,' Edgar."

"The bird kid," he explained. "Elliot Finch."

"You contacted him?" Edgar nodded. "How? And why?"

"I reached out to him through his website. I liked what I saw the other day and wanted to give him a few tips on security and graphics. Hope you don't mind, but I dropped your name. He seems to like you."

"I'm a raven."

"What?"

"Never mind. So, what, you left a message for him?"

"No, Ray. We IM'ed for about forty-five minutes."

"IM'ed?"

Edgar gave me another one of those looks, as if he were talking to someone who didn't know how to program a DVR.

"Instant-messaged," he explained. "Instant messaging is like talking on the phone, but you just send text messages back and forth in real time."

"I know what IMing is, Edgar. But why don't you just talk on the phone if you're going to have a forty-five-minute conversation?"

"Because we have computers now."

"We also have cell phones."

He was growing more exasperated with me. "It's just . . . it's . . . it's a way of communicating that some of us feel more comfortable with. I like this kid."

"He gives good IM?"

"Ha." Edgar was getting the fake laugh down real good. "We," he went on, "are planning to collaborate on a website."

"Sounds like he's *your* little friend now."

"He's really into bird-watching, as you know. And, like me, he agrees there's an untapped market out there screaming for a halfway decent bird-watching site."

"I didn't know you were that into it, Edgar. I thought your uncle was the bird-watcher in the family."

"I used to go out with him a lot," Edgar said. "But then I got interested in video games, computers, and technology." He looked off into space for a moment and said, "I spend way too much time inside. But now, I can combine all that and maybe make some money in the process."

"How do you make money off a bird-watching site?"

"Ads," he said. "Binoculars, clothing, high-tech birding equipment. We figure the people who subscribe to our site all need the same kinda stuff. We'll start with Central Park and then build from there."

I nodded approvingly. "I got to hand it to you, Edgar. You're always thinking."

"Yeah," he said. "Cuts into my sleep, but whatta you gonna do? We're gonna meet up this weekend and go over the details."

"Meet up?" I asked. "Like, in person?"

"Yes, Ray. Like, in person. I hope it goes well. He's a nice kid and all, but he struck me as a little . . . off."

"He remind you of anyone?"

"No. Did he remind you of anyone?"

I smiled. "Nope. Just asking."

"We're gonna have coffee at Starbuck's."

Of course you are, I thought. Before I could tease him a little more, my phone vibrated in my front pocket. I'd forgotten it was there. I checked the caller ID and recognized Allison's number. I squelched the urge to say "hurray" and took the call.

"Hey," I said, hiding some of my enthusiasm.

"Hey, yourself. You busy?"

"Just chatting with Edgar here at The LineUp. Creature-of-habit stuff. You?"

"Finishing off the latest—and hopefully last—piece on the basketball daddy."

"You don't call him that in the paper, I hope."

"Give me a little more credit, Ray. Besides, it seems the woman making the accusations—the baby mama—has done this before. Most of the major sports, too. This is the first time she's gone down to the college level, though."

"Well, good for our basketball star."

"Yeah. I know it's a better story the other way, but it's nice to see one of these go this way once in a while. He seems like a decent kid."

It was good to hear Allison say that. She was a sharp reporter, but I had concerns about her desire for a good story getting in the way of her being a good person.

"So," I said. "Does that free you up a bit? I was thinking maybe we could do dinner tomorrow?"

"That's a real possibility," she said. "But"—her voice got low and sexy now—"I've got something that might be more interesting."

I spun my stool away from Edgar.

"What's that?" I asked.

"Paulie Sherman."

"What about him?"

"Okay," she began. "I went to my editor today with the info on the Quinn kid being in the hospital. I sold him on the idea there at least *seems* to be a connection between the three boys and what's happened to them."

"Yeah?"

"He's given me the go-ahead to make the connection."

"Beyond the fact they were all friends, attending the same school?"

"The same *private* school, Raymond. These are families of more than a little influence. Including Dougie's. His uncle being a lawyer and all. The last thing my bosses want is a pissed-off lawyer making trouble for the paper. I've been instructed to tread lightly."

"So what's the deal?"

"I've set up an interview for tomorrow afternoon with Paulie's parents."

"They agreed to an interview?"

"Reluctantly," Allison said. "I told them the piece might not even publish. They knew Dougie, and they're friendly with the Quinns. I spoke with the father. He didn't come right out and say it, but he's curious about what might be going on. They've agreed to give me a half hour."

"Good."

"It gets better."

"How so?"

"I need a photographer."

"And your boss said yes?"

"No, my boss said no."

"How's that better, Allison?"

She paused for a few seconds and said, "You own a camera, Raymond?"

Holy shit.

"Yeah," I said, thinking of the digital one I use at school to take pictures of graffiti or injuries to students. "But I've been told by Murcer, Douglas Lee, and my uncle to stay away from the case."

"You afraid of getting into trouble with your uncle, Raymond?" She did a pretty good imitation of a middle school girl.

"I'm concerned about stepping over the line—again—and impeding an active investigation, Allison. I've probably done that already, but my name has kept me out of trouble. I don't think I can push it much more."

"Okay," she said. "If you don't want to do it . . ."

"I didn't say I don't want to do it." I took a deep breath and listened to the silence on the other end of the phone. "Half an hour?"

"Thirty quick minutes," she said. "We're in, we're out, and then I let you take me to dinner, tough guy."

Another pause. I spun around just enough to grab my beer. Edgar gave me another of his "What's up?" looks. I ignored him and finished off my pilsner. I wasn't sure why I was making a big deal over this. I knew what my answer would be.

"Okay," I said. "I'm in."

"There you go," she said. "Tomorrow at one."

"I'll have to leave work early."

"I think you can come up with something to tell your boss."

"Shouldn't be a problem. Where am I meeting you?"

She gave me the Shermans' address. Riverside Drive. Nice neighborhood, three blocks from where their son was killed. I wondered if they'd move.

"I'll be there," I said.

"Looking forward to working with you, Raymond," she said. "And to dinner."

"Me, too. Thanks, Allison."

"Thank *you,* Mr. Donne."

I hung up and slipped the phone back into my pocket. A brand-new beer was waiting for me when I turned back to Edgar.

"What was all that about?" he asked.

"Allison and I are going to meet with Paulie Sherman's folks tomorrow. He was the kid killed on his skateboard. Friend of Dougie's."

"Right. Good for you, Raymond. Nice to see you being your own man. The heck with what the detective, the lawyer, and your uncle tell you to do."

"No, Edgar. They're right, but . . ."

He gave me a few seconds, and when he realized I had no end to that sentence, he repeated himself. "Good for you, Raymond."

"Yeah," I said. "I guess we'll see about that."

Chapter 22

"SO, OLIVIA," I SAID TO THE girl seated to my right, "*does* your mother have sex with people in order to support her drug habit?"

Olivia's mouth fell open. "'scuse me, Mr. Donne?"

I picked up the statement she had just signed, took my finger, and touched the phrase in question. "Is," I said, "your mother—and I'm quoting here—'a crack ho'?"

"No."

"Okay then." I picked up the other paper and turned to its author, seated on my left. "Devona. Is your mother a"—I used my finger again to find what I was looking for—"a 'big fat black bitch'?"

Devona looked at me and then over to Olivia. "Not the bitch part."

"But she is big?"

"Yeah, kind of."

"And, of course, she's black?"

"Yeah."

"So your objection to Olivia's statement is, your mom's not a bitch?"

"I guess."

"Okay." I took both statements, turned around, and put them on my desk. The three of us were seated in a triangle in the middle of my office. "And this all jumped off because . . . tell me again, Olivia."

Without even thinking about it, she got right into it. "What happened was Devona was talkin' smack about me on the playground."

Devona was about to interrupt. I raised my finger and said, "Let her finish."

"Sayin' I'm a two-timer and I let boys feel me up."

"You heard her say this?"

"No," Olivia admitted. "Veronica told me 'bout it."

"So you didn't actually hear Devona say anything?"

"She called my moms a crack ho."

"She admits to that, but that was after you called *her* mom a big, fat black bitch."

Olivia looked down at her feet. "Okay."

"Devona," I said, "did you say those things about Olivia?"

"No." Devona folded her arms across her chest.

"Why would Veronica make that up?"

"I don't know. Ask her. She always instigatin' and shit." She realized the word she had just used. "Sorry."

"It's okay." I looked at the two girls. "You two ever have a beef before?"

They both shook their heads no.

"So this all got started because you"—I motioned with my head at Olivia—"heard Devona said something you didn't actually hear yourself."

Olivia shrugged. "I guess."

"Let's be clear here, then. You two almost got into a fight and risked getting suspended because of some he said–she said crap?" I paused to let that sink in. "If Ms. Levine hadn't been there and stepped in, we would be having a completely different conversation right now. With your parents. They got nothing better to do than take time out of their day because somebody said something somebody else didn't say?"

I wasn't quite confident of my grammar there—but I think I got my point across, because both girls shook their heads and whispered, "No."

"Okay then. Let's all be glad this didn't get out of hand. Olivia, you have something you want to say to Devona?"

Olivia looked at me. "Sorry."

"Tell her, not me."

She faced Devona. "Sorry I called your moms a big, fat black bitch."

I looked at Devona as she fought back a smile. "I'm sorry I called your moms a crack ho."

"Okay," I said. "What happens now?"

"Whatta you mean?" Devona asked.

"How do I know this is over? That you two aren't just blowing smoke in my face and this jumps off again after school?"

"Nah, it won't, Mr. D," Olivia said, then held her hand out to Devona. "We cool."

Devona gave it a light slap and held hers out to Olivia, who returned the gesture. "Yeah," Devona said. "We cool."

"Okay," I said. "I'm going to trust you two." I stood up and walked over to my desk. "I'm also going to have a talk with Veronica. Her name's come up before in things like this, and she never seems to be the one sitting in my office apologizing. Let me talk to her, not you two."

"Okay, Mr. D," Olivia said. "Thanks."

"Yeah," Devona said. "Thanks."

"You're welcome. When you get the chance, you might also want to thank Ms. Levine. You're lucky she was there."

They both nodded. After I wrote them late passes to class, they left my office.

I gave my principal some bullshit excuse about having some personal business to take care of on Long Island, and he didn't push it. Ron was too busy looking at his computer screen to have a conversation, and that was okay with me.

I grabbed a buttered bagel and a coffee by the subway station. The subways were running great, so a little more than thirty minutes later, I was outside the Shermans' apartment on Riverside Drive. Allison got there about a minute after I did.

"You are prompt," she said, giving me a quick kiss on the cheek.

"And courteous." I reached into my backpack and pulled out the camera.

"And prepared," Allison said. "Like a Boy Scout."

"Not exactly."

She looked at my camera. "You know how to use that?" When I didn't respond, she said, "Remember, you are a photographer today. After I introduce you, you are to take a few pictures and remain silent. Got it?"

"What if I have a question?"

"You won't. Photographers don't have questions, reporters do." She reached out and grabbed my arm. "Promise me. No questions."

"Okay," I said. "No questions. I promise."

"It'll be good practice for you. Sitting and listening."

"Are you implying I talk too much and don't listen enough?"

"Oh, please. Not just you. Most men." She touched my face and lowered her voice. "Consider this a test. If you pass, there might be something in it for you."

I got that warm feeling in my chest again. "Okay," I said.

"Good boy."

We walked inside and were greeted by a uniformed doorman. Allison took out her newspaper ID and explained to him that we were expected by the Shermans.

The doorman stepped over to the house phone, told someone on the other end we were here, then pointed to the elevators.

"Be nice to them," he said. "They've been through a lot."

"Do you know the family well?" I asked, and got slapped on the arm by Allison. I looked at her. "You said no questions for the Shermans. You didn't say anything about the doorman."

After giving us a confused look, the doorman said, "Known 'em since they moved in. Knew Paulie since he was just a pup."

"What kind of kid was Paulie?"

"All boy," he said, a sad smile crossing his face. "Lots of life in that one. It was all his mom could do to keep the lad in his stroller. He was walking at about nine months."

"What about lately?" I asked. "Anything out of the normal?"

"Geez. The kid was a teenager. What the hell's normal about that?"

I laughed. "You know what I mean. Normal for Paulie."

The doorman—his name tag said AL—thought about that. After a while, something came to him.

"He'd leave here all cranky some days," Al said. "Got his skateboard under his arm, but a real scowl on his face. Wouldn't even say hi. Be back an hour later, and he's back to being the happy kid. Moody, I guess you'd say. Even for a teenager."

"Were you working the night he was killed?"

"Nah. I'm the day guy. I'll pull some doubles now that the holidays are here, but I'm mostly seven to four." He got quiet for a few seconds. "Came in the next morning, though, and felt something was wrong as soon as I walked through those doors." He shook his head. "Maybe it was coming off Bobby, the night guy, but I felt it. Something bad happened. You ever get that feeling?"

"Yeah," I said. "Sometimes."

Allison looked at her watch and said, "I don't want to keep them waiting. Thank you for speaking with us, Al."

"Yeah," he said. "Don't put none of what I said in the paper, okay? Don't want the residents to think they got themselves a Chatty Cathy for a doorman."

"I won't."

We both thanked him and took the elevator up to the tenth floor. Somehow, Allison was able to keep her hands off me for the entire ride. We walked down the long hallway toward the apartment, and I heard a door open ahead of us. Into the hallway stepped a rather tall man. He had on a blue shirt and well-pressed khakis. He was holding a glass of something in his right hand.

"Ms. Rogers?" he asked.

When we were a few steps away, Allison offered her hand.

"Mr. Sherman," she said. "Thank you again for agreeing to the interview."

"We'll give you thirty minutes, Ms. Rogers."

"Allison," she said and then turned to me. "This is my photographer."

Who, I surmised, was to remain nameless. I stuck out my hand. "Mr. Sherman, I'm very sorry for your loss."

"Yes," he said softly. "Thank you."

He stepped aside and motioned for us to go inside the apartment. As I passed by him, I didn't smell any alcohol. I wouldn't have blamed him if I had, but it seemed he was just drinking water. We walked through a small hallway and entered the living room area. The far wall was almost completely windows, which opened up to an amazing view of the Hudson River and New Jersey.

"Is that all the equipment you have?"

It took me a moment to realize he was speaking to me.

"Yes," I said, just as an attractive woman walked into the room. I guessed her to be in her early forties, but an Upper West Side early forties. I could easily picture her drinking gin and tonics at the club after a tough game of tennis. She wore a sleeveless blouse that showed off her toned and tanned arms and almost enough makeup to cover the dark puffiness under her eyes. She confidently stepped over to Allison and introduced herself as Natalie Sherman.

"Please," Mrs. Sherman said, "have a seat." She gestured to the couch.

"Actually," Allison said, "if you don't mind, I'd like you and Mr. Sherman to sit on the couch for a photograph."

"Oh," she said, surprised at the request. "I suppose that's fine. Matthew?"

"Fine," Mr. Sherman said. "Is a photograph really necessary?"

"It's a way to put a face—two faces—on the story," Allison explained.

The Shermans walked over and sat on the couch as if they were not used to being next to each other. They looked at me with awkward smiles. Allison took the seat to the left of the couch.

"Don't worry about the camera," she said. "We'll just talk, and my photographer will take a few shots as we do so."

Mrs. Sherman squirmed a bit, uncomfortable on her own couch. "You're not going to ask us to hold a picture of Paulie, are you?"

"No," Allison said with a slight grimace. "I don't like those shots. We'll just get a few with the two of you on the couch having a natural conversation."

"There's nothing 'natural' about this conversation, Ms. Rogers," Mr. Sherman said. "Our son is dead."

"I'm sorry, Mr. Sherman. I just meant I don't want the picture to seem posed."

"If you ask any questions I deem are out of line, this interview's over. Are we clear about this, Ms. Rogers?"

"Completely, Mr. Sherman." Allison cleared her throat in an attempt to gather herself and gain some control.

I remembered from my days as a cop, nothing made me more uncomfortable than trying to do my job around people who had just lost a loved one. And when it was a parent losing a child, the grief just covered everything like a thick layer of ash.

"Would you mind," Allison said, "beginning by telling me what you both do?"

Mr. Sherman sighed, bored by the question. "I'm a personal financial adviser and money manager," he said. "Natalie manages the household."

"I used to be in advertising," Mrs. Sherman said. "I left when we decided to have kids, and I never went back. I volunteer at the kids' schools once a week." She added the last part as if we were due an explanation.

"How many children do—?" Allison stopped herself, not sure how to phrase the question. To her credit, Mrs. Sherman sensed the awkwardness.

"Paulie has a little sister," she said. "Chelsea. She's at school right now."

"We didn't want her around during this," Mr. Sherman said.

"I completely understand." Allison wrote something in her notebook. "Did you know Douglas Lee?"

"Douglas was a guest in our home many times," Mrs. Sherman said. "He was a delightful young man with impeccable manners."

I hid a small smile behind my hands and camera. Dougie had obviously charmed the hell out of this woman. Judging by the look on his face, not so much the father.

"Did Douglas give you any indication he was in any sort of trouble?" Allison asked.

"Not the kind of trouble that would get him killed," Mr. Sherman said.

"*Any* kind of trouble?"

"Well"—Mrs. Sherman now—"both boys were concerned about their grades slipping. During the past couple of months, they both complained about not sleeping a lot. That was new for Paulie. He never seemed to stress over grades before."

"That was part of the problem," Mr. Sherman said.

"What was?" Allison asked.

"Paulie needed to focus more on his grades and his future. He fought us tooth and nail when we placed him at Upper West and decided to put him on medication."

"Medication for what?" Allison asked.

More squirming from Mrs. Sherman. Her skittishness reminded me of Paulie, the night I had met him outside Dougie's wake. Mr. Sherman rubbed his eyes.

"Paulie," he said, "had a mild case of attention deficit disorder. We figured a private school, smaller classes, and a low dose of medication would get him back on track. Help him get ready for college."

"Did it work?"

"It did at first," Mr. Sherman said. "Paulie had a good year academically last year and was on his way to another good one this year. But then he started losing the focus again, not caring as much about his work. Late for curfews. We were about to come down real hard on him when . . ." He shut his eyes. He'd said enough.

Allison turned to Mrs. Sherman. "When did you notice the change?"

Mrs. Sherman put her hand on her husband's thigh. Neither one of them seemed comforted by the gesture.

"A few months ago," she said. "He began to fall back into his old habits. Late with assignments. Forgetting about homework. That's when we noticed he wasn't sleeping well. He had always been a good sleeper." She took a deep breath, and something resembling a smile crossed her face. "We used to joke that it took a lot of energy to be Paulie." She paused. "He was always . . . so full of energy."

Allison jotted down some more notes. This allowed some time for Mr. and Mrs. Sherman to compose themselves, and for me to take a couple of quick photos of the grieving parents on the couch. Mr. Sherman took his wife's hand off his leg and held it. I glanced at my watch and was happy to see our thirty minutes were almost half over.

"And," Allison said, "Douglas also complained about not sleeping?"

"He didn't have to," Mrs. Sherman said. "I could see it in his eyes. One time he actually dozed off on our couch."

"What about Jack Quinn?" Allison asked.

"What about him?"

"Did you know him well?"

"He didn't come by as much as Douglas. Hardly ever. The two of them—Paulie and Douglas—always seemed to be meeting Jack outside his apartment. On the east side of Central Park."

This last comment brought a barely audible snort from Mr. Sherman, whose eyes were still shut. Allison heard it, too, and leaned forward a few inches.

"What is it, Mr. Sherman?"

Mr. Sherman picked his head up and opened his eyes. They were wet and red, fighting back tears.

"We didn't care much for Jack Quinn," he said. "He struck us—me— as a trust-fund kid who felt he didn't have to work to get what he wanted. He was not a good influence on Paulie." He noticed Allison writing that down. "Please don't put that in your story, Ms. Rogers. I don't want to come off as . . . just don't write that."

Allison nodded. "I understand." She drew two lines through what she had just written. "But the three boys were close?"

"Very much so," Mrs. Sherman said. "They even went away together at times. Just this past Columbus Day they went up to the Quinns' home in Rhinebeck for the weekend. I have some pictures around here somewhere. Would you like to see them?"

"I would, if it's not any trouble," Allison said.

"It's no trouble at all," Mrs. Sherman said as she stood. The perfect hostess. She seemed glad to get off the couch. "They're in Paulie's room. I'll be right back."

As she exited the living room, Mr. Sherman leaned back into the couch.

"Paulie came home from that trip," he said, "asking us why *we* didn't have a second home like the Quinns."

"What did you tell him?"

"I told him if he really wanted a second home, he'd better come up with another way to pay for college. Paulie didn't understand. Christ, what teenager does? One of the drawbacks of private school is that you hang around with people who have more than you do, and you start to question why. It was a constant conversation with Paulie. I know it may not seem like it, with this apartment and two kids in private school, but we struggle financially to give the kids what they need."

Allison nodded. I took a picture of the two talking. Mrs. Sherman returned, holding an envelope. She remained standing as she handed the envelope to Allison.

"I don't think," she said, hesitating to let go of the envelope, "I'll ever get used to going into his room."

"I can't imagine," Allison said as she waited for Mrs. Sherman to release her grip. When she did, Allison opened the envelope and slipped out the photos. I stepped over to get a better look.

There were only six pictures—all of them with two of the three boys in them, the third boy apparently serving as the photographer. It occurred to me there seemed to be no grown-ups around to take pictures or to supervise. The trio was all smiles back then. Not even two months ago. The backgrounds showed the Hudson River, the red and orange leaves of fall, an old Victorian home. Upstate New York in early October. It must seem like years ago to Paulie's parents.

"Very nice," Allison said as she put the pictures back in the envelope. She handed them to Mrs. Sherman.

"Yes," Mrs. Sherman said, holding the envelope with both hands as if hoping the life and energy of the photographs would course through her. "They had a good time."

"And we," Mr. Sherman said as he got up off the couch, "are just about out of time, Ms. Rogers." He looked at his watch. "I have a conference call in ten minutes."

"Just one or two more questions," Allison said, "and we'll be on our way." She looked at her notebook. "Did Paulie often go out at night with his skateboard?"

Mr. and Mrs. Sherman exchanged glances, not happy with the question.

"No," Mr. Sherman said, his eyes still on his wife. "It was not something he did often. Every once in a while . . ." He stopped mid-sentence.

"Every once in a while," his wife picked up, "if it was a nice night and Paulie had completed all his homework, we'd let him take his board out for a quick ride before getting ready for bed." She paused, thinking about what she'd just said. "I know it may not sound like the best parenting idea. But it was an incentive for him to finish his work, and it's always well-lit outside. And that was the night of Dougie's wake. So we felt he needed some release. He was never out for more than half an hour."

"And that Thursday night?" Allison asked.

"We were running a bit hectic that night. Matthew"—she looked at her husband—"was on the phone with a client in Singapore. I was putting Chelsea to bed. She was up later than usual, and she was quite a handful." She paused. This was painful for her to remember. "By the time things got settled down, I realized Paulie had been out for almost an hour."

"What did you do?"

"I called his cell phone," Mrs. Sherman explained. "He always had it with him, and we wouldn't let him out at night without it." She closed her eyes. "It went right to his voice mail. That wasn't like him to not have it on."

Allison wrote that down and waited for Mrs. Sherman to continue. It was Mr. Sherman who spoke next.

"Natalie came into my office. I had just finished my call and was placing my client's order. She told me Paulie had not come back up yet." He thought about that as he chose his next words. "I admit it, my first reaction was anger. We give him a special privilege, and he's taking advantage of it, you know? I put my jacket on and went outside to find him. I know he likes to skate in Riverside Park."

Mrs. Sherman took a few tentative steps toward her husband and then stopped. She turned to face Allison instead.

"Don't imply that we're neglectful parents, Ms. Rogers," she said. "We know it wasn't the best idea to allow him out at that time, but . . ."

"I won't imply anything, Mrs. Sherman," Allison said.

"I went over to the park," Mr. Sherman continued. "I was about to go down the hill leading to the basketball courts, where he liked to skate sometimes. That's when I noticed the flashing lights up the block." He slowly sat back down on the couch. "I knew right away it was Paulie. He never stays out more than half an hour. That was the rule." He balled his hands into fists and pounded on his thighs. "That was the rule."

Mrs. Sherman took a few more steps toward her husband. She stopped again, and this time turned to look out the window. I wondered what she saw out there.

Allison closed her notebook and looked at me.

"I think we have enough, Mr. and Mrs. Sherman," she said. "I know this was hard for you, and I truly appreciate your time. We are very sorry for your loss."

Her eyes still looking out at the Hudson, Mrs. Sherman said, "Thank you."

Mr. Sherman said nothing. He just sat on the couch, his fists resting on his knees.

"We'll see ourselves out," Allison said, moving toward the front door. "Thank you again."

I followed Allison into the hallway. She turned around and shut the door quietly, as if trying not to wake a sleeping baby. When she looked at me, I saw her eyes were filled with tears. She leaned with her back against the wall.

"That," she said, "fucking sucked."

"You got that right," I said. I reached out and touched her hand. "You okay?"

"I will be," she said, standing on her own now. "You get some good shots?"

"A few, yeah." We started walking toward the elevator. "I don't know if they're good enough for your paper, but . . ."

"Please," she said. "I'm sure they're better than the ones I would have taken." She laughed a little as she pressed the DOWN button for the elevator. "That would have been a little awkward, huh? 'Excuse me, Mr. Sherman, but would you mind pounding your fists again? I missed it the first time. And this time, show more grief.'"

"I'm glad I could help."

The elevator arrived, and we stepped inside. We rode down to the lobby in silence. After thanking Al the doorman, we walked outside to Riverside Drive. A cold breeze was coming off the Hudson, and Allison and I both zipped our jackets. We slipped our hands into our pockets and exchanged awkward looks. It felt kind of like not knowing if a date was over.

"Too early for a drink?" I suggested.

"God knows I could use one after that," she said.

"What if I offered you a late lunch as well?"

"I might have to take you up on that."

"I know a good sushi place over on Amsterdam."

"*You* know a sushi place?"

"Yes, Allison. I know a sushi place." I smiled as she slipped her arm through mine. "I've never eaten there before," I admitted. "But they have good Japanese beer and a decent happy hour."

"Is there such a thing as an *indecent* happy hour?"

"Not in my experience," I said, and led the way to the restaurant.

Chapter 23

I POURED ALLISON ANOTHER sake. "Feeling any better?" I asked.

"Yeah," she said. She pointed at her sake vase. "Of course, a couple of these will make most things better."

"I agree." I took another sip of Kirin. I like Japanese beers. Not as much as I like the American craft beers, but definitely better than the mass-produced American stuff. It's the one thing I would admit to being a snob about: for every beer advertised on TV, there are thirty better that most people never heard of. I was planning on having a Sapporo for my next one.

"Thanks again, Ray. Having someone else there always makes it easier."

"You're welcome," I said. "That about as bad as it gets?"

She took another sip. "Not even close," she said. "Interviewing the families of four recent high school graduates who thought they could make it through the flashing lights, around the barrier, and over the train tracks before the train got there. That's as bad as it gets."

"Wow," I said. "Where and when did that happen?"

"Westchester. Three years ago."

"They all die?"

"Three of the four. The fourth one—the driver—wishes he had."

"Were they drinking?"

"Yep. Coming back from a graduation party. Had their whole lives in front of them. All four college-bound. Thought they were invincible."

I finished off my beer. "I remember those days," I said. "Stupid shit was done."

"Most of us make it through. Those who don't, sometimes make the papers."

Our food came. We'd ordered the sushi platter for two, which I figured a lot of couples probably do. Not because we were a couple, but there *were* two of us, and it seemed the thing to order. After the waiter informed us which fish was which, I asked him for a Sapporo, and Allison asked for another vase of sake. Neither one of us had to be back at work until the next day, so . . .

"What about you?" she asked. "What was your worst day?" Before I could answer, she winced. "Oh, right. Sorry."

"It's okay," I said. "I don't blame myself as much as I used to."

"Do you think about it a lot?"

"Only every time I pass a fire escape," I said, more than a touch of bite in my voice. *Stupid.* "Sorry."

"No, no. I understand, Ray. I still flinch whenever I see a Jeep."

"Yeah," I said. "It's kind of always there."

The waiter came by with our drinks. I asked for two sets of chopsticks and he handed them over. Again, Allison looked surprised.

"My sister taught me," I said. "She said it'd impress women."

Allison took her wooden set and separated them. "Tell your sister she's right."

"I'll be sure to do that."

We ate without talking for a while. I liked the way Allison dug right in. There was none of that picking around, asking if I wanted a certain piece. She knew what she wanted and she took it. It was just sushi, but I admired the attitude. When she really liked a piece, she made a low moan.

"What other advice did your sister give you?" Allison asked.

I swallowed a piece of tuna and took a sip of beer before answering.

"To take things as they come," I said. "And to keep in mind you need time and space in a relationship."

She moved her chopsticks through the air in a circular motion and said, "Is that what we have here, Raymond? A relationship?"

Great, I thought. *Haven't had this conversation for a while.*

"I don't know what we have here, Allison."

"Good answer." She took a sip of sake. "You passed the test, you know."

"The keep-my-mouth-shut-and-listen test at the Shermans?"

"That's the one."

I leaned forward and lowered my voice. "Remember the offer you made the other night?"

"No, Ray," she said. "I was so blasted out of my mind, it's all a blur."

"Okay, no need to ruin the mood with sarcasm."

She raised one of her chopsticks up to her mouth and ran it over her lower lip.

"What mood is that, Ray?"

I didn't answer. I just kept watching that lucky chopstick make its way around her mouth.

"Are you propositioning me, Mr. Donne?"

"Yes," I said. "I am."

"Does that make you feel better about it? Now that it's your idea?"

"No. I just think that—"

She turned the chopstick around and placed it on both my lips. "Shhh," she said. "Do that thing again where you don't talk so much."

Two hours later, we were at Allison's apartment in her bed. The curtains were pulled, the lights were turned off in favor of scented candles, and her head was resting on my chest. I couldn't see her face, so I wasn't quite sure if she was smiling, but you would have had trouble wiping the one off my face with a rake. Allison sighed.

"What?" I asked.

"Daytime sex fucking rocks."

"I agree." I moved my arm so I could rub her shoulder. "Feels like we're getting away with something. Like we know there are things to do, but we had sex instead. I half expect my mother to come through the door asking why I didn't make it to school."

She patted me on the stomach. "It's okay, Ray. Your mother has no idea who I am or where I live."

"Good. Now I can relax."

And I did. I found myself staring up at her ceiling, feeling my eyes get droopy and letting them close. I took in the scent of the candles and the scent of Allison. I could have stayed that way for many hours. Allison had other ideas.

"So," she said. "What are you thinking?"

"I'm thinking this feels real good right now. You?"

"I mean about the three boys."

We just had sex and now she wants to talk about this?

"I wasn't thinking about the boys, Allison," I said, squeezing her shoulder.

"Well, *I am* and now *you are*." She rolled onto her side and propped her head up with a couple of pillows. "I'm getting more and more curious about what happened to put the Quinn boy into the hospital."

Looked like we were going to have this conversation. I took a few more pillows and put them behind my back as I sat up. I looked down at Allison. "Yeah, me, too. You still thinking of heading over to the hospital?"

"Tonight. I'll catch the nurses on a shift change. There's always a better chance to talk with them on their way out."

"You really think you'll get information out of any of them?"

"I told you," she said, "some of them get real chatty after a long shift. What do we want to know exactly?" She didn't wait for an answer. "Why Jack's there, right?"

"Right."

"I can get a nurse or an aide to give that up without them even realizing they did."

"Is that something they teach in journalism school? Getting people to reveal confidential information?"

She sat up. "Don't get all high and mighty on me now, Raymond. *You* went to the hospital. And you just passed yourself off as a photographer to a grieving family."

"Number one: that's not a crime," I said. "Number two: it was your idea."

"Doesn't make it right, and you had no problem agreeing to it. You were just as curious as I was to meet Paulie's parents." She readjusted the pillows behind her back. "Do I sometimes have to cross some ethical line to get a story? Damn straight. If I didn't, I wouldn't be long for this business. Shit, the way newspapers are now, I may not be long for it anyway. You'll be able to get everything off the wire or the Internet."

"No," I said. "You're right. It just seems a bit—"

"Hey," she interrupted. "You got into this for a reason. You were trying to help Mrs. Lee find the truth about what happened to her son. I agreed—not completely selflessly—to help you. You know how this works. You can't stop in midstream because you don't like the way things are going."

"I never said I wanted to stop," I said.

"No, but you're starting to question my methods. I don't appreciate that."

That warm and fuzzy post-coital feeling was almost gone. I closed my eyes and tried to get some of it back. It wasn't working.

"Okay," I said, opening my eyes and looking at Allison. "You're right."

"Damn straight, I'm right," she said. "Your sister teach you how much women love to hear those two words? 'You're right'?"

"No. I had to figure that one out for myself."

"See," she said, throwing her legs over mine. "You're smarter than you look."

"I get that a lot."

"Keep that up, and you might get something else."

"You mean . . . this is not a one-night stand?"

She leaned in and kissed me. "It's the afternoon, Ray. Let's talk about the night later."

"Fine by me," I said, and kissed her right back.

Chapter 24

IT WAS A SLOW NIGHT AT THE LineUp, and it didn't look like it was going to pick up anytime soon. Nobody was playing pool, and only three people were sitting at the bar. A couple of retired cops who were watching the news with the sound off. And, of course, Edgar.

I poured myself half a pint of Brooklyn Pilsner and went over to where Edgar was playing with his laptop. I must have been standing there for a minute before he acknowledged my presence.

"Raymond," he said. "Absolutely brilliant idea Mrs. Mac had, putting Wi-Fi in."

"Wasn't that your suggestion, Edgar?"

"Oh, yeah." His eyes were still on the screen, but he was grinning. "So, why are you here tonight?"

"Mikey called me this afternoon," I explained, leaving out the part about getting the call while in Allison's bed. "Said he forgot he had an early-morning fishing trip tomorrow and asked me to cover his shift for him."

"Cool beans. Can I get another one of these, please?"

I took his glass and filled it up with Bass. I also grabbed a small can of tomato juice and brought it over to him.

"On me," I said. I must have been bored because I heard myself say, "What're you looking at?"

"Thanks." He held up a finger, telling me to let him finish. It took him less than a minute. He sipped a bit of his ale, opened the tomato juice, poured a small amount into his glass, and took another sip. "Ahh."

I pointed at his laptop. "More about bird-watching?"

"Nope," he said. "Did you know the Quinns have a house up in Rhinebeck?"

"Yeah," I said. "Paulie's mom said the boys were up there recently."

"Well, I entered the name 'Quinn' into a search engine I'm fond of, along with 'Rhinebeck.' After a few more clicks, I was able to get his address."

"That doesn't sound right," I said. "Is that legal?"

"I don't use the popular search engines," he said, as if that explained whether it was legal or not. "Then I punched in the address." He paused, making me wait.

"And?"

"And," he said, pleased I had taken the bait, "it seems there was a rash of home invasions on his block a few months ago."

"How'd you find that out?"

"Local paper has a 'Police Beat' column. The usual for a town like Rhinebeck. The occasional loud-party-noise complaint, DWIs coming off the bridge, small stuff like that. The one interesting item was this."

He spun his laptop around so I could see the screen. He pointed to the item in question. Five homes had been broken into. The article did not mention what—if anything—had been taken from the houses or if anyone had been hurt. In fact, the article mentioned very little.

"Notice anything interesting, Raymond?"

I read it slower this time. "No," I said. "I don't."

"Look at the addresses."

I did and realized what he was talking about. The addresses were consecutive even numbers. All the break-ins took place on the same side of the block.

"That *is* interesting."

"Thought so." Edgar turned the screen back around. "And one of those five houses is owned by Mr. John R. Quinn Sr."

I gave that some thought. Someone—probably more than one person—had broken into five houses in a row in the same evening. That took either some set of balls or very little brains.

"How'd they get into the houses?"

"Article doesn't say. A lot of times, people in a town like that get complacent, leave their doors unlocked."

"What was the date of the break-ins?"

"October tenth," he said.

A lightbulb went off. "That's when the boys were up there. Columbus Day weekend."

"That's when everyone who owns a home in Rhinebeck is up there, Raymond. Second week of October is primo leaf-peeping season."

"So the homes had people in them." I realized something else I had neglected to notice. "They say what time the break-ins occurred?"

"Sometime after midnight. All the homeowners were tucked safely in their beds. No one heard a thing."

"Hmmm," I said. "I wonder what was taken."

"There might be a way to find out." Edgar punched a few more keys and then turned the laptop back around to me. "Here's the sheriff's office number," he said.

"I can see that. What good does that do me?"

"Call 'em up."

"Edgar," I said, "they're not going to give me that kind of information. It looks like they don't even want the local paper to know."

"They might," he said, "if they thought you were . . . you know . . . a cop."

"Great idea, Edgar. Impersonating an officer. You want me to lose my job?"

"You call 'em up. Say you're investi—*looking into*—a homicide down here in the city and need some info on the break-ins because your victim had visited one of the homes broken into. You never have to say you're a cop. Maybe you'll luck out and get some Barney Fife who thinks he's talking to NYPD and will read off the report."

"Don't call them 'Barney Fifes,' Edgar. Small-town cops have to be just as sharp as the ones down here. Especially in a town like Rhinebeck. All that money."

"I'm just saying it doesn't hurt to make a phone call." He paused for a second. "If that doesn't work, have your girlfriend call. Or your detective buddy."

"Oh, yeah, Dennis would be all over that."

"Your girlfriend, then."

"She's not my girlfriend," I said.

"Okay. Whatever she is, she's press, and they may give her the four-one-one."

I looked over at the screen, at the number for the sheriff's department. Edgar was right: a phone call wouldn't hurt. Maybe they'd tell me, maybe not. Worst case was, I'd be right back where I started.

The front door opened and two customers walked in. A young couple, early twenties. Good. That gave me something to do while I pondered the wisdom of making the call. I took their drink order and the guy's credit card, which I placed on the register. I stepped back over to Edgar, who was giving me his whatta-ya-got-to-lose look. I pulled out my cell phone, looked at the number for the sheriff, and dialed. Edgar's grin went around to the back of his neck. I turned so I didn't have to look at him.

"Sheriff's department," the voice on the other end said.

"Yes," I said, trying to sound official. "This is Raymond Donne, New York City. Whom am I speaking to, please?"

"The Sheriff's department," he repeated, and then waited for me.

"My name's Raymond Donne. I'm . . . looking into a homicide down here in New York City." I paused to let that sink in, maybe impress the small-town cop. "Which may be connected to a case your department is involved in."

"And which case are you referring to, sir?" He didn't sound too impressed, but he wasn't blowing me off, either.

"Series of home invasions. Columbus Day weekend."

I heard the sound of computer keys being punched and waited. I didn't have to wait long.

"Who'd you say you worked for?"

"I'm looking into the case on behalf of the family of a murder victim down here in the city." That was close to true. "He was visiting one of the homes on the block where the break-ins took place."

"You private?" he asked.

"You could say that. Yes."

Another pause. "What's the address of the home he was visiting?"

I told him and heard the computer keys again.

"That," he said, "was one of the homes that was broken into, so I guess there's not much more I can tell you, Mr. Donne. Is that all?"

I was about to get hung up on. "No," I said. "I was wondering if you could tell me if anything was taken from the homes."

"Why would you need to know that, sir?"

Good question. No Barney Fife, this guy. With nothing brilliant coming to mind, I said, "Just filling in the details for the family."

"Of your murder victim?"

"Yes."

"Whom you say you're looking into this for?"

"Yes."

"In what capacity, sir?"

I thought we'd established that. "In a *private* capacity, Officer."

"Deputy," he corrected me. "So, basically you want information from an incident report, but can't actually tell me why?"

"It's privileged information," was the best I could come up with.

"As opposed to an official incident report?"

"That's not what I meant, Deputy. I just—"

"The garages," he said.

"Excuse me?"

"Garages," he repeated. "Nothing was taken from any of the homes."

"Nothing?"

"That's what I said, sir. According to the homeowners, there was nothing taken from any of the residences. However, they all reported their garages had been entered sometime during the early morning hours, and the trunks of the cars had been broken into."

I waited. "What was reported missing?"

"They all reported their trunks had been broken into, but nothing had been taken."

"Really?"

"Yes. All the residents were quite clear on that point."

"Right," I said. "Any ideas who committed the break-ins?"

"A few," he said. "But as this is an active investigation, I have told you all I am allowed to tell you—*more* than I'm allowed to tell you. I'm sure you understand. Garage doors and trunks opened, nothing taken. Anything else I can do for you, Mr. Donne?"

I couldn't think of a thing. "No," I said. "You've been quite helpful, Deputy . . . ?"

"You're welcome, sir. Good luck with your investigation."

"Thanks."

We both hung up. I turned back toward Edgar.

"So?" he said.

"Nothing was taken from any of the houses that were broken into."

"For real?"

"That's what the deputy told me." I told Edgar about the car trunks.

"Shit," was his response. And then, "You know what I think?"

"Yeah," I said, coming to what I believed was the same conclusion he'd arrived at. "A bunch of kids having a little fun."

"And what bunch of kids do we know for sure—?"

"Dougie, Paulie, and Jack. Who were up there," I added, "seemingly without adult supervision."

"Nice kids," Edgar said. "Fucking richies."

"Dougie was not a 'richie,' Edgar."

"No. He just hung around with them." He took another sip of beer. "I tell you, Raymond. I read about this stuff all the time. The biggest influence on kids' behavior is their peer group. Parents and—no offense—teachers can do all they want, but when it comes right down to it? Kids'll do what their friends'll do. Nine times out of ten."

I had no answer for that. Edgar was right. It was my job to know that kind of stuff. I just always thought Dougie would be the one out of ten.

"Hey, barkeep!" The guy behind me. I'd forgotten about them.

I spun around and walked over. "Another round?"

"Yes," the guy said. "Please."

I got them two more drinks, apologized for the wait, and told them the round was on me. That got a smile out of both of them, and they touched glasses. I'm a decent bartender, and I didn't want them thinking I was unaware of my mistake. This way, especially if they were new to the neighborhood, they'd be more likely to come back. God knows we needed folks like them on nights like these. "Hardly worth turning the lights on," the owner, Mrs. Mac, would say. But she'd never think of closing this place. The LineUp meant too much to too many people—many of them cops and ex-cops—so she was willing to weather through the slow times. "Besides," she'd told me more than once, "what am I gonna do? Sell the bar and move to Florida?"

I checked on the retired cops, and they both agreed they were fine and really should be heading home soon. I offered to buy them a round, and suddenly their plans had changed. It looked like they'd be staying a bit longer. The golden years.

Edgar got my attention and waved me over.

"So," he said, barely over a whisper, "whatta you thinking?"

"About what?"

"The break-ins. The boys. The Quinn house."

"I told you what I thought, Edgar. The boys were pulling a stupid prank. I think that's what the deputy was alluding to, but didn't have the authority to share it with me. The kids were smart enough to make sure it looked like the Quinns' garage was also broken into. Just a group of bored kids having fun."

Edgar's face registered disappointment. "So you don't think it's important?"

I patted his arm. "You did good work. Not every piece of information turns out to be helpful. The trick is figuring out which pieces are."

"I gotcha," he said, nodding his head. Another lesson learned.

I looked at my watch. It was almost midnight, and I didn't think we'd be getting an unexpected rush anytime soon.

"Half hour, folks," I said to the small crowd. "Early night tonight." They all nodded in agreement. I got the guy and his girlfriend one more drink and closed out his credit card. The two ex-cops were okay, and Edgar asked for one more round.

"Y'know," Edgar said, "it's kinda like putting together a jigsaw puzzle that has too many pieces."

I smiled at my pupil. "That's as good a simile as I could've come up with."

"Look at me," he said. "I'm talking in similes."

"Yes," I said, and took a sip of beer. "Look at you." A thought hit me. "Hey, Edgar. While you have your laptop all warmed up, would you mind looking up another name for me?"

His face lit up. "Not at all. Shoot."

"Matthew Sherman," I said.

His fingers danced along the keys. "Related to Paulie?"

"His dad. He's a money manager. A financial advisor. Something like that."

"Okay," Edgar said, punching a few more keys. "Matthew Sherman, Real Estate. Matthew Sherman, DDS. Matthew Sherman, Riverview Management?"

I thought back to the Shermans' apartment and the wall of windows overlooking the Hudson. "Yeah," I said. "That's probably it."

"Okeydokey." Edgar clicked on something and turned the screen around. "This your guy?"

It was. Right next to the company name and slogan—"Private and Personal Financial Services"—was a picture of Paulie's father. His arms were folded across his chest, and he had a serious look on his face. His white shirtsleeves were rolled up, and his red power tie was loosened. Ready for battle. Exactly the kind of guy you'd want protecting your family's assets. I clicked on *Services* and got a list of what you'd expect: *Portfolio Management, Trust Funds, Inheritance Strategies, Stocks and Bonds Investments, Commodities.* The guy seemed to have it all covered.

"Anything about him in the papers?" I asked. "Trade journals?"

Edgar spun the computer back around and worked the keys. He had that look on his face that told me he'd be a while. I took the time to clean some glasses and wipe down the bar. By the time I was done, so was Edgar.

"Whatcha got?" I asked.

"Nada," he said, his voice registering surprise.

"Nothing?"

"Nada much." Edgar smiled at his joke. "This guy takes the 'Private and Personal' for serious. I checked a few services, some investment websites, and the name Matthew Sherman comes up less than half a dozen times. That's pretty impressive. He must be very careful and very good."

"That's rare, I guess? Someone in that business?"

"Yeah," Edgar agreed. He took another minute and punched a few more keys. "He's not even named in the initial stories about his kid being killed. Papers just say 'The victim's parents were not available for immediate comment.' Low profile."

"Seems like it," I said. "I wonder why he agreed to be interviewed by Allison and without a lawyer."

"Maybe he got past his initial grief and wanted his kid's story out there."

"Maybe. Thanks, Edgar."

"No problem. Anything else before I shut down?"

I thought about that. "No," I said. "I think that's it for the day." I looked behind me: my four customers had already left. *Great. I never said good-bye.* This case was turning me into a crappy bartender. I turned back to Edgar. "I think it's time to go home."

"You're right." He shut down his laptop. "I got an early morning."

"What're you doing?"

"Actually," he said, "I'm heading uptown to see our friend Elliot."

"Going bird-watching?"

"There's a . . . I don't know what he called it . . . a club fair? All of Academy's clubs are having an open house. Recruiting members for the second half of the year."

"How does that involve you?"

"Elliot said he could use an extra hand with his bird-watching club, so I volunteered. I gotta meet with the headmaster first. Get cleared." Edgar's face turned serious. "Elliot's the only member, now that . . . y'know."

Dougie. "Yeah," I said. "I know."

"Anyways, since we're gonna be business partners, I figured I'd head up there and see what the kid's got."

"You mean face-to-face?" I teased. "You're not going to IM him?"

"That's funny." His face told me it wasn't. "Hey, you wanna come along? You know how I am with meeting new people."

I did know. I was surprised Edgar knew.

"I'm not sure," I said. "I got kind of a busy day tomorrow." I didn't.

"Ahh, come on, Ray. I'll pick you up. We'll be there in no time."

It would be something to do, I thought. I walked with Edgar to the front doors, shut the lights, and we stepped outside so I could lock the place up.

"Maybe," I said, turning the key. "What time are you leaving?"

"I can pick you up at eight thirty."

I gave that some thought. "All right, but can you get me back by one? I need to hit Muscles's tomorrow, and I have a date with Allison tomorrow night."

"Yeah," he said. "It starts at nine. All over by noon."

"Okay. Cool. Eight thirty."

"I'll bring the coffee and bagels," Edgar said.

"I'll need them both," I said. "Thanks."

Chapter 25

SATURDAY MORNING TURNED out to be surprisingly pleasant. The temp was in the low forties, and if there was a cloud in the sky, I didn't see it. Except for a few small, gray mounds melting along the streets, the snow was pretty much gone. Edgar and I were driving over the Williamsburg Bridge. With little humidity and smog, and the early-morning sun shining on the skyscrapers, Manhattan looked like it was in high-definition. One of those mornings when I couldn't imagine living anywhere else.

Then I remembered we were driving right past the same tennis courts where Dougie had been killed. Maybe there were other places to live.

"What did I tell ya, Ray?" Edgar said. "No traffic on the bridge, we cruise up the FDR, exit at Ninety-sixth, cross the park, hang a louie, and we're at the school in just over twenty minutes."

I raised my coffee cup in a nonchalant salute. "When you're right, you're right." To get my mind off Dougie, I said, "You think you'll find parking by the school?"

"You nondrivers are all alike." He took a bite of his bagel. "Betcha we find a spot along the park less than three blocks from Upper West."

As it turned out, if I had bet him I would have lost. Fifteen minutes later Edgar pulled into an empty space along Central Park, and we finished our coffees and bagels on the short walk to the school.

We saw a few people on the steps leading up to the school building. Most of them walked indoors, but two small groups had formed off to the side. One boy, about sixteen, held a sign attached to a stick that read,

UPPER WEST ROADRUNNERS. He was talking to two boys, a girl, and a couple of grown-ups. The other sign read, FOR THE BIRDS, and was held by none other than Elliot Henry Finch. He had a box at his feet and was talking to no one.

"Elliot," I said, as Edgar and I climbed the steps.

"Ray," he said. "This is a surprise. I was expecting only Edgar." He turned to face my friend. "It is nice, as I have heard people say, to finally put a face with the name, Edgar. I am Elliot Henry Finch."

"Edgar Martinez O'Brien," Edgar said, shaking Elliot's hand. Edgar looked around the steps and the front of the building and said, "Where's the group?"

"It appears we are the group. I would like to wait a few more minutes before we head off into the park." He reached into the box and pulled out two pairs of binoculars. He handed one to Edgar and one to me. "I am hoping for a few more people."

I couldn't tell if he believed that or not. It was hard to read this kid's face.

"Great day for it," I said, going for optimistic.

"Actually," Elliot began, "I would have preferred to introduce newcomers to the group's activities in October or April. Those are the peak bird-watching months along the Ramble, but I am not in charge of scheduling the open house." He looked up at the sky. "Although today is a good day weather-wise, I am not sure how successful we will be when it comes to spotting the more interesting birds."

We stood there on the steps in awkward silence for almost a minute. It was broken by Edgar.

"In the meantime," Edgar said, "I've had a few ideas for the bird-watching site. Potential advertisers. Logo design."

"Excellent," Elliot said. "As have I." He reached once again into his box, pulled out a walkie-talkie, and handed it to me. "Ray, I have to introduce Edgar to the headmaster, and then I would like to speak with Edgar privately. Is that rude?"

I shook my head. "No, Elliot. I understand completely." I turned on my walkie-talkie and put the strap of the binoculars around my neck. *Look at me, I'm a bird-watcher.* "I'll take a walk over to the park. Radio me when you two get there."

Without a word, they walked off in the other direction. I headed toward Central Park. I got about a half block, when I recognized the man walking my way. It was Mr. Rivera, the computer teacher. He looked at the walkie-talkie in my hand and the binoculars hanging from my neck and smiled.

"You joining Elliot's bird club, Mr. Donne?"

"Not quite," I said. "I'm here with a friend."

I explained the relationship between Edgar and Elliot and how Edgar didn't want to come alone for his first meeting with his future partner.

"Birds of a feather, so to speak," Rivera said.

My turn to smile. "That's good."

"Yeah, every once in a while the computer guy makes a joke."

"I've heard of that happening. You going to the open house?"

"Yeah. I run the after-school computer club. I've got one of my seniors up in the lab giving the introduction."

"I won't keep you, then," I said.

"No, it's cool. Truth is, Sheila practically runs the group anyway. I'm just the mandatory faculty advisor."

"Nice work if you can get it."

"Yeah. Hey, anything new on Douglas?"

"Not that I know of," I said. "You heard about Jack Quinn?"

"Of course. It's a small school." He shook his head. "Lot of shit going on lately."

"Yeah," I agreed. "Seems like it."

We both thought about that. When we were done thinking, I spoke.

"I met Jack's sister last week."

"Alexis," he said. "How'd that come about?"

I told him about my trip to the hospital and running into the sister, the father, and Dougie's uncle.

"What did she have to say?"

"She denied being Dougie's girlfriend. Made it seem like they barely knew each other. 'My brother's best friend' is the way she put it."

Rivera shrugged. "Maybe I got it wrong. Wouldn't be the first time."

"Or she was just too out of it to give me a straight answer."

"She was high?"

"Took one of her mom's anxiety pills. To help her through the crisis."

"Jesus," he said. "Sometimes it seems like everyone's on something. How was Mr. Quinn?"

"Appreciative, at first. His daughter could have run into a lot worse than me in that situation. Then when he found out who I was and why I was there, he threatened me with his lawyer. Who just happens to be Dougie's uncle."

"Sounds like it was a fun visit."

"That's one way to describe it."

He laughed. "I can imagine. Was Dad there when Alexis denied her relationship with Dougie?"

"No. Why?"

He nervously looked over my shoulder, up toward the school. When his eyes returned to me, he lowered his voice.

"Quinn senior? Never struck me as the most ardent defender of racial diversity."

"Really? I got the feeling he was the reason Dougie attended Upper West."

"Like I told you the other day, we *unofficially* have to have a certain amount of minority students. That number falls below . . . let's say ten percent—and the school looks bad. As a board member, Quinn knows that. Doesn't mean he likes it. I would imagine he probably viewed Dougie as the 'right kind' of black kid."

"Not from the projects," I added.

"Right. A nice smile, no tattoos. Hardworking boy and his single mom make a great photo for the brochure, but not necessarily someone he'd want his daughter to bring home to dinner, if you know what I mean."

Cynical guy, Rivera. I liked that.

He looked at his watch. "I really should head up to the computer lab," he said. "Sheila's good, but the parents are going to have a few questions for me about exactly where their after-school fees are going." He stuck out his hand. "You won't repeat any of what I told you, right? About Jack and his dad?"

"I wouldn't even know whom to tell," I said. "Take it easy."

"You, too."

As we walked off in different directions, I realized the little interest I had in bird-watching had suddenly disappeared. When I got to the stone wall separating Central Park from the sidewalk, I cleared off a spot big enough to sit on and did just that. With little else to do except watch traffic make its way north up Central Park West, I put the binoculars up to my eyes and checked out the apartment buildings on the other side of the street. *Damn.* This was a Peeping Tom's dream come true. Hundreds of windows, many of them with the shades pulled down and not too many on street level. But, still, if looking into other people's homes was something you were into, book a room and head on over to the Big Apple.

"You can get into trouble doing that, you know," a voice said.

I lowered the binoculars and looked into a couple of familiar faces. I couldn't quite place them, but some time in the past week . . .

"Mr. Donne," the boy said. "Jack Quinn."

Right.

"We met outside the funeral home. This is my sister, Alexis."

I slid off the wall and walked over to him. If Alexis recognized me, she didn't show it. I wondered if she remembered anything from the afternoon we'd met.

"Hey, Alexis. Raymond Donne."

"Hello," she said. *Nope, not a flicker.*

I turned to Jack. "How are you?"

"What do you mean?"

"Last I heard," I said, "you were in the hospital."

He looked at me blankly, no idea what I was talking about. I couldn't think of what else to say when he said, "I'm just messing with you, Mr. Donne." *Funny kid, this Jack.* "Bad case of food poisoning. They released me this morning," he explained. "I started feeling a lot better yesterday, but they wanted to keep me overnight for observation. And bill my dad's insurance company for one more day."

"Wow," I said. "And you're up and about."

"I guess." He shrugged. "I wanted to get over to the school. They're having their club thing today, and my dad says I need to have more on my transcript than just good grades if I wanna get into a good college. My folks insisted Alexis come along in case I get all woozy or something." An idea suddenly came to him. "Why are *you* here?"

I raised the walkie-talkie and binoculars. "Helping out a friend," I said, and told them about Edgar and Elliot.

"That's funny," he said. "Elliot's bird club was one of the ones I wanted to join. Supposed to hit the Ramble today."

"You're into bird-watching?"

"I'm *into* being out of the building. You know how us kids with ADHD are." He wiggled his fingers and waved his arms. "Gotta keep moving. Can't be in one place for too long."

"Doesn't bird-watching require a decent amount of attention?"

"They've done studies of kids with ADHD, what happens when you put us in the woods, surrounded by nature. Most of our symptoms just disappear. Guy wrote a whole book about it: *Last Child in the Woods.* Said a lot of us are just suffering from *nature*-deficit disorder." He snapped his fingers. "You're a special ed guy, right? You should know this stuff."

I did, but kept my mouth shut. Alexis looked at her watch as if she were late for a dinner date.

"I'm sorry about your friends, Jack."

"Huh?" he said. "Oh, yeah. Dougie and Paulie. That was some bad shit. I loved those guys. Y'know, Paulie was killed the night of Dougie's wake."

I watched for a reaction from Alexis. She just looked bored.

"I heard that."

"That's fucked up, y'know. We took the subway back to the city together that night. I was one of the last people to see him alive."

"Yeah," I agreed. "That is— You talking to anyone about it?"

"Whattaya mean? Like a counselor?"

"That's what I mean, yeah."

"Nah. Therapy's for those who can't handle reality. Like my sister." He playfully slapped Alexis's arm. Her face showed no sign of humor. "What happened to Dougie and Paulie sucked big-time, but that's life, y'know."

"That's a pretty harsh bit of reality, Jack."

"Hey, like my dad says, 'Whatever doesn't kill you . . .'"

He stopped when he hit upon the irony of those words. Neither one of us had much to say after that.

"Well," I said. "I'm glad to see you're doing better, Jack."

"Better than what?" *Fucking with me again.*

"Better than a kid with a bad case of food poisoning."

"Right." He looked at his watch. "Okay. We gotta run." He grabbed his sister's hand—*who was watching whom?*—and turned to catch the green light. He raised his hand as he crossed the avenue. "See ya soon."

"Yeah," I said. "Take it easy. Hey!" I called, walking over to him. "You mind doing me a favor?"

A brief look of annoyance crossed his face, but disappeared as he crossed back to my side of the avenue.

"No," he said. "Not at all."

I took off the binoculars and handed them and the walkie-talkie to Jack.

"Tell Elliot I forgot about an errand I have to run," I said. "And tell Edgar I took the subway home."

"Is that it?" he asked, obviously not used to delivering messages.

"Yeah, Jack. Thanks."

"Not a prob, Mr. Donne. See ya."

"Have fun, you guys."

"Always do," he said as they crossed the avenue again. "Always do."

Chapter 26

"THAT LOOKS LIKE IT HURTS a bit, Raymond."

"It's a little . . . uncomfortable, yeah."

"That's because," Muscles said, "coming in every Saturday *is not* the same as coming in three times a week. I seem to remember explaining that to you *last* Saturday. Now, if there were three Saturdays in a week, we wouldn't be in so much . . . discomfort."

"*We?*" I said, not trying to hide my grimace as I pushed myself into standing position on the leg press machine.

"Don't you think it pains me to see you like this? Especially when you've been making such progress over the past six months?"

"I've had a pretty busy week, Muscles."

"We're all busy, Ray. It's a matter of priorities. Okay, stop." I did and watched as he moved the pin up one notch, reducing the weight by twenty pounds. "Don't get too excited," he said. "What I want you to do now is count to five as you press up, and then count to five as you come back down. One Mississippi, two Mississippi, like that. Breathe out on the way up; breathe in on the way down. Can you remember all that?"

"I'll do my best."

"I know you will." He patted me on the shoulder. "You give any more thought to the clinical trial I was telling you about?"

"Not really," I said, completing one ten-second rep. I loved how Muscles would start a conversation with me as I was working out. Kind of like a dentist who asks you a question when you've got a mouthful of cotton and novocaine. "Still time to sign up?"

"They want the names of possible test subjects by next week."

I did another rep. " 'Test subjects'?"

"Sounds better than 'lab rats,' don't it?"

"Slightly," I answered, then did three more ups-and-downs silently, breathing in and out every ten seconds. "Tell me again: what do I have to do?"

Muscles repeated what he had explained to me last week: the forms, the drug tests, an MRI, the personal interview, and the medical history. He closed with the reminder that, for my efforts, I would be given a thousand dollars.

"I like that last part," I said. "And it's safe, right?"

"They wouldn't be doing a U.S. trial if it weren't," Muscles said. "That's what the overseas tests are for."

"Less regulation in other countries."

"Bingo. Less regs, less risk to the company, less press if something unexpected happens."

"Negative side effects."

"You're catching on," he said. "These companies have an obligation to their shareholders. Anything that might cut into their bottom line is scrutinized to hell."

"And this one has no side effects?"

He laughed. "There's always side effects when you put something foreign into your system, Ray. It's the R&D guys' job to minimize those side effects."

"What's an acceptable side effect?"

"With this supplement," he said, "I think the literature said headaches, upset stomach, dry mouth. Nothing serious enough to slow things down at this point."

I did a few more reps on the machine while I thought about Muscles's offer. I wasn't desperate, but I could always find a use for an extra thousand bucks, especially with the holidays coming up and my new . . . relationship.

"All right," I said. "Sign me up."

"Excellent. I have all your vitals and contact info. I'll shoot them an email this afternoon. You'll probably hear from them in a day or two."

"You think I'll get paid before the holidays?"

"No idea. You can bring that up when you talk to the company."

"Okay." I did one more rep. "How many more of these I gotta do?"

Muscles used his fingers to count. "What was that, seven? Do thirteen more, then hit the ab machine for three sets of fifteen. And don't even think of heading out before you do the calves, lats, and a half hour on the treadmill."

"Thanks, Muscles."

"You can thank me by showing up on Monday." He gave my thigh a playful punch. "But, yeah. You're welcome." He leaned his clipboard up against the wall, pointed at it, and said, "Fill in your numbers and drop the sheet off at the front desk."

"You got it," I said.

As soon as he left, I rubbed my thigh and finished up on the machine.

Chapter 27

"SO," ALLISON SAID, SLOWLY slipping her hand out of mine as we stopped in front of her apartment. "This is where I get off."

I took her hand again and pulled her into me for a kiss. When we were finished, she gave me the look I could feel in my gut. "You know, Raymond. It is a long subway ride back to Brooklyn."

"It is at that," I said, making a big deal out of looking at my watch. "And the trains do run pretty unpredictably at this time of night on Saturdays."

"Well, so much for one-night stands." She took my hand and led me to her front door. As she opened her purse to take out her keys, I heard the sound of footsteps behind us. I turned to see what was happening and got taken out at the knees and knocked to the ground.

"Allison!" I yelled.

I looked over and saw someone had an arm around Allison's neck. Whoever it was wore a ski mask. I tried to get up, but a second person behind me squeezed the back of my neck and pushed me back down. A raspy whisper told me, "Do that again and your girlfriend gets hurt." To accentuate this point, my attacker squeezed harder.

"What the hell do you—?" This time I got smacked in the head.

"Ah, fuck!" I could see Allison's attacker was holding something against her throat. "Goddamn it," Allison said, her voice filled with fear and anger. "Just take my fucking purse!"

Her attacker pulled her closer and whispered into her ear. With the knife pressed up against her neck, all Allison could do was listen. With my neck being squeezed and my knees screaming in pain, I could only watch. I tried to get up, but my attacker kicked me in my right knee, dropping me to the ground.

"Don't" the raspy whisper said, "fucking do that again."

I turned my head to get a better look at my attacker. He was wearing the same type of ski mask as his partner.

"Okay," I heard Allison say. I looked over and Allison addressed me. "Ray," she said, the knife still against her throat. "They're going to leave now. Don't get up."

"What do you mean, don't get—?"

"Ow!" Allison yelled. When she could speak again, she said, "Just don't get up. Okay, Ray? Please."

The hand on my neck squeezed harder.

"Yeah," I said. "Okay."

I watched as Allison's attacker turned her around and pressed her face against her front door. Again, he whispered into her ear. I could hear her crying now, nodding her head slowly. Her attacker released his grip. Allison kept her face against the glass door. Her attacker walked over to me and quickly kicked me in the stomach.

"Don't" he whispered, "even think of following us."

By the time I straightened myself up, both attackers were sprinting toward the avenue. I got to my feet and limped over to Allison. I touched her on the shoulder and she screamed.

"It's okay," I said, my own voice just above a whisper. "It's me. They're gone."

She turned toward me, still crying. "Oh my god, Ray."

"I know," I said. "It's over now." I leaned over and picked her purse off the ground. *Why hadn't they taken it?* I gave it to Allison. "Let's go inside."

She took her keys out and opened both sets of doors. When we were safely inside, I took out my cell phone.

"What are you doing?" Allison asked.

"Calling nine-one-one," I said.

"They said . . . he said, no cops."

I punched in the three numbers anyway. "They always say that, Allison. Why the hell didn't they take your purse?"

She stepped over and grabbed the phone out of my hand before I could make the call.

"They weren't after my fucking purse, Ray."

"Then what . . . what did he whisper in your ear?"

"He was . . ." She started sobbing again. I put my arms around her. "He was telling me," she began again, "to stop writing about Dougie."

"About Dougie?" I said. "Why the hell—?"

"I don't know, Ray," she said, her anger coming back. "I would've asked but I had something real pointy pressed against my neck."

I pulled her close again. "I know. I'm sorry. I was just thinking out loud. I mean, who the fuck were those two?"

"Just take me upstairs. Please."

"We need to call the cops."

"I know," she said, pressing the button for the elevator then looking over at the front door. "Let's just do it upstairs, okay?"

"Okay."

The door to the elevator opened and we stepped in. She pressed the number for her floor, her hand shaking. In this light, I could see a small wound just under her chin. She got a look at herself in the elevator mirror and gasped.

"Shit. I'm bleeding."

I took her hand. "We'll take care of that upstairs, too."

"Okay. Thanks." And then she collapsed.

"You sure you don't want us to call an EMT, ma'am?" the taller of the two cops—his name tag read JOHNSON—asked, looking at the Band-Aid I had just placed over the wound on Allison's neck. "They can take a look at that."

"No," she said. "I'm good."

She reached up and touched her fingers to the Band-Aid. With her other hand, she squeezed my left knee. We were seated on her love seat. Officer Johnson sat in the recliner, while his partner looked down at the street where the assault had taken place.

"Nobody else on the street, huh?" he asked, still looking out the window.

"It's a quiet block," Allison said. "That's why I moved here." She caught the irony of her words and laughed. "I thought I'd be safe."

"Nah." The cop at the window turned and walked toward us. His name tag *also* read JOHNSON. *I bet that was good for more than a few chuckles back at the precinct.* "My sister just moved into the city," he said. "From the Island. I told her make sure you get a place on an avenue, good and busy. These quiet side streets . . ."

"And nothing was taken from your person?" the first Johnson asked.

"No," Allison said. "I told you. He threatened me and told me to stop writing about Douglas Lee."

"The boy who was murdered?" the second Johnson asked.

"Yes."

"And you never saw their faces?"

"No. I told you—" She turned to me. "Why do they keep asking me the same questions, Ray?"

"Victims—" *Bad choice of words.* "People who've been involved in assaults like this sometimes remember more details as they start to calm down. You'd be surprised what people remember ten minutes after they say they couldn't recall a thing."

"And you," First Johnson said to me, "you're a teacher?"

"Yes."

Second Johnson came over and took his partner's notebook. He studied it for a few seconds. "What'd you say your last name was, sir?"

I was waiting for them to catch on. "Donne," I said. "First name, Raymond."

I'm not sure who made the connection first, but both Johnsons let out a "holy shit!" at the same time.

"You're Chief Donne's nephew."

"Since birth," I said.

First Johnson stood up as if being called to attention. "We should really get a supervising officer down here."

"No," I said. "We're fine. We don't need any special treatment." I looked at their worried faces. "And if anybody asks—and I doubt they will— I'll tell them the both of you were more than thorough and professional."

That eased the tension in their faces. Second Johnson gave First Johnson his notebook back and they exchanged glances. They weren't quite sure of their next move, so I decided to help them out. I stood up. Slowly.

"Thank you both," I said. "Officers . . . Johnson and Johnson." I shook my head and allowed myself a small laugh. "Sorry. How much shit do they give you back at the station over that?"

"Quite a bit, sir," Second Johnson said. "Lieutenant's got a real good sense of humor. But we're used to it."

"I hope so." I shook both their hands. "Thanks again, guys."

"Yes," Allison said from the love seat. "Thank you, officers."

Both of them actually reached up, tipped their caps, and said, "Ma'am."

I walked them to the door and, after they left, made sure to secure the three locks Allison had there. I went back over and sat next to her. She put her arm around me, and we both leaned into the softness of the couch.

"What happens now?" she asked.

"They file their reports, see if any crimes of a similar nature were—"

"Similar nature?" She practically jumped to her feet. "How many assaults are there going to be where the victim was warned to stop working on a news story, Ray?"

I leaned forward but stayed on the couch. "You're right," I said, keeping my voice level. "But it's standard operating procedure in a case like this. Nothing'll come of it, but they gotta check."

"And in the meantime . . ."

I stood up. "In the meantime, you go to work, live your life."

"Always looking over my shoulder? Scared to go home?"

"Allison," I said, "what would your reaction have been if I said to stay at home, don't go out until the cops catch those two?"

She thought about that. "You're right. I would've been pissed and accused you of being overprotective."

"That sounds like you."

She smiled, stepped over to me, and wrapped her arms around me. "Sorry," she whispered. "I'm just angry and scared."

"I know," I said, then came up with an idea. "How about you commute from my place for a couple of days? It's a quick shot by subway into work."

She released me and held me at arm's length. "You know," she said, "for a tough guy, you can be pretty thoughtful."

"Don't let that get around." I kissed her. "Now go pack. It's getting late."

Chapter 28

IT OCCURRED TO ME AS I LAY in bed, my arm around Allison with the early-morning sun sneaking through the curtains, that this was the first Sunday in a while I'd awakened with a woman next to me. I tried to remember the last time that had happened and time-traveled all the way back to my college days, before I had joined the police. I made a mental note to do this more often.

I slowly removed my arm, rolled off the bed, and went to the kitchen to put on a pot of coffee. There was nothing much in the fridge, so I figured I'd better head down to the avenue and do a little quick shopping. Back in the bedroom, I was slipping on a pair of jeans when Allison turned over.

"Leaving me so soon?" she said, her eyes barely open. "Typical male."

"I'm gonna run down and get some bagels and lox and the Sunday *Times*."

"Oooh, the competition."

I forgot about that. "You want me to pick up your paper, too?"

"Nah. I see enough of that at work. Besides, the Sunday *Times* rocks." She sat up. "Wanna do the crossword together?"

"I don't think I'm ready for that level of commitment."

She threw a pillow at me. "Just hurry back, okay?"

"There's coffee in the kitchen."

"Thanks. Go."

I went.

When I got back, Allison was at the kitchen window, drinking coffee and checking out the skyline. She had put on one of my Brooklyn Brewery T-shirts and a pair of boxers. I cleared my throat so as not to frighten her. She turned and raised her mug toward me.

"You score another two points for the coffee," she said. "Where'd you get it?"

I held up the bag of breakfast. "Same place I got these," I said, moving into the kitchen. "Manhattan does not have a monopoly on primo coffee and good food, you know. That"—I pointed at her cup—"is from Hawaii."

"Impressive," she said, turning to face the city. "This view is to die for, Raymond."

I put the bag down on the table and came up behind her. Wrapping my arms around her waist, I said, "Yeah. I could stay here all day."

"I was thinking . . ."

"Yeah?"

"How did those two last night know where I live?"

"That's a good question," I said. "My best guess would be they followed you home from work one day."

"How did they know when I—we—would be getting home last night?"

"More than likely, they followed us from your place to the restaurant and back."

She put her coffee down on the countertop and turned into me.

"That's fucking creepy," she said. "I'm being stalked?"

"*We,*" I said. "Last night, *we* were being stalked."

"Doesn't make it any less creepy."

"No, it doesn't."

"What do we do now?"

"I think we're doing it," I said. "You stay here for . . . a while, and we go on with our lives. Tomorrow, you go to the paper and I go to school. We'll just be a lot more aware of what's going on around us."

I pulled her in close and hugged her. After about a minute, I said, "It's all going to work out."

"What the hell does that mean?" she asked.

"I don't know. My mom used to say it a lot."

She snorted and broke the hug.

"I could really go for that breakfast now."

"Go start on the paper," I said. "I'll bring everything into the living room."

"Score another point for you, Raymond."

"What, exactly, do I get with all these points?"

"Let's see how breakfast goes," she said. "Then we'll talk."

Less than an hour later, I was clearing our plates off the coffee table. Allison was leaning back on the couch, the *Times Magazine* up against her thighs, and tapping her forehead with a pencil.

"Five letters," she said. "'Mysterious award.' Starts with an *R*."

I popped the last piece of bagel into my mouth and followed it with a sip of coffee. "Raven."

"What? Like the bird?"

"Like the poem by Poe. The Raven is a big award in the mystery writing biz."

"Mystery writers give awards?"

"Hey," I said. "Journalists do."

"Careful, tough guy. You don't want to start *losing* points, do ya?"

"Not yet." I got all the dishes into the sink, all the leftovers into the fridge, and all the garbage into the trash. I went back into the living room and sat on the couch next to Allison. I closed my eyes. "I'm a raven, you know."

"Excuse me?"

"The kid from Dougie's school? Elliot?" I said. "With the bird-watching club?"

"What about him?"

"He said I was a raven."

"Was he trying to compliment you?"

"Ravens are smart, playful, and enjoy starting trouble."

"Hmmm," Allison said. "Insightful kid. I wonder what kind of bird I am."

"You," I said, finding her thigh with my hand, "are more in the *Canidae* family."

"I'm a dog?"

"I was thinking, more like a fox."

She tossed the magazine onto the coffee table, lifted her other thigh, and straddled me. She put her mouth next to my ear.

"Wanna redeem some of those points now?" she whispered.

"Oh, yeah," I said, slipping my hands under the T-shirt that, as far as I was concerned, now belonged to her. "Absolutely."

She took my ear into her mouth and gently tugged on it with her teeth. I ran my fingernails down her back to just above the boxers. There's something about that spot that kills me. Allison moved her head until our mouths met. They were happy to see each other. She broke off the kiss and leaned back. She pulled up the bottom of the T-shirt and was about to take it off, when a thought crossed her face. She turned and faced my curtainless window.

"Nobody can see in, right?"

"Nope. We're the highest building around."

"Good."

She removed the shirt and went back to kissing me. I slowly ran my hands up her sides, and I believe we both "ooohed" at the same time. Then the phone rang.

"You wanna get that?" she asked.

"What do you think?"

"Good answer."

After four rings, the machine picked up.

"Ray? This is Elliot Henry Finch. I have something that might be of interest to you regarding . . ."

"Shit," I said to Allison. "I should get that. It's the kid from Dougie's school."

"The bird kid?"

"Yeah."

"Okay." She got off me and slipped the T-shirt back on. "Don't be too long."

"I won't be." I got to the phone and picked it up. "Elliot," I said. "It's Ray. Sorry. I just got in and I was screening. What's up?"

"Screening?" he asked, obviously not familiar with the concept.

"Yeah. It's when you let the machine pick up, the caller starts to talk, and then you can decide whether to pick up."

"So, you are deceiving the person calling you into believing you are not at home . . . and then you either pick up the phone or you do not, depending on whether the caller is someone you wish to speak to at that moment."

"Yes."

There was silence from the other end for a few seconds. I looked over at the beautiful female on my couch as Elliot pondered the situation.

"So," he finally said, "I should be flattered."

"You should be," I said. "You got through the screen."

"Even though you deceived me?"

"I didn't know it was you, Elliot. When I did, I picked up."

"Thank you, Ray."

"You're welcome. So, what's up?" *And please make it quick.*

"I am on Finch's Landing, as I am every day at this time."

"Okay . . ."

"And I am looking at something that may be of interest to you."

"What is it, Elliot?"

"Are you aware Jack Quinn is no longer hospitalized?"

"Yes."

"Are you also aware he had planned a trip abroad?"

"No, Elliot. I wasn't. How do you know this?"

"Jack posted a message on my site this morning. He wrote he was happy to be out of the hospital, but disappointed he would have to cancel his trip to Beijing until further notice."

"Beijing?" I said.

"Yes," Elliot said. "According to the post, he was to leave Tuesday evening."

It was still a few weeks until the public schools would break for Christmas, but that was the joke about private schools: the more money you pay, the fewer days you go.

"Are you guys going on break already?"

"No, Ray. Which is part of the reason I believed you would be interested."

"The other part being . . ."

"Jack Quinn was a friend of Dougie and Paulie."

"Can you read the whole post to me, Elliot?"

"Yes." He cleared his throat. "'Thanks for all the calls and cards, folks. Glad to be awake and back in my own crib.' What does that mean, Ray? 'My own crib'?"

"It's street talk, Elliot. It means his apartment."

"Oh." Again, he cleared his throat. "'Missed most of you all. Disappointed I won't be going to Beijing again Tuesday night, but my travel buddy is gone, and I don't wanna be flying solo to that part of the world, especially after one A.M. Taking a few more days off from school. See ya when I see ya. Jack.' That is all he wrote, Ray."

Cool and mysterious kid, this Jack Quinn. Too much of each for my taste. He was doing nothing to ease my bias against private school kids.

"Ray?"

"Yeah," I said. "Sorry, Elliot. I was thinking of the message. Trying to make some sense of it."

"Maybe," Elliot said, "it does not make much sense. According to his sister's message a few days ago, Jack was in bad shape. Now that he is feeling better does not necessarily mean that he is thinking . . . normally."

"You've got a good point there," I said. "Anyway, thanks for calling."

"You are welcome," he said. "Will you be seeing Edgar this evening?"

"I don't think so. Why?"

"He is the friend you were speaking about the first time we met, right?"

"Yes," I admitted. "You do remind me of him."

"After meeting him yesterday, I will take that as a compliment, Ray."

"That's how I meant it, Elliot. I'll talk to you soon."

"Why?"

Gotta choose your words very carefully around this kid, I remembered.

"No reason," I said. "I just meant I'd like to talk to you again."

"I would enjoy that as well, Raymond."

"Good-bye, Elliot."

"Oh," he added. "About that screening thing you do?"

"Yeah?"

"You really should look into caller ID."

"Thanks, Elliot. I'll do that."

"Good-bye, Ray."

I put the phone back, and Allison gave me a weird look.

"What was that about?" she asked.

"I need to get caller ID." The look got weirder. "He wanted to tell me about a strange post Jack Quinn made on his site." I told her about the post and Finch's Landing.

"Cute," she said. "Any idea what Jack meant by canceling his trip to Beijing?"

"None at all. But like Elliot just said, the kid's just come out of the hospital. How much sense is he supposed to make?"

"Good point."

"Now," I said, walking over to her and lifting her shirt. "Where were we?"

She raised her arms above her head. "An even better point, Mr. Donne."

Having never made it to the bedroom, we were intertwined on my couch. She was still sitting on me, and neither one of us felt like moving. Our breathing seemed to be synchronized, and we both had our eyes closed. That's when the phone rang again.

"Wow," Allison said. "You always this popular on Sunday?"

"Not for a long time now."

She gave me a playful slap on the shoulder as the machine picked up.

"Mr. Donne," the voice on the other end said. I recognized it right away.

"That's Dougie's mom," I said to Allison.

She rolled off my lap. "Pick it up."

I jumped off the couch and got to the phone. "Mrs. Lee. How are you?"

"Not so good at the moment, I'm afraid," she said. She sounded tired and confused. "Not so good at all. I'm sorry to call you on a Sunday, Mr. Donne."

"That's not a problem, Mrs. Lee. What's wrong?"

Silence, except for the sound of breathing.

"Mrs. Lee?"

"I'm sorry," she said. A little more silence. "Is it possible for you to come over to the house, Mr. Donne?" She didn't sound good at all.

"Are you okay, Mrs. Lee? Do you need me to call nine-one-one?"

"Oh, no," she said quickly. "Nothing like that. Just you. Please."

I looked at the clock on my DVR. It was just before two.

"I'll be right there, Mrs. Lee."

"Thank you, Mr. Donne." She hung up.

Allison pulled her T-shirt on and gave me a concerned look. "Is she okay?"

"She didn't sound like it." I went into my bedroom. "I'm going over there. You can stay here, finish the puzzle, watch TV, whatever."

She stepped into the room as I was dressing. She had the boxers back on.

"Why don't I come with you?"

"Thanks, but she asked for me, and she didn't sound like she was in the mood for too much company."

"Okay," she said, not happy with my answer. "When will you be back?"

"In time to take you downstairs for Chinese food."

"All right." She stepped over and gave me a hug. "Be careful, okay?"

"I'm just going over to Mrs. Lee's, Allison."

"And last night we were just going to my apartment."

I nodded and hugged her back. "Gotcha."

When I got down to the street, I found Uncle Ray in front of my apartment. He was standing outside the door, cigar in his mouth, studying the buzzers.

"Number five," I said as I exited the building.

"I'd probably know that," he answered, "if you had names next to the numbers. Or—God forbid—I were ever invited by."

"Consider yours an open invitation, Uncle Ray. What's up?"

He took the cigar out of his mouth and smiled. "'What's up?'" he repeated. "That's good, Nephew. Why the hell didn't you call me last night?"

"It was a Saturday night," I said. "I had a date."

"I know. With Allison Rogers, the journalist."

"How'd you know—? Who called you?" I asked. "Johnson or Johnson?"

"Their CO called me. Captain Doherty. Do I have to explain to you again that simply by virtue of our sharing a name, you cannot have official contact with the police in this city—especially if you're assaulted—without my knowing about it?"

"I didn't want to make a big deal out of it."

"You," he said, "didn't want me knowing you still had your nose in Murcer's case. Still hanging around with the girl from the press."

"It was a date, Uncle Ray. It had nothing to do with the case."

"Until the assault, you mean."

I noticed his town car parked across the street with no one in the driver's seat.

"Where's Smitty?" I asked.

"Went to have a smoke."

"Can't he smoke in the car?"

"I don't like people smoking in my car."

I looked down at his cigar. "Really?"

"I don't like *other* people smoking in my car. And don't change the subject. Why are you still hanging around with the reporter, Raymond?"

"We were on a date, Uncle Ray. It's what people do when they like each other."

He took a drag off his cigar and let it out slowly. "You both okay?" he asked.

"Yeah. Thanks."

He took the rest of the cigar, pressed the lit end into the brick wall, and tossed it into the street.

"Take me upstairs and make me a cup of coffee," he said. "I gotta be somewhere in an hour and don't want to sit in the car. We need to talk some more about this."

He stepped toward the door. I put my hand on the door handle and said, "I'm just on my way out, Uncle Ray." I realized I couldn't tell him I was going to see Mrs. Lee. "How about we talk tomorrow?"

He looked me in the eyes for about five seconds and smiled. "You got the girl up there, don'tcha, Ray?"

How the hell— "How the hell did you know that?"

"You got that look in your eyes. Like you just got laid, and it's gonna happen again as soon as you get back. You're screwing the lady reporter. Jesus, Ray. You can't find a nice schoolteacher?"

I shook my head and smiled. "We thought it would be safer if she stayed with me for a few days," I said.

"I bet you did, Nephew." He took me by the elbow. "Where you going? I'll have Smitty swing you on by."

"That's okay," I said. "It's a quick shot on the subway."

"On a Sunday? You can wait a half hour for the G train. Let Smitty take you. It'll save you time and get you back to your girlfriend that much quicker."

"She's not my— Thanks anyway, Uncle Ray. I'd rather take the train."

"You'd rather," he said, "not have me know where you're going."

Someday I'll put one past my uncle. Today was not that day.

"I'll be fine, Uncle Ray. Let's talk in the next few days."

He grabbed me by the elbow and held me this time. With his eyes fixed on mine, he said, "You stay out of this case, Ray. You've been lucky so far. Luck runs out, kiddo."

"I'm out, Uncle Ray. I just got some errands to run." I gently removed his hand from my elbow. I was surprised he let me. "Listen, I got ten days off coming up in a few weeks. Why don't you and Reeny come over for dinner? You can even bring Smitty."

"That's cute," he said. "I'll talk it over with Reeny. She's always bugging me to take her into the city anyway."

"Good. Let's talk this week and set it up. We'll do an early dinner, and then you guys can hit Manhattan."

"You gonna bring your girlfriend?"

"If we're still seeing each other, I'll invite her. I'm sure she'll be completely charmed."

"Keep spreading it, Raymond. Pretty soon you'll be up to your knees in it."

"I hear you, Uncle Ray."

"I hope you do, Nephew. I truly hope you do."

"Thank you for coming so quickly," Mrs. Lee said as she opened the door.

We stepped inside and, when we got to the living room, I said, "What is it, Mrs. Lee? Did something happen?"

"No," she said. "Well, I guess something *did* happen, but I don't . . ."

I pointed to the couch. "Would you rather sit and tell me?"

"No," she said, a touch of determination in her voice now. "I need to show you something, and the sooner I get it over with, the better." She took a deep breath. "It's in Douglas's room."

She started off in that direction, so I followed. The door to Dougie's room was shut. Mrs. Lee turned to me and took another breath. She put her hand on the doorknob, turned it, and stepped inside. Again, I was right behind her.

She flicked on the light switch. The room had been straightened up since the last time I was in there. Everything had been picked up off the floor, and the bed had been completely stripped.

"I've been cleaning up," Mrs. Lee said.

"I can see that."

"I'm donating everything to Goodwill. Not the pillows, of course, or the stuff on the walls, but everything else." She paused. "I was told it would help."

"That sounds like good advice," I said.

"It was," she agreed, then she stepped over to the closet and slid open the door. "Until I started in on the closet and Douglas's clothes."

I looked into the closet but still had no idea what she was talking about. "What's wrong with the closet?"

She reached into the pocket of one of Dougie's jackets, then handed me a photograph of Dougie and Alexis Quinn, embracing, nose-to-nose. It certainly looked like they were more than just acquaintances.

"I'm not saying there's anything wrong with that," Mrs. Lee said. "It's just, Douglas never mentioned any girls to me, and I have no idea who that is."

"Jack Quinn's twin sister," I said. "I met her outside the hospital the other day."

"Were they serious?"

"Not according to what she told me."

Now that I thought about it, Alexis probably didn't want her relationship with Dougie to become common knowledge. An Upper West Side white girl with a black boy from Williamsburg might play well with their friends, but from what Mr. Rivera had told me, I doubted Mr. Quinn would approve.

"Is this why you called me over, Mrs. Lee?"

She shook her head and reached into another jacket pocket. Again, she handed me what she had pulled out.

"That," she said. "That's what is wrong, Mr. Donne."

It was an amber prescription pill bottle. The label had Paulie Sher-man's name on it and said the container originally had ninety doses of a drug I was quite familiar with as a special ed guy. I opened the bottle. There were five white pills left.

"I don't know what Douglas was doing with that," Mrs. Lee said. "He was not taking any medications. Why would Paulie give him that? I don't even know that doctor or that pharmacy. They're in Manhattan." She pointed at the pill bottle. "Do you know what drug that is?"

I nodded. "If the label's correct," I said, "it's one of the most widely prescribed medications in the nation, used to treat Attention Deficit Hy-peractivity Disorder."

Mrs. Lee gave me a blank look.

"ADHD," I said.

"Oh, my Lord. Douglas was not taking any medications, Mr. Donne. He was never diagnosed with anything like that. After he left you, Upper West Academy did a full evaluation. They never said anything about atten-tion problems."

But, I remembered, Mr. Rivera had told me both Paulie and Jack were on medication for ADHD. I looked at the label again. "Did you call anybody about this?

"No," she said. "I found that and called you."

My curiosity started to rise and, before it got me in trouble again, I said, "I think you need to call Detective Murcer, Mrs. Lee. This is some-thing he needs to know about."

Instead of agreeing with me, she got a look on her face. I waited.

"There's more," she finally said.

"Okay . . ."

She pointed inside the closet. "In there," she said. "All the way to the right on the floor. In the shoebox."

"I have your permission to go in there?" *Cop instinct,* I thought. Getting the owner's okay before conducting a search, preventing some smart-ass lawyer from declaring the evidence obtained from said search inadmissible. The proverbial fruit from the poisonous tree. *Good thing I wasn't a cop anymore.*

"Yes," Mrs. Lee said. "Please."

I stepped into the closet and slid all of Dougie's hanging clothes to the left. I moved to the right, bent over, and picked up the shoebox. It was heavier than I thought it would be. I took two backward steps out of the closet.

"It was under a bunch of his sports jerseys," Mrs. Lee explained.

I opened the box and immediately realized why Mrs. Lee was so upset. Inside was a gallon-sized baggie filled with blue-and-white capsules. I guessed somewhere between two and three hundred of them.

"Wow," I said, because I didn't want to say "holy shit" in front of Mrs. Lee.

"Yes," she said. "You can see why I called *you*, Mr. Donne."

I nodded. "I *can* see why you called me, Mrs. Lee. But I gotta tell you, this is even more reason why you should call Detective Murcer."

She shook her head. "So he can have more reason to believe that Douglas was involved in drugs?"

Good point. But the shoebox I held was proof Dougie *was* involved with drugs. How, I didn't know. But in some way.

"I'm not sure what you want me to do, Mrs. Lee. This is pretty serious stuff."

I opened the baggie, took one capsule out, and rolled it between my fingers. There was a four-digit number, followed by two letters, printed on it.

"Why would Douglas have those, Mr. Donne?"

"That's a real good question, Mrs. Lee. You obviously . . ." *Of course she didn't.* "Did Dougie ever . . ." *Of course he didn't. . . . Okay, time for a cop question.* "Was there *anything*—now that you are aware of what Dougie had in his closet—that would make you believe he was involved with drugs or drug use in any way?"

She shook her head. "Like what, Mr. Donne?"

"Was he getting a lot of phone calls at night he didn't want you hearing? Did he have more money than he should have?"

As Mrs. Lee listened to my questions, her eyes filled with tears. "Now you sound like that detective when he first came over here."

"Because," I said, "these are the kinds of questions Murcer would ask if he knew about Dougie's stash." *Nice choice of words, Ray.* "If he knew this stuff was here."

Her eyes overflowed, and the tears ran down both cheeks. *It looked like she was real glad she had called me now.* I reached out and put my hand on her elbow.

"I'm sorry, Mrs. Lee," I said. "But the truth is, Douglas was into something, and he was doing a pretty good job hiding it from you."

"I know," she said through the tears. "I know." She wiped away the tears with the back of her hand. "Like I told you that day, he'd been having trouble sleeping and he was snapping at me a bit. I just thought it was Douglas being a teenager."

"These," I said, rattling the pill bottle, "are stimulants. That's why they work so well reducing the symptoms of ADHD. If Dougie were taking them, that's most likely why he was having trouble sleeping. They've also been known to have other *adverse* effects on kids' behavior. Loss of appetite. Mood swings." I looked at the single blue-and-white capsule I held. "These other ones, I don't have a clue."

She nodded. "What I don't know is . . . what do I do now?"

"You're telling me you didn't call anyone else about this? A friend? Someone from the church? Dougie's uncle?"

"Oh, no," she said. "I didn't know who else to call."

"Okay. Good." *No, Ray. Not good.* "I mean, for right now, no one else knows about this except you and me. It buys us some time to think."

"Think about what?"

"What to do with this," I said, shaking the baggie filled with capsules. "I honestly don't see how we can keep this from Murcer." She was about to say something, but I kept going. "For now," I said, "we say nothing to anybody."

"Okay." She sounded relieved.

I took a few more capsules out of the baggie and put them, loose, in my pocket. Then I zippered up the baggie and put it back in the shoebox before returning it to its original hiding place in the corner of the closet floor. Then I put the amber pill bottle into my other pocket.

"Let me think on this, Mrs. Lee. The first thing that comes to mind is contacting the doctor who prescribed these pills and the pharmacist who filled the order. I can do that tomorrow, after school."

"Okay," she said, nodding her approval. "Then what?"

"Honestly?" I said. "I have no idea. But I have to tell you, if I find out Dougie was involved in any ille—*questionable*—activity, I am going to have to let Detective Murcer know." Before she could protest I added, "It'll help him find whoever killed Dougie, Mrs. Lee. There's no way this is not connected."

I watched as she struggled with that concept. I had basically just told her Dougie had probably been killed over drugs. Just what the cops told her the morning she'd lost her son. Again I found myself wondering if she was sorry she had called me.

"Okay," she whispered. "If that's what it takes to find out who killed my boy, so be it." She looked me dead in the eyes. "But I will tell you, Mr. Donne. My hand to God." She raised her right hand above her head. "My Douglas was not dealing drugs. Whatever reason he had these pills, and the marijuana they found on his body, he was not dealing."

"You're preaching to the choir, Mrs. Lee," I said, putting my hand on her arm. "I just hope I'm not the only one singing."

Chapter 29

NOW, WAKING UP NEXT TO A woman on a *Monday* morning—I was pretty sure that had *never* happened to me before. Allison got up first and went right to the bathroom. As she showered and put herself together for the day, I made a pot of coffee and took out some of yesterday's bagels. I chose some clothes for the day and jumped in the shower as soon as she got out. By seven thirty, we were finally doing something together: drinking coffee. I was on my own when it came to the bagels.

"I'm not an early-morning eater," she explained. "For me, it's coffee until about eleven o'clock."

"That's not a real healthy way to start your day."

"Yeah, well, whattaya gonna do, right?" She finished her coffee and placed the cup in the sink. "You still planning on heading uptown after school?"

"Yeah."

When I got home last night, I showed Allison what Mrs. Lee had discovered in her son's closet, then told her what I was planning on doing about it.

"I figure I'll hit the pharmacist first," I said. "Then the doctor's."

"And you still don't think you should call Detective Murcer about this?"

"I will call him. Just not yet."

"Because you want to know something before he does?"

"Because I promised I wouldn't until we know what those capsules are."

"Same thing, Raymond." She went into the living room. "You want to get into some sort of pissing contest with him? Or maybe you just need to prove to yourself you can still do the cop thing."

I followed after her. "Where the hell is this coming from? Haven't we both been bending the rules just a little bit, Allison?"

"Yes, Ray. We have." Her eyes filled up with tears. "And then Saturday night happened. Or have you forgotten about that?" She took a deep breath. "We could have been killed."

I stepped forward and put my arms around her. There were a lot of things I wanted to say right then, but I uncharacteristically kept my mouth shut and just held her. We stayed that way for a few minutes.

"I'm sorry," she finally said. "I'm just scared, and I don't like being scared."

"No one does," I said. "Look, I'm just going to head uptown, talk to a pharmacist and a doctor, and see what I can find out. If I find out anything worth going to Murcer about, I will. That's a promise."

"Okay," she said. "We just need to be real careful, Ray."

"And we are." I let go of her. "What about you? What does your day look like?"

"I'm gonna try and stay in the office all day." She reached down and picked up her bag. "I have to start putting my notes together into something resembling a narrative. I'll try calling the Quinns, see if I can get a comment or some info on Jack. I'm not buying that food poisoning story. And then"—she paused—"I'm going to try and set up an interview with Dougie's mom."

I wasn't too keen on that idea. "Why do you have to bother her?"

"I'm not *bothering* her, Ray. I need to interview her for the story." She held her hand up, predicting my interruption. "A lot of what I know comes from you. I appreciate your help, but I'm not going to print hearsay just because I think the source is kinda cute and he lets me wear his T-shirts to bed."

"It's as good a reason as any other."

"Better than most, actually, but I've got rules I have to follow."

"You're right," I said. "Just go easy on her."

"Aw, gee, Ray." She smacked my arm. "And I was gonna bring my garden hose and stun gun."

"That's not funny," I said, fighting back a smile.

"Yes, it is. You just like being the only wiseass in the room."

"I told you, baby." I pulled her into a hug. "I'm a raven."

Even ravens sometimes have to go to work.

"Yo, Mr. D, I'm telling you, I didn't go nowheres near her desk. I was sitting, doing my work. Why I wanna take her cell phone, anyway?" He reached into his pocket. "I got my own phone, don't need hers."

"That," I said, pointing at Alberto's phone, "should be in your book bag or locker and turned off. If Amanda followed that rule, we wouldn't be having this conversation."

"That's what I'm saying." He shut the phone off and put it in his bag. "I don't need her bootleg phone. I got my own."

I've learned over the years that kids who steal from other kids usually have a reason why they *didn't* steal from other kids. And it's almost always the same reason: "I don't need to steal her fill-in-the-blank." Kids who are unjustly accused don't usually tell you *why* they didn't do it. They just say they didn't do it. That's really the only answer an innocent kid should come up with.

"So," I said to Alberto, "if I were to go through your book bag right now, I wouldn't find Amanda's cell phone?"

"Nope." He reached down, picked up his bag, and zipped it open for me to see inside. "You can look, Mr. D. Ain't no phone in here 'cept mine's."

I got up and walked around my desk to where Alberto was sitting. I made a show of looking into his bag, even though we both knew what I'd find. Or rather, what I wouldn't.

"Okay," I said. "What if we were to check your locker?"

"You can do that?"

Bingo. "Yeah," I said. "I can do that."

"Don't you need, like, a . . . search warrant or something?"

Just like the punks at the bus stop, I thought. *They all know their rights.* I liked Alberto. He struck me as the kind of kid who saw an opportunity, took it, and now wishes he could go back and undo what he'd done. He was no punk, and part of my job, the way I saw it, was to prevent him from becoming one. But I needed his help.

"No, Alberto. I do not need a search warrant. I can search your locker anytime I want for any reason I want. Search warrants are for cops and"—I paused for dramatic effect—"I don't think we need to get them involved. For *now*."

Alberto zipped up his bag and placed it back at his feet. He kept his eyes away from mine.

"So here's what we're going to do," I said. "I'm real busy for the next few periods." I looked at my watch. "I'll pick you up from your seventh-period class, and we'll go to your locker together and make sure the phone didn't somehow end up there. But," I said as I went behind him and put my hands on his shoulders, "if Amanda's phone is found and returned to her before seventh period, I'll obviously have no need to search your locker. How does that sound, Alberto?"

He nodded. "That sounds cool, Mr. D. That's fair."

"Good. Now, what do you have this period?"

"Lunch."

"Go to lunch. I'll check in with Amanda at the end of sixth period."

"Okay," Alberto said as he stood up. "Cool. Thanks, Mr. D."

"For what?"

He had no answer for that. "Just thanks."

He left my office and hurried off to lunch. Or maybe his locker. I was sure I'd find out later. My phone rang.

"You have a visitor," Mary informed me.

"Who is it?"

"A Mr. Smith," she said. Then she lowered her voice. "But he doesn't look like a Smith to me."

"I'll be right down."

It took less than a minute to make it to the office. Except for Mary, the room was empty. I gave her a quizzical look.

" 'Mr. Smith,' " she said, "has asked that you meet him outside."

"Outside?" I asked. "What's up with that?"

"I'm just the messenger, Mr. Donne. Why don't you run back up and get your jacket. It's cold out there."

"He say what he wanted?"

"Just to talk to you. Then he said he'd meet you outside. He didn't seem too comfortable waiting around the office."

"What'd he look like?"

"Raymond," Mary said, as if that were one question too many. "He's right outside. Why don't you go see for yourself?"

"Thanks, Mary."

I decided not to run back upstairs for my coat. If this Smith guy wanted to talk, he could do it inside where it was warm. I went out through the set of double doors and was greeted by a burst of cold air. There was nobody waiting on the steps, but somebody in a big, puffy, black coat was leaning against the metal railing, his back to me. As I walked down the steps and over to him, I said, "Mr. Smith?"

The guy turned. It took me a second.

"Tio," I said, not even close to hiding the surprise in my voice. "What's up?"

"Teacher Man," he said, taking his right hand out of his pocket and offering it to me. "Just wanted to drop by and say *gracias*."

"Okay." I shook his hand. "For what?"

He smiled. "For the heads-up on Jerome Dexter."

"Oh, yeah." I got a bit worried now. "How'd that go?"

"Me and a coupla my boys had a face-to-face with the young Mr. Dexter," he said. "Made it clear to him it would be in his best interest to start rockin' some colors other than the Family's. Told him to trash them beads, too."

I buried my hands in my pockets. I noticed two boys across the street wearing what looked like the same jacket as Tio. They had their hands in their pockets also, and Saints caps on their heads.

"And . . ." I said.

Tio smiled. "And that's all, folks. For a kid who don't seem all that bright, he got wise to our position pretty quick."

I lowered my voice. "You didn't hurt him?"

"Teacher Man. I made you a promise and I kept it." The smile grew. "But we made it quite clear to the boy that if we heard he was wearing our colors again, the next conversation would be a bit more . . . nonverbal. Know what I'm sayin'?"

"I do," I said. "You couldn't have told me this inside? Where it's warm?"

He shook his head. "I ain't real comfortable in school buildings since I dropped out. Don't like the way they smell, y'know?"

I didn't, but just nodded. The wind was starting to pick up. "Is that it?"

"Nah, man. I didn't come all this way just to say thanks. Coulda done that over the phone."

I guessed this was where I was supposed to ask what he *did* come all this way to say. So I did.

"Just wanted to let you know," Tio said, "I owe you one."

Really? The top guy in a gang owes me one? I couldn't wait to tell my mother.

"That's okay, Tio," I said. "I'm just glad you took care of it the way you did."

"Nah. That was some good lookin' out you did. Way I run things, I don't need no knucklehead wannabe out there causing trouble. You gave me a righteous heads-up and I owe you. I don't owe too many people. So when I do, I want them to hear it from my face. Not over the phone, feel me?"

"I feel you, Tio." I didn't know what else to say except, "I'll let you know if I need something. Right now, I need to head back into work."

He took his hand out again and we shook. He pulled me in closer to him.

"I ain't fronting, Teacher Man. You need something, you let me know."

"I'll do that. Thanks for coming by."

"You got it," he said. He turned around and raised his hand to say good-bye.

I watched as his two boys crossed the street, and the trio walked away from the school. I went back inside, freezing, but with a stupid grin on my face.

Three fifteen. School was out and the kids were gone. It was a bit too cold for them to hang around the building, so clearing the block didn't take all that much time. Not a bad day. No fights, only one kid caught cutting, and Amanda's cell phone had made a miraculous reappearance. I hoped Alberto had learned from this.

Chapter 30

I TOOK THE L TRAIN to the 1 train, then walked the three blocks from the Seventy-ninth Street stop to the pharmacy that had filled Paulie's prescription. It was probably one of the last independent pharmacies in the area, which meant I wouldn't be able to do my grocery shopping, use an ATM, or get my digital photos processed. What I was hoping to do was find out if the pills in the bottle were what the label said they were. I stepped up to the register and asked the girl if I could speak with the pharmacist.

"And what is this in regards to?" she asked.

I pulled out the amber bottle, shook it, and gave her the truth. "I'd like to know what these pills are."

She nodded knowingly and excused herself as she went to the back room. She returned less than a minute later followed by an older man, who wore a light blue pharmacist shirt and half-frame reading glasses. His shirt had the name of the pharmacy stitched in red just over his name, WARREN. He motioned for me to meet him at the end of the counter by the condoms and breath mints.

"How can I help you?" Warren asked.

I showed him the pill bottle. "I was hoping you could tell me what these are."

He took the container, pushed his glasses farther up the bridge of his nose, and checked out the label. I had ripped off the part of the label that had Paulie's name on it. I left the name of the drug alone.

"You have reason to believe they're not what they say they are?" he asked.

"That's about right," I said.

"Found them," he looked at the label again, "in your son's room and don't know how they got there?"

I gave him an awkward smile. "How'd you know that?"

"I get parents in here six, seven times a month asking me to identify pills they found in their kids' rooms."

"Good to know I'm not the only one," I said, going for slightly embarrassed.

I was half expecting some sort of lecture, but all he said was, "Gimme a minute. I'll run it through the database."

He stepped back over to the computer at the other end. I took the opportunity to check out my prophylactic options. If this thing I had with Allison kept on moving forward, I'd need to stock up. I grabbed a twelve-pack of condoms—optimist that I was—just as the pharmacist returned.

"Well," he said, "Good news, I think. They are what the label says they are."

"For ADHD, right?"

"Yep. I take it these were not prescribed for your boy."

"No," I said. "They were not. And you're sure they're ADHD meds?"

He took one of the pills out of the container and pointed at the small numbers and letters imprinted on it.

"Got a program." He pointed over to his computer. "I just enter the code and the color of the pill. If it's in my database, it tells me what it is."

"Cool," I said as I reached into my pocket and pulled out one of the blue-and-white capsules. "Would you mind doing that for this one, too?"

He gave me a concerned look. He was about to say something, but I cut him off.

"I know," I said. "My son and I are going to have a long talk tonight."

He thought about that for a few seconds. "Okay," he said, taking the capsule from my hand. "Gimme another minute."

"I appreciate it, Warren. Thanks."

He went back to the computer and started working the keys. Even from the other end of the counter, I could see the confused look on his face. He punched the keys again, and the confused look remained. He shook his head and walked back to me.

"No good news?" I asked.

"No news at all," Warren said. "Ran it twice and didn't get a hit. You find this in your son's room, too?"

"Yeah," I said. "What does it mean when you don't get a hit?"

"Could be it's not in the database yet. Sometimes it can take a month or so for it to be entered. Happens once in a while."

"What do you do when it does happen?"

"Put a call in to Poison Control. Takes them a day or two, but they can usually identify what the medication is."

I reached out my hand for him to give me the capsule back. When he didn't, I said, "Can I call them?"

"Doesn't work that way," Warren said. "I have to give them my license number. I take it you're not a pharmacist, right?" He grinned.

"Right," I said and looked at the capsule. "Can I have that back now?"

"Maybe when you tell me what's really going on here." He held up the capsule. "You really find this in your kid's room?"

I took a moment to decide how much truth I was willing to share with Warren. I went for three-fourths.

"No," I said. "A friend of mine found it in her kid's jeans and asked me for help. She's a single mom and doesn't want her son jacked up because of this."

"That's why she sent you?" he asked. "She's too nervous to come herself?"

"Something like that."

As Warren considered that, he rolled the capsule around his palm with his fingers. He gave me a look that told me he was assessing if I was telling the truth. The whole thing took about ten seconds.

"Here's what I'll do," he finally said. "There's a lab I use here in Manhattan. It usually takes them a day or two to run the tests and ID the meds. Thirty bucks."

"Two days?"

"They can do a rush job, but it'll cost you another twelve."

"I can do that," I said.

"I also have to call this in to Poison Control today. Depending on what they tell me, I'll either call you or the FDA."

The Food and Drug Administration? Shit. "Is that really necessary?"

"Hey. I have a legal obligation here. If I can't ID this, I have to call it in." He paused. "You came to me, remember? I'll do what I can to help you with the independent lab and all, but I'm not going to risk my license over it. Go ahead and tell your single-mom friend you did what you could."

"Can you give me a heads-up if you have to call the FDA?"

"I'll call you as soon as I get the lab results," he said. "It'll take at least a day before Poison Control gets back to me. Then you're going to want to have a conversation with your friend. You seem like an okay guy. I wouldn't recommend you get into hot water with the feds because of a kid who's not even yours."

"I hear you, Warren." I gave him my hand. "You got something I can write my name and number on?"

"Yeah." He went over to the register, grabbed a piece of paper and a pencil, and handed them to me. "Here ya go."

"Thanks." I wrote my name and cell number, then handed it back to him.

"No problem. Tell your friend I said good luck."

"I will," I said, and turned to leave the pharmacy.

"Hey!" Warren called to me.

I looked back. "Yeah?"

"You gonna pay for those or what?" He pointed to my hand.

I looked down and smiled. Then I walked to the register and handed the girl the pack of condoms. I also asked her to add in the forty-two dollars for the lab work.

"That'll be cash," I said, before grabbing a pack of breath mints. "And these."

"Smart combo," the girl said, ringing up my order.

"Yeah," I agreed. "I'm nothing if not smart."

My next stop was the office of the doctor who had prescribed the ADHD meds to Paulie. It was only a few blocks from the pharmacy. As I walked over, I tried to think of anyone I knew from my days as a cop who could help me get out in front of this mess with the mysterious blue-and-white capsule. For the moment, I came up empty.

I walked into the doctor's office and was pleased to see the waiting room empty. The receptionist was on the phone. She raised one finger at me and mouthed, "One minute." I took the time to look up at the high-def TV in the waiting room and watched as the weather guy on NY1 explained why we may not be getting the same snow that was going to dump six inches on the DC–Baltimore area the next day.

"Yes," the receptionist said. "Can I help you?"

"I certainly hope so," I said, stepping over to her window. "I'd like to see Dr. Williams."

She picked up a clipboard and a pen. "Have a seat and fill these out. Be sure to sign the bottom of page two, and I'll need to make a copy of your insurance card."

"I'm not here as a patient," I explained. "I just want to talk with Dr. Williams."

"Oh," she said, withdrawing the clipboard. "What is this in regards to?"

"A patient of his."

"I'm afraid Dr. Williams is not allowed to talk about—"

"Paulie Sherman," I said, interrupting her.

"Oh." She picked up the phone. "And your name is . . ."

"Raymond Donne."

She punched one of the buttons and spun her chair around so I couldn't hear what she was saying. Half a minute later, she spun back around.

"Dr. Williams will be right out."

"Thank you."

I went over to the waiting area and took a seat, then I picked a *People* magazine off the coffee table and leafed through it. I must be getting old. I didn't recognize ninety percent of the people in there. *I need to get out more. Or watch more crappy TV.*

"Mr. Donne?"

I looked up into the face of a guy about my age. Another sign of getting older. Used to be, all the doctors were older than I was. He wore dark pants and a white doctor's jacket. I got to my feet and said, "Dr. Williams." We shook hands. "Thank you for seeing me."

"Well," he said, "you've caught me in a rare slow period. We had a cancellation. What's this about Paulie Sherman, and who are you?"

"I'm looking into the murder—" I waited a beat—"of one of Paulie's close friends. Douglas Lee?"

"I'm afraid I don't know any Douglas Lee, Mr. Donne."

"He was the boy who was murdered last week. Under the Williamsburg Bridge."

"I read about that," he said. "Sad story. But I still don't know him or what he has to do with me."

"This"—I reached into my pocket and handed him the pill bottle—"was found in Douglas Lee's closet." I handed it to the doctor.

He looked at the label. "Again, I'm not permitted to discuss any of my patients without patient or, in this case, parental consent."

I nodded. "Even the dead ones whose prescription medications end up in the possession of another dead kid?"

"Even those, Mr. Donne. Patient-doctor confidentiality applies even after the patient had passed away."

"Passed away?" I said, finding it easy to sound offended. "Paulie was run over by a bus and Douglas Lee was stabbed to death. They didn't just 'pass away,' Doctor."

"Lower your voice, please," he said. "Regardless of how it happened, I am bound—both legally and ethically—not to talk about the deceased patient." He paused for a few seconds. "Who did you say you worked for?"

"I represent the family of Douglas Lee." *That lie was coming easier.*

"In what capacity?"

"Private," I said, before I could take it back.

"Then you know what I'm talking about. If you went around breaking your clients' confidentiality, how long do you think you would stay in business?"

"Point taken," I said. "But maybe you can answer one question for me."

"I doubt it," he said.

I took the pill bottle back and pointed at the label.

"It says here this contained ninety doses. Is that the normal amount?"

"Let me see that." He took the bottle and read the label again. I could tell he had something to say, but was weighing it against his professional obligations. "No," he said after a while. "The usual prescription is thirty doses. That allows me to monitor progress and effectiveness every month."

"So, it's possible for someone to change the amount?" I asked. "To get more?"

He handed me the bottle. "That would be possible, yes. You would have to look at the original prescription. I suppose you could change the number of doses, and a pharmacy may not notice. I wouldn't want to testify to that, though."

I slipped the bottle back into my pocket.

"You're not being asked to testify, Doctor," I said. "Not yet."

"Okay, then," he said. "If there's nothing else . . ."

"No, Doctor. That's it for now. Thank you for your time."

He turned to go and suddenly thought of something. "Mr. Donne," he said, stopping at the door he'd come through. "You never showed me your license."

"You never asked to see it," I said, and made a quick exit out to the street.

Chapter 31

WHEN I GOT HOME, MY STOMACH reminded me I hadn't eaten since breakfast. The number "1" was flashing on my answering machine. I pressed the button and listened to Allison telling me she'd be working late and not to wait for her to eat dinner. I checked my cell phone, and she had left the same message there. I went to the kitchen and took two hot dogs and two buns out of the freezer. I put some water in a pot to boil for the hot dogs and stuck the buns in the microwave for sixty seconds. *Yum*.

I went back to the phone and called my mom. I left a brief message on her machine and told her I'd try her again in the next few days. She'd probably call me back in a few hours. Rachel's machine also picked up, and I left a similar message. I opened my cell phone, retrieved Mrs. Lee's number, and used my landline to call her. She picked up after two rings.

"What were you able to find out?" she asked after we exchanged quick hellos.

I told her about my visits to the pharmacist and the doctor.

Silence. "I really think you should call Detective Murcer," I said. "You also might want to consider calling your brother-in-law, Mrs. Lee."

"Oh, Lord," she said. "Do you think it will come to that? The FDA?"

"Right now, I don't know. But it wouldn't hurt to have a lawyer on your side if it does. I know how that sounds, but he is family."

"Yes," she said, as if just remembering that. "He is."

"I'll give you a call tomorrow after I hear from the pharmacist."

"Thank you again, Mr. Donne. For everything."

"Let's speak tomorrow."

I ate most of my dinner watching the Manhattan skyline through my windows. It looked like more snow was coming, so I brought the rest of my meal into the living room, fell into the couch, and flipped on the Weather Channel.

"Ray?"

I opened my eyes and saw Allison smiling down at me and shaking the keys I'd forgotten I'd given her. Not a bad way to wake up from an early-evening nap.

"Hey," I said.

"Looks like you had quite a party, huh?"

I sat up and looked at the coffee table. Half a hot dog sat by itself on a plate next to two empty beer bottles. Video of snow falling in the Midwest was on the TV.

"Oh, yeah," I said. "Sorry you missed it. Got crazy there for a while. You make it through the day okay?"

"I was a bit jumpy, and I probably looked over my shoulder more than is socially acceptable. But yeah, I'm okay." She picked up the remains of my hot dog and took a bite. "Yum. Ketchup *and* mustard."

"Don't eat that," I said. "I can make you one."

"I had a pretzel on the way home," she said, finishing the hot dog in another bite. Then, realizing what she'd just said, added, "I mean, the way here."

She wrapped her arms around me and we kissed. When the kiss was over, she held me at arm's length. "Honey, I'm home," she teased.

"Why must you smother me, woman?"

"Man!" She slapped my arm.

I laughed and looked at her neck. "I see you removed the Band-aid. Let me see."

She raised her chin to give me a better look. Up close, cleaned, and almost two days later, it didn't look so bad. Something clicked.

"You didn't get a good look at the weapon that did this, did you?"

"No, Ray. I was scared and it was up against my throat. Why?"

"I was just thinking," I said. "Looking at your . . ."

"Yeah?"

I touched her neck gently. "This is similar to the wound Murcer described on Dougie's neck. Right under the chin."

She reached into her bag to pull out a small mirror and looked at her wound. I watched as the reporter's lightbulb went off. "You're right."

"That could explain the warning to stop writing about Dougie."

"It could," she agreed. Another fifteen seconds of silence.

"So," I finally said. "How was the rest of your day, dear?"

"I stopped by the hospital to see if I could get some more info on Jack Quinn."

"And . . . ?"

"He was discharged on Saturday, very early morning."

"Okay," I said. "We knew that. Did you ask about the food poisoning?"

"The nurse I spoke with didn't seem to buy into that. But she did strongly imply it was drug-related."

"Which drugs?" I thought back to the ADHD meds and those other capsules Dougie had hidden in his closet.

"She wouldn't say."

I told her what the doctor and pharmacist had said.

"There's another connection between the boys and drugs," she said.

"It'd be one hell of a coincidence if it wasn't. I mean, Dougie was in possession of Paulie Sherman's ADHD meds and another unknown drug. Jack Quinn ends up in the hospital, and maybe it was an overdose of something." It was hard to say what came out next. "I think it's time we call Murcer ourselves."

Allison smirked. "He'll be so glad to hear from Nancy Drew and Encyclopedia Brown. How do we explain how we just happened to come across this information?"

"Good question," I said. Then it came to me. "You," I began, "can claim you got a phone call and—as a journalist—are under no obligation to reveal a confidential source. Isn't that in the Constitution or something?"

"Not quite. But maybe Murcer won't push it," she said. "I could always tell him the call was anonymous. It's good info, and he should be happy to have it. I'll also have to tell him about Saturday night's assault." She closed her eyes. "That protects me," she said. "What about you?"

"I got a phone call from Dougie's mom," I said matter-of-factly. "There's nothing to suggest I was impeding anything. He'll give me some shit for not calling him sooner—you'll probably get the same shit—but I can handle that. I get worse from the parents at school."

"Okay," Allison said. "Sounds like half a plan at least." She looked at her watch. "Murcer's probably gone for the day. I'll call first thing tomorrow. It's early. You got pay-per-view?"

"Yeah," I said, and handed her the remote. "Find something not too chick-flicky, and I'll pop some popcorn."

"You're a cheap date, Raymond."

"There's a rumor I'm easy, too."

We kissed again, and she gave my butt a slap. "We'll see about that." She pointed the remote at the TV. "Now, get that popcorn."

Chapter 32

I GRABBED MY USUAL cup of coffee at the deli right outside the subway entrance. I thought about picking up a paper, but figured I'd had enough "news" lately. I looked up at the clouds and could smell snow in the air. Angel and his dad were standing on the steps in front of the building when I got to school. Both looked cold, and neither looked happy. Angel clearly had been crying.

"Mr. Rosario," I said, stopping a step below them. "What's going on?"

He let out a deep breath as he shook my hand, looking like someone who'd just received bad news or was about to report some.

"I was on the phone with my union rep yesterday," he said.

"Yeah?"

"He told me to expect this thing with the kid at the bus stop to drag out for a while. He said maybe even a year."

"Jesus," I said. "Did you get a lawyer?"

"With what?" he said. "I ain't getting paid during the suspension. We were practically living check-to-check before this. I gotta go with the union's lawyer, and I'm not the only case he's working on."

Damn. "Did you get the collection from the school?"

"Yes, it was very generous. I'm not used to being on the receiving end of charity, but . . ." He took a deep breath. "Thank you. It'll cover half a month's rent, but it don't look like things are gonna work out very soon."

"Yeah," I said. "Do you have anybody you can stay with for a while? Friends or family?"

He nodded and put his arm around Angel. "That's why we're here."

"I'm not sure what you mean."

"I got a cousin, runs an auto repair and body shop up near Kingston. Been asking me for years to come up and work with him."

"Okay."

"Got himself a nice house up there, too. Whattaya call it?" It came to him. "A mother-daughter. He and his family got the first floor, the basement, and the backyard. The upstairs he made into an apartment. Two small bedrooms, bathroom, kitchen. Separate entrance. The works."

"So you're here to . . ."

"I been in touch with the middle school near my cousin's place," he said. "I gotta get Angel discharged from here before they let me enroll him up there."

Angel started crying again. His whole life was about to change, and none of it was his fault. His dad pulled him close.

"It's too good a deal to pass up," the father said, as much for Angel's sake as for mine. "Rafael—that's my cousin—said I can have the upstairs, and the rent'll come out of some of what I make at the shop." He shook his head. "I hate to leave here, but I gotta look out for Angel."

"I get that," I said. "When does all this happen?"

"Gonna be on our way up day after tomorrow. My cousin's sending down a moving van; we'll put what we can in it and that's that."

He had this all worked out. This was a good man dealing with a bad situation.

"You know," I said, "I took a trip over to the bus stop last week. To see if I could talk some sense into this Hector kid."

"Really?" he said, surprised. "How'd that go?"

"Kid's a first-class knucklehead. I even had my uncle give it a shot."

"The cop?" Angel asked, breaking his silence.

"The *Chief*," I reminded him.

"And?"

"And Hector's too stupid to be scared of much. He thinks this lawsuit is going to end all his troubles and set him up for life."

"Yeah, as he fucks around with mine."

I looked at Angel and touched his shoulder. "How're you doing with all this?"

He shrugged. "It sucks. We didn't do nothing and now we gotta move." He looked at me with tears in his eyes. "I like this school. This is where all my friends are at, and now I gotta start at a brand-new school with new kids and new teachers. Don't know no one."

"Any cousins up there?"

"Yeah, but they're all younger than me."

Mr. Rosario removed his arm from around Angel and put his hands in his pockets.

"I explained to Angel," he said. "Gonna have to make the best outta this. Life throws some nasty stuff at you sometimes. Gotta move on the best you can."

"That's a good attitude," I said. "But if you had your way . . ."

"I'd stay here in the Burg. Grew up here. Hell, all *my* friends are here, too. But I got other things I got to think about. Like working a decent job and Angel getting to school safe every day." He looked up at the sky. "Maybe this is the way it's supposed to be. Maybe it's all part of a plan."

That's a conversation for another day.

"So," I said, "you have to meet with the pupil accounting secretary."

"She the one does the discharges?"

"Yeah."

"That's the one I hafta see then." He turned to his son. "Let's go, Angel."

They made their way to the front door. Mr. Rosario had his hand on the handle when a thought came to me.

"Mr. Rosario?"

He turned. "Yes?"

"You're not leaving for two days, right?"

"Thursday, right."

I walked up to where the two of them stood. I put my hand on his arm and gently pulled Mr. Rosario to the side, out of earshot of Angel.

"Why don't you wait a day on the discharge?" I said.

"I'm here now, Mr. Donne. We got a lot of things to do before Thursday."

"I know, but a lot can happen in a day."

"What? You think Hector's gonna have a revelation or something? You think there's a chance in hell he's gonna drop the charges?" He lowered his voice. "Come on, man. You said so yourself. He ain't scared of shit. This lawsuit is his Lotto ticket. Ain't nothing gonna change his mind about that."

"You're probably right." I paused to think about what to say next. "Do what you have to do at home. Come back tomorrow and, if nothing's changed, you go through with the discharge."

"What does that mean, Mr. Donne? If nothing's changed?"

I had an idea but decided it was best not to tell him. It might not work, and I didn't want to get his hopes up.

"A day," I said. "That's all I'm asking."

There must have been something in my eyes because Mr. Rosario looked straight at them, seemed to find an understanding, and nodded.

"Okay," he said. "But what're you gonna do?"

"I'm going to make a phone call," I said. "Then we'll see what happens."

After homeroom ended and the hallways were cleared for first period, I went to my office and used my cell to make my phone call. I left a message. Five minutes later, my cell chirped. I recognized the number as the one I'd just dialed.

"Raymond Donne," I answered.

"Talk to me."

I did. When I was done, the voice said, "Check with you later."

I went over to my desk and filled out some forms that needed to be faxed over to the district office before the end of the day. As much as I hated paperwork, I had to admit that once in a while I welcomed a break from the various crises I found myself as dean dealing with on an almost daily—sometimes hourly—basis. I finished most of it just as first period ended. I canvassed the halls and, when I got back to my office, my cell rang again.

"Raymond Donne."

"Mr. Donne," the voice said. "Warren from the pharmacy."

"Yeah. How are you? Did the lab results come back already?"

"Yes, sir. Your extra twelve bucks was money well spent. Lab's open twenty-four hours a day, seven days a week."

"So whatta you got for me, Warren?"

"What I got for you, Mr. Donne, is very interesting."

"Good interesting," I asked, "or bad interesting?"

"Not quite sure yet, but . . ." I could hear the sound of a computer printer running. "It says here, part of what your friend's kid had in his pockets was a nonprescription dietary supplement."

"Vitamins?" I asked.

"That's part of it," he said. "The B vitamins, mostly. The kind of stuff they put into those energy drinks. Then"—he paused, I assumed to read the printout—"it's got a bunch of . . . Do you know what nootropics are?"

"Say again?"

"No. Uh. Troe. Pix."

"I don't."

"They're nonprescription cognitive enhancers, and this little pill's got . . . nine of them. Basically, what they do is raise the level of acetylcholine in the brain. That's a neurotransmitter that increases the brain's ability to take in and remember new information. Works kind of like that ADHD med your friend's kid had." He paused. "It's an over-the-counter smart drug."

Smart drugs. I've known for a while that college and high school students were using ADHD meds for off-label use. They'd pop them when they had an all-nighter or a big test they had to study for. Problem was, many of those meds are addictive.

"So, this capsule," I said, "with all these cognitive enhancers and B vitamins . . . this is approved by the FDA?"

"That's the beauty of them. They don't have to be. They're dietary supplements. All the stuff's been approved already. That's the part of your friend's pill that's kosher."

"And the part that's not?"

"Donepezil."

"Which is?"

"Mainly prescribed to patients with Alzheimer's to treat dementia. It helps the patients think more clearly and process information better. Unlike the nootropics, donepezil *is* a prescription drug and, to my knowledge, has never been combined with nootropics."

"What would be the benefit of combining them?" I asked.

"Donepezil improves, or at least slows down the loss of, mental functioning. Memory, attention, reasoning, and language skills."

I thought about that for a bit, then said, "So, by combining them, you're basically making—"

"A *super* smart drug," Warren said. "In *theory*. But donepezil comes with a whole list of potential side effects, some of them pretty serious: depression, nervousness, insomnia. Any combination of donepezil with dietary supplements would need to be tested prior to it being made available to the public."

I thought back to my conversation with Muscles. "Clinical trials," I said.

"You got it," Warren said. "The question is: How did your friend's kid get this combination?"

That was a good question, I thought.

"Could someone combine the two by themselves?" I asked.

"They'd have to have access to some pretty sophisticated laboratory equipment to do it right and make it safe," Warren said. "That kind of hardware runs into the hundreds of thousands and is not easy to come by."

"But all the big pharmaceuticals have them, right?"

"The biggies do, sure. Smaller ones contract out."

And the only pharmaceutical company in Dougie's life was Ward Fullerton, whose head of research and development just happened to be the father of one of his best friends. *Shit on a stick. What the hell had these kids gotten themselves into?*

"Okay, Warren," I said. "Thanks a lot. You've been more than helpful."

"Don't thank me so quick, Mr. Donne. I gotta call these results in to the FDA."

"I thought Poison Control would do that."

"They will, but I got my obligations, too."

Right. "Okay." I said. "I appreciate the help."

"Thank you, sir," Warren said. "And good luck to your friends."

It was way too late for that.

Chapter 33

WHEN THE BELL RANG at the end of the day, I headed outside, cleared my kids off the streets, and, despite the cold, decided to walk home. Maybe I'd hit the fish store and pick up something for dinner—tuna steaks, maybe—and a bottle of white wine. I needed some air, some movement, and some space.

I wasn't quite sure how to process all the new information that had come my way over the past few days: the threat to Allison to stop writing about Dougie; the drugs in Dougie's closet; the fact that one of those drugs was more than likely under the FDA's radar. How did those capsules end up in Dougie's closet? How did Jack Quinn's father, a head guy over at Ward Fullerton, play into all this? I should just take everything I knew—or thought I knew—to Murcer and let him sort it out. Allison and I had not told him about Saturday night's attack yet, so he was already going to be pissed. Would he agree that the similarities between Allison's and Dougie's wounds were a connection? Or would he take me for the wounded ex-cop I was and tell me to stay the hell out of his sandbox?

Just as my head was beginning to spin, my phone rang. I didn't recognize the number, but answered it anyway. Maybe the caller would have all the answers I was searching for.

"Ray," the voice on the other end said. "This is Elliot."

"Hey. What's up?"

"I hope I am not interrupting something important."

"I'm just walking and thinking, Elliot. What's going on?"

"I wanted to share with you a few postings that appeared on Finch's Landing the past few days. They appear to be in response to Jack's posting from the other night about canceling his trip to Beijing."

"I thought we had agreed his posting didn't make sense."

"We had," he said. "But now that others are responding, I have realized that, just because we did not understand something, does not mean it did not make sense."

This kid was good. "Okay, Elliot. Shoot."

"Excuse me?"

"Share them with me."

"One says, 'Too bad about the trip to Hong Kong getting nixed. Anyone have suggestions for other travel plans?'"

"Hong Kong?" I said. "Jack said he was going to Beijing."

"I know. That is why I said they 'appeared' to be in response to Jack's posting."

"Right."

"Another one says, 'I knew Jack would come out of the hospital disoriented, but why do we have to suffer?' Do you think the pun was intended, Ray? Dis*oriented*?"

"Yes, Elliot. I believe it was."

"Because Beijing and Hong Kong are both in the Orient—"

"I get it, Elliot. I just don't know what it means."

"I do not enjoy puns very much. Especially when used in crossword puzzles."

Different strokes, I thought.

"Who posted those responses, Elliot?"

"It is my policy, Ray, not to identify any of the members of Finch's Landing. I can tell you, however, one of the members attends Upper West, and the other attends another private school. Why is that important?"

"It may not be. I'm still at the stage where I'm asking a lot of questions. You ever get to that place, Elliot?"

"I believe it is one of the most effective methods of learning, Ray. I have also found it useful to understand what questions need to be asked."

Like a jigsaw puzzle, Edgar had said. With too many pieces.

"You'd make a good teacher, Elliot."

"Thank you, Ray," he said. "You did mean that as a compliment?"

"Absolutely. Listen, if there's nothing else . . ."

"That was the only reason I called. There is nothing else at this time."

"I appreciate your calling."

"And I appreciate your answering. Good-bye, Ray."

"Good-bye, Elliot."

Before I put my phone away, I saw the little icon that told me I had a voice mail waiting for me. It was Allison.

"Hey, Ray. It's Allison. No word back from Murcer. I'm going out with some friends tonight. I've had these plans for a while and kinda spaced on them until today. I'm gonna stay over at a girlfriend's, so don't wait for me to eat or come by your place tonight. Call me if you want, or I'll see you tomorrow. Bye."

Back to the bachelor life. So, I wouldn't be stopping off at the fish place or the liquor store. I tried to think about what I had in the fridge and came up with a big zero. I could go shopping. Or I could have another in a long line of dinners at The LineUp. And just so the evening wouldn't be a complete waste, I decided to call Edgar.

"Raymond," he said. "What's the haps, man?"

"Edgar," I said. "How'd you like me to buy you dinner?"

"Whoa. Sure thing. Just tell me where and when."

"The LineUp. Tonight at six thirty. But I need a favor."

"You mean," he said, "I hafta earn my dinner?"

"Don't think of it like that, Edgar. Think of it as two friends doing a solid for each other. Quid pro quo."

"I failed French," he said. "What's the favor?"

"I need you to find out anything you can about Ward Fullerton."

"The pharmaceutical company?"

"That's the one."

"What kind of information am I looking for?"

I thought about that. "Any of the legal stuff. The stuff we touched on the other day, but more in-depth. Licenses, lawsuits, clinical trials. Stuff like that."

"Okay, Ray. That may take some time."

"Then make it seven o'clock."

"Sounds like a plan, man."

This time after closing up my phone, I kept it closed. I had a couple of hours before meeting with Edgar, so I decided to spend some of them at Muscles's.

Muscles wasn't there, the young girl with the big blue eyes working the front desk informed me as I signed in. He was doing a rare—and presumably very profitable—home visit. "Make sure you tell Muscles I was here," I said.

She looked down at the sheet. "You got it, Mr. Donne." Only she pronounced it like it rhymed with "bone."

I went through the same routine I had gone through with Muscles on Saturday. I should have come by yesterday, but even with the extra day off between workouts it felt pretty good. Muscles was right: I needed to come at least three times a week if I wanted to keep seeing progress. Now, if he could get me into that clinical trial and it showed results, I could realistically get back to my pre-accident self. Who said there are no second chances? With a little work and the proper pharmaceutical assistance, you could probably even squeeze out a third or fourth chance.

I finished the workout and took a quick shower. As I passed the front desk, I thanked the receptionist and reminded her to make sure Muscles knew I'd been by. She said, "Sure thing," gave me a smile, a wink, and an adorable finger-wave good-bye. Then she ruined the whole thing by calling me "sir."

I got to The LineUp half an hour early. I figured I'd grab a quick, relaxing beer before dealing with all of the questions I expected from Edgar. I figured wrong.

There he was, sitting in his usual spot, clicking away at his laptop. On the seat next to him was his computer bag, which he removed when he saw me enter the bar. "Saved you a seat," he said. "And I waited to order since, you know . . ."

"Since I'm buying?"

"Yeah. That's it."

Mikey came over.

"Edgar will have his regular," I said. "And I'll have the Brooklyn Pennant."

"No pilsner tonight?" Mikey asked, hand at his chest, pretending to be shocked.

"I've been jonesing for baseball for a while, so Pennant is as close as I'm gonna get. Go on ahead and put in a couple of burgers for us, too. And a big plate of o-rings."

"Ketchup *and* Tabasco?"

"Absolutely," I said, and Mikey went away.

"Okay," Edgar said. "Ward Fullerton. Corporate offices and labs are over in New Jersey. We knew that. Not much happening on the legal front for the past few years besides the boring stuff. Renewing licenses, some patent work, wrapping up and settling an old class-action suit for a drug they took off the market three years ago. The only thing of recent interest on this side of the Atlantic is their stock has been steadily declining in value over the past twelve months. Nothing catastrophic, mind you, but I imagine the shareholders are not a bunch of happy campers."

Mikey came by with our drinks, silverware, ketchup, and Tabasco sauce.

"What did you mean," I said, " 'this side of the Atlantic?' "

"I didn't find enough info in the U.S. papers to feel I'd earned this fancy meal," he said as he took a sip of his Bass, then poured in some tomato juice. "So I checked out some of the major overseas media outlets. The London *Times* had a little tidbit about six months ago about a drug trial in Nigeria that didn't go so well for our friends at WFP."

"They get into any details?"

"See, that's where the lawyers and PR guys really earn their money, Ray. The less news that hits the papers, the less the news hits the stock price."

I sipped some ale. "But they must have said something."

"Not much," he said. "But I found a press release from one of those sites that swears Coca-Cola is plotting world domination. They 'reported' Ward Fullerton had been conducting trials in some orphanages in Nigeria. The tests had to be terminated due to, and I quote, 'unforeseen and harmful side effects.' "

"What were the side effects?"

"Didn't say. Just that some of the kids involved—all kids, by the way, in their mid-teens—had to be hospitalized, and Ward Fullerton subsequently made substantial donations to the orphanages."

"Payoffs?"

"If you read between the lines, yeah."

"What were the drugs designed for?"

"Good one, Ray. Then you can ask me what the Colonel's secret blend of seven herbs and spices is."

"So," I said. "Bad, mysterious drug causes bad, mysterious side effects—but money makes it all go away."

"Welcome to Big Business 101. This shit's been going on since we were using rocks and seashells for currency. As long as you keep putting up those crooked numbers, everything's fine."

"Yeah," I said. "But if these CEOs ever tried to sell pot or crack in the projects, then they'd be looking at some real time."

"If they had more melanin than money? Absolutely."

Our food came at the exact moment my appetite went away. I downed the rest of my ale and asked for another. While I waited, I thought about the bag of drugs in Dougie's closet. Wherever it had come from, I'd bet a shitload of money it had made a stopover in Nigeria.

Did Dougie steal the drugs from Jack Quinn's father? Did Jack steal the drugs and ask Dougie to hide them? For what? Who the hell kept non-approved pharmaceuticals where teenagers could get their hands on them? Now I was starting to feel the puzzle didn't have *enough* pieces.

No, Uncle Ray would have said. The pieces are there, probably in plain sight.

There was something in the back of my brain, tapping its fingers on the door to my memory. I poured some ketchup on my plate and mixed in some Tabasco sauce while I waited for the door to open. I dipped in an onion ring and took a bite.

"The break-ins," I said, loud enough to grab the attention of a few people across the bar.

"What?" Edgar asked.

"The break-ins," I repeated. "Up in Rhinebeck."

"What about them?"

"The deputy told me none of the victims reported anything stolen."

"Right."

"All the car trunks were popped and left open. So we all just wrote it off as a prank—most likely pulled by Dougie, Paulie, and Jack. Boys being boys."

"What does that have to do with Ward Fullerton?"

I figured it was time I shared the story with Edgar.

"If I tell you something," I said just above a whisper, "you promise not to tell a soul. Not even an *online* soul."

He moved his stool closer to mine. "Yes, Ray. Of course not."

I proceeded to tell him about the bag of drugs Mrs. Lee had found in her son's closet. Then I told him about my trip to Warren, the pharmacist, the results of the lab tests on the drugs, and that Warren had said he'd never heard of that combination before.

"Smart drugs, huh?" Edgar asked.

"*Super* smart drugs. That's what Warren called them."

"So," Edgar said as I finished. "You think those drugs Dougie had are the ones Ward Fullerton was testing in Nigeria?"

"I do," I said. "And what if Mr. Quinn thought hiding the drugs in a locked trunk in a locked garage up in Rhinebeck was a decent temporary solution, but the boys somehow found out and wanted to get their hands on them? These are smart kids, remember. It would be too obvious if they just broke into the Quinns' garage . . ."

"So they break into *five* garages, figuring there'd be less suspicion on them. But don't you think he would have figured out his kid stole the drugs?"

"You're right. There's no way he wouldn't have."

"But why the hell would he want to hold on to a bunch of drugs that were causing negative side effects?"

"I don't know," I said. "They had to cost millions to produce. Maybe he just couldn't bring himself to get rid of them. Could be, the company didn't know he still had some. Maybe he wanted to use the old ones to help with research on the next?"

"I don't know."

"Maybe that's why we're not pharmaceutical executives, Edgar."

"Okay. Then what reason would the boys have for stealing the drugs?"

"That," I said, "is a piece of the puzzle we haven't found yet." I watched as a grin slowly took over Edgar's face. "What?" I asked.

"You said 'we.'"

"I guess I did, didn't I?" I gestured with my head toward his laptop. "Anything else you can think of that might help us out?"

"Not at the moment. No." He clicked some of the keys, then turned the laptop around to give me a better view. "But I was looking at Elliot's website today and noticed something a bit odd."

"Odd how?"

"Jack's first post after he gets out of the hospital is about some trip to Beijing."

"Yeah," I said. "Elliot told me about that and the other two. One about Hong Kong and another about Jack being '*disoriented*.'"

"Was he really planning a trip to China?"

"If he were, it would have meant missing two weeks of school . . . When did he say the trip was scheduled?"

Edgar scrolled back to Jack's post. "Tuesday night. Well, after one A.M. Technically, that's Wednesday morning. Hey, that's tonight."

"And Elliot told me their school doesn't break for the holidays until—*Shit*."

"What?"

"Beijing and Hong Kong are both cities in China."

"I knew that."

"Jack wasn't planning to go to *China*, he was planning on going to see *Chee-nah*. It's spelled the same as China."

"You lost me, Ray."

"China is the leader of the Royal Family on the other side of the bridge. The one who dug her nails into me after my meeting with Tio. She told me they'd seen me over at the tennis courts where Dougie was killed when I first met with Murcer and Allison. She warned me to stay away."

"You think she mighta killed Dougie?"

"I don't know. That *is* her turf."

"What's she got to do with Jack Quinn?"

"I don't know that, either."

"So," Edgar said, "according to this, he won't be showing up tonight."

"That's what he says." Then my ex-cop's lightbulb went off. "I wonder if China knows that."

Chapter 34

JUST LIKE DOUGIE, I also had a shoebox in my closet. I didn't want anyone to know about mine, either.

I took the shoebox out of the closet and brought it over to the coffee table. I placed it down gently and removed the lid. An old T-shirt was wrapped around something I'd sometimes forget I had. I unwrapped it and picked it up. It seemed heavier than I remembered and felt awkward in my hand. I guessed that's what happens when you don't hold something for so many years. Like an old baseball glove or a newborn baby.

My off-duty gun.

There was no practical reason for me to still have it. I certainly hadn't foreseen a time when I'd need it again. It was part of my past, given to me by my uncle upon my graduation from the Police Academy. Getting rid of the gun would have meant giving up a physical link to my past life. Some people hold on to pictures of ex-lovers, favorite pairs of worn-out sneakers, college drinking mugs. I held on to my old off-duty gun. Most ex-cops do.

Like many cops, my off-duty gun was a .38, snub-nosed revolver. Some cops chose an automatic, but, as Uncle Ray explained to me years ago, they can jam or misfire. Revolvers don't. It was—big surprise—made by Smith & Wesson, was black, and held five bullets at a time, which made it easier to carry than the ones that held six.

"Black's the color you want," my uncle had said. "If I had my way, I wouldn't allow any cop to carry the silver ones. All they do is give the bad guys a nice and shiny target to aim at."

I went into my bedroom and opened up the top drawer. Behind my socks and underwear were three more mementos: a box of bullets, my ankle holster, and my speed loader. I always stored the gun in one room and the ammunition in another. It was safer that way. Too many gun owners kept their guns loaded, making them much more likely to shoot someone in their own family. I had no family to worry about, but gun safety is drilled into you as a cop. Some habits are hard to break.

I left the speed loader where it was, brought the bullets and the holster into the living room, and sat down on the couch. I opened up the gun and looked at the five empty chambers. The thought of bringing an unloaded gun with me crossed my mind, but then I remembered something else Uncle Ray used to say: "If you bring a gun into a situation, you'd better be prepared to use it." I opened the box of bullets, took out five, and slid them into the chambers. I closed up the gun, made sure the safety was on, and placed the gun in the holster.

I rolled up my right pant leg, wrapped the holster around my ankle, and fastened it into place. I put the pant leg down and stood. I walked around the apartment as if trying on a new pair of shoes. After a few minutes, it began to feel a bit more comfortable. I kept looking down, thinking I'd see a big bulge by my ankle, but it looked normal. No one would be able to tell I was carrying. I sat on the couch again to double-check the safety. All set. Except, of course, for the fact I was no longer licensed to carry a concealed weapon. Nothing I could do about that now, other than leave the gun at home, but there was no way I was going to face China and her girls with nothing but my wit and charm. I'd tried that once and ended up with a bunch of notches on my wrist. What if they were the ones who had attacked Allison and me the other night? Who knew what they'd do when they caught me in their territory again?

But catch me I hoped they would.

An hour later, I was standing by a bench outside the locked tennis courts next to the office where Murcer, Allison, and I had had our talk with Terrence, the maintenance guy. During the subway ride over, I couldn't shake the feeling my few fellow travelers on the train could tell I had a gun strapped to my ankle. When a transit cop walked through the car, it felt like the gun was burning a hole into my leg. He had walked right on past me into the next car, unaware of how fast my heart was racing.

I reached into my jacket pocket and took out my cell to check the time. It was a few minutes after one, and the cold breeze coming off the East River was starting to cut through me. I pulled my zipper up as far as it would go, readjusted my hat so it covered more of my ears, and shoved my hands deeper into my pockets. I figured I'd wait for an hour. If China didn't show, I'd head for home and try again the next night.

A solitary tugboat made its way up the river. Traffic on the Williamsburg Bridge was predictably light for this time of night, and a subway train rattled along on its way into Brooklyn. I figured I'd hail a cab back home, since I planned on being here till at least two in the morning, and probably wouldn't feel like walking to the subway station and waiting God knows how long for the next train.

"Yo!"

The voice came from behind me. I turned to see China and one of her girls as they walked toward me. They were also wearing winter jackets, but theirs were open, so I could see the Saints jerseys and beads underneath. Too tough to worry about the weather, neither wore a hat or gloves. China gave me a look that said she was expecting someone else. Most likely Jack Quinn.

"Whatchoo doin' here, Mister Man?" China asked, looking around. "Thought we agreed you got no more business this side of the bridge."

"Some other business came up," I said. "Made me change my mind."

"Maybe we change it back for you." The two girls stopped about ten feet away from the fence that separated us. They smiled. "You came by at the wrong time."

I heard something behind me and looked over my shoulder at two more of China's girls coming around the small building. They stood with their hands in their pockets, blocking the only exit out of the fenced-in area. I faced China again.

"I just need to talk," I said, showing my open hands.

China smiled. "Must be real important, you coming all the way out here in the freezin' nighttime."

She and her partner took a few more steps toward me. I heard the girls behind me move as well. I stepped on the bench with my right foot and raised the pant leg.

"This time," I said, "I'm a bit more prepared."

Looking at the gun around my ankle, China laughed. "Where you get that thing? Toys"R"Us?"

"Actually . . ." I removed the gun from its holster and held it at my side, pointing at the ground. "It's from my old job."

"What, you used to be five-oh, or something?" They all laughed at that.

"Yep."

I watched as her eyes went from my gun to my face. She studied my eyes, checking for any signs of a bluff. Looked like the funny stuff was over now.

"So," she said. "You come across the bridge to do us or something?"

"I came across the bridge," I said, "to talk with you." I held up the gun and then put it back to my side. "This is so I don't get hurt." I called over my shoulder. "Why don't you two join your friends?"

The two girls behind me looked to China for permission. China nodded, and the girls went behind the building and reappeared on the other side of the fence.

China put her hands over her pockets. "Whatchoo wanna talk about, Mister Man? Something more 'bout that kid who got hisself killed over here?"

"That's part of it, China. First, I'd like to know what connection you've got to a couple of Upper West Side kids."

She smiled, sniffed, and ran an index finger under her nose.

"Don't know nothing about shit like that," she said.

"Yeah," I said. "I figured that's what you'd say. But I'm not the cops, China, and I don't believe you. How do you think I knew to come here tonight?" I tapped the gun against my thigh. "I bet if I went through your pockets right now, I'd find some real interesting stuff."

She looked at her girls, then back at me.

"That why you're here?" she said in disbelief, slapping her pockets. "You wanna rip me off for what I'm carrying?"

"Goddamn it!" I yelled. "That's part of your problem. You don't listen, and you assume everyone thinks like you do." I tapped the gun against my thigh again. Harder. "I said I want to *talk* to you. If I wanted what's in your fucking pockets, I'd have it already and be on my way home."

"Okay," she said. "Don't give yourself a heart attack, Mister Man." She paused for a bit and gestured for her girls to come closer to her. "Yeah, okay. We did some biz with these two white boys. Coupla times a week."

"That why you're here tonight?"

China nodded.

"You using or selling?" I asked.

"Little of both."

"These white boys. Did you ever get their names?"

She laughed again, this time nervously. Then the laugh disappeared.

"We just called 'em Peanut and Cracker Jack. Like from the song, 'Buy me some peanut and Cracker Jack,' y'know?"

"Why'd you call them that?"

"Don't know when it started," she said, "but Peanut's all small and shit, and Cracker Jack 'cause he's giving us drugs, y'know? That was his real name, too. Jack."

Paulie Sherman had come down here with Jack Quinn. The "travel buddy" Jack had mentioned in his post on Finch's Landing. Probably didn't want to come down here all by himself this time of night.

"What kind of drugs did Jack sell you?"

"Just some good prescription shit."

"What kind of prescription stuff?"

She shook her head. "Don't know the name of it, it just kept us goin', y'know? Smoke a little weed, take some meddies. Last all night."

I thought back to the drugs I'd taken out of Dougie's closet.

"Were they pills?" I asked. "Or capsules?"

"What's the fuckin' difference?"

"A pill's like a . . . like a small white M&M," I said. "A capsule's bigger. A lot of times they're two different colors."

She gave that some thought. "Pills. Yeah, they was pills."

The ADHD meds, I thought. They were stimulants, so it'd make sense that if you took them while smoking pot, the high would last longer, maybe be more intense.

"And we didn't *buy* from him exactly," she said.

"What's that mean?"

China smiled and looked at her girls. To me, she said, "Okay if I go into my pockets, Mister Man?"

I tightened the grip on my gun. "If you do, make it slow and easy."

She did. When her hand came out, she held a large plastic baggie of what I assumed was marijuana.

"See," she said, "we didn't buy those pills. We traded, 'cept he used one of them fancy white-boy words." She searched her memory. "*Bartered*," she finally said. "He gave us stuff he came by easy, and we gave him stuff *we* came by easy. He even asked for some beads that last time. I remember *that*."

Now it made sense. Jack had no backup. That was why he posted he wouldn't be able to make the trip tonight. He was letting his clients know he wouldn't be able to provide them with any pot for a while.

"You ever see Peanut and Cracker Jack with a black kid?" I asked. "About my height? Seventeen years old?"

"The kid that got killed?"

"Yeah."

"Nah," China said. "Jus' the two of them." A thought came into her head. "*Did* see a kid on a bike, coupla weeks ago. Coulda been black. Inside the courts. He wasn't *with them* with them, but he coulda been *waiting* for them, I guess. And there was another kid, hanging around outside the courts, smoking. Had a hoodie on. Kept moving all over the place, stomping his feet like he was all cold and shit."

"When was this?"

"Like I said, a coupla weeks ago."

"Maybe three Saturdays ago?"

"I don't know, Mister Man. I don't remember *last* Saturday."

Of course not. With all the shit she'd been popping and smoking, I might as well have been asking about last year.

"There was one thing a bit wacked," she said.

"What's that?"

"Cracker Jack was real wired up that night. Like he was on some sort of shit. Most times, he's cool like ice."

"How'd you two arrange these meets?" I asked.

"We just hooked up every Tuesday and Saturday."

"You call him, or did he call you?"

"No, man. Like I said, it was *every* Tuesday and *every* Saturday. Same time, right after the lights go out. Jack said no phone calls. Something about how he didn't want no record of us meeting."

Sharp. Maybe he'd put his business deal with China on his college application.

"Did he show up this past Saturday?"

"Nope. Didn't show up Tuesday, neither."

That was the day I'd met Jack's sister outside the hospital. He was still in the hospital Tuesday.

"Jack ever say how they got down here?"

"Nah," she said. "Figured they rich, white boys. Probably took a cab." She motioned with her head to the north. "Get off at that exit up there and walk on down."

That made sense. I tried to think of some more questions, but nothing came to mind. She'd pretty much confirmed what I needed to know: Paulie and Jack were down here dealing—*bartering*—and Dougie might have come along once. Based on what China had told me about the bike and the beads, it had to be the night he was killed.

Which put Jack and Paulie at the top of the suspect list. Maybe that was why Paulie skateboarded into the bus. He couldn't handle what he'd been a part of. But who was the mysterious kid in the courts with Dougie? Finch? Had Jack talked him into getting involved?

"How'd you hook up with Peanut and Cracker Jack to begin with?" I asked. "I don't see you running in the same social circles."

"We run into them on the courts one night," China said. "They be skateboarding and smoking and shit. We was gonna take their stash and run them back home to the white folks, but then Cracker Jack come up with this idea for the trade, y'know?" She smiled and shook her head. "That is one smooth-talking white boy."

"And the only thing you remember out of the ordinary from that night three weeks ago was—"

"That boy was tight, yo."

"You have any dealings with the kid on the bike or the other one?"

"Nah," she said. "We got our shit and went off to party. If that was the night the kid got killed, we ain't seen shit. Everything was 'copacetic' when we bounced. That's another white-boy word he used."

"All right," I said to the group. "You can go." I waved my gun in the direction of the closest park exit, put my leg up on the bench, and slipped the .38 back into its holster.

"Hey, Mister Man?"

"Yeah?"

"You think Peanut and Cracker Jack comin' by tonight?"

I thought of the dead kid and the one who'd just come out of the hospital.

"I seriously doubt it."

"Shit, man. We ain't seen them in, like, two weeks. Kinda jonesing for them pills. What the fuck we supposed to do now?"

"I don't care," I said. "Why don't you go home and get some sleep?"

I started off out of the park and walked to the small turnoff a few blocks north. With any luck, I'd catch a quick cab and be back home and in bed before two.

Chapter 35

WHEN I WOKE UP the next morning, I felt hungover. I hadn't had a drop to drink the previous night, but I was working on maybe three hours of sleep. That's what happens when you stay out till all hours, talking to gang members about their drug deals with Upper West Side private-school kids.

I took my coffee into the bathroom and stepped into a hot shower. I let the water pound my face, hoping it would help the coffee wake me up. After fifteen minutes of that, I dried off, went into the kitchen for another cup, and did some stretches against the wall to get more of my blood flowing. I'd gone to work with less sleep than this before. It'd be rough, but I'd get through.

I had it all planned out: I'd get the kids into the building, clear the halls after homeroom, then call Dennis Murcer myself since he hadn't gotten back to Allison. Even though I had a lot of good info to share with him, I was not looking forward to making that call. I was prepared for a major lecture, a couple of threats, and a description of the many ways I had impeded his investigation into the murder of Douglas William Lee. And, for the most part, he'd be absolutely correct. But he was a smart guy and a good detective. We were good friends once. He would listen.

When I got to school, Angel Rosario and his dad were standing on the front steps, just like the day before. They both had their hands in their pockets and were doing a little bounce to stay warm. Mr. Rosario came down the steps to greet me, while Angel remained several feet away.

Mr. Rosario reached out, grabbed my hand, and squeezed it.

"Thank you, Mr. Donne," he said, his eyes wet. "Thank you."

"For what?" I asked. Playing ignorant was becoming one of my more developed skills.

"For making that phone call yesterday."

"Oh."

"*Oh*'s right." He smacked his hands together and let out a huge laugh. "I got a call from my union rep last night."

"Yeah?"

"That kid Hector dropped the charges."

"No shit?"

"According to my rep, he walked into the precinct yesterday about two o'clock—with his lawyer—and dropped the charges. It's over."

"Holy shit," I said. "Any idea why he had the change of heart?"

"I don't think he said." He gave me a look. "But you know, don't you?"

"How would I know?"

"Yesterday," he said. "You told me to hold off on discharging Angel. That you were gonna make a phone call." He wiped his hand across his mouth. "Who'd you call, Mr. Donne? Your uncle, the chief?"

"No," I said. "I told you. We tried that and it didn't work."

"Then who?"

I let out a deep sigh. "I really can't tell you, Mr. Rosario. I just can't."

"Whatta you mean, you can't? You make a phone call and then— *bam!*—the biggest problem in my life disappears. Who else do I got to thank?"

No way was I going to tell him about my call to Tio. The less Mr. Rosario knew, the better for all of us.

"Someone owed me a favor," I said. "I told that someone you needed it more than I did. I guess he heard me."

Angel's father looked at the ground and shook his head. When he looked up again, tears in his eyes, he said, "Ever since Angel's mother died, it's been only me and him, y'know?"

"It's gotta be tough."

"It is, but you get through it by being tough." He looked over at his son, still standing on the steps. "That's what I try to teach him. To be tough, but also smart. You lose your mother at that age and . . . shit, you *gotta* be tough. But you also learn you can't rely on anyone but your family." He wiped a tear off his cheek. "Your mom's gone and you start having problems believing in your family. I mean, if a parent dies then anything can happen, right? And then this shit with Hector goes down, and I can't do shit because I tried to be tough to solve my kid's problem."

"You did what you thought was right, Mr. Rosario." I put my hand on his arm. "You were protecting your son."

"I thought I was, but look what happened."

"And now it's over."

"Thanks to you," he said.

I looked over at Angel. "What does he know?" I asked.

"Just that the charges were dropped. I thought you could tell him the rest."

I shook my head. "He doesn't need to know that. He just needs to know it's over, and his dad's a good man."

"But I—"

"You asked me for help. I asked someone else for help. That's all that happened here. We both knew the right people to ask."

He gave that some thought. "So, you don't want to tell Angel?"

"He doesn't need to know more than he knows. It's over."

He took my hand again. "Well, I thank you, Mr. Donne. And please thank the person you called. For me."

"I'll do that," I said, pretty sure I wouldn't. "When do you go back to work?"

"My rep said I could start today, but I think I'll go in tomorrow. Everything's happened so quick. I need to get my mind straight."

"You gonna take Angel home with you?"

"I can do that?"

"He might need a little time to get his head straight, too. Spend some time with you without the case hanging over your heads."

He smiled and looked back at his son. "Angel, come on down."

Angel did as he was told, and his father wrapped his arm around him.

"Mr. Donne says you might wanna take the day off with me. Get some breakfast, maybe go into the city?"

Angel looked at me like someone had just told him he'd won the lottery.

"I can do that?" he asked, sounding exactly like his dad.

"What am I going to do?" I said. "Call your father?"

They both laughed and then thanked me again. I watched as the father and his son walked away. And just like that, I was glad I'd gotten out of bed that morning.

The first time I called Murcer, the call went directly to his voice mail. As instructed, I left a brief message with my name and number, and the time I had called. The second time I called, an hour later, I was informed by the mechanical voice that the subscriber I was trying to reach had a full mailbox and would not take any further messages. I decided to try again in a few hours. Maybe Dennis was too busy solving other crimes to answer his phone or even check his messages.

I called Allison, expecting the same results, but was pleasantly surprised when she actually picked up.

"How are you feeling this morning?" I asked.

"Like I spent five hours drinking margaritas with a bunch of girl-friends I hadn't seen in six months," she said. "And how did you spend your evening?"

"You want the full story or just the good parts?"

"I'm hungover, Ray. Just gimme the good parts."

So I did. I told her about my visit to Jack's doctor and pharmacist, and what the pharmacist had told me about the potential side effects of those capsules. Then I went into my conversation with China—Allison was impressed how Edgar and I had figured that part out—and about how China had a bartering deal with Jack and Paulie, and how she apparently had seen Dougie at the crime scene the night he had been murdered. I also told her about the mysterious, hooded kid bouncing around outside the tennis courts.

"You went down there," Allison said, "at that time of night all by yourself?"

I figured I had missed out on getting lectured by Murcer, so maybe I deserved this. She was not going to like what she heard next.

"I had protection," I said.

"What, you brought condoms with you? What do you mean 'protection'?"

"I'm an ex-cop, Allison."

"So, what? You called up some old cop buddies?"

"Not exactly."

"'Not exac—'? Oh, tell me you didn't do what I think you did, please."

"Depends on what you think I did."

A long pause followed and then, "You brought a gun with you, didn't you?"

"I had to bring something."

"No, you didn't, Ray. You didn't have to go down there at all. Didn't we agree that I would call Murcer?"

"Yeah," I said. "But that was for *yesterday*. This was last night."

"Don't even. Do you realize the danger you put yourself in? I know at least part of you does. That's why you brought the gun. What if you had to use it, Ray? Did you think that far ahead? How that could have completely fucked up your life?"

I guess I hadn't. I didn't know what to say.

"Damn it, Ray. You're smarter than that. At least, I thought you were. I'm going to call Murcer again. Leaving out the part about the gun, of course."

"I already tried. Twice. I left a message and now his box is full."

"I'll call the precinct then. Maybe they know where he is. You don't have any plans for after school, do you?"

"No."

"Then I'll try to set up a meeting with the three of us. We'll tell him what we know and let him take it from there."

"He's not going to be happy."

"At this point," Allison said, "I don't care. We've got enough for him to, at the very least, pick up the Quinn kid for questioning. I'm sure dear old dad will have a lawyer there quicker than—*crap*."

"What?"

"That might be Dougie's uncle."

"Oh, yeah," I said. "I almost forgot about that."

"Doesn't matter," she said. "Lemme see if I can reach Murcer. Keep your phone with you, okay?"

"Yeah." I said. "Okay."

She was silent for a little while. "Sorry I got all pissy with you, Ray. It's just that . . . you made some decisions last night and didn't think how they might affect . . . others."

I couldn't help but smile at that. I was glad she couldn't see my face.

"Like my mother?" I said. "And Rachel? Uncle Ray and . . ."

"Screw you, Ray," she said, but I could hear the smile in her voice. "I'll call you after I talk to Murcer."

"I'll be here."

"You better be," she said, and hung up.

Chapter 36

THE REST OF THE DAY WENT by pretty quickly. I had to deal with a couple of kids cutting class and making out behind the curtain in the auditorium. I think I got there just in time, because the boy's shirt was unbuttoned and the girl had kicked her shoes off. Two other geniuses figured that, since their regular math teacher was absent and the class was being covered by a sub, they might as well give themselves an extra gym period and snuck in after the phys ed teacher had taken attendance. The math sub realized they were cutting, got a message to me, and I caught the two playing basketball in the gym. They actually asked me if I could wait until the game was over before taking them back to math. This was the kind of stuff they didn't go over in teacher school.

After a last-period meeting with my principal and the two assistant principals regarding what would and would not be allowed during the holiday parties many teachers had planned for their classes, and then discussing the topic of how many school safety officers and how many parents were needed to chaperone the holiday dance, I had five minutes to run up to my office and get my jacket before dismissal. My cell phone rang on my way back down. I looked at it, hoping it was Murcer getting back to me. It was Allison.

"You get in touch with Murcer?" I asked.

"Nope. I did leave a message for him at the precinct, though. Said it was urgent."

"Good idea. You coming over tonight?"

"That's the plan, but I need to take it easy. Let's just order in some Chinese and drink lots of tea and water."

"Sounds good," I said. "I even have a full bottle of ibuprofen in the cabinet."

"I'm past that stage," she said. "Now I'm onto the detox part of the program."

I laughed. "I'm gonna hang out here for a bit, do a little paperwork. I'll be at my place at around five."

"I'll try to make it by six. I've got to put the finishing touches on a piece about some Upper East Side lady's poodle who got lost then found by some kids in the projects behind Lincoln Center."

"Maybe the dog just wanted some culture."

"Yeah, maybe. Anyway, I'm working it as 'Rich Dog Found by Poor Kids.'" She paused. "I'll call you when I'm on my way. You can order the food and I'll pick it up."

I could get used to this. "Cool."

"Later."

A few minutes later, I was outside clearing the sidewalk of post-school stragglers, which didn't take long because of the cold breeze picking up. Low temperatures and rain always got the kids moving faster. I could almost smell the snow that was headed our way. On my walk home, I got another call.

"Hello?"

"Raymond," the now-familiar voice said. "This is Elliot."

"Hey, Elliot. How are you?"

"I am fine. I need to talk to you."

"Okay." I waited. Then I realized I'd have to ask for it. "Go ahead."

"No," he said. "Not on the phone."

I decided to put on my teacher voice. "Elliot, I'm just getting off work and have things to do tonight. If you need to talk to me, now's the best time."

He paused for a few seconds. "Okay, then. Forget it."

"I don't want to forget it." I sighed. "Can you at least tell me what it's about?"

Another pause. "I have some information about Douglas," he said. "And something about drugs from Jack."

"Drugs? Who told you this, Elliot?"

Silence, then, "Douglas did. A few days before he . . ."

"Okay, Elliot." I didn't like the hesitation in his voice. "Where are you now?"

"No, not now," he said. "Tonight. Seven o'clock."

"Elliot, I told you I have plans for tonight."

He waited a few beats. "Okay. Forget it."

"I don't want to . . ." I took a breath. "Okay. Seven o'clock. Where do you live?"

"No," he said. "Not at my apartment. The Ramble."

"The Ramble?"

"In Central Park. Where you were supposed to go bird-watching with us the other day."

"Why the Ramble? Your folks are okay with you going out there at night?"

"I am not a baby, Ray." Another pause. "I have a lot of homework to do. My parents sometimes let me go out and do a little night birding if I get my work done."

I thought of the Shermans letting Paulie skateboard after dark.

"Okay, Elliot," I said. "Seven o'clock at the Ramble."

"On the bridge," he said. "When you enter the—"

"I know the bridge. Seven o'clock."

It took him five seconds to say, "Thank you, Ray," and he hung up.

What the fuck? Now I had to call Allison and change our plans, because Elliot had something to tell me about Dougie and couldn't do it over the phone. Maybe it was about the night Dougie was killed. Maybe *Elliot* was the mysterious bouncing kid.

I called Allison back. She apparently recognized my number, because she answered. "This better be good, tough guy. I told you how busy I am."

I told her about my phone call from Elliot and my plans for seven o'clock in Central Park.

"Why does he want to talk to you?"

"He didn't say. He didn't say much, in fact. My guess is he needs a grown-up to talk to, and since Dougie trusted me . . ."

"Jesus, Ray."

"He said Dougie told him something about some drugs at the

Quinns'. I'm just not sure if he means Paulie's prescription or those un-identified capsules Mrs. Lee found."

"You think Jack and the boys were trying to sell them?"

"I don't know," I said, and something from the part of my brain that stored last week's memory clicked in. "Remember when I had that conversation with Dougie's father?"

"At the bar, yeah."

"He told me Dougie had told him he was going to get him help. To make him better. Something about connections at school."

"You didn't tell me that."

"I didn't know what to make of it."

"And now?"

"Part of the drug Ward Fullerton had their problems with was designed to treat the symptoms of dementia and stimulate a chemical in the brain that helps with memory retention and learning. If not for the side effects they experienced in Nigeria, they'd probably be doing clinical trials here in the States within the next year or so."

"But they *did* have side effects. Enough where they had to scramble to save the company's ass."

"I know," I said. "But that might explain what Dougie said to his dad. About getting better."

"That's quite a stretch, Ray."

"I know, but think about what we know about the last weeks of these kids' lives. Their parents said Dougie and Paulie were both experiencing abnormal mood changes and problems sleeping."

"Two side effects of donezepil. You think the kids were taking those clinical trial meds?"

"Maybe. And Jack and Paulie were on ADHD medications. Stimulants." *Shit.* "A side effect of some of those meds is suicidal thoughts."

Allison caught on. "Paulie Sherman. Holy fuck, Ray."

"All right," I said. "We're getting way ahead of ourselves. I'll call you after I find out what Elliot has to tell me."

"Definitely," she said. "Should you try Murcer again?"

"Yeah, just to cover our asses."

"What if he's still not picking up?"

"Then, I guess we'll have to cover each other's asses," I said.

"Any other time, I'd have a smart answer for that, Ray. Call me later."

After we hung up, I called Murcer again. No luck, so I phoned the precinct. I was told he was still out, so I left my own 'urgent' message. I asked that he call me ASAP, but left out the part about meeting with Elliot Finch. I didn't want to hear I was overstepping my bounds again. I already knew that.

I went home to eat. Alone. I was hungry, and the night had the potential to be a long one. Another after-dark trip to a city park. I thought about my off-duty gun, now safely stored away in the back of my closet. I didn't think I'd need it tonight. At least, I hoped not.

Chapter 37

AT SIX FORTY-FIVE, I was standing outside Central Park, hands in my pockets, watching my breath turn to mist and disappear into the night. Some flakes had started to fall and, if the local news was to be believed, we were still expecting up to six inches by the morning. Not enough to cancel school in the city, but more than enough to make getting around tomorrow a bit slower and a whole lot messier.

I was early, so I walked around to get my blood flowing. I used the old street cop's trick of stamping my feet every thirty seconds to help stay warm. It may have looked weird and gotten me a few strange looks, but it worked. I don't really mind the cold weather; it's the standing around part that gets to me.

Five minutes later, I called Allison again and got her voice mail. Since I already had the phone out, I tried Murcer. No luck. I looked at my watch and decided to head into the park. It'd take me a few minutes to get to the bridge by the Ramble, and I didn't want to give Elliot any reason not to stick around.

I arrived at the bridge just before seven o'clock. There was no one there to greet me. It was full-on nighttime in the city now, and the snowflakes were beginning to increase in size and number. There was light coming from both sides of the bridge. The vision of falling snow was straight out of a Hallmark card.

"Mr. Donne?"

I turned, expecting to see Elliot, but instead saw Jack Quinn walking toward me. His hands were in his pockets—*didn't anybody wear gloves anymore?*—and he had on the same ski jacket he'd worn to Dougie's wake, the lift ticket still hanging from the zipper. The ski hat he was wearing was white and pulled down over his ears. His long blond hair spilled out the sides.

"Hello, Jack," I said.

He stepped toward me, looking behind me and then over his shoulder. "Thanks for coming."

"Where's Elliot?"

"He had to go home." He turned around again, checking for something. At this hour, in this cold, I doubted we'd see anyone. Maybe that was the point.

"What's this about, Jack? Elliot told me he had information about Dougie."

"Elliot made the call for me. I told him what to say."

That explained all the pauses.

"So *you* have information about Dougie? Couldn't you have just told me over the phone? Or better yet, called the detective in charge?"

He took a deep breath and let it out slowly. It looked as if he were smoking an invisible cigarette. He closed his eyes, concentrating on his next words.

"I killed him," he said, like he was telling me he'd dropped an expensive vase.

I let those words sink in before responding. Even after five years as a cop, I'd never heard that before. The most I'd gotten was someone telling me he'd snatched a lady's purse or decided to take a ride in a car that wasn't his. Murder confessions were new territory for me.

"You killed Dougie?" I said.

"Yeah," he said, then mumbled something I couldn't hear.

"What was that?"

"I said, I think so," he said louder.

"You 'think so'? Jack, you either did or you didn't."

"I did. I killed him."

He sounded like he was trying to convince both of us.

"All right, Jack," I said. "Don't say anything else. I'm going to reach into my pocket and take out my phone."

He looked nervous. "Why are you doing that? I didn't say to do that."

"I didn't ask," I said, my phone still in my pocket. "I'm calling the police."

"No!" he screamed, and then backed away a few steps. "No police." His voice got shaky and then he lowered it. "Please. Not yet."

"Jack," I said as calmly as I could. "You just confessed to murder. I know the detective in charge. Tell him what you told me. He'll help you get out in front of this. You'll need a lawyer. Things'll go a lot easier—"

"Fucking lawyers!" he screamed. In a much calmer tone, he added, "His uncle's one, you know? Dougie's?"

"I know. That's not the one I would call, though." I felt like moving closer to the kid, but had the feeling he'd jet out of there if I moved so much as an inch. I stayed where I was, put my hand in my pocket, and touched my phone. "Jack," I said. "Tell me what you want to do about this."

I knew what I wanted: to get him out of the park, into a cab, and down to Murcer.

"I don't know," he said, looking at me as if he were five years old. "Elliot said I could trust you. That you would know what to do."

"Then *trust* me, Jack, when I say we need to get you to the police."

He thought about that. "Are they going to tell my mom and dad?"

Holy shit, I thought. *You just confessed to murder, and you're concerned about your parents finding out?*

"They'll have to know, Jack. You're under eighteen and—"

"What if I sign something?" he asked. "Can't I waive my rights or something and not get my parents involved?"

He couldn't do that, I knew. What I said was, "That's a good question for the detective. That's why we need to go see him. He'll know what to do."

"He was going to tell on us, you know." Now he *sounded* like he was five.

"Who?" I asked.

"Dougie. He was gonna tell on us: that we'd stolen the drugs and we were taking them, and they were making us act all different. He was gonna get us in a lot of trouble." He stamped his feet, and yelled, "You don't rat out your friends, Dougie!"

Shit. This kid was going off the deep end fast. I needed to get him out of the park and into a cab two minutes ago.

"Paulie and I wouldn't have told on him. We were buddies. We . . . Paulie's dead now, too, you know. Fuckin' skateboarded into a bus. The fuck was *that* about?" He took a step toward me. "Can ya tell me what the fuck that was about, Mr. Donne?"

"It was the drugs, Jack," I said, taking a step toward him. "Maybe that's why Dougie felt the need to stop you guys. That's why you ended up in the hospital, right? The drugs?"

He nodded his head yes.

I took another step closer. "You ready to go talk to the police, Jack?"

"He's not going anywhere with you, Mr. Donne."

I turned around as Jack's sister, Alexis, stepped onto the bridge from the same direction he'd come. Again, no jacket. Just a volleyball hoodie.

"Jesus Christ," Jack stage-whispered. "It's my sister."

Alexis walked around me and took her brother by the arm.

"It's time to go home now, Jack."

Jack didn't resist. He just hung his head and stared at the snowy ground.

"Alexis," I said, moving in front of the twins. "Jack just confessed to killing Douglas Lee."

A voice from behind me said, "My son did no such thing, Mr. Donne."

I turned. It was John Quinn Sr.

"Hey, Dad," Jack said. "Where's Mom?"

Ignoring that, the father looked at me. "He's obviously still feeling the effects of his medications. He left the house without telling us. We came to the park, heard him yelling, and found him here with you." He looked over at his kids and back at me. "If you leave now, we'll just take Jack home and consider this matter closed."

"Jesus Christ," I said. "What world do you people live in?"

"The kind of world," he said, "where grown men don't meet with young boys late at night in the park, Mr. Donne. What world do *you* live in? First, you harass my daughter, and now I find you doing the same to my son?"

"Your son asked me to meet him here."

He looked at his son. "Is that true, Jack?"

Jack gave that a lot of thought before answering. "No," he said, obviously scared to death to give any other answer.

"You see, Mr. Donne. My son contradicts your version. I suggest you leave."

"I have a witness," I said. "Elliot Finch."

"Who?" Alexis said, finally speaking. "The retard?"

Oh, fuck these people. I pulled my phone out of my pocket.

"Either way," I said, "I'm contacting Detective Murcer. I'll tell him Jack told me he killed Dougie, and he and his friends stole drugs from you. The drugs Jack had Dougie hide in his closet. Those drugs were responsible for Paulie Sherman's death."

Mr. Quinn looked surprised. It was clear this was the first time he'd heard that Dougie was in possession of his drugs. He recovered quickly.

"First of all, Mr. Donne, Jack will deny having anything to do with Douglas's death. And from what I understand from Jack, it was Douglas who stole the drugs." Already, he was spinning the story in his favor. "Jack just told me the boy was up there the weekend the drugs were taken."

"Is that the card you're going to play, Mr. Quinn. Blame it on the black kid?"

"It doesn't matter what color Dougie was, he—"

"Your daughter's *boyfriend,* Mr. Quinn? It didn't bother you he was black?"

For the second time that night, Quinn senior blinked. He turned to face Alexis.

"It's not true, Daddy," she said.

"Wanna see a picture, Alexis?" I asked. "One that Dougie's mom gave me?"

"Shut up, Mr. Donne," she said, the fear and agitation in her voice almost palpable. "Daddy, I swear . . ."

"We'll talk about this at home, Alexis," he said. "We are leaving, Mr. Donne. I think you should do the same."

I knew I couldn't let them leave the park with Jack. I needed to stir the pot that was this fucked-up family.

"I think you *should* go ahead and call the police, Mr. Quinn," I said. "I'll do the same and take my chances with my story against yours. I have your drugs now. You can explain how they got into the hands of your son's murdered friend. And your daughter can explain how she was not all . . . hot and heavy with the murdered black boy from Williamsburg."

"I told you to shut the fuck up!" Alexis screamed. I watched as her hand came out of her jacket pocket, holding a knife. She raised it and came charging at me. I was about to sidestep her, when she lost her footing on the thin layer of snow and barreled into me, sending us both to the ground. My knees screamed out in pain as they hit the cold bridge. Alexis's weapon flew out of her hand and onto the snowy ground a few feet away. I could see now it wasn't a knife. It was a lock pick. I put that together with the hoodie she was wearing.

"You," I said to Alexis as I struggled to get to my feet. "*You* killed Dougie."

"You don't know what the fuck you're talking about. You said so yourself. . . ." she said, barely able to catch her breath to get the words out. She started crying and pointed at her brother. "You said Jack did it. That he confessed."

"Alexis!" her father yelled. "Don't say another word." He ran over to grab the lock pick off the ground.

"Oh," I said to Mr. Quinn. "You definitely need to call the police."

His self-assured arrogance was now gone. He held the lock pick out in front of him, waist-high, as if warding off an attack from an invisible enemy. For someone so skilled with words, he seemed to be at a complete loss for them now.

His son, however, was not. He turned to his twin sister.

"You told me I killed Dougie."

"Shut up, Jack," Alexis said.

"Yes, Jack," Mr. Quinn said. "Shut up."

"No!" Jack screamed. "I will not shut up. You're both always telling me . . ." He looked at Alexis. "You told me I did it." He turned to me. "I only wanted to scare him, you know? He was gonna tell on us, and I was gonna get in trouble." He looked at his dad. "I just wanted to scare him, but things got out of control, and I was high and shit. Alexis told me I lost it and that I killed Dougie." Now it was his turn to cry. "I just wanted to scare him."

"With what?" I asked.

"This." He reached into his jacket and pulled out a pocketknife.

That was not the weapon that had been used to stab Douglas William Lee eleven times, but I would bet good money it was the weapon that had inflicted the wound under his chin—and Allison's. The murder weapon was the lock pick in his father's hand. Of that, I was sure.

"Mr. Quinn," I said. "I think you're going to need more lawyers."

Alexis sat up and pulled her knees into a hug.

"I'm sorry, Daddy," she cried. "Dougie was going to tell his uncle everything. About the drugs. About him and me. He was going to ruin everything." She tucked her head between her knees and her chest. "He was going to ruin *us*. Our family."

Again, Quinn senior could think of nothing to say, so he just mumbled, "Shut up." He looked at both his children as if deciding which one to go to. In the end, he chose neither. He moved toward me. The look on his face was primal now, the look of a father protecting his offspring. I took a step back.

"Mr. Quinn," I said. "Put the lock pick down."

"Don't you tell me what to do, Mr. Donne. These," he said, looking over at Jack and Alexis, "these are my *children*."

"Then get them the help they need."

I looked around and thought about running, but didn't think I'd get too far on the slippery bridge with my bad knees. If I let him get close enough, maybe I could get the lock pick away from him. Judging by the look on his face, that was a big maybe.

"You're making things worse," I said. "People know I'm here to see your son."

"No one knows Jack came here for sure," Quinn said. "Jack's all confused. If the police ask, we'll say he snuck out without our knowledge." He turned to his son. "Whose phone was used to call Mr. Donne, Jack?"

Jack seemed surprised by the question. "Elliot's."

"See?" Quinn said to me. "No record of *my son* calling you and only—maybe—the word of a child of limited capacity."

"You underestimate Elliot, Mr. Quinn."

He took a step closer. He could have reached down and helped his daughter off the ground. Instead, he glared at me. "And you underestimate me."

"Daddy?" Alexis pleaded from the snowy sidewalk.

"Just shut up, Alexis," he said, wiping some snow from his face. "You've caused enough trouble as it is."

"Daddy," she repeated.

He looked down at her with disdain. "I told you to shut—"

He was interrupted by Alexis lunging at his legs. They both seemed surprised as he lost his balance, and father and daughter became entangled in each other on the snowy ground. Jack stepped over to them. It looked as if he were going to help them up. Instead, he started crying and raised the pocketknife above his head.

"Jack!" I yelled, running over to the trio. He waved the knife in my face.

"Get away, Mr. Donne," he said. "Just stay the fuck away!"

Jack looked down at his father and sister. Both were still on the ground, brushing the snow off their legs. Jack let out a scream that could only be described as primal. He raised the knife again and looked unsure as to whom he wanted to hurt more.

"Don't do it, son!" a voice from behind us yelled. "Drop the weapon!"

All four of us—the three Quinns and I—looked over to see Detective Murcer aiming his gun at Jack. Behind Murcer was Allison.

The knife still above his father and sister, Jack screamed again. "Fuck!"

Taking advantage of Murcer's distraction, I reached out and grabbed the lock pick from Quinn senior's hand. I put it in my pocket and looked at his son.

"Put the knife down, Jack. It's over now."

There were three feet between us now, and he seemed clueless as to how we'd gotten there. His eyes went from me to the pocketknife in his hand, over my shoulder to Murcer, and back to me.

"Jack," I said. "Give me the knife. Please."

His eyes filled with tears. "Am I in trouble, Dad?"

Jack collapsed to the ground in a kneeling position, all alone. He lowered the knife. I moved over and snatched it from him. Behind me I could hear Murcer talking into his radio, stating our location and requesting a squad car.

"Am I in trouble, Dad?" Jack repeated. No one made a sound.

"Everybody stay right where you are," Murcer ordered.

I looked at the three Quinns as Allison came over and put her arm around me.

"I see you finally got through to Murcer," I said.

"Just covering your ass, Ray," she said.

Murcer came over and took the two weapons from me, then removed two plastic bags from his pockets. After securing his evidence, he turned to me and smiled.

"I called your sister," he said.

"I know."

"We're getting together next week."

"Dinner's on me," I said.

Chapter 38

"A FEW MORE OF THOSE," I said, "and I'll ruin my dinner."

"Well, then, Mr. Donne. You go right on ahead and ruin it."

I took two more cookies off the tray Mrs. Lee was holding. Dinner could wait. Then she gave the tray to her brother-in-law.

"So the drugs I found in Douglas's closet . . ."

"Were taken from the Quinns' car up in Rhinebeck," I said. "Mr. Quinn didn't even know they were gone until a week or so ago. When the police investigated the break-ins, they spoke to Jack. When Mr. Quinn confronted his son about it, Jack denied knowing anything. When his father kept pushing, Jack figured the best way out was to put the blame on Dougie."

"The dead black kid," Mr. Lee said.

"Yeah. Jack knew his dad would believe that without question."

"You should have told me about those drugs immediately, Gloria."

"And the father just kept them there?" Mrs. Lee asked, ignoring her brother-in-law. "In the trunk of his car? That just sounds to me like negligence."

"The firm," Mr. Lee said, "is looking into what the industry protocol is. But I'm sure that storing them in your car is not it. John Quinn is going to have a lot to answer for. To the company and the FDA. He's also going to face charges of bringing an unapproved drug back into this country without documentation, and he'll be looking at endangering the welfare of a child. He's going to jail. The only questions are for how long and whether it's going to be federal."

"I hope he has a good lawyer," I said.

"It won't be me. The firm has relieved me of all my files and obligations regarding Ward Fullerton. As of now, I'm on paid leave."

"For how long?" I asked.

"Until they let me go outright," he said. "My firm's going to need a scapegoat, and they have no reason to look past the lawyer in charge. I'll wait them out for a big severance package and take some time to figure out my next move."

Dougie's mom took a seat on the couch, then took a sip of hot chocolate.

"But this drug," she said again. "Douglas thought it would help his father?"

"I think he did when this whole thing started. But it was designed to help kids," I reminded her. "It's made to work with the chemicals in the area of the brain in charge of learning and memory. The boys, led by Jack Quinn, were, to some extent, conducting their own clinical trials."

She shook her head. "But why?"

"Jack could be quite convincing and clever. It was his idea to put those beads around Dougie's neck and plant the marijuana after Alexis killed him. He sold his friends on the possibility of higher grades and a shot at the better colleges. Remember, Jack was living in the academic shadow of his twin sister. That's a lot of pressure in that world." I took another sip of hot chocolate. "The same drug would have been of no use to someone with a traumatic brain injury like Dougie's dad. His issues are physical, not chemical."

"The booze doesn't help," Mr. Lee said.

"He thinks it does," I said. "And in this culture, if the doctor doesn't prescribe something, you can do it yourself. At happy hour prices."

Mrs. Lee shook her head. "I can't believe that the brother and sister—twins, for Lord's sake—would go after each other like that."

I thought back to something Rivera, the computer teacher, had told me last week. *They eat their own in this zip code.*

"As soon as they get out of rehab, they're in for a rough ride. They're only sixteen, but murder's murder. They'll be lucky to be charged as minors."

"And they were the ones who attacked you and Ms. Rogers?"

"Yes."

Mrs. Lee shook her head. "And what about the Sherman boy?"

"The combination of the drugs from the Quinns' car and his ADHD medication most likely triggered suicidal thoughts. After witnessing Dougie's murder, Paulie was a plane crash waiting to happen. Those pills also put Jack Quinn in the hospital."

"Those poor children."

"Those *poor* children," Mr. Lee said, "grew up with every advantage, Gloria."

"No, Douglas," Mrs. Lee said, shaking her head. "They most surely did not."

"Well," I said, taking a final sip of my hot chocolate. "I have to be going."

"I hope," Mrs. Lee said, "you're leaving because you have dinner plans with that lovely Ms. Rogers."

"As a matter of fact, I do."

"Good for you, Mr. Donne." She stepped forward and hugged me. "Thank you again for all you've done for this family. Would I offend you if I said, 'God bless you'?"

"No, ma'am. You would not."

"Then God bless you, Mr. Donne."

Douglas Lee, Attorney at Law, stood and offered me his hand.

"Thank you, Mr. Donne," he said. "I know I wasn't as kind to you as I could have been, but under the circumstances . . ."

"No need to apologize, Mr. Lee."

"I never said I was apologizing."

"No," I said. "I guess you didn't." *Fucking lawyers.*

Two minutes later, I was heading for the subway into Manhattan. I planned on staying the night at Allison's and taking the next day off.

God bless me indeed.